The bestselling novels of
TOM CLANCY

EXECUTIVE ORDERS

The most devastating terrorist act in history leaves Jack Ryan as President of the United States...

"UNDOUBTEDLY CLANCY'S BEST YET."

—*Atlanta Journal-Constitution*

DEBT OF HONOR

It begins with the murder of an American woman in the back streets of Tokyo. It ends in war...

"A SHOCKER CLIMAX SO PLAUSIBLE YOU'LL WONDER WHY IT HASN'T YET HAPPENED!"

—*Entertainment Weekly*

THE HUNT FOR RED OCTOBER

The smash bestseller that launched Clancy's career—the incredible search for a Soviet defector and the nuclear submarine he commands...

"BREATHLESSLY EXCITING!"

—*Washington Post*

RED STORM RISING

The ultimate scenario for World War III—the final battle for global control...

"THE ULTIMATE WAR GAME . . . BRILLIANT!"

—*Newsweek*

PATRIOT GAMES

CIA analyst Jack Ryan stops an assassination—and incurs the wrath of Irish terrorists...

"A HIGH PITCH OF EXCITEMENT!"

—*Wall Street Journal*

THE CARDINAL OF THE KREMLIN

The superpowers race for the ultimate Star Wars missile defense system...

"*CARDINAL* EXCITES, ILLUMINATES . . . A REAL PAGE-TURNER!"

—*Los Angeles Daily News*

CLEAR AND PRESENT DANGER

The killing of three U.S. officials in Colombia ignites the American government's explosive, and top secret, response...

"A CRACKLING GOOD YARN!"

—*Washington Post*

THE SUM OF ALL FEARS

The disappearance of an Israeli nuclear weapon threatens the balance of power in the Middle East—and around the world...

"CLANCY AT HIS BEST . . . NOT TO BE MISSED!"

—*Dallas Morning News*

WITHOUT REMORSE

The Clancy epic fans have been waiting for. His code name is Mr. Clark. And his work for the CIA is brilliant, cold-blooded, and efficient . . . but who is he really?

"HIGHLY ENTERTAINING!"

—*Wall Street Journal*

continued...

Tom Clancy's
NET FORCE™

Created by
Tom Clancy and Steve Pieczenik

BERKLEY BOOKS, NEW YORK

TOM CLANCY'S NET FORCE ™

A Berkley Book / published by arrangement with
Netco Partners

PRINTING HISTORY
Berkley edition / February 1999

The Penguin Putnam Inc. World Wide Web site address is
http://www.penguinputnam.com

ISBN: 0-425-16172-2

BERKLEY®
Berkley Books are published by
The Berkley Publishing Group, a member of Penguin Putnam Inc.,
375 Hudson Street, New York, New York 10014.
BERKLEY and the "B" design are trademarks
belonging to Berkley Publishing Corporation.

PRINTED IN THE UNITED STATES OF AMERICA

10 9 8 7 6 5 4 3 2 1

Acknowledgments

We'd like to thank Steve Perry for his creative ideas and his invaluable contributions to the preparations of the manuscript. We would also like to acknowledge the assistance of Martin H. Greenberg, Larry Segriff, Denise Little, John Helfers, Robert Youdelman, Esq., Richard Heller, Esq., and Tom Mallon, Esq.; Mitchell Rubenstein and Laurie Silvers at BIG Entertainment; the wonderful people at The Putnam Berkley Group, including Phyllis Grann, David Shanks, and Tom Colgan; our producers on the ABC mini-series, Gil Cates and Dennis Doty; the brilliant screenwriter and director Rob Lieberman; and all the good people at ABC. As always, we would like to thank Robert Gottlieb of the William Morris Agency, our agent and friend, without whom this book would never have been conceived, as well as Jerry Katzman, Vice Chairman of the William Morris Agency, and his television colleagues. But most important, it is for you, our readers, to determine how successful our collective endeavor has been.

Tom Clancy's

NET FORCE™

1

"Okay, Commander," Boyle said. "We're clear."

Steve Day stepped out into the muggy autumn night from the cooler air-conditioned restaurant, surrounded still by the wonderful odors of exquisite Italian cooking. Already on the sidewalk, Boyle, Day's chief bodyguard, spoke into his link. The limo was there, but Boyle was a very careful young man, one of the FBI's finest. Only after he spoke did the limo's electrically locked rear door click open. The whole time, Boyle looked everywhere but at Day.

Day nodded at the driver, the new guy. Larry? Lou? Something like that. As he slid across the cloned-leather seat, he was feeling pretty good. Nothing like a seven-course meal and three kinds of excellent wine to put a man in a good mood. Umberto's was new, but it was at least a four-star eatery—or would be as soon as somebody got around to ranking it, though Day hoped that wouldn't be anytime soon. It never failed. As soon as he found a new out-of-the-way place with decent food, it was quickly "discovered'' and reservations were impossible to get.

True, he was the Commander of the recently established Net Force, still the flavor of the month in Washington power circles, but that didn't cut much ice when rich Senators or even richer foreign diplomats were in line ahead of you. Even restaurant owners in this town knew which backsides to kiss first, and top of the list sure wasn't a political appointee as far down the food chain as Day was. For now, anyway.

Still, the meal had been great: al dente pasta and artery-clogging sauce and shrimp, and salad and palate-cleansing ices. Day was both pleasantly full and slightly tipsy. Good thing he didn't have to drive.

His virgil cheeped at him.

Boyle slid in next to Day, closed the door, then tapped on the bullet-proof Lexan partition with one knuckle.

The driver started the car as Day unclipped the virgil from his belt and looked at it.

His Virtual Global Interface Link—virgil for short—had a flashing telephone icon in the upper right corner of the small LCD screen. He touched the icon and a number blinked onto the screen. Marilyn, calling from home. He looked at the timesig. Just after eleven. She must have gotten back from her DAR meeting early. Those gab sessions usually ran past midnight. He grinned, tapped the phone number twice and waited for the connection.

Not much bigger than a pack of cigarettes—he'd given *those* up twenty years ago, but he hadn't forgotten how big a pack was—the virgil was a terrific toy. It was a computer, a GPS unit, phone, clock, radio, TV, modem, credit card, camera, scanner and even a little weavewire fax, all in one. The GPS could tell you where you were anywhere on the planet—and because he was a ranking FBI officer, it didn't have the fudge-factor that commercial civilian units came with, so it was accurate to within five meters. You could link to anybody with a phone or computer, via a scrambled hyperdigital channel so dense they called it a pipe and that would take an expert codebreaker a month of Sundays to tap into. This particular unit would, with the proper code, allow Day to access the FBI and Net Force mainframe DNAs, with their vast information stores. Had he been so inclined, Day could have grabbed a pinch of the powdered sugar that came on the cheesecake he'd had for dessert, dusted a fingerprint left on a plate by his waiter and had it checked, ID'd, and a full history on the man back to him before he'd finished eating.

It was great living here in the future, a mere decade after the turn of the century. If 2010 had such wonders, what might it look like in another twenty or thirty years? He was looking forward to finding out, and with advances in medicine, he could pretty much expect to do so.

The virgil's speaker said, "Hi, Steve."

"Hi, Marilyn. What's up?"

"Nothing much. We got done early. I was just wondering if you might want a late supper."

He grinned at the virgil. He didn't have his camera on, so she couldn't see the smile. "I just left Umberto's," he said. "I think I'll pass on eating for the next couple of weeks."

She laughed. "I understand. You coming home?"

"On the way."

He had a condo in the city, but most nights he tried to get across the river and to the house. The kids were grown, but Marilyn and the dog still liked to see him now and again.

He tapped the virgil and re-clipped it to his belt, which needed a little attention. He loosened the buckle a couple of holes and slid the Galco paddle holster with his SIG .40 around toward the front a little so it wouldn't dig into his right hip. He could have carried one of the new-model wireless KTs—kick-tasers—that were supposed to be better than a gun, but he didn't really trust them. Yes, he was a political appointee for the current job, but he'd been in the field a long time to earn the spot. He trusted his old-fashioned pistol.

Moving the gun helped. While he was at it, he undid the Velcro on his Kevlar vest's side panels and re-tabbed them a little looser, too.

Next to him, Boyle fought to keep his grin under control.

Day shook his head. "Easy for you to laugh. You're what—thirty? Still bulking up at the gym three or four times a week, right? Us fat old desk jockeys don't have time to stay in shape."

Not that he was *that* much out of shape. Five-eight, maybe 190? He could drop a few pounds, but hey, he was fifty-two last June and he was entitled to carry a little extra baggage. He'd earned it.

They were on the narrow street behind the new projects, the shortcut toward the expressway. It was a dark and dreary part of town, with streetlights broken out and dead, stripped cars lining the road. Another of the instant slums, going down fast even before the original paint had dried. In his opinion, the current welfare philosophy needed major work; of course, it always had. Though things were getting better, the future still had a way to go to pick up all of its passengers. There were streets in D.C. he wouldn't walk alone after dark; gun, vest, and virgil notwithstanding. An armored limo made him feel a little more secure—

There came a terrific bang, a flash that strobed the limo's interior a sudden bright orange. The car rocked up on the driver's side, hung for what seemed like forever on two wheels, then fell back and hit the street hard.

"What the hell?"

Boyle already had his pistol out as the limo fishtailed, slewed and slammed into a streetlight post. The post was fiberglass. It snapped off at bumper level and fell on the limo, spraying shattered glass in a tinkly rain upon the car's trunk.

Day saw a bulky man in black run toward the car from out of the sticky night. The man wore a watch cap pulled low but not covering his face. He had blond hair, a scar running through his right eyebrow. He was smiling.

Day thought he caught a flash of movement at the rear of the limo, but when he looked, he didn't see anything.

"Go!" Boyle yelled. "Go, go!"

The driver tried. The engine roared, the wheels screeched, but the car didn't move. The stench of burning rubber filled the car.

Day thumbed the emergency scramble button on the virgil, and was already reaching for his own pistol when the man in black reached the limo and slapped something on the door. Whatever it was thunked metallically. The man turned and sprinted away, back into the darkness—

"Out!" Boyle screamed. "He's stuck a limpet on the door! Out!"

Day grabbed the door handle on the driver's side, jerked it up, dove out and hit the ground in a sloppy shoulder roll.

There came the repetitive bark of a submachine gun, followed by the *spang! spang! spang!* of jacketed teeth chewing at the wounded limo.

Day rolled again, looking for cover. Nothing. Nowhere to hide!

He glanced back at the car. Saw and felt time become mired in heaviness. Boyle exited the car, gun working, tongues of orange fire stabbing into the dark, but it was like a slow-motion scene in a movie.

Boyle jerked as the small-arms fire beat at him, slammed into his torso.

In a small corner of his mind, Day knew that most submachine guns used pistol ammunition and that the vests he and Boyle both wore would stop any handgun round. As long as they didn't—

—blood and brain matter sprayed from the side of Boyle's temple as a bullet exited there—

—as long as they didn't think to shoot for the head!

Damn, damn! What was going on? Who were these people?

In the limo, the driver kept trying to pull away, the roar of the engine continuing. Day could smell the exhaust, the burned tires—he could smell his own fear, too, sharp, sour, overwhelming.

The mine attached to the rear door of the limo went off—*blam!*

All the glass in the limo blew out. It sleeted in all directions—some of it hit Day, but he was only dimly aware of it touching him.

The car's roof peeled up a little in the back, leaving a fist-sized gap. Smoke, bitter and acrid, washed over him in a hot wave.

The driver hung partway out of his window, boneless.

Dead. The driver and Boyle were both dead. Help would be coming, but he couldn't wait for it—if he did, he would be dead, too.

Day came up, took two or three quick steps, jinked right for two more steps, then cut left. Broken-field, came back to him from football in high school thirty-five years ago.

Gunfire tried to catch him, but failed to connect solidly. A bullet tugged at his jacket, punched through under his left arm. He felt a sense of outrage. The goddamned jacket was Hong Kong silk, it had cost him six hundred dollars!

Another round smashed into his chest, right over the heart. He'd never worn the titanium trauma plate, had just used a trifold of Kevlar stuffed down in the trauma pocket over the heart like a lot of agents did, and the impact hurt like a bastard! Like he'd been hit with a hammer, right on the sternum! Damn!

But it didn't matter. He was up, he was moving—

A black figure appeared in front of him, waving a flashing Uzi. Even in the night and murk of his fear, Day saw the man wore bulky combat armor under his black jacket. Day had been taught to shoot to the center of mass first, but that wouldn't do now, no, no, the SIG .40 wouldn't hurt the attacker that way any more than the Uzi's 9mm's were hurting *him*!

Still running, Day lifted the SIG, lined the glowing tritium dot of the front sight on the man's nose. Day's vision tunneled—all he could see was the face. The green nightsight dot bounced around, but he squeezed off three shots as fast as he could pull the trigger.

The armored attacker dropped as if his legs had vanished.

All right! All right! He had taken one of them out, he had created a hole, it was just like in football when he'd been the quarterback so long ago.

Now, go through the hole, *fast,* head for the goal line!

He caught motion peripherally, glanced to his left, and saw another man, also in black. The man held a pistol in two hands. He was as still as a painting. He looked as if he were at the range, ready to practice.

Day felt his bowels clench. He wanted to run, shoot, defecate, all at the same instant. Whoever these guys were, they were professionals. This wasn't any street gang looking for somebody's wallet. This was a hit, an assassination, and they were good—

It was his final thought.

The bullet hit him between the eyes and took away everything else he might ever think.

In the backseat of the Volvo station wagon, Mikhayl Ruzhyó looked into the cargo compartment behind him at the body of Nicholas Papirósa. The body lay on its side, covered with a blanket, and the smell of death seeped into the air despite the covering. Ruzhyó sighed, shook his head. Poor Nicholas. It had been hoped there would be no casualties—it was always hoped to be so—but the fat American had not been as old and slow as expected. They had underestimated him—an error. Of course, it had been Nicholas who had been responsible for the intelligence about the FBI Commander, so perhaps it was fitting that he was the only casualty. Still, Ruzhyó would miss him. They went back a long way, to the days in the Foreign Intelligence Service, the SRV. Fifteen years. A lifetime in this business.

Tomorrow would have been Nicholas's birthday; he would have been forty-two.

In the front seat, Winters, the American, drove, and Grigory Zmeyá rode in the passenger seat, mumbling to himself in Russian.

Their last names—even Winters—were not those bestowed upon them by their fathers. They were jokes. Ruzhyó meant ''rifle.'' Nicholas had named himself ''cigarette.'' Grigory called himself after the Russian word for ''snake.''

Ruzhyó sighed again. Done was done. Nicholas was dead, but so was the target. The loss was therefore acceptable.

''You doin' okay back there, hoss?'' the American said.

''I am fine.''

''Just checkin'.''

The American had said he was from Texas, and either he was or his accent was a passable fake.

Ruzhyó looked down at the pistol on the seat next to him, the one with which he had killed the man who had killed Nicholas. It was a Beretta 9mm, an Italian weapon. It was a fine piece of machinery, well made, but it was also big, heavy, with too much recoil, too much noise, too much bullet for Ruzhyó's taste. When he had been *spetsnaz* and involved in *mokrie dela*—wet affairs—he had carried a little PSM, a 5.45mm pistol. The round it fired had been perhaps half as large as those in the Italian gun, and the weapon itself was much smaller than this piece. True, he'd had the armorer tune it for him; but still, it had always been sufficient to do the job. It had never let him down. He would have preferred that weapon to this one, but of course, that would not do. This had to look as if the killing was by someone inside this country, and a Russian assassin's weapon would ring enough alarms to raise the dead man. The Americans were not altogether stupid in these matters.

He frowned at the Beretta. The Americans had this obsession with size; to them, bigger was always better. Their policemen would sometimes empty handguns containing eighteen or twenty high-powered and large-caliber rounds at their criminals, missing each time, what they called "spray-and-pray." They did not seem to understand that a single shot from a small-caliber weapon in the hands of an expert was much more effective than a magazine full of elephant-killing bullets in the hands of an untrained idiot— as many of the American policemen seemed to be. The Jews knew this. The Israeli Mossad still routinely carried .22's, weapons that fired the smallest commercially available rounds. And everybody knew Mossad was not to be taken lightly.

But at least the FBI man had died well. He had taken one of them with him and that had been unexpected. He had hit Nicholas three times in the head. Once might have been an accident; thrice, certainly by intent. He had seen the body armor, known what it was, shot for the head. Had he been a bit faster, he might have gotten clear of the initial attack.

In the front seat, the Snake muttered something, loud enough for Ruzhyó to hear. He gritted his teeth. Ruzhyó did not like Grigory the Snake. The man had been in the army in 1995, one of the units that had stomped into Ruzhyó's homeland of Chechnya to kill and rape. Yes, yes, Grigory had been a soldier, just following his orders, and yes, this mission was more important in the long run than any grudges Ruzhyó might have against the Snake, so he would endure the man. But perhaps one of these days, the Snake would speak of his beautiful Medal for Action in Chechnya once too often, and if that day came near enough to the end of the mission so he would not be vital, Grigory Zmeyá would go to join his ancestors. And Ruzhyó would smile while he throttled the stupid oaf.

Not today, however. There was still much to be done, bridges to be crossed, objectives to be achieved, and the Snake was still necessary.

Which was lucky for him.

Alexander Michaels was only half asleep when the small monitor on the nightstand next to his bed lit. He felt the pressure of the light against his closed lids, and rolled toward the source and opened his eyes.

The screen's blue Net Force background came up and the computer's vox said, "Alex? We have a priority-one com."

Michaels blinked, and frowned at the timesig on the monitor's upper right corner. Just past midnight. He wasn't awake. What—?

"Alex? We have a priority-one com."

The computer's voice was throaty, sexy, feminine. No matter what it said, it always sounded as if it were asking you to go to bed with it. The personality module, including the vox program, had been programmed by Jay Gridley, and the voice he'd chosen for it was, Michaels knew, a joke. Jay was a great tech, but a better cook than he was a comedian, and while Michaels found the vox irritating, damned if he would give the kid the satisfaction of asking him to change it.

The Deputy Commander of Net Force rubbed at his face, combed his short hair back with his fingers, and sat up. The small motion-sensitive cam mounted on the top of the monitor tracked him. The unit was programmed to send visuals unless he told it otherwise. "All right, I'm up. Connect com."

The voxax—voice-activated—system obeyed his command. The screen flowered, and the somewhat-harried face of Assistant Deputy Commander Antonella Fiorella appeared. She looked more alert than he felt, but then she had the graveyard watch this week, so she was supposed to be alert.

"Sorry to wake you, Alex."

"No problem, Toni. What's up?" She wouldn't be calling him if it wasn't vital.

"Somebody just assassinated Commander Day."

"What!?"

"His virgil sent out an alert. D.C. PD rolled on it. Time anybody got there, Day, his bodyguard Boyle and the limo driver, Louis Harvey, were all dead. Bombs and submachine guns, looks like. Maybe twenty minutes ago."

Michaels said a word he seldom used in mixed company.

"Yeah," Toni said. "And the horse it rode in on, too."

"I'm on my way."

"Virgil's got the address." A short pause. "Alex? Don't forget the assassination protocols."

She didn't need to remind him of that, but he nodded. In the event of an attack on a senior federal official, all members of that unit had to assume it might not be the only attack planned. "I copy that. Discom."

His assistant's image vanished, leaving the Net Force

blue screen. He slid off the bed and started pulling on his clothes.

Steve Day was dead? Damn.

Damn.

2

Red and blue lights from the D.C. police patrol cars strobed the street with primary carnival colors, an effect appropriate to the circus of activity now going on. It was pushing one in the morning, but there were dozens of people lining the road, held back by police officers and bright plastic crime-scene tape. More curious onlookers peered down from nearby buildings. There was something to see, too, what with the blasted limo, the litter of shell casings, the three bodies.

It was a bad neighborhood to die in, Toni Fiorella thought. But then, when you got right down to it, any neighborhood was a bad one to die in when death came from a hard and sudden sleet of submachine-gun fire.

"Agent Fiorella?"

Toni blinked away her thoughts on mortality and looked at the police captain, who had, judging by the size and shape of his sleep-wrinkles, been roused from his bed. He was an easy fifty, nearly bald, and certainly, at this moment, a most unhappy man. Dead federal agents in your yard, on your watch, were bad things to wake up to. Real bad.

"Yes?"

"My men have come back from their initial canvass."

Toni nodded. "Let me guess. Nobody saw anything."

"You should go into law enforcement," the captain said. His voice was sour. "You have an eye for detail."

"Somebody in this crowd must have outstanding warrants for something," Toni said. She waved one arm in accusatory benediction.

The captain nodded. He knew the drill. When a cop was killed, it didn't matter if he was local, state or federal, you did what you had to do to find whoever did it. Squeezing some low-life drug dealer or even a citizen with too many parking tickets for information was penny-ante stuff. Whatever it took. You did *not* let cop-killers slide.

Toni looked up, and saw the new Chrysler town car glide to a stop just outside the police barricade. Two men, the bodyguard and the driver, got out first and scanned the crowd. The bodyguard nodded at the passenger in back.

Alex Michaels alighted, saw Toni and headed for her. He held his badge case up, and was waved through by the cops blocking the street.

Toni felt that mixed rush of emotion she always felt whenever she saw Alex for the first time on any given day. Even in the middle of all this carnage, there was a certain amount of joy, of admiration, even of love.

Alex's expression was not grim, but as he habitually wore it, neutral. He didn't let himself show that he felt such things, even though she knew it had to be causing him great pain. Steve Day had been his mentor and his friend; his death must be stabbing deep into Alex's heart, though he would never let on, even to her.

Maybe even especially to her . . .

"Toni."

"Alex."

They didn't speak as they toured the murder scene. He squatted and examined Steve Day's body. She caught a flash of tightness in his face, a quick flex of jaw muscles as he looked at Day. Nothing more.

He rose, moved to the limo and looked at the other dead agents and the ruined auto. FBI and local police agents still circled around with light bars and videocams, covering the entire street. Forensic techs drew circles around each of the spent shells on the street and sidewalk, noting the location of each empty hull before they bagged it. Somebody would do the super-glue steam on those shells, the fine mist of cyanoacrylate ester that could, when done properly, find a fingerprint on a sheet of toilet paper; and they would do the biological-activity scan that could find a germ in an ocean. But Toni figured that coming up with useful prints or DNA residues wasn't going to be likely. It was almost never that easy. Especially on something as well planned as this obviously had been.

After he'd gotten as good a look as he wanted, Alex turned to her. "Okay. Lay it out."

"As nearly as we can tell so far, it was an assassination, Commander Day the target. A bomb under a manhole cover kicked the limo into a light pole. The door in the rear was blown open—probably a marine limpet of some kind—and the passengers were cut down by several attackers. From the ejected brass patterns, there were three or more shooters. Porter will run the ballistics stuff, but he's pretty sure from what he's already seen they were using 9mm's, at least a couple of submachine guns, and one handgun."

She kept her voice level, as if talking about sports stats. She came from a family of expressive Bronx Italians who wore their hearts on their sleeves and who laughed hard or cried hard as needed. It was tough to keep the emotion from her words—she'd liked Steve Day and his wife—but it was her job.

"Boyle and Day both returned fire. Boyle managed to get off twelve rounds, Day three. Porter has come up with a couple of deformed handgun slugs found on the street whose impact shapes indicated they hit something harder than Kevlar and bounced off. He'll have to run the nose prints to be certain, but—"

Alex cut her off. "The assassins wore armor, probably military-grade ceramic or spider-silk plate. What else?"

"Over here."

She led him to a spot behind Day's body. The coroner's people were bagging the corpse, but Alex didn't spare them or his friend a glance; he was all business now. "Day's brass was found there, there, and over there." She pointed at small chalk circles a few meters apart on the street. She moved a couple of steps, and pointed at the street again. "There's a small, congealed blood ooze, right there, and a spray pattern of blood and brain tissue angled that way, behind the blood," she said. She waited, knowing he would make the connection.

He made it. "Somebody tagged one of the assassins, despite the armor," Alex said. "Day would have known to shoot for the head. But the killers took the body."

"D.C. Police have set up roadblocks."

He waved this off. "This was a professional hit. The shooters won't get caught in a roadblock. What else?"

She shook her head. "Until we get the lab work, I'm afraid that's about it. No witnesses have come forth. I'm sorry, Alex."

He nodded. "All right. Steve—Commander Day—ran Organized Crime for a long time. Crank up the system, Toni. I want to know everything about everybody Day ever talked to in his tenure at OC, anybody who had a grudge. And anything current we are working on. This looks like a

New Mafia operation, it's their style, but we don't want to overlook anything.''

"I've already got teams on it," she said. "Jay Gridley is running the system stuff."

"Good."

He stared at the street, but his eyes were focused on something a million miles past it.

She wanted to reach out, to put her hand on his arm, to help him carry the sudden load of pain she knew he shouldered, but she held her ground. It would not be appropriate here and now, she knew, and she did not want him to close that door, to turn away from her if she offered comfort. He was a good man, but he kept himself bottled up, never let anybody get too close. If she was ever going to slip past his iron wall, it would have to be with the greatest of care and subtlety. And, she knew on some level, it would be unfair to use the death of his friend to do it.

"I'll go with Porter to the lab," she said.

He nodded, but otherwise did not respond.

Michaels stood in the middle of a run-down street in the middle of a run-down night, beset with the stink of burned gunpowder, hot camera lights and death, the sounds of police radios and working investigators, the buzz of onlookers held at bay by bored street cops. In the background in the distance, the whine of a maglev passenger train passing at speed, dopplering its way toward Baltimore.

Steve Day was dead.

It hadn't really sunk in yet. He'd seen the body, seen that the light behind Day's eyes was gone, leaving nothing but a shell, a hollow form where nobody lived any longer. Intellectually, he knew it, but emotionally, he was numb. He'd known other people who had died, some of them close to him. The reality of it never became true until days, weeks, months later, when you realized they were never

going to call or write or laugh or show up at your door
with a bottle of champagne again.

Dammit, somebody had put out a good man's lights,
snuffed him like a blown-out match, and all Alex Michaels
was left with at this moment was the heat of his own anger.
Whoever had done it was going to pay—he was going to
make it happen if it was the last thing he ever did!

He sighed. There was nothing else to be done here. The
killers would be a long way away by now, and all the door-
knocking and witness-interviewing wouldn't turn up anything immediately useful. The shooters weren't hiding in
one of the run-down buildings, and even with a photograph-
ically accurate description of the assassins, it wouldn't do
the investigators much good—they wouldn't be locals. The
public didn't know it, but professional killers seldom got
caught. Nine out of ten icemen who *were* caught were
turned in by the people who'd hired them, and Michaels
didn't see that as very likely in a high-profile operation such
as this. Those responsible would know the authorities
would not be satisfied merely with locking up triggermen.
Nobody would be giving up *anybody* in this kind of deal.
If this was a mob job and the bosses got nervous, the shooters would likely disappear into a lime pit two kilometers
past the end of the road in Nowhere, Mississippi. And
maybe the guys who shot *them* would go away, too.

Net Force had access to the highest technological resources on the planet, the fastest computers on the net, a
wealth of information beyond measure. The agents on-line
and in the field were also the best and brightest, culled from
the cream of the FBI, the NSA, the nation's top universities
and police and military agencies. And none of it would help
if the assassins hadn't made some kind of mistake. If Net
Force didn't get some kind of break. Michaels had been in
the business too long to try to pretend otherwise.

Then again, even professional killers weren't perfect.

Now and then, they did slip up. And if they'd made the slightest slip here, something so small it could only have been seen with an electron microscope, Alex Michaels was going to move the entire solar system if necessary to find it.

His virgil cheeped.

"Yes?"

"Alex? Walt Carver."

Michaels let another small sigh escape. Walter S. Carver, Director of the FBI. He'd been expecting the call.

"Yes, sir."

"I'm sorry about Steve. Anything to report?"

Michaels gave his boss what they had. When he was done, Carver said, "All right. We've got a meeting with the President and his National Security Team at 0730 at the White House. Put together what we've got. You'll be doing the presentation."

"Yes, sir."

"Oh, and as of now, you're Acting Commander of Net Force."

"Sir, I—"

Carver cut him off. "I know, I know, but I need somebody in the chair and you're him. I don't mean to sound dismissive of Steve's death, but Net Force is responsible for a whole lot more than one man's fate, no matter who he might be. Everybody will bump up a notch, Toni will take your old job. I'll need the President to sign off on it, but we should be able to get you confirmed as Commander in a few days."

"Sir—"

"I need you here, Alex. You aren't going to let me down, are you?"

Michaels stared at the virgil. He didn't have any choice in this. Shook his head. "No, sir. I won't let you down."

"Good man. I'll see you in the morning. Try to get some

sleep—you don't want to sound like a zombie when you lay this out. Full assassination protocols are in effect, you understand?''

"Yes, sir.''

"Go home, Alex.''

Michaels stared at his car, at the bodyguard and chauffeur who stood watching and waiting. He had a little over six hours to put together a presentation for the President of the United States and his hard-nosed security advisors—not to mention Alex's own boss at the FBI—and supposedly get some rest, too. That last part sure wasn't going to happen.

He shook his head. About the time you thought you were in control, life sure had a way of setting you straight. *Think you're in charge, pal? Here, chew on this: Your immediate superior just got murdered, probably by the Mob, you just got promoted, and tomorrow, a presentation to the most powerful man in the world will probably make or break your career. How does that make you feel?*

"Like shit,'' Michaels said aloud.

A traffic cop nearby said, "Excuse me?''

"Nothing,'' Michaels said.

He headed for his car.

"Home, Commander?'' his driver said.

Commander.

The driver already knew about the promotion. Well. One thing was certain. Michaels was damn sure going to use that promotion to take care of this business. Steve Day was his friend.

Wrong. Day had *been* his friend. Michaels wasn't going home, no matter how tired he was.

"No. To the office.''

3

Vladimir Plekhanov wiped some of the ever-present dust from the inside of his window and looked down upon the city. Despite the installation of air conditioners and weekly visits from a cleaning woman, there seemed always to be a layer of powder everywhere, fine as talcum, but much darker. Of course, the dust was just dirt now. He remembered a time when much of it had been soot from the crematoriums, the remains of soldiers, civilians and invading Russians. That was a long time ago, almost twenty years, but as he grew older he spent perhaps more time in his room of old memories than he should. Well. Even though he had much to live for yet, and a most rewarding future in mind, he was sixty and should be allowed a glance backward from time to time, yes?

From his vantage point in the corner office on the sixth floor of the Computer Wing of the Science Building—formerly, and briefly, the Military Headquarters Building—he had a good view. Here was the new downtown bridge over

the Sunzha River; way over there, the massive Makhach-
kala Pipelines, delivering their ever-more-precious black
fluid to the waiting tankers on the Caspian Sea. Just there,
the remains of the barracks where Tolstoy had served as a
young soldier. And there, in the distance, the Sunzha Range
of the mighty Caucasus.

As cities went, this one was not bad. It was hardly a
village—nearly half the population of the entire country
lived here—but even so, at less than three quarters of a
million people, it was not an overly large city. And in a
beautiful country it was.

Oil was still the lubricant that ran Grozny's economy,
though it was running out, bleeding away faster than it
could have been replaced by ten thousand dinosaurs dying
and instantly rotting each day—a thing even Steven Spiel-
berg and all his movie magic could not provide. The flare
stacks at the refinery ran day and night, spewing fire and
smoke into the skies, but in the not-too-distant future those
fiery towers would go dark. Chechnya needed a new base
for its economy. A base that he, Vladimir Plekhanov, was
going to provide. For even though he had been born a Russian, he was as much Chechen as any man. . . .

The sound of his computer's telephonic program interrupted Plekhanov's musings upon his Grand Plan. He
turned away from the window, walked to the door of his
office and smiled at his secretary, Sasha. He then closed
the door quietly but firmly before turning to his state-of-
the-art workstation. "Computer, sound dampers on."

The machine hummed and obeyed the vox command.
"Dampers on," it said.

Plekhanov nodded at the machine, as if it could see and
understand his gesture. It could not—but he could have
programmed it to do so had he wished.

"Yes?" he said in English. There was no visual mode
on this line, nor would he have wished for one. Of course,

the communication was secure—as secure as the best Russian military encryption program could make it. Plekhanov knew this because he himself had written the program under contract to the Russian Army, and there was no one likely to hear this communication remotely capable of breaking it. Perhaps some of the Net Force operatives might, but they would be . . . otherwise occupied just at the moment. He smiled. Still, he spoke English because Sasha had not two words of that language; nor did anybody likely to be passing by.

"The job is done," said the voice from thousands of kilometers away. It was Mikhayl, amusing himself by using the name Ruzhyó—thus, Mikhayl the Rifle. A violent man, but loyal, and most adept. The proper tool for the mission.

"Good. I expected no less. Any problems?"

"Nicholas unexpectedly decided to retire."

"How unfortunate," Plekhanov said. "He was a good employee."

"Yes."

"Very well. You are moving into the new quarters?"

"Yes."

Even though the link was encrypted, old habits died hard. Their *spetsnaz* days were long past, but still deeply ingrained. Plekhanov knew that the hiding place was San Francisco, so there was no need to say it aloud. Should some nascent mathematical computer genius manage to miraculously obtain a recording of this conversation—and even more miraculously, decode it—what would he have? An innocuous dialogue between two unidentified men, bounced off so many satellites and through so many relays as to be untraceable, filled with generalities so bland as to mean nothing. A job? Someone named Nicholas retiring? A move? There was nothing there.

"Well. Continue as planned. I will contact you when further work is required." He hesitated a moment, then realized one more thing needed to be said. Communism was dead and rightfully so, but the workers still needed approbation to feel a sense of accomplishment. A good manager knew this. "You did well," Plekhanov said. "I am pleased."

"Thank you."

That ended the conversation.

Plekhanov leaned back in his chair. The Grand Plan was progressing exactly as he had intended. Like a snowball rolling down a hill, it had begun small, but by the time it was done, it would be vast and unstoppable.

He pushed the intercom buzzer on his desk. A few seconds passed, and nothing happened. He pushed the button again. Still no response. He sighed. The intercom was broken again. If he wanted tea, he would have to go and tell Sasha. He was on the way to being the most powerful man in the world and he had to work in an office wherein the simplest devices were in need of repair. He shook his head. That was going to change.

And that would be but the smallest of changes. . . .

Wednesday, September 8th, 7:17 a.m.
Washington, D.C.

Alexander Michaels had felt better. As his chauffeur maneuvered the car toward 1600 Pennsylvania Avenue, he shuffled through the hardcopy printouts yet again, ordering his thoughts as best he could. The town car was bracketed fore and aft by bodyguard vehicles, governmental-gray cars whose drivers and passengers carried enough hardware to sustain a small war. The protocols were pretty clear about what must be done in the event of a high-level federal assassination. The genesis of these protective measures went all the way back to Lincoln. Most people didn't realize that the murdered President had not been the sole target of Booth and his fellow plotters.

Michaels had been to the White House several times, although always as a backup to Steve Day, never on the hot seat himself. And he had every scrap of information the FBI had on the assassination on tap, all duplicated on a small disk capable of holding gigabytes of material, nestled inside a coded plastic case, ready to load into the White House's Secure System. Should something happen to him, anybody who tried to break open the disk's case would be in for a hot surprise when ten grams of Thermoflex went up with enough heat to melt the case, the disk and the fingers of anybody stupid enough to be holding both.

The White House Secure System was a set of special computers without any links to the outside world, along with state-of-the-art antivirals and sweepers installed, so once his information was installed there, it would be safe.

Still, he was tired, had drunk too much coffee, and he wanted nothing more than to find a bed far away from all this and sleep for a week.

Well, too bad. That's not what you signed on for, now is it?

The virgil cheeped.

"Yes?"

"Alex? You ready?"

The Director. "Yes, sir. I should be there in about five minutes."

"Anything new I should know about?"

"Nothing substantial."

"All right. Discom."

The procession arrived at the West Gate. Alex alighted, was checked by the metal detectors, bomb sniffers and an HOS—a hard-objects scanner—this latter a new device designed to keep ceramic or plastic guns and knives from sneaking past. He checked his taser, got a receipt and visitor badge, then ran the gamut of Marine sentries at the door who checked his ID. The Situation Room where his meeting was scheduled was one of the older ones, one level down, under the Oval Office.

Another pair of Marines inspected his badge as he exited the small elevator, and a trio of Secret Service agents in suits nodded or spoke to him as he headed toward the Situation Room. He knew two of them, one of whom had been with the Bureau back when Alex had been stationed in Idaho.

"Morning, Commander Michaels," his old Idaho friend said.

"Hey, Bruce." The term "Commander" still made him uneasy. He hadn't even *wanted* this job. He sure as hell hadn't wanted it at the cost of Steve Day's life. The silver lining here was that being in charge gave him the best chance of catching Day's killers. And he was damned sure going to do that.

A final check, the thumbprint scanner, and the door opened to admit Alex.

Inside, Director Carver was already seated at a long table shaped like the office above the room, sipping coffee from a china cup. Standing to his left was NSO Assistant Director Sheldon Reed, making a call on his virgil. A middle-aged secretary in a tweed skirt and white silk blouse sat at a small table off to the side, a steno pad in front of her and a voxax unlinked recorder next to the pad, that next to a computer station. A Marine in dress uniform poured coffee from a silver pot into a cup balanced perfectly on a saucer, then set the steaming brew down next to Carver on the right—that would be Alex's seat, and the server would know he took it black. Hardcopy reports duplicating the ones Michaels carried were inside sealed folders that lay upon the table in front of each chair.

Carver smiled his professional smile at Alex and nodded at the seat next to him. Alex was halfway there when the door opened and the President and his Chief of Staff, Jessel Leon, entered the room.

"Good morning, gentlemen." The President nodded at the secretary and smiled. "And Mrs. Upton. I've got a busy schedule, so let's get right to it. Walt?"

"Mr. President. Around midnight, Steve Day, the Commander of the FBI's Net Force, was assassinated. You know Alex Michaels—I've bumped him into Day's chair. He'll lay out the situation as we now know it."

"Helluva way to get a promotion," the President said, nodding at Michaels. He sounded a little nervous. Worrying that maybe he'd be the next target? "Okay, let's hear it."

Michaels took a deep breath, as quietly as he could. He walked to the computer, opened the coded disk packet he carried and handed the disk to the secretary. She inserted the disk, and ran the viral scan. It took all of five seconds. "You're set up for voice command," Mrs. Upton said to him.

"Thank you," Michaels said. "Computer, image one, please."

A holographic projector in the ceiling clicked on, and a three-dimensional image of the assassination scene, photographed from a police helicopter less than eight hours ago, blossomed in the middle of the table.

Michaels began to lay it out. The explosion, the attack, the dead and suspected dead. He did it methodically, taking his time. He had the computer show other views as he talked. After ten minutes, he paused and looked around the table. "Any questions so far?"

"Any other unusual activity regarding federal officials last night?" That from the President. Yes, that was a prudent question. Who might be next?

"No, sir."

"Anybody step forward to claim responsibility, terrorist groups, like that?"

"No, Mr. President."

"Anything on the bombs?" Reed asked.

"The charge under the manhole cover was a U.S. Army antitank mine, and the explosive's taggants identified it as part of a batch that supposedly went into the ground in Iraq during the Gulf War. Likely dug up by some farmer with a metal detector and sold on the black market. Or maybe diverted by a quartermaster before it ever got to Iraq. No way to tell at this point."

"The limpet on the door was untagged, but our lab says it's Israeli small-marine surplus, about five years old."

"Probably pick up one of those at a good-sized gun show," Reed said. He smiled to show it was a joke. He sounded nervous, too. Not really afraid, but a little edgy. Understandable.

Michaels continued: "No prints or DNA dregs on the expended brass, all of which were identical. From the bullets removed from the victims and cars, the ammunition appears to have been factory-loaded Federal 147 gr. 9mm Luger FMJ round-nose, and would have been subsonic from either a pistol or a submachine gun. Extractor marks on the casings show that both types of weapons were used. So far, recovered tags from the gunpowder show the lot numbers to be parts of shipments that went to Chicago, Detroit, Miami and Fort Worth."

"Good luck tracing that," Reed said. "And those guns are probably in the bay by now."

"All right, we have the facts, such as they are," the President said. "How about a theory. Who did it, Mr. Michaels? Who are they going to come after next?"

"Computer, image twelve," Michaels said.

Another holoproj appeared, also from the air, but this one showing a different scene, recorded in daylight.

"This is an FBI archive image of the scene of the killing of Thomas 'Big Red' O'Rourke in New York City last September. The method of attack was remarkably similar. A bomb went off under the Irish mobster's armored limo, the doors were blown off by limpets, O'Rourke and his bodyguards were killed by multiple rounds from 9mm pistols and submachine guns."

"There have been other killings like that, haven't there?" the President said.

"Yes, sir. Joseph DiAmmato, of the Dixie Mafia, in New Orleans last December, and Peter Heitzman in Newark this past February. The FBI's Organized Crime Unit believes the hits were ordered by Ray Genaloni, head of the New York City Five Families, but the investigation is still pending."

"Meaning you don't have anything concrete yet," Reed said.

"Nothing a federal prosecutor wants to take into court, no."

The President nodded. "So it looks like what we're talking about here is mob related? Not some kind of terrorist activity?"

Michaels was careful with his next words. "Sir. At first glance, it would seem a strong possibility."

Carver said, "If I may, Alex?"

Michaels nodded, happy to let his boss take over. He hoped his relief didn't show too much.

Carver said, "Commander Day was head of the FBI's Organized Crime Unit for several years. During that time, many of the top people in the major New York families were arrested, and half of those were convicted and put away. Genaloni's father and older brother were among those imprisoned. The mob wouldn't lose any sleep over Steve's death. And they tend to have long memories."

" 'Revenge is a dish best served cold,' " the President

said. "Isn't that a Sicilian proverb?" He looked a bit more relaxed than he had. The mob wouldn't be gunning for him.

He stood, glancing at his watch. "I hate to cut this short, gentlemen, but I have pressing matters elsewhere. It looks like this is some kind of mob thing, and while I regret the loss of Commander Day, I can't see that national security is at risk here." He glanced at Reed, who shook his head.

Or their own asses, Michaels thought.

"Okay, Walt, I *would* like to see this cleared up. Keep me apprised. Gentlemen. Mrs. Upton."

With that, the President and his Chief of Staff left.

Carver moved over to where Michaels stood near the computer. "Well, that wasn't so bad, was it?"

"No, sir."

"All right. We'll start some heat Genaloni's way," Carver said. "The man won't be able to pee without somebody watching him from inside the bowl. I want you to get your computer people digging."

"Yes, sir."

"Talk to Brent Adams at OC. He'll be told to cooperate. We aren't going to have a turf war here—I'm giving this one to you. The President of the United States has just told us he wants to see this cleared up, and it did not sound like a request to me."

"No, sir."

"That's it. I want situation reports daily, sooner if anything breaks. Anything else you can think of?"

"No, sir. We'll keep you in the loop."

"Good man."

Not until he was back in his car and well away from the White House did Michaels allow himself to relax. This high-level stuff was risky. He would rather be in the field, training new agents, anything, than playing with politicians and security advisors. Here, a misstep, one word out of place, and you'd be counting paper clips the rest of your career. So now, aside from his personal agenda, he had it straight from the top: Find out who killed Steve Day.

Find out—or else.

Fine. No problem. That was exactly what he planned to do, and he had the resources to do it.

4

Toni Fiorella was in the small gym practicing *djurus* when two members of the newest class of FBI mainline recruits came in. There were maybe a dozen people already working out—lifting weights, using the flywheel bikes or punching the heavy bag, but most of them were regulars, instructors or people assigned to Training HQ. The trainees tended to stay in their own gym, which was just fine with her. Newbies, most of them fresh out of law or accounting schools, tended to think they knew everything, and that the Bureau should feel honored they had chosen to grace it with their wonderful presence.

She shifted into a right-front stance, most of her weight on her forward foot, knee bent, did the windshield-wiper-like two-handed block to control the center, left, right, then shot her right elbow upward in a short, tight strike to an imaginary opponent's head. She slapped the elbow with her left hand to simulate the hit, slid the left hand under the right arm, where it stood ready to sweep away an opponent's return punch, then shot the straight right and left punches that followed.

This was the first *djuru,* and a very simple sequence.

One of the newbies, a tall, muscular man in blue spandex bike shorts and a matching FBI-trainee T-shirt, looked at Toni, then chuckled and said something to his buddy.

The second newbie was a short and compact man, a bit on the pudgy side, with a thick bar of eyebrows. He laughed in return.

Toni ignored the two, did the left punch and chambered that arm by her hip, then stepped forward with her left foot, to mirror the moves she'd just done.

Day's death had affected her more than she would have thought, and Alex's state of mind was also weighing heavily on her. She'd come to the gym to burn off some of her frustration at not being able to reach out to Alex the way she wanted. The workout wasn't helping much, and she wasn't feeling particularly charitable just now.

She finished the series of steps and strikes, made the backfist turn and started back the way she'd come, starting into the second *djuru*'s pattern. In Bukti, there were eight short forms, or *djurus,* that many *sambuts*—prearranged fighting sets—and techniques beyond counting based on those few simple routines.

Spandex and Eyebrows had faced off against each other; they danced back and forth, sparring. Even though she knew she should have been concentrating on her form— her guru would have frowned at her lack of attention—she watched the two men peripherally. Spandex threw a lot of high round and spinning kicks, most of them to the head, while Eyebrows barked several *kiais,* the karate-style guttural yells used for focus, as he backpedaled and ducked or blocked the kicks.

She figured Spandex for one of the Korean styles, Eyebrows for a Japanese or Okinawan fighting form. Both men looked fairly adept, though Spandex was better.

She saw Spandex grin, then launch a flying-spinning back-kick.

Right out of a bad action movie, she thought. She kept her pace even, trying to pretend she didn't notice them. Her expression gave her away, though—she couldn't stop the smile completely.

Spandex caught it, and he was not pleased.

He did a quick bow to Eyebrows to show he was done, then turned to face her. "Something funny, ma'am?" He had a strong Southern accent. Alabama, Mississippi, maybe.

Ma'am. Well, he wasn't paranoid, because she *was* laughing at him, however hidden she tried to keep it. And, truthfully, she hadn't really tried very hard to hide it. She had to watch this, the feeling of superiority she got when she saw one of the other Oriental fighting styles. Everybody thought their own system was better; she *knew* hers was.

Toni was about to the end of her set anyhow. She stopped. She knew she didn't look particularly imposing in her old black sweats, wrestling shoes and sweaty headband. And at five-five and a hundred and thirty pounds, she was almost a foot shorter and probably seventy pounds lighter than Spandex. But his tone irritated her.

"No," she said. "Nothing funny."

"Really? I thought maybe you were, you know, amused by my form or something."

"No. It's not amusing," she said. She started to turn away.

Eyebrows decided this was a good time to jump in. He said, "My friend here has a second-degree black belt." He waved at her, as if to take in the form she'd been practicing. "I bet he could teach you some things."

"I'm sure he could," Toni said. Yeah, how to move wrong. But she kept her mouth shut as she headed for her towel. Might as well shower. She wasn't going to be able to concentrate with these two bozos flexing and being macho. She'd grown up with a houseful of brothers; she knew once the testosterone got to flowing, it was like the full-moon tide, there was no stopping it. Pretty soon, these two would be spitting on the ground and adjusting their crotches, or as close as they could get to it indoors.

Manhood was a tricky business. She ought to know better than to mess with it by now.

"So, what is that little shuffle thing you were doing?" Spandex said. He and Eyebrows grinned at each other.

Little shuffle thing. Oh, boy.

She turned back to face the pair. "It's called a *djuru,*" she said. "The style is *Pukulan Pentjak Silat Bukti Negara-Serak.*"

Spandex gave her a big grin. "Sounds like some kind of Thai food with peanut sauce. You, uh, have any rank in it?"

"We don't have belts. You're either a student or a teacher. I'm a student."

"Well, it looks very nice," Spandex said. "Even though I never heard of it."

Nice.

Toni smiled. There were a lot of things she generally let pass when she heard them from obnoxious men, and condescension had to be high on her list, since she got so much of it. She was only twenty-seven—that got comments, a woman—more comments, and Italian—that one was usually good for three or four Mafia jokes. She wondered why it was men felt the need to behave with her as they sometimes did. Not all men, not all the time, but enough so that it was sometimes a chore dealing with them. More than sometimes, it seemed to her.

Another day, in a better mood, she'd have smiled and shaken her head and turned away, let the boys have their fun. But right now, she didn't much feel the milk of human kindness flowing through her. It had been a long, crappy night, and was shaping up to be a long and crappier day. She didn't need this. *And know what?* She didn't have to take it.

So she said, "I'm sorry your education has been so narrow."

Spandex frowned. He knew an insult when he heard it. "Excuse me?"

She smiled wider, as sweet as she could make it. "Which part didn't you understand?"

"Look, ma'am, there's no reason to get snotty."

"Oh, I agree. So, you're a black belt, is that right?"

"That's right."

"Tell you what. Why don't you come over here and see if you can hit me? And I'll show you how my little shuffle works."

Spandex and Eyebrows exchanged glances. Spandex hesitated, and she knew why. This was a no-win situation for him. If he whacked her, he was a big bully picking on a little woman. If she whacked him, his manhood would be in great jeopardy.

"I don't think so, ma'am. I am an expert. I wouldn't want to hurt you."

"I wouldn't worry about that," she said. "I don't think it's likely."

She knew this was not a good thing to be doing. Her guru would be irritated in the extreme to know she was egging this guy on, but she couldn't seem to help herself. The trainee was so arrogant it rose from him like steam from a fresh-cooked hot dog on a winter's day in the Bronx.

Eyebrows waggled the hairy bar at Spandex. "Hey, you don't have to hit her hard. You can pull it. Just show her a couple of your moves."

Spandex grinned. A chance to shine? How could he pass that up? "All right, ma'am."

He walked closer. When he was about three meters away, he stopped. Bowed. Dropped into a narrow horse stance and edged forward, hands lifted, one high, one low. "You ready?"

She almost laughed. Might as well send her a telegram. "Oh, yeah."

He was fast—and he was smarter than he looked. He didn't try one of the flashy and stupid high kicks. He scooted, stepped in, and fired a quick, hard right punch at her chest, right leg leading. It was a good shot, in balance, aimed where it wouldn't cause her any great damage if she missed deflecting it. Kept his other hand up to cover.

Perfect.

He probably expected her to step back and parry, but that was not how it went in her version of *silat,* not in this situation. She double-blocked with both hands open, stepped toward him, set her left foot down in a front stance and ducked under his outstretched arm as she swung her right elbow into his ribs under the armpit. Made a nice hollow thump when she hit him. Stopped him cold.

Surprised the hell out of him, too.

Her feet were already in place. *Base—*

She reached up behind him fast, caught his left shoulder with her left hand. *Angle—*

At the same time, she reached up and across with her right hand and laid it on his forehead, elbow down. *Leverage—*

Those things done, she pushed forward, then tugged down and back at his shoulder at the same time she swept his head backward.

Base, angle, leverage. If you had all three, the technique always worked. No exceptions.

She had all three.

Spandex went down like a chainsawed redwood, hit the
mat flat on his back. She could have followed up with el-
bows, knees, whatever, but instead she moved back two
steps. She didn't want to hurt him. Just embarrass him.

The entire sequence, from the time of his punch until she
stepped away, had taken just under two seconds.

He rolled up and started for her. "Bitch!"

Well. So much for "ma'am."

He probably had a sequenced attack planned, a favorite
combination of kicks and punches, fakes, sweeps, before
the killer shot that usually worked for him when he sparred
for points. If she stood there and let him get to it, it could
be dangerous.

She didn't let him get to it.

As he launched a left jab to set her up, she stepped outside with the two-handed block, alligatored his arm with
both hands just above his elbow, pivoted, dropped all her
weight to one knee and pinwheeled him. Some of the boxing styles did teach their students how to do a little grap-
pling and how to fall, but apparently Spandex's was not
one of them.

He did a half-flip, and slammed into the mat on his upper
back again, hard enough to knock his wind out. This was
all simple stuff, right out of the first *djuru*. Why work any
harder than you had to?

Toni came to her feet, waiting to see if he was going to
try a third attack.

Spandex was not so foolish. This time when he got up,
he held out one hand in a *no mas* gesture. Lesson over. He
knew when he was overmatched.

Toni felt pretty good, despite knowing she should not
have felt that way. Then she glanced at the entrance to the
gym.

Alex Michaels leaned against the wall, watching her.

• • •

Michaels walked over to where Toni stood. He was in decent shape. He ran three or four miles most days, did a little triking and had a Bowflex machine in his condo for resistance work, but it had been a long time since his hand-to-hand training in the military, and later when he'd joined Net Force. Computer geeks didn't spend too much time in real-world hot-field situations. He thought he could handle himself in most one-on-one situations, but he would not have particularly wanted to take on the big guy just getting up off the mat, and after watching Toni toss the poor joker around like a Frisbee, he *sure* wouldn't have wanted to take her on. He knew from her file what the fighting system was, though he didn't know much about it. Amazing.

"Very interesting," he said. "It's called *silat*? Where did you learn it?"

She wiped at her face with a towel. "There was a little old Dutch-Indonesian woman who lived in my neighborhood when I was about thirteen. Her name was Susan DeBeers. She was in her sixties, retired, her husband recently dead. She liked to sit on the stoop of the building across the street, smoke a small carved meerschaum pipe and enjoy the spring sunshine. One Saturday, four gang-bangers decided they wanted her spot. She got up to leave, but it wasn't fast enough for them. One of them tried to speed her up with a kick."

Toni slung the towel over her shoulder. "These guys were eighteen, twenty, had knives and sharpened screwdrivers tucked into their pockets. I was waiting for a bus, I watched the whole thing. It took maybe fifteen seconds, and I couldn't tell you to this day exactly what she did to them. Here was this little old potbellied woman smoking like a chimney who pounded and threw four thugs around like tennis balls, kept her pipe in her mouth the whole time, didn't work up a lather. She put all four of them into the emergency room. I decided I needed to learn whatever it was she knew.''

"She had a school?''

"No. I walked across the street a couple of days later—took me that long to get my nerve up—and asked her if she would teach me. She just nodded and smiled and said, 'Sure.' I trained with her until after I graduated from college and moved to Washington. Whenever I go home to visit my folks, I work out with her.''

"She must be getting up there,'' Michaels said.

"Eighty-two on her last birthday,'' Toni said, "and I still wouldn't want to try her head-to-head.''

"Amazing.''

"It's a very scientific art, based on leverage and angles. It assumes you'll be fighting with multiple opponents, all of whom will be bigger and stronger than you. So it relies on technique and not muscle, which in my case is a good thing. Normally, women didn't get into it very far, but Guru DeBeers' husband traveled a lot. He wanted her to have something to protect herself.'' Toni stopped. "But I won't bore you with any more esoteric fighting stuff.''

"No, I'm interested. How does this compare with something like boxing or judo?''

"Well. Most of the older arts come from countries long civilized. Things like Chinese kung-fu, Korean taekwondo, Japanese jujitsu—they've had hundreds, even thousands of years to refine the techniques. Along the way, some of the really ugly stuff got replaced with more spiritual aspects. Fighting to the death tends to get frowned on in civilized company. Which is not to say that an expert in any of these arts isn't dangerous. A good kung-fu or karate stylist will surely hand you your head if you don't know how to stop him.''

"I hear a 'but' in there,'' he said.

She grinned. "A lot of *silat* came out of the jungle only

two or three generations ago. There are hundreds of styles, although most of it wasn't practiced in public until Indonesia gained independence in 1949. It's real primal stuff, designed for one thing—to cripple or kill an attacker. It's not civilized. It is as deadly and efficient as they could make it. If a technique didn't work, the player who used it either wound up maimed or dead, so that piece didn't get passed on.''

"Interesting.''

She grinned. "What you saw here? That was the Bukti, the simple stuff. The parent art, Serak, is a whole new ballgame. *Really* nasty, and a lot of weapon work—sticks, knives, swords, tridents, even guns.''

"And you're supposed to be a nice Italian girl from the Bronx. Remind me not to get on your bad side.''

"Hey, Alex?''

"Yeah?''

"Don't get on my bad side.'' She laughed. "Okay, so what's up? You didn't come here to watch me beat recruits up, did you?''

"No, it's business. We've got another problem,'' he said. "Somebody just blew up the main subnet server at the Net Force post in Frankfurt, Germany.''

"You mean the CIA post.''

"Right. Net Force being chartered to operate in this country only, except in cases of international emergency and requiring Presidential authorization for such operation, of course what I meant was the CIA listening post.''

That got a grin from her. "Memorized that right out of the charter, huh?''

"Why, whatever do you mean, Deputy Commander Fiorella? Net Force would never do anything illegal.''

She smiled wider. He kind of liked that, making her smile. The idea that an FBI unit set up to do computer monitoring would be restricted to the United States was fairly foolish. There were no borders on the net; the web stretched everywhere, and while you could access most of it from anywhere, certain systems were easier to log into with a certain amount of proximity. The CIA was willing to lend its name to Net Force from time to time, in exchange for certain favors they couldn't get on their own. The CIA wasn't supposed to operate *within* the United States, but *nobody* really believed it did not.

"Let me clean up and let's go see," she said.

5

An incoming tankbuster rocket hit the building behind Colonel John Howard's Net Force Strike Team, no more than twenty feet above their heads. The missile exploded on impact, blasting a blackened crater in the eighty-year-old structure. A shower of brick fragments and glass pattered down around the half-dozen soldiers where they crouched behind a twisted metal Dumpster. It was a sharp rain, but the least of Howard's worries at this point. They had to take the sucker with the missile launcher out fast!

"Reeves and Johnson, flank, left!" Howard said. It wasn't necessary to yell—all of them wore LOSIR headsets built into their helmets; he could have whispered and they'd have heard him loud and clear. The line-of-sight infrared tactical com units had a short range and worked pretty much only if you could actually *see* the person you were talking to; on the other hand, they wouldn't be picked up by an enemy with a scanner unless you could see *him,* too, and that was the reason to use them. "Odom and Vasquez, suppressing fire! Chan and Brown, go right! On my command . . . three . . . two . . . one—*now!*''

Odom and Vasquez opened up with their H&K assault subguns, unleashing a canvas-rip full-auto barrage of high-cyclic 9mm's from hundred-round drum magazines.

Reeves and Johnson bailed left and dodged their way across the street, stutter-stepped for the cover of a big tractor-trailer. The truck was long dead, the tires burned and melted away, the metal of the cab and trailer pock-marked with old bullet holes and darkened by soot and graffiti.

Chan and Brown bailed right, adding fire from their weapons as they ran broken-field lines across the killing zone.

The modified SIPEsuits the team wore should be enough to stop most of what the locals had to throw at them. The vests and pants were of cloned spider-silk hardweave, and held pockets of overlapping ceramic plates that would turn pistol or rifle bullets, provided they weren't armor-piercing hotloads. Helmets and boots were Kevlar, with titanium inserts. The backpack CPUs were shockproofed and double-ceramic-plated. The tactical comps encrypted radio, satellite uplinks and downlinks, gave heads-up ghost displays, with motion sensors, IR and UV spookeye scans, terrain maps, even instant flare-polarizers built into the helmets' retractable blast shields. The Net Force suits weren't as heavy as regular Army issue, since they had no SCBA, no distill, no biojects. For this kind of assault, in and out in one day, they didn't need full infantry bells and whistles; even so, the suits added twenty pounds to a wearer.

Howard popped up and shoved his Thompson submachine gun over the top of the Dumpster, cooking off several three-round bursts at the hidey-hole where the guy with the rocket launcher was. The tommy gun was definitely low-tech, an antique built in 1928, and had first belonged to an Indiana sheriff during Prohibition. Howard's great-grandfather, being black, wasn't officially allowed on the force in those days, but the white sheriff he'd worked for knew a good man when he saw one, regardless of his color, so there was an unofficial Negro who spent twenty years making good money enforcing the law, even if it was off the books. When the sheriff died, he left the tommy gun to Grampa Howard. They called it a Chicago typewriter in those days.

No time for a stroll down memory lane now, John! Duck!

The rocket man had kept his head down, too, but somebody in the stairwell with him let loose a return blast of small-arms fire that pinged and clanged against the heavy Dumpster. Its battered steel was still thick enough to turn the bullets. Howard was glad of it, too, suits notwithstanding.

"Fire in the hole!" Reeves's voice over Howard's com interrupted the sounds of gunfire.

The grenade Reeves tossed into the stairwell went off. More shrapnel spanged against the Dumpster, and the stink of burned explosive washed over Howard, along with smoke and dust.

Two seconds passed. All shooting stopped.

"Clear!" Johnson yelled.

Colonel Howard stood. He saw Johnson grin at him and give him a thumbs-up gesture. Howard returned the grin. His men—well, five men and a woman—stood at the ready, weapons seeking possible targets as they scanned the street and buildings for more trouble. It would be stupid in the extreme for a local to stand up and wave hello to the nice Americans just at that moment.

Howard tapped his helmet flatpad, toggled on his heads-up display and got a digital time-read. He usually kept the display off when things actually got hot—he didn't want to be shooting at phantoms created by his computer. You were supposed to ignore such things with enough practice, but when real bullets started zipping past, it was amazing how many well-trained soldiers opened up on a heat-sig icon or a flashing timer in a heads-up display.

"Good job, people, but let's move. We've got six minutes to get to the rendezvous point."

The team started to move out—

Abruptly, the men, the street, the buildings faded. They went ghostly, transparent, then blinked out.

"Priority call, John," a crisp military voice said.

Howard blinked, raised the VR eyeband and sighed.

He was in his office at the Net Force HQ, and the firefight in Sarajevo had been a computer simulacrum, not a real battle. It was nothing to keep playing at when there was a priority call on-line. "Put it through," he told his computer.

The head-and-shoulders image of Net Force's civilian Commander, Alexander Michaels, appeared over Howard's desk.

Howard nodded at the holoproj. "Commander Michaels."

"Colonel. We have a situation I thought you might want to monitor."

"The explosion in Germany?" Howard said.

"Yes."

"My people are already aware of it. Are we talking about an insertion here?" Howard couldn't keep the interest out of his voice.

"Not in Frankfurt, no," Michaels said, "it's too late for that. But I've got all our listening posts and subnets on alert, especially in the European theater. Better make sure your Strike Teams are ready."

"My Strike Teams are *always* ready, Commander." He felt the stiffness in his voice, but could not help that, either.

He had yet to get used to taking orders from a civilian, a man whose father had been a career Army noncommissioned officer, but who had never spent any time in the service himself. Yes, the President of the United States was the Commander in Chief of the military, and yes, the current one hadn't done any time in the service, either. But he was smart enough to let his generals do their jobs. Steve Day had been Navy, and that was bad enough; Howard wasn't sure about Alexander Michaels yet.

"I didn't mean to imply otherwise, Colonel."

"Sorry, Commander. We're on Alert Status Two. I can have my top ten teams airborne in an hour—half that if we go to AS-One."

"I hope it won't come to that."

"Yes, sir," Howard said. But what he hoped was that it *would* come to that. The sooner his troops got a chance to show what they could really do in a hot zone, the happier he was going to be. If you were going to be a warrior, you needed a war now and then—or a police action at the very least.

"I'll keep you apprised," Michaels said. "Discom."

"Sir."

But Howard wasn't worried about that. He had his own wireheads working the nets. If Michaels's crew got it first, it wouldn't be by much.

Best he put them to work to be sure they didn't miss anything. He reached for the com again.

When he went on-line, Plekhanov still used old-style helmet and gloves, even though the newer systems didn't need either. These days, holoproj imagery could englobe a viewer's field of vision with a simple eyeband no wider than a pencil, and the reader software behind a computer's holocam could pick up finger-jive command language and translate it as accurately as even the best gloves. But he liked the gloves, was used to them. Just as most keyboarding was now Dvorak pattern instead of Qwerty, another system he hadn't switched over to. He didn't care what anybody said. Forty-five years of muscle memory just didn't go away and allow itself to be replaced by something else simply because the new method was more efficient.

He waved the web to life and said, "Olympic Peninsula Trail."

The VR gear took over, producing an image of a temperate rain forest, a narrow path bounded on the sides by tall Douglas fir, thick ferns and patches of assorted fungi—mushrooms, toadstools and the like. Early July afternoon sunshine slanted down through the dense canopy of evergreens and alder trees, and painted the forest with slats of light and dark. Insects buzzed, birds chirped; a pleasant warmth, not overly hot here in the shade, suffused the woods.

Plekhanov was dressed in sensible hiking clothes: a khaki shirt and shorts, knee-length polyprop socks, wafflestomper trail boots. He also wore an Irish rain hat. He carried a stout walking staff his own height, and a small day pack containing a rain poncho, a water bottle, a plastic bag of trail mix, a compass, a flashlight, matches, a basic first-aid kit, a Swiss Army knife and an emergency cell phone/ GPS unit. Though he planned to keep to the trail, it was always better to be prepared than not.

In his day pack, he also had the sealed packet he was to deliver.

He walked along the edge of a stream, listening to the cold and clear water burbling over smooth stones. Here and there, he saw small fish in quieter pools. He enjoyed the scent of fir, the feel of the humus-padded earth under his hiking boots, the empty trail, devoid of other humans.

After walking briskly for a time, he stopped and had a drink of water. While he was resting, he examined his watch. The device was a match to the one he had carried for more than fifteen years, a Russian analog-mechanical pocket watch. It was a Molnija, big, heavy, mostly steel, with an eighteen-jewel movement. This model had the hammer and sickle and star on the back and an inset of the Kremlin on the hinged front, and was a commemorative model celebrating the Russian victories in the 1941–1945 war. After the breakup of the Soviet Union, cash-poor Russia had sold everything that wasn't nailed down to anybody with the money to buy it, and such watches had gone for ridiculously small amounts. If you could find a non-digital timepiece this well made and sturdy in the West—and you could not—it would have easily cost ten times as much as he had paid for this one.

He thumbed the button, and the hinged cover popped open. He looked at the Roman numerals. Almost time for his meeting at the big rock on the coast. He snapped the cover closed. He needed to hurry. At the rock—a massive chunk of weather-beaten stone near the juncture of the Pacific Ocean and the Straits of Juan de Fuca at Cape Foulweather—Plekhanov would deliver his packet to a courier. The courier would take the package by fishing boat—in this scenario, at least—to a certain fat man who had access to certain systems, and the fat man would, in exchange for the packet of valuables—in this case, binary "jewels" he could sell—cause to be put into effect a small series of electronic "snowballs." By the time these reached their destinations, some of them would be no larger, just like balls of hard ice, but some would be veritable avalanches. Whatever was needed.

A small animal darted across the path in front of Plekhanov—a rabbit or perhaps a raccoon?—and there was a commotion in the ferns as the creature passed through. The man smiled. This was one of his favorite trips. He much enjoyed the counterpoint to the reality. Walking along a wooded trail was as far removed from computers and nets as the moon was from the Earth. No small irony here.

Naturally, such musings turned his attention to technology, and the uses to which he had been putting it of late. Most of it had been in VR or sublinks. Not all, of course. Sometimes the real world needed real actions.

The physical destruction of the CIA/Net Force post in Germany had been one such action, crude, but necessary. Too much electronic tampering with programmers as adept as the best of Net Force's hackers would send up a warning flag. A bomb, on the other hand, could come from any wild-eyed radical. There had to be some alternation. The kind of software and viral attacks he was about to launch on systems in several of the Commonwealth of Independent States, in the Baltics, even on a Korean or Japanese system or two, just to keep people guessing—well, those would be of a different nature.

There were going to be hundreds of programmers and systems engineers cursing and sweating soon, and much chaos to rectify. When chaos came, his talents were going to be in great demand. And who better to fix things than the man who knew exactly how they had been broken?

The trail wound to the left, then the right, and broke out of the forest into a sandy area dotted here and there with sedge grasses or stunted ground cover. Surf pounded on the rocky shore only a kilometer or so away. He saw the fishing boat anchored well offshore, and a high-bowed dory motoring from the larger vessel toward the shore. Come to see him, to collect what he carried, then to do his bidding. The weather was going gray, fog rolling in, and it was also growing chilly. Appropriate for this scenario.

Here was VR power, the ability to create such visions, but VR power was but a small part of his talents.

He laughed aloud. It was good to be in control. And it was going to get better, very soon.

6

Ray Genaloni put the phone's receiver down gently. "Excuse me, but isn't this supposed to be a secure line?" He did not raise his voice. He might have been asking about the weather. He pointed at the flashing red diode on the little electronic tap-detector connected to the telephone's base. "That doesn't look particularly *secure* to me."

Luigi Sampson, his enforcer, as well as the Vice President in charge of Security for Genaloni Industries—the more or less legal side of the operation—shrugged. "The feds. They got stuff we can't get commercially."

Genaloni ground his teeth together. He mentally counted, slowly.

One . . . two . . . three . . .

He had been working to control his temper for most of his forty years, and he was a little better at it than he used to be.

. . . four . . . five . . . six . . .

Twenty years ago, when Little Frankie Dobbs had given

him a similar shrug for something that had pissed Ray off, he had beaten Little Frankie's head in with a Louisville Slugger. Killed the idiot, ruined a nine-hundred-dollar suit with blood spatter, and had to beg his father for forgiveness because Little Frankie was almost a made guy and the son of an old friend besides.

... seven ... eight ... nine ... ten.

"All right," Ray said, feeling a little more in control, even if his anger was still hot and churning in his belly. As long as it didn't show, that was the thing. He had come a long way since Little Frankie. He wasn't going to fly off the handle and start doing stupid stuff, not now. He had a degree in business from Harvard. He was the CEO of a major company, not to mention head of the Family and all *those* businesses. Take it easy, find out what's going on.

He looked at Sampson, who sat on the couch across the desk from him. "All right, Lou. Who is behind this?" He waved at the phone.

"It's coming out of the FBI's Net Force," Sampson said.

Genaloni adjusted the Windsor knot on his two-hundred-dollar silk tie. Calm. That was the way. Calm. "Net Force? That's computer stuff. We aren't into that in any major way."

Sampson shook his head. "Somebody knocked off their head guy in D.C. last week. They're looking at us for it."

"Did we do it and somebody forgot to tell me?"

"We didn't do it, Boss."

"Then why, pray tell, are they looking at us for it?"

"Somebody wants them to think it's us. Whoever cooled the FBI guy used the same MO as our Ice Team."

"Why would somebody want the feds to think we killed one of them? Never mind, I know the answer to that. So the question is, *who* is trying to put this one on us?"

Genaloni leaned back in the massage chair, a four-thousand-buck unit full of motors and top-of-the-line electronics under a carefully distressed brown leather cover. The chair hummed and sensors measured and weighed and adjusted springs and cushions to support the small of his back. He'd injured his back on a dare when he'd been fourteen, jumping sixty feet off a dock into the East River. That had been stupid two times: one, for the jump; two, for the polluted water. He was lucky he hadn't gotten hepatitis while he'd been thrashing around in that crappy water, almost drowning from the pain. And his back had been giving him trouble on and off ever since.

"I don't know, Ray. We've got our people looking, but no leads yet."

"All right. Keep at it. Find out who is trying to give us grief. Let me know as soon as you get it. And since I can't trust my own phones, get a message to the Selkie. Put him on standby."

Sampson said, "We can handle this in-house, Ray. I got people."

"Humor me, Lou. You know, me being the boss and all?"

Sampson nodded. "Right."

After Sampson had left, Ray touched a control on the chair and allowed the motors to rumble and massage his aching back. He didn't need this kind of problem. The legit enterprises now brought in more money than the graybiz. There were some corporate takeovers and a couple of merger possibilities in the works, and he did not want the feds breathing down his neck while those were in flux. Whoever was doing this had made a mistake, a bad mistake. One more generation and his family would be respectable, as legitimate as any other family whose fortunes had begun with bandit ancestors somewhere back in history. His grandkids would rub shoulders with Kennedys, Rockefellers, Mitsubishis—no hint of scandal or illegality. The ends justified the means. Respectability was worth it, even if you

had to kill a bunch of people standing between you and it
to get there.

Mikhayl Ruzhyó stood on a street corner in Chinatown,
looking at a storefront with live white ducks penned in the
window. It was as interesting as anything he'd seen in this
city, the ducks. He had ridden on the famous cable cars,
and they were, in his opinion, much overrated. He had
viewed the Coit Tower in the distance. Gone to Fisherman's
Wharf and eaten fried shrimp. He had seen the famous bar
where women with a fondness for filling their breasts with
bathtub sealer had danced naked. Too, he had watched
many homosexual couples walk past on the streets, holding
hands and doing things that would have gotten them arrested back home.

And now he watched ducks, destined to be somebody's
dinner, waddle back and forth in the window of a Chinese
grocery. Such an exciting life.

He smiled to himself. He was no Country Ivan, come to
a big city for the first time. He was a man of the world.
He had spent time in Moscow, Paris, Rome, Tel Aviv, New
York, Washington, D.C. But none of those places were
home. Where he wished more than anything to be was at
his small farm on the outskirts of Grozny. What he wanted
to do was arise at dawn, go outside on a frigid winter morning with hoar frost thick on the ground and split wood for
the stove, using his muscles like a man should. He wanted
to be feeding the goats and chickens and geese, milking the
cow, then warming his hands by the fire as Anna fried eggs
in fragrant goose grease for his breakfast. . . .

He turned away from the placid fowls, which knew not what fate awaited them. Anna was five years gone, taken by the cancer that had eaten her life all too quickly. At least she had not died in pain. He'd had enough contacts to provide her with medicine for that. But no cure had been possible, even with the best doctors in the country on call. Plekhanov had seen to the doctors. Ruzhyó would always be in the Russian's debt for his help during Anna's final days.

What he wanted was impossible. The farm was still there, his brother working it, but Anna was not, and so it meant nothing to him anymore. Nothing.

He started to walk, paying only as much attention as needed to potential threats as the Chinese locals and tourists moved past him, ogling the displays in various shops. Here a place where imported brass was peddled, there a store specializing in stereo music players and small computers, over there a place that sold shoes.

When Anna died, nothing had been left to him. After a dark, bleak time he could hardly remember, Plekhanov had reminded him of his old desire to see his country prosper. And Plekhanov had offered him a way to help achieve that, by doing what he already knew how to do best: *mokrie dela*—the wetwork. Before Anna's illness, he had put that away, retired, but afterward? What did it matter? One place was as good as another. If a thing pleased Plekhanov, that was sufficient reason to do it.

No, he could not go back to the life he had lived before. Never again.

The communications device Plekhanov had provided him buzzed on his belt. Ruzhyó looked around, sharpening his perceptions, alert for anybody taking notice of him. If he was being watched, he could not detect it. There was no reason for anybody in this city to watch him, even to know he existed, but one did not survive in this business for very long by being less than careful. Plekhanov wished for him to survive, so he did what was needed to do so.

He pulled the com unit from his belt. Only three people should have this number: Plekhanov, Winters the American, and Grigory the Snake.

"Yes?"

"There is another job," Plekhanov said.

Ruzhyó nodded at the speaker, even though there was no visual link. "I understand," he said.

"I shall contact you later to supply the details."

"I am ready."

Plekhanov disconnected the link. Ruzhyó clipped the com unit back to his belt, adjusting it slightly. He was used to the weight of a gun on that hip, and even a small gun was much heavier than the little communications device, but he carried no gun now. This was not Chechnya nor Russia, where he had official standing. Here, you normally did not carry weapons, unless you were police or some sort of governmental agent, especially in this city. Guns were banned here. They had a statue in a park somewhere, made of metal from melted guns. Besides, he was not a man who felt naked without a pistol on his belt. He knew a dozen ways to kill somebody using his hands, or a stick, or other available materials. He was well trained in such things. Yes, he would obtain a gun when it was needed, but unless he was working, no.

In a land of sheep, even a toothless wolf is king.

Another job. Fine. He was ready. He was always ready.

The secure line bleeped, and Mora Sullivan smiled as she waved her hand over the phone to activate it. The unit was wireless, shielded, and its transmissions and receptions encoded. The signal was routed and rerouted a dozen times. Each new call took different pathways in a random pattern through the net and comsats and back, so that tracing the unit to her location would be impossible. And her outgoing vox signal was scrambled—without a coded receiver, the binary code could not be translated. The speed, pitch, tone and cadence of her speech were electronically altered by her computer, so that on the other end of the connection, she sounded male, with a deep Midwestern American TV announcer's voice. The effect on a listener was that of a powerful middle-age man who had perhaps smoked or drunk too much at one time. The vox-scrambler was good enough so there was no hint of electronic trickery in the sound it produced, and it would fool the most sophisticated voxprint reader attempting to match it to her own. Not that it would ever come to that.

"Yes?"

"You know who this is?"

It was Luigi Sampson, Genaloni's enforcer. "I know who this is," she said.

"Would you be available to perform a service for us in the near future?"

"I can make myself available."

"Good. If you would stand by for the next week or so, we will pay your customary advance against the service fee."

The Selkie smiled. Her standby advance was twenty-five thousand dollars per day, whether she did a job or not. A hundred and seventy-five thousand just to be available for a week in case somebody decided upon a target was not a bad bit of change. Her fee for a job itself varied according to the complexity and danger involved; a quarter of a million was her starting price. If the client came up with a target, she would deduct the standby from the total payment. She wasn't greedy. And Genaloni was one of her best customers, worth two million to her last year. Another six or eight months and she would be able to retire, to leave the game. She had almost enough put away to do so now, pushing ten million, which had always been her goal. With that much, she could spend a million a year in earned interest and never have to touch the principal. And there she would be, not yet thirty, wealthy, able to go anywhere she pleased, to do anything she wanted. Nobody would have a clue who she had been in her previous life; nobody would ever suspect the petite red-haired Irishwoman, daughter of an IRA man who didn't have two nickels to rub together when he died, of being the Selkie, the highest-paid freelance assassin on the planet. Besides her current identity, she had paper and electronic trails already laid for her new life, so that should her background and wealth ever be questioned, they would easily pass inspection.

Her father's early lessons with a gun or knife or bomb had certainly paid off. Of course, he probably wouldn't be pleased at some of the people she'd worked for since he'd died, but his cause was not hers. Once the British decided to leave Ireland to its own sorrows, that whole long-running mess had ceased to have any meaning, even though the players refused to just quit and leave it at that. Something that established just didn't go away, even if its reason for being did.

Her mother, bless her, had been a hardheaded Scot, and had taught her children, all seven of them, to value a shilling.

Sullivan smiled again. That was where she had come up with her *nom de morte,* from her mother. The old stories her mother had told her children late at night, when the telly was on the blink and the radio unable to pick up anything, were full of changelings and curses and magic. The Selkies were the seal-folk, full of the *were,* able to shapeshift from men to seals and back again. She had always liked that image, of appearing to be one thing while really being another.

Nobody knew who she was. She had never met a client

face-to-face, save once, and that client was no longer among the living. She was a faceless assassin, one that most people thought a man, and the best there was at it, too.

Of that her father would have been proud, she was sure.

And, it seemed, she was about to go out on the hunt again.

7

One of the reasons Alex Michaels liked the condo in which he lived was the size of the attached garage. It was a two-car unit, and there was plenty of room for his hobby, which had been, for the last month, a thirteen-year-old Plymouth Prowler. It had replaced a '77 MG Midget that he'd spent a year and half rebuilding. He'd enjoyed that, gotten a nice profit for it, but the little English car couldn't hold a candle to the Prowler for looks.

Designed by the legendary Tom Gale for Chrysler as a concept car in the early nineties, the Prowler finally saw production four years later. It was essentially a slicked-up hot rod, a rear-wheel-drive, two-seat convertible roadster, painted a brilliant deep rich color known as Prowler purple. Since it wasn't old enough to be a classic, it had all the bells and whistles of a street car—air bags, power disc brakes, power steering and even a power rear window—but what it really was was a big kid's toy. It also had a manual transmission, smaller tires on the front than on the rear, exposed front wheels with just hints of fenders and a tachometer mounted on the steering column.

He'd been too young for the glory days of hot-rodding in the late forties and early fifties, days portrayed in rebel movies old before he was born in 1970. But his grandfather had told him stories. Told him tales about the Eisenhower years when he'd owned a primer-gray '32 Ford he'd souped up and taken to drag-race a quarter mile Sunday mornings in the summers on the cracked concrete runways of a shut-down airport. He'd filled Michael's mind's eye with chopped and channeled Chevys and Mercurys and Dodges that sometimes wore twenty hand-rubbed coats of candy-apple-red metalflake paint, with hubcaps called spinners or moons or fake wires. Showed him the stacks of old hot-rod magazines that had gone dry and yellow with time, but whose fading pictures still revealed the cars. He had smiled happily as he'd told a young Alex Michaels about im-promptu races in the middle of town at every stoplight on any given Friday night, and of drive-in malt shops and rock and roll music blasting from AM radios, when gasoline had cost twenty cents a gallon for ethyl and nobody who was anybody walked anywhere when they could drive.

Some kids grew up wanting to be cowboys in the Old West of the 1870's. Michaels had wanted to be James Dean in the post-World War II 1950's. . . .

He smiled as he rubbed creamy-gray degreaser into his palms, then over the rest of his hands. The stuff had that sharp, perfumed stink that reminded him of Grandaddy Michaels, who had started to teach him how to work on cars when he'd been fourteen.

You could have eaten off the floor in the old man's shop, so clean had it been, with its big red rolling-chest of Crafts-man and Snap-On tools always at the ready. The old man could strip an engine, drop a transmission, break down a rear end, and when he was done there was never a trace of oil or grit left on the concrete floor of the workshop. He'd been an artist.

He hadn't lived long enough to see the Prowler. A heart attack had dropped him at seventy, but Michaels was sure his grandfather would have approved of the latest project, with a few reservations. Yeah, it wasn't as frill-free as the old man would have liked—he hadn't held much with air bags or power anything—but it was mostly an analog machine in a digital world, and it sure looked like one of the old hot rods. Drove nice, too, though Michaels hadn't gotten a chance to do much of that yet. Several parts of the engine were on the workbench, including the electronic fuel-injection unit, which was much in need of work or outright replacement. The last guy who'd owned the car had apparently tried to fix it on his own, and just as apparently, had not known which end of a screwdriver was which.

Michaels wiped much of the grime from his hands on a red shop rag, tossing the cloth into a steel rag bin when he was done. His grandfather had been a bug about spontaneous combustion, though the idea of a hand-cleaner rag bursting into flame seemed far-fetched to Michaels. The rest of the grease should come off just fine in the shower.

The doorbell rang. Hmm. Must be his driver. He was early; he wasn't supposed to show up for another half hour. The assassination protocols were still in effect—for another few days, anyhow—so one of the guards posted out front would have intercepted anybody who didn't have clearance to approach his house.

Michaels reached for the intercom. "Larry?"

"Not that I noticed," a woman's voice said.

"Toni?"

"Yep."

"Come around to the garage, I'll let you in." He hit the control for the electric gate lock that allowed access into his yard, then tapped the garage-door opener as Toni rounded the corner.

"Wow. So this is the new car?"

He grinned. "This is the beast."

She stepped into the garage, and put one hand on the right rear fender. "It looks great."

"I'd offer to take you for a ride, but she's not on-line at the moment." He waved at the part on the workbench.

"Fuel injectors clogged?" she said.

That surprised him. It must have shown in his face.

Before he could say anything, she shrugged. "I grew up with a house full of brothers. Cars were big status symbols in our neighborhood. The boys always had one beater or another up on jacks, trying to keep it running. I picked up a little bit about them on the way. This a V-Eight?"

"A V-Six," he said. "A 3.5 liter, 24-valve single over-head cam, but it'll develop just over two hundred horsepower at 5900 RPM. It's not a muscle machine like the Dodge Viper—one of those will blow the doors off a Corvette—but it'll scoot right along." Toni was tough, beautiful—and she knew about cars. There was a combination a lot of men would appreciate in a woman, him included.

Dangerous road, Alex. Better stay off it.

"Let me know when you get it running," she said.

"I will. So, what brings you here so early?"

"We've had some developments."

His house phone rang. He nodded at Toni. "Just a second." He walked to the wall, intending to get rid of who-ever it was.

"Hello?"

"Hi, guess who!"

"Susie! How are you?"

"Great, Dadster. Mom said I should call and thank you for the skates."

For a moment, he went blank; then the empty spot was filled with panic. Her birthday was yesterday! Jesus, how could he have forgotten that? And what skates was she talking about? Had Megan covered for him? That would be a first.

"How was the party, hon? I'm sorry I couldn't be there for it."

"It was terrif. All my friends came, except Lori, but she's got the flu, so that's okay, and even Tommy Jerkface Stupid Dumb Head came."

Michaels grinned. At seven—no, eight, now—Susie had never been shy in expressing herself. Tommy must be the new boy she liked. The worse the names, the more the like. He felt a pang of sadness, another stabbing sensation in his gut. It was a long way from Boise to Washington, D.C. He was missing all of Susie's best moments.

"How's your mother?"

"She's fine. She's making breakfast. We got to sleep in because it's a teacher work day. You want to talk to her?"

Michaels suddenly remembered that Toni was there in the garage. He flicked a glance in her direction, but she had squatted down next to the Prowler and was looking at the front struts. The pants she wore pulled tight across her tight rear end. He looked away. It was not something he should be noticing while talking to his daughter.

"No, I'll talk to her later, hon. Give her my love."

"I will. When are you coming out to visit, Dadster?"

"Soon, baby, soon as I can get loose."

"Got a crisis, huh?"

For a moment, he wondered how she knew that. But she didn't let it lie very long. "That's what Mom said, you got a crisis, why you couldn't come to my party. She said you always got a crisis."

"That's the truth, baby. Never a dull moment."

"I gotta go. I just heard the microwave go off, so the waffles are done. I love you, Dadster."

"I love you, too, Susie. Say hello to your mom for me."

"Bye!"

He hung up. He missed her. Missed Megan, too, even though the divorce had become final more than three years ago. It hadn't been his idea to split up. Even after the decree, he'd still had hope. Somehow, they'd get together, work things out. . . .

He turned his attention back to Toni, who had come up from her squat and was now leaning over the engine compartment, looking inside. He moved to stand next to her. "My daughter," he said.

"How'd she like the skates?" Toni said.

He blinked at her as she leaned back from the car and looked at him. "*You* sent them?"

"I—well, yeah. You were up to your eyeballs in things, so—yeah. I hope that wasn't out of line."

He shook his head. "Not at all. You saved my butt. I can't believe I forgot. Her mother would have never let me live it down. Thank you, Toni."

"I'm still your assistant," she said. "My job is to make you look good."

Well. He had hired her because of her credentials, and she'd been very good at her job. But she was proving to be a lot more than that.

He became aware they were standing only half a meter apart. She was an attractive woman, she smelled clean and fresh and he wanted to hug her. But he was her boss, after all, and he was afraid the hug might be misinterpreted. Especially given that his feeling right at that moment wasn't exactly platonic.

Oh? his little inner voice said. *Maybe you're really afraid a hug won't be misinterpreted at all, hey? What if she likes it?*

He suddenly felt the need to wipe his hands again. He turned, took a couple of steps and grabbed a fresh shop rag. "So, what's up?"

Toni felt a stab of disappointment. She had felt the heat in him, thought for just a moment he might reach out to her, literally, and her breath had caught in anticipation. Yes. Yes, do it!

But—no. Instead, Alex turned away from her and began wiping his already clean hands on a cloth. Became all business again.

Damn. She had a sudden flash of fantasy—lying with him right here, making passionate love in this wild purple car of his.

Wishful thinking, Toni.

Still, it had definitely been a good thing to have sent that birthday present to his daughter. His gratitude had been real enough. She felt that, too.

"You want the bad news? Or the worse news?"

"God."

Thursday, September 16th, 7:50 a.m.
Quantico

"Colonel? I think maybe you ought to saddle up," Michaels said.

"Sir?" John Howard sat forward in his office chair, his back suddenly straight and tense.

"According to a coded message intercepted by CIA listening post at the U.S. embassy in the Ukraine, a physical attack is planned on the station there, likely in the next few days. We'd like two things. One, you take a platoon or so of your best to augment the Marine guard at the embassy and head off any attack. Two, and more importantly, we wouldn't be real unhappy if you could find out who is behind it while you're sitting around waiting for the shooting to start.''

Howard grinned at the blank screen. *Yes!* "Won't the Ukrainians, uh, *frown* on us wandering around in their country chasing terrorists?''

"Officially, yes. Officially, you and your troops won't be leaving the embassy, which is U.S. territory. Unofficially, the local government won't get in your way. We've got a Dad Tee policy in effect for this operation.''

Howard grinned again. Dad Tee, from the acronym DADT—Don't Ask, Don't Tell—a policy spawned long before the Clinton Administration had made the term popular. What that meant was, as long as he and his men didn't get caught doing something too blatant, the host country could—and would—pretend it didn't see them. If he didn't burn down the capitol or assassinate the President while CNN had a camera on him, they'd be okay.

"I'll have my teams in the air in thirty minutes, Commander Michaels.''

"Don't break a leg, Colonel. Take an hour or two. The pertinent information is being downloaded to your S&T computer even as we speak. Your contact at the embassy will be Morgan Hunter, the CIA station chief, but it's your operation.''

"Sir.''

After he hung up, Howard couldn't keep the grin from his face. Finally. A field operation, and not a virtual one. The real thing.

He found himself breathing faster, and with a sudden urge to visit the bathroom. This was it.

"Time to rock and roll,'' he said to the air. "Rock and *roll!*''

8

In his office, Jay Gridley prepared to ride the net.

Cyberspace wasn't really like the old movies that had first depicted it, Gridley knew. But virtual reality constructs—VRCs—did use imagery to help a webwalker navigate the web. The images could be almost anything a user wanted. There were hundreds of standard commercial overlays, from cities with freeways, to old Western towns, to space flights. And there were tens of thousands of shareware scenarios to be had on the web. Some of the best software you could get was free. Download or timeshare the ware, and the net could be anything anybody had ever bothered to program. If you couldn't find anything that suited you, you could create your own vehicle. You didn't even need to be a programmer; any fool could do it. WebWeaveWare these days was easier than paint-by-numbers.

Gridley had several favorite travel pieces he used when he donned his VR gear and went on-line. He did the finger

weave to access the command mode, waved the web to life
and said, "Dodge Viper, Bavaria."

The VR gear gave him an image of a mountain road in
a somewhat-stylized German landscape. He was inside an
RT/10 Viper, a black convertible roadster with broad white
racing stripes, driving down a steep switchback. There
would be a border crossing coming up soon. He clutched
and downshifted from sixth into fifth, tapped the accelerator
and grinned at the crisp breeze ruffling his long black hair.
He enjoyed the classic James Bond movies, even though
saying, "Gridley, *Jay* Gridley," didn't have quite the same
ring to it. . . .

The border crossing loomed. A single uniformed soldier
stood behind a black-and-yellow-striped pole blocking the
road, a submachine gun held at port arms.

Gridley downshifted and braked. The roadster rumbled
deep in its muscular throat as it rolled to a stop.

The guard said, "Your papers, please."

The guard smelled like cheap aftershave and stale sweat,
with a touch of cigarette tobacco thrown in.

Gridley smiled, reached into the pocket of his tuxedo—
well, if you were gonna play, you might as well go all the
way—and removed his passport.

Eventually, he would have to program himself a female
passenger to complete this scenario. A sultry redhead, perhaps, or a dark and deadly brunette. A woman afraid of the
speed, but excited by it nonetheless. Yeah. . . .

In the real world, an electronic password was tendered
to a gate server on the web, bits of binary hex code pulsed
from one system to another, but in VR, the visuals were so
much more pleasing and much more intuitive.

A cursory inspection, then the guard returned his passport, nodded curtly and raised the barrier. Gridley had come
this way before. There was never any problem.

Around the next curve, the mountain road turned suddenly into an autobahn, with traffic zooming past at speeds in excess of 160 kilometers per hour. He tromped the Viper accelerator, laid rubber—first . . . second . . . even in third—upshifted when the engine peaked in fourth, then fifth gears, achieved sixth as he merged with the flow of cars and trucks barreling along.

James Bond's old Astin-Martin, and in the later movies the BMW, would never have kept up with the Viper. It had a top speed of around 260 kilometers per hour, with an eight-liter, ten-cylinder engine that would get one to that top speed with unbelievable rapidity. It was a rocket with wheels.

He was in the netstream now, his program running smoothly. He liked the freeway image, but he could, if he wished, switch to a more leisurely hike along a stream, or a bicycle tour of France, although that kind of sudden program change did tend to jar one somewhat.

Ahead was an exit sign: CyberNation.

Gridley frowned. There had been a lot of infospew lately about CyberNation, a VR "country" that was accepting not only tourists, but residents. They—whoever the programmers were who'd created the VRland—were offering a whole bunch of computer perks if you were willing to "emigrate" to their creation—if you were willing to give up your electronic citizenship in your own country for theirs, a thing that seemed unlikely. He hadn't checked into it himself, but it was an interesting idea. Some day, in his copious spare time, he'd have to see what all the fuss was about.

He glanced at the analog clock inset into the car's dashboard—no digital gauges for this beast.

A sleek Jaguar passed the Viper, and Gridley smiled at it. Oh, yeah?

He goosed the Viper, felt the jolt of acceleration even in sixth gear as the car surged forward and began to gain on the Jag as if it were standing still. He flew past, seeing the frowning driver's face. Gridley grinned. The Jag didn't have any more, and the Viper wasn't even close to red-lining the tach. So long, pal!

He was still feeling pretty full of himself when he saw the wreck about half a mile ahead of him. A big semi had flipped and turned onto its side, the trailer now blocked all the lanes on his side of the freeway. Traffic was lined up for a quarter mile, and the line was getting longer fast.

Damn!

Gridley hit the brakes—carefully, they were top-of-the-line disk but not little-old-granny ABS—and started down-shifting. Fortunately, the Viper was as good at stopping as it was at going. He pulled to a halt behind a big Mercedes full of men in hats, then checked his rearview mirror to see that the Jag was also slowing to a stop behind him.

What the virtual image meant was that someone had bol-lixed the system link he was using. Whether by accident or on purpose, he couldn't say.

A European-style siren dopplered and hee-haw-hee-hawed toward the wreck on the other side of the Autobahn, blue lights flashing. That would be the cops—or the diag-nostics—coming to see what was what.

Traffic was now at a standstill on his side of the highway. Gridley vaulted over the Viper's low door; fortunately the tux had plenty of stretch. He'd just mosey over to the cops and see if he could find out what was going on. Surely an Americanized Thai in a tuxedo could get a few answers, especially in his Bond persona. . . .

Tyrone Howard rode the net, wind blasting his bare face—well, bare except for the old-style aviator goggles he wore. These were the only protection he had on the big Harley Davidson XLCH that rumbled along at more than a hundred miles an hour. A classic bike, they didn't make them anymore, and one he was still several years away from being old enough to drive even if he could find or afford one. The thing with VR was that you could do stuff you couldn't do in RW—the real world.

He was in L.A., had just skirted a fender bender that blocked most of the Hollywood Freeway going north, hauling butt toward the valley when the reminder vox he'd set up warned him of the time. His dad was on the way home, and he'd only have a couple of minutes to visit before he had to take off again. He couldn't tell Tyrone where he was going or anything—that was secret stuff—but at least they could say good-bye. His dad had been excited, even though he had tried to hide it. Too bad Mom was down in Birmingham, visiting her sister. She'd be sorry she'd missed Dad.

He pulled the bike onto an off-ramp, geared down and rolled into a parking lot. When he shoved his World War I aviator goggles up onto his forehead, the VR band also went up in RW, and all of a sudden he was back in his room. He blinked. RW always looked so . . . *pale* compared to VR. Like *it* was the imitation, and virtual was the real place.

Just in time. He heard the front door open.

"Tyrone?"

"Hey, Pop!"

Tyrone got up, and nearly tripped on his own feet. Jeez! He was constantly knocking stuff over or slipping and sliding. Grandaddy Carl said that his dad had been the same way at thirteen, couldn't walk down a ten-foot-wide hall without bumping into both walls nine times. Tyrone found that hard to believe, that his dad had ever been that clumsy. Or that *he* would someday grow out of it.

When he reached the living room without destroying any furniture, he saw his dad there, in Net Force fatigues, neutral gray pants and shirt over spit-polished black boots. Behind his father, Master Sergeant Julio Fernandez stood by the door, dressed similarly.

"Hey, Tyrone," the sergeant said.

"Hey, Sarge. How's it goin'?"

"Not bad, for an old Hispanic." He grinned. Fernandez had retired from the RA—Regular Army—at the same time Colonel Howard had left. They went way back, had known each other for twenty years. They'd joined Net Force at pretty much the same time. His father had told him that Sarge had said if the colonel could work for civilians, he could manage it, too. But Sarge's love for computers was below zero, and Tyrone thought that was kind of strange, given that that was the business Net Force was in.

"I wanted to stop by before we took off," his dad said. "I've already called your mother. She'll be back on the commuter flight arriving at eighteen hundred, so you'll only be on your own for a couple of hours. Think you can handle that?"

Tyrone grinned. "I dunno, Pop. That's pretty scary. After I get home from school, I'll be alone in the house for all that time. I could starve. Maybe die of terminal boredom."

"Life is hard. Mrs. Townsend is running the car pool today, right?"

"Right." Rick Townsend's mother had the duty this week; next week it would be Arlo Bridger's mom, the week after that, *his* mom. The co-op car pool made getting to school and back a lot easier than catching the bus. He was on the mid-morning schedule this semester, so he didn't have to be there until nine-thirty.

His dad grinned back, then came over and hugged him. "I don't know when I'll be back. You take care of your mother. I'll call when the situation permits."

"Yes, sir."

His dad turned away. "Okay, Sarge. Let's roll."

"You're the colonel, Colonel."

His dad squeezed Tyrone's shoulder once more, then did a crisp pivot and headed for the door.

Tyrone felt a sudden coldness in the pit of his belly. His dad never let on about whether his assignments were dangerous or not, but for him to come home when he didn't have to pick up any gear or anything, for all of a whole minute, just to tell him good-bye—well, that made Tyrone nervous.

Where was Net Force posting his father? And what kind of trouble might be there waiting for him?

Thursday, September 16th, 7:15 p.m.
Grozny

Plekhanov was in his office in front of his computer. There was no one around this area, and probably no one on the entire floor. The government could not afford to maintain a night shift, though had he wished it, Plekhanov himself could have paid for it. One of the advantages of being a computer expert of his caliber was that stealing money electronically was not a problem—as long as one did not get too greedy. A million here, a million there, and pretty soon, it added up.

His communication software had reached out and connected him to the Rifle, and now their business was almost completed.

"Are we clear on what needs to be done, Mikhayl?"

"*Da*, we are clear."

Plekhanov frowned. It was not good that Ruzhyó used a Russian word, though there was not a chance in ten million that anybody would know it. Still, despite that, Plekhanov did not wish to take even that risk. But he would not speak of it during this conversation.

"The specifications for clothing, hardware and vehicles are in the secure file. Use the second account for funds," he said. "Take as much as you need, we want to do a good job."

"Yes," Ruzhyó said. "A good job."

"Is there anything else?"

"No, I believe that is everything."

"Good hunting, then."

"Thank you."

After the connection had been broken, Plekhanov leaned back in his chair and considered his next action. There were so many small details that must be attended to if the plan was to continue to work properly. A call here, a shaft of information there, a few words whispered into an influential ear at this juncture, all added to the momentum and kept things rolling along.

Everything was going according to plan.

Thursday, September 16th, 8:20 a.m.
San Francisco

Ruzhyó felt a little better. It was always good to have a specific chore, a job to be done, regardless of the constraints. He had already set up his contacts with suppliers; the gear they would need for the next step could be assembled in less than a day. Ruzhyó had known what the step would be, even though it had been a tentative plan until the call confirming it. Knowing it gave him some leeway, and he had exercised it.

Now, he had to call the Snake and the Texan and get them set. This would be tricky, and in one way, probably more so than the assassination of the federal agent, but not so dangerous. This time, they would have the law on their side.

In a manner of speaking.

Thursday, September 16th, 1:15 p.m.
Quantico

In his office, Commander Alex Michaels frowned at the young man sitting across the desk from him.

"All right, Jay, what exactly does this mean?"

Gridley shook his head. "I dunno, Chief. I went for a ride on half-a-dozen major highways—netways—and there were wrecks on all of them. Plus a bunch of others I didn't get around to. The cops—ah, the sysops—didn't have any big problems clearing most of them, although the Australian pileup was a real bastard. It was simple stuff, but traffic slowed down everywhere."

"But we're not talking major sabotage? And it didn't seem focused on one particular system?"

Jay shook his head. "Well, sort of and no. No piece of it was a biggie, but taken altogether, it adds up to major. Time is money, especially on the commercial roads, and there was a lot of stuff got shuffled because of some of the delays. If some big portion of that was diverted into one pocket, the guy wearing that jacket could retire and buy Cleveland, if he wanted. Though I can't imagine he'd want to. But as far as we can tell, nobody got rich off the snafu—least we haven't found who or how yet."

Jay paused, blinked, then stared into space as if he'd gone into a trance.

"Jay?"

"Oh, sorry. Far as I can tell, no one system was hit any

harder than another. It was spread over dozens of links fairly evenly. I've got houndbots sniffing, but none of 'em have run anything to a source. Whoever built this program is good, real good, 'cause he slipped it past a bunch of safeguards and the only people who caught him was us.''

Gridley smiled, obviously pleased with that fact.

"So Net Force systems were unaffected?''

"Yep. He tried, but he bounced off our wards. Guy's not as sharp as he thinks. He doesn't know who he's messing with. We'll run him down.''

For no reason at all, Michaels had a sudden flare of suspicion. *Unless he wanted us to think he couldn't get past our guards.*

"All right. Go and find whoever did this. Let me know how it progresses.''

"You got it, Chief.''

Gridley stood and sauntered from his office. Once the young man was gone, Michaels leaned back in his chair and pondered the situation. Since Steve Day's death, something hadn't felt right. He couldn't quite put his finger on what it was, but he felt as if somehow Net Force was under attack. It could be nothing more than the professional paranoia of course, that went with the job, but if it wasn't, if somebody *was* out to damage Net Force, who was it? And more important than that, why?

He waved a hand back and forth over his com unit.

From her office next door, Toni said, "Yes?''

"Hey, Toni. Anything new?''

"Sorry, Alex, no.''

Day's murder still hung over the unit like a heavy thundercloud: dark, threatening, unresolved.

He started to say something to his assistant, but decided to hold off. He didn't want to sound like the little boy crying wolf; besides, there was enough on his plate to worry about: the murder investigation, the situation in Ukraine, the other net problems. Better to keep his unfounded suspicions to himself, unless something else came along to give them some weight.

9

Colonel John Howard leaned back in the jetliner's seat and nodded at Sergeant Fernandez next to him. Probably one of the smartest things Net Force had ever done was to lease several 747's, then outfit them for fast tactical flights. The big Boeing jets were a long way from the old bone-jarring military transports that were little more than hollowed-out aluminum shells, so noisy you couldn't talk or even think straight. Aside from the comfort factor, there was a very practical reason for this choice: A 747 with civilian markings could land in places where a U.S. military cargo plane would get a Stinger missile up the spout for being stupid enough to try.

"Okay, Julio, let's run through it one more time."

The sergeant shook his head. "Begging the colonel's pardon—"

"There would be a first," Howard broke in.

"—and no disrespect intended," Fernandez continued,

ignoring Howard's comment, "but the colonel must have
a brain like a sieve."

"Thank you for your neurological opinion, Dr. Fernandez." He rolled his finger in the "continue" sign. "Move
along."

Fernandez sighed. "Sir. Ukraine is about the size of
France, holds fifty-two million people, has an elected President, and a four-hundred-fifty-person parliament called the
Verkhovna Rada. The U.S. Embassy is in the capital of
Kiev, at 10 Yuriya Kotsubinskoho. The building used to be
the Communist Party precinct and Communist Youth
League HQ, before the Ukrainians kicked the Commies out
in '91. There are one hundred and ninety-eight American
employees and two hundred and forty-four Ukrainian na-
tionals working at or for the embassy."

Howard smiled, but kept it to himself. Sarge never told
it the same way twice.

Fernandez continued. "Kiev has a population of three
million, covers forty-five by forty-four kilometers and sits
on the Dnieper River, which runs all the way to the Black
Sea. This time of year it's still warm, though mostly over-
cast and about to get rainy. About seventy-five percent of
the population is Ukrainian, twenty percent are Russian, the
rest are Jews, Byelorussians, Moldovans, Poles, Armenians,
Greeks and Bulgarians. Counting yourself, there might be
three people of African descent in the country, although
some of the Crimeans and ethnic Mongols are a bit dark.
You *will* draw a crowd on the streets, sir."

Howard waved him off. They had argued about this for
half the trip. According to Fernandez, there was no way
the colonel should be on this operation. He should sit back
at the embassy and direct traffic by radio and satlink. Sir.

"Go on."

"Sir. The city is eight time zones ahead of D.C. It has
an okay subway and surface street system, lousy radio and

TV stations. You can get the CNBC Superstation until noon, and CNN after six p.m., and yesterday's *Wall Street Journal* and *New York Times* if you go to a big hotel and are willing to pay half your retirement for a copy of either. If you go into a public bathroom, best you take your own toilet paper, you will need it.

"Money is the 'hryvnia,' and one of ours will get you two of theirs at the legal exchanges. The water is okay to bathe in if you let it run a few seconds for the lead to settle out, but you don't want to drink it without boiling it, due to bacteria and intestinal parasites. Radiation levels from Chernobyl are mostly normal, but don't eat local mushrooms, berries, or game animals unless you want to maybe be able to read at night without using a bedside lamp.

"If you drink alcohol and drive and get caught, you'll probably get thrown into jail, unless it is the militia that catches you, in which case you'll probably be shot on the spot. They drink like fish here, but they *walk* when they get potted. Zero tolerance for drunk drivers and more power to 'em.

"A lot of folks still speak Russian, but the official language is now Ukrainian. The most useful phrase you'll want to know in Ukrainian is, '*Probachteh, deh cholovee-chy tualeht.*' "

Howard said, "Which means?"

" 'Excuse me, but where is the men's room?' "

Howard grinned, and shook his head. "Keep going."

Fernandez droned on, but now Howard was only listening with half his attention. Despite his sergeant's concern over his brain leakage, he did know this material. He was just burning it in deeper. Better to be sure than sorry.

Unfortunately, Sarge was right about him not skulking around on the streets of Kiev. He'd been to China, and everywhere he had gone people had come up to him to stare, and sometimes to touch him. Black wasn't just dif-

ferent in some cultures; it was amazing. No way could he
move around surreptitiously with that kind of attention on
him. And yet, the idea of sitting in an embassy command
room trading comments with the CIA station chief while
his teams went hunting for a terrorist lair did not appeal in
any way, shape or form. He was a soldier, a field man
before he joined Net Force, and he did not want to spend
any more time behind a desk than he had to.

"—weapons and sub-rosa field gear are scheduled to arrive by diplomatic pouch at approximately 0945, local time.
Although diplomatic *shipping crate* would be more appropriate. FedEx is bringing it in. Ain't that something? We
don't need bombers, we can just FedEx it to our enemies,
have 'em sign for it, then set it off. Boom."

Howard made an appropriate grunt to show he was still
awake. So—how was he going to do it, get out on the
street? Some kind of disguise? Makeup, maybe? It was his
operation, and he ought to be able to post himself to the
active side of it. Maybe he could let his units scout things
out, then get there for the finale, if it came to that. There
had to be a way. He'd already sat out too many wars.

"—crime is on the rise and we are advised not to go
down dark alleys late at night alone." Fernandez grinned.
"Bet the local muggers will go into major pucker-factor if
they jump one of ours and find themselves target-laser-
painted and staring down the barrel of an H&K subgun."

"Let's not be shooting the locals, even the muggers, if
we can help it, Sarge. This is supposed to be a surgical
operation, in and out like a lance, no more damage than
necessary. We don't want any incidents we can't sweep
under a thin rug."

"Certainly, sir. I'll make sure the boys keep the barroom
brawls to an absolute minimum."

Howard grinned and shook his head again. There was no
better man to have at your side or watching your back than

Julio Fernandez. He had trouble working a computer that a six-year-old could operate with ease, but when push came to shove, he was the best. He could pin a fly to the wall with his throwing knife, then shoot its eyes out with whatever hardware he happened to be holding, either hand and you pick 'em.

And a bunch of half-baked local radicals were about to discover that making threats against a United States embassy was an extremely stupid idea.

Friday, September 17th, 1:25 p.m.
New York City

Luigi Sampson, Security Chief for Genaloni Industries, left the midtown Chinese restaurant, flanked by two bodyguards. Despite his position and ancestry, Sampson did not like Italian food. He did enjoy Chinese cuisine, however, and large amounts of it. For lunch, he had consumed an order of hot and spicy chicken, hard wheat noodles, sweet and sour pork, lemon duck and snow crab in peanut sauce, as well as two beers and three cups of tea. There had not been enough of the meal left to bother packing into little paper containers.

Sampson used a toothpick as he strolled toward his chauffeured automobile, parked illegally in front of the restaurant. He flicked bits of his meal into the air, to fall upon the sidewalk.

In the plain one-color, four-door sedan across the street, Ruzhyó looked at Winters, the driver, then at Grigory the Snake, seated in back. "Are we ready?"

"I am ready," the Snake said.

"Go to it, hoss."

The three of them wore identical charcoal suits, not too

expensive ones, with shined black-leather shoes, dark sun-glasses and new, short haircuts. In addition, each of them carried cards and badges that identified them as Special Agents of the United States Federal Bureau of Investigation. These IDs were, of course, forgeries, but the best that money could buy, and as such, would pass any examination up to destructive tests.

The license plate of the car had been switched, and the one it now wore had come from a vehicle currently parked in the FBI lot, not that far from where they now were.

The Snake still looked like a big, dumb Russian to Ruzhyó, even with his disguise, but there was no help for that. Besides, big dumb Russians and big dumb Americans looked much alike.

Winters was the best driver among them. It was his country, and he needed to stay at the wheel.

Ruzhyó adjusted the pistol in the holster behind his right hip. It was a SIG .40, a no-nonsense flat-black German combat weapon, very expensive and dependable, and was carried by many FBI agents. They looked the part, even the Snake.

"All right. Let us go."

Ruzhyó and Grigory the Snake alighted from the car and started across the street.

The bodyguards noticed them immediately. One of the guards said something to Sampson, who paused in picking his teeth, looked at the approaching men and grinned. He laughed and said something to his men. Ruzhyó could not hear, but he had an idea of what it might be. These men would have no love for their own federal authorities.

As Ruzhyó and the Snake drew near to the trio, Sampson said, "Good afternoon, boys. You guys're with the Bureau, right?" He smiled at the two guards, to show how adept he was at recognizing federal agents.

This was exactly as Plekhanov and Ruzhyó had planned.

Give people something close to what they expected and they would fool themselves, you did not need to say a word.

Ruzhyó affected the flat Midwestern American accent he had practiced. "Luigi Sampson? I'm Special Agent Arnold, this is Special Agent Johnson." He held his badge case up in his left hand to show the ID card and badge just as real agents did, always keeping their weapon hand clear. He nodded at the Snake, who glared at the bodyguards.

While their IDs were fake, the names were not—Agents Arnold and Johnson were assigned to the New York office. "We'd like you to come with us and answer a few questions."

"Sure thing, boys." To the nearer guard, Sampson said, "Verification?"

The bodyguard had a small computer flatscreen he tapped commands into. After a beat, he said, "They're on the list."

"Call the lawyers and the boss. Tell 'em." Sampson flicked the toothpick into the air with his thumb and middle finger. "Third floor of the Federal Plaza, right?"

"That's the *twenty*-third floor, Mr. Sampson. You've been there before," Ruzhyó said.

Sampson's grin increased. He thought his crude test was enough. He was a fool, more so for believing he was clever. Wise men always left room for new things; fools thought they knew it all already. "Always glad to help out my government. Let's go."

In the back section of the car with the Snake, Sampson said, "So, what's it all about, boys?"

As Winters pulled away, Ruzhyó noted one of the bodyguards step into the street to make a note of their vehicle's license number. Good. He looked at Sampson. "You work for the Genaloni crime family. You have personally killed six men, and ordered the deaths of more than a dozen others. You and your ilk are responsible for drugs on the streets, prostitution, smuggling, gambling, other illegal activities too many to list.''

"Whoa! That's slander, Agent, 'cause it ain't true. I'm a security man for a legitimate company. Better be careful what you say—you could get sued, you know. Our lawyers don't have enough to do."

"You are criminal scum," Ruzhyó said. "And you will pay for it very soon."

Sampson laughed. "Good luck proving it, pal. Better men than you have tried." He leaned back into the seat, his face going hard. "I'll be back on the street in time for dinner."

"You will not," Ruzhyó said.

"Yeah? Well, you're stupid if you think that."

"No. You are the stupid one—*you* believe we are with the FBI."

The look on Sampson's face was a mix of fear and disbelief, but by then the Snake had his gun out and pressed it into the man's side. "And you would be *extremely* stupid to attempt to move," the Snake said. The Russian accent was so thick in his voice you could lean against it without falling.

"Jesus!" Sampson said.

"Afraid he ain't gonna be offering you much help, hoss," Winters said.

"What the hell is going on? Who are you? What do you want?"

"To feed the wolves a poisoned bait," Ruzhyó said.

The criminal frowned. He did not understand. Nor would he have time to worry over it. Fate had reached into the lottery basket and closed his cold hard fingers.

Luigi Sampson's number had been drawn.

10

Ray Genaloni was mad enough to kill somebody with his bare hands. The man who stood in front of his desk, one of Luigi's bodyguards, was not delivering good news and he was the only target of opportunity—but that would be a bad idea, to kill him. Instead, Ray kept his temper held down, as if pressing a lid on a boiling pot to keep the steam from escaping.

"Excuse me, Donald," Genaloni said, "but what exactly do you mean the FBI doesn't have him?"

"We sent the lawyers, Boss. The feds say they didn't pick up Luigi."

"But you and Randall say they did?"

"We had just come out of Chen's. There were two of 'em, another one in the car. Luigi made them, and Randall and I know feds when we see them. Their IDs checked out, they are on the New York Bureau list, the car they were in had no-hit plates—which we ran through our police contacts and found they were blind-issued to the New York

City FBI motor pool. They got him, all right.''

"Then why are they telling the lawyers they never heard of him?"

Donald shook his head. "I don't know."

Genaloni sat silent for maybe fifteen seconds. He saw the bodyguard's sweat. Good. Let him be nervous. Finally, he said, "That's all. Go find something to do."

After the bodyguard left, Genaloni sat and stared at the wall. What the hell were the feds up to? Why were they putting the squeeze on him? Luigi was stand-up, they could threaten him with anything they wanted and he wouldn't give them shit, but We-ain't-got-him was a new game. And it was one he didn't like. They were up to something and whatever it was, he didn't fucking *like* it.

Fine. They want to play cloak-and-dagger? No problem. He had a knife sharp enough to shave with just sitting around doing nothing. All he had to do was reach out and grab it. *We'll just see about this crap.*

He picked up his phone. "Scramble, code two-four-three-five, Sunshine," he said.

The phone said, "Scrambled."

He punched in a number.

We'll just see about this crap.

"I understand," Mora Sullivan said, knowing her voice would not give her away.

She waved the phone off, stood and began a measured pacing.

Three steps this way, turn, three steps back, turn, then repeat, as she began to assimilate the assignment. The Selkie did not sit and meditate. Yes, she could be still when necessary, when the stalk required it, but at this stage the Selkie thought best when she moved, when she was on her feet, exploring avenues, watching for side roads, scheming.

She could become anything, anybody, and the world was

her chew toy, but this would be a dangerous one. There could be no room for error. Nearly always on her assignments there was wiggle room, space for small mistakes. Though she never left anything undone if she knew about it, there had been occasions when she had made errors. Tiny things, those errors, not wide pathways upon which a pursuer could have traveled to catch her. But now and then, she *had* missed something. She was the best, but even the best could overlook some bit of business, realizing it only afterward, when it was beyond her control to repair.

Step, step, step, *turn*—

People had not noticed the little clues she had accidentally dropped, because most people never thought to look for them. And eventually the links had rusted away under time and weather, become no more than stains on her trail, small, dark blotches that offered nothing to normal vision.

But this time? This time there would be a microscope turned upon her actions. Police officers, no matter what their organization, were special cases. First and foremost, the police protected their own. The message was simple: You may do many heinous acts and escape, but killing a cop is not one of these acts. Do so, and you rise to the top of the list, never to be removed until you are caught or killed—preferably killed. Sullivan knew this. Her father had been one of those who had gunned down a policeman, and paid for that with his own life. The policemen who had caught him had executed him, and it had been no chore for the killers to justify their revenge, no chore at all.

Step, step, step, *turn*—

Killing her target would not be the problem. That was the easy part. An assassin who was willing to be caught or to die herself could pretty much take out anybody in the public eye, from the President on down.

Getting away with such an assassination was another thing. Especially when the best and brightest lights of the top anticrime organization in the world would be shined into your escape tunnel. There would be no wiggle room on this one, no errors permitted. The smallest clue would be found, magnified, analyzed, tested, followed.

The thought was both scary and attractive. The Selkie thrived on the risk. She enjoyed epinephrine as if it were a fine wine, savoring the jolt it gave. The truth was, she could walk away tomorrow and live a long and well-supplied life. Once you had more than a few million working for you, you didn't really *need* more. She had a goal and she would reach it because she always reached her goals, but she was self-aware enough to realize that for her, the game was as important as the get. And this would be a challenge. She'd never deleted an FBI agent before, especially one who was head of a sub-agency.

Step, step, step, turn.

So, the plan would require a meticulous surveillance, an undivided attention to every possible problem and enough time to make certain everything was covered. *Everything*.

Before she left, she would take on a new identity. She would become a woman who belonged in Washington, D.C., who had reason to be near her target, who would pass any inspection if necessary.

Sullivan stopped pacing, and grinned to herself. Already, the adrenaline bubbled in her, made her skin and muscles tight, gave her breathtaking rushes.

She was a creature of the *were*. She could change her look as easily as some people changed their clothes, could become anything she wished.

Already the Selkie's metamorphosis had begun.

Saturday, September 18th, 4:19 p.m.
Los Angeles

Ruzhyó stood on the moving walkway at the Los Angeles Airport, heading for the car-rental pickup. According to the pilot, the temperature outside was nearly body heat. It might be fall, but summer was not done with this country— it had been almost that warm on the East Coast when he'd boarded his flight.

The business in New York had gone well. Less than twenty-four hours after they had kidnapped him, Luigi Sampson was no more.

Well, Ruzhyó thought, that was not strictly true. The chopped-up pieces of the criminal were by this point a semiliquid goo inside a large, glass-lined holding tank filled with a very strong acid. It had been necessary for the Snake to carve the dead man into sections small enough to fit through a pressure-valve opening atop the containment vessel, a chore that affected Grigory not in the least. He had an uncle who was a butcher, and had worked in his uncle's shop summers before entering the military. The tank was for storage of a corrosive used in etching steel at a metal-finishing plant in New Jersey. The solution, of which the criminal was fast becoming a part, was generally used in small amounts; by the time the workers got around to tapping the tank for their work—the second of two such storage vessels—the late Luigi Sampson would be merely organic contaminants, and unlikely to be noticed save as perhaps a slight discoloration as he was sprayed with the acid over masked sections of steel plate.

The acid was very strong. But to be certain, the Snake had hammered out all of the dead man's teeth, and the American Winters had sprinkled these teeth one by one over the side of a ferry to Staten Island, interspersed with handfuls of popcorn he had thrown to the seagulls that followed the ferry.

The FBI disguises were likewise no more. The IDs and clothes had been burned and the ashes flushed away; the badges had been pounded to flat scrap and put into a metal-recycler station. The car's plates had been switched back, the automobile itself returned to the agency from which it had been rented with more fake identification. The guns had been wiped clean, packaged, marked "Rock Samples," then mailed to a large post office box rented to a non-existent person in Tucson, Arizona, where they would sit until the rental expired or the post office tried to find the box holder, whichever occurred first, and months away in any case. Disposable items, all.

Such a ruse would not work again—the Genaloni organization would now be alerted. But it was not necessary.

It was remotely possible that the bodyguards might be offered pictures of the real agents Ruzhyó and Zmeyá had impersonated, but it was most unlikely. Genaloni's suspicion and natural distrust of the authorities would be enhanced, and he would not turn to them for aid in finding his man even if he did believe them, which he would not. The crime boss would not pursue the matter with the federal authorities, and they, in turn, having other things to do, would quickly forget about it.

The FBI would think Genaloni had killed one of his own. And Genaloni would think the FBI was out to get him. The former was incorrect, but the latter was now true. Genaloni, according to the research Plekhanov had supplied, was not a patient man. He would likely do something rash. And if he did not, then Ruzhyó would do it *for* him—or at least it would seem so.

Giving one's enemy something else about which to worry was an old but still useful device. Plekhanov knew history well, and he was a master manipulator. A good man to have on one's side in a conflict. A bad man to have as an opponent.

There were other small things Ruzhyó and his crew could do to further harass both Net Force and the criminal family they had set upon each other, small things, but each adding a bit more to the load.

Sooner or later, even the strongest camel will collapse under one more additional straw added to its load.

It was Ruzhyó's job to supply the straws.

Sunday, September 19th, 2:30 a.m.
Kiev

John Howard was just a little peeved at the CIA station chief. Morgan Hunter was maybe forty-five, hair gone gray, but still pretty good shape, to judge from the fit of his suit and the way he moved. And he'd been a Company man for twenty-odd years, had worked in Chile, done a stint in Beirut, then in Moscow after the breakup, before landing here. So he ought to know his business.

"I'm sorry, Colonel, but what can I say? None of our contacts among the local radicals have squat on this, outside of the original reports. We haven't been able to run it down."

"The clock is ticking, Mr. Hunter."

They were in the small conference room in the sub-basement, a room Howard had been given for his operation. There were landline phones, computers, printers, television monitors and other such impedimenta on the tables and walls.

The CIA man gave him a superior smile. "I am aware of that, Colonel. We *wound* the clock, so we know. As you might recall, we brought it to your agency's attention in the first place. An agency that is here more or less by our invitation, sir."

Howard was making ready to reply when Julio Fernandez entered the room. He gave the colonel an uncalled-for snappy salute and said, "Sir, we might have something."

"Go ahead, Sergeant."

Fernandez glanced at Hunter, then back at his commanding officer. Howard had to work to keep his own grin in check. The look said much, not the least of which was: *Is it okay to talk in front of this jerk, sir?*

Hunter caught it, and his jaw muscles flexed.

"Sir, Lucy—that's Lucy Jansen, Third Team—made, uh, *friends* with one of the guys on the short list." He handed Howard the list with a name circled in red. As Howard looked at the name, Fernandez continued. "Guy speaks German, so does she, so that gave them something in common. They, ah, connected in a local bar and after five or six glasses of vodka, the guy let it slip about having an old wire-guided missile launcher he was gonna have a chance to use real soon."

Howard felt himself ratchet into alertness. "Go on."

"Lucy is working the guy. She's gonna get back to me in a couple of hours."

Howard looked at Hunter.

The other man shrugged. "Could be something. Could be a drunk trying to impress a woman."

Howard nodded. "True. But the guy is on your list." He turned to look at Fernandez again. "Keep me posted on this."

"Yes, sir." Another crisp salute, then Fernandez turned and marched away.

"I'll see if I can get some more background on this man," Hunter said. He pointed at the list.

"Good idea." Howard hesitated for a moment, then decided there was no point in losing the cooperation of the

CIA man. "Sorry about before. I'm still a little jet-lagged."

"No problem, Colonel. We've all been there. I want these guys as much as anybody does. If we do our jobs right, we'll get them."

"Amen."

The two men smiled again, and this time the expressions were real.

Maybe it was nothing, but Howard didn't think so. All of a sudden, he had a fluttery sensation in his belly. This was it. This would lead them into the radicals' den.

11

When the phone rang, Alex Michaels was in his garage, working on the Prowler. He was fairly certain he knew who was calling. He wiped his hands on the greasy rag and reached for the receiver.

"Hello?"

"Dadster!"

"Hey, Little Bit, how you doin'?"

"Great. Well, except for I fell while I was skating and kinda wrecked a knee pad."

He felt a stab of concern. "You okay?"

"*I'm* fine, but the knee pad is like, you know, scraped silly."

"Better it than you."

"That's what Momster said."

In the background, he heard Megan: "Let me talk to Daddy for a minute, hon."

Michaels felt his belly twist, his bowels go cold and tight.

"Mom wants to talk to you."

He took a deep breath. "Sure. Put her on."

"Bye, Dadster."

"Bye, Little Bit."

Time stretched. Aeons rolled past. Civilization decayed, fell into ruin. . . .

"Alex?"

"Hi, Megan. What's up?"

"Susie, why don't you go make Mom a cup of coffee, okay?"

Michaels suddenly felt as if he was in free fall.

A moment passed. "Look, Alex, I know you put your job at the top of your list, but your daughter still thinks the moon rises in her father's shadow. Are you going to be able to break loose and come to her play?"

The years of arguments threatened to break out again—fresh blood from old wounds never healed, at least not on his heart. He didn't want to fight with her. "That's in October, right?"

"You remembered. Amazing."

She could still cut him with her sarcasm as easily as a new razor-sliced paper.

This whole deal with Day's death would probably be over by then; if not, it was doubtful it would still be boiling so hot he couldn't step away from the stove long enough to see his daughter's second-grade play. He said, "I'll be there."

"You sure?"

"I said I'd be there." She could always do that, too, spark him to anger without raising her voice, with the most innocent phrase. *You sure?* If she'd called him a damned liar, it would have sounded exactly the same to him.

There was an uncomfortable pause. In the last year they were together, there had been more of those uncomfortable moments than anything else. Not so much anger as resignation. The inevitable end of their marriage had oozed to-

ward them like a glacier, slow but inexorable, grinding flat
everything in its path.

She said, "Listen, there's something else. I'm seeing
someone. I wanted you to hear it from me."

The coldness in his belly hardened into shards of liquid
oxygen so frigid they stopped his breathing. When he found
his voice again, he put everything he had into keeping it
level, light, mildly curious.

"Anybody I know?"

"No. He's a teacher at Susie's school. Not her teacher."

"Well. Congratulations."

"We aren't about to get married, Alex, we're just seeing
each other socially. You've been dating, haven't you?"

He waited just a little too long before he replied: "Sure."

"*Jesus,* Alex."

And *that* summed up years of discussions, too. He hadn't
been with another woman since he and Megan had split.
He'd thought about it a few times. Certainly he still noticed
attractive women, even had brief fantasies. But he'd never
acted on them. Once the fantasy passed, the reality was still
out there, the risk. And he still missed Megan, despite all
that had happened. She'd been the love of his life. She
always would be. If she called and asked him to come
home, he'd go, even if it cost him everything else—the
condo, the car, the job. He hadn't known that before, but
he knew it now. Too late, of course. It wasn't going to
happen. They were divorced. She was seeing another man.
Maybe even sleeping with him.

It further churned his stomach, made him want to throw
up, the idea of Megan naked with another man, laughing,
making love, doing things he and she had once done. What
was worse was knowing that she wanted another man—
and not him. Knowing that she would *enjoy* it . . .

Michaels shook his head. He had to get off this track.

He didn't have the right to feel this way anymore—if he'd ever had that right.

"I have to go. Tell Susie I love her."

"Alex—"

"Good-bye, Megan. Take care."

He put the phone's receiver gently back into the cradle, then looked at the purple car upon which he now spent each spare minute. Usually, he was able to fend off the feelings about Megan. As long as he kept busy, as long as he didn't let himself stop and think about it, he was fine. But when he heard her voice, when her words caused him to paint a picture of her in his mind, it was impossible.

Maybe there was a magic spell somewhere that would erase all the bad between them; maybe there were some magic words that would put them back together as they had been when Susie had still been in their future, or even when she'd been a fat and laughing babe toddling around that big old house in Idaho.

Maybe there were such words—but Alex Michaels had not found them.

Sunday, September 19th, 11:15 a.m.
Washington, D.C.

Toni Fiorella had just gotten off the phone with her mother, a Sunday morning ritual that usually ran twenty or thirty minutes before Mama began getting antsy: "This must be costing you a fortune, baby," Mama would say.

No matter how many times Toni had told her mother she could afford a couple of hours of long-distance charges a month between Washington and the Bronx, it didn't seem to sink in. Mama remembered the days when long-distance phone calls had been a major luxury, reserved for birth or funeral announcements, maybe a quick ring on holidays. And the idea of getting a computer and simply using E-mail or voxtrans was out. Mama did not hold with such things.

For the last fifteen minutes while they visited, Toni had been puttering around the kitchen. She'd rinsed dishes, put them into the washer, wiped the counters and chopping block, even dust-mopped the floor. The apartment was small, but the kitchen was bigger than usual in a place this size, and the vinyl floor looked enough like real wood to fool most people at first glance. A nice place.

As she was putting the dust mop away, the phone rang. Was that her mother calling back for something?

"Hello?"

"Deputy Commander Fiorella?"

"Yes?" The voice had a familiar sound, but she couldn't place it.

"This is Jesse Russell. We, uh, met the other day."

A Southern accent, the voice. Wait—she had it. "Spandex."

"Ma'am?"

Toni hadn't realized she'd said the word aloud until he'd responded. She flushed, glad the visual wasn't on. "Sorry, Mr. Russell, never mind. What do you want?"

"Well, ma'am, I wanted to apologize. For that business in the gym. I was showing off for Barry and I kinda put my brain on hold. I shouldn't have acted that way. It was stupid and I'm sorry."

Toni grinned. Well, well. Would wonders never cease? An asshole apologizing. And because she knew she shouldn't have done what *she* had done, she could be gracious about it now. "It's all right, Mr. Russell, forget about it."

"No, ma'am, I'm not likely to forget that anytime soon. I was, uh, wondering if maybe you might be willing to show me some more of the style sometime? You know, so I could see what you did instead of decorating the floor with my backside?''

Toni chuckled. Maybe he wasn't so bad after all. He had a certain charm. She said, ''If we run into each other at the gym, sure.''

''Well, Miz Fiorella, if you could tell me when you might be working out again, I could arrange my schedule to break loose for a while. They keep us pretty busy in class, but we are allowed some free time now and then.''

Toni thought about it for a second. Was this guy hitting on her? Or was he really interested in learning *silat*? Background in another art was a hindrance sometimes, but not always. And Guru kept telling her she needed students, that she'd never really master the art until she taught it.

''I sometimes do mornings, but I usually work out on my lunch hour, noon to one. You could drop by if you want.''

''Oh, yes, ma'am, I want.''

''Might as well drop the 'ma'am' and 'Miz Fiorella' stuff. I'm Toni.''

''I'm Rusty to my friends,'' he said. ''Thank you. You gonna be at the gym Monday?''

''Unless something comes up.''

''I'll see you there, ma'am—I mean, Toni.''

She found herself smiling as she put the dust mop away. Spandex—Russell—had been pretty much a typical macho idiot from his reactions both before and immediately after she'd decked him. But this call, assuming there weren't any hidden agendas in it, made up for some of that. Most people deserved a second chance most of the time. Lord knows she'd stepped into things she'd regretted, and had been glad to be on the receiving end of somebody's forgiveness.

People could change. She had to believe that. And he wasn't all that bad-looking, either.

She immediately felt a twitch of disloyalty. Whatever else Russell might be, he was not Alex, in no way, shape or form. Alex was who she wanted. And sooner or later, if she worked hard enough, maybe he would want her, too.

But a student wouldn't be so bad. And who knows? A good-looking student might give Alex a jolt, show him Toni was somebody to look at. It couldn't hurt.

Sunday, September 19th, 11:15 a.m.
Quantico

Jay Gridley cranked up the big motor on the Viper, and left a trail of smoking rubber as he popped the clutch and burned up the freeway's on-ramp. Why not? He didn't have to buy new tires in VR.

He had spent a good part of the last few days cruising the net, looking for more roadblocks, but so far, nothing out of the ordinary. Oh, yeah, sure, there were traffic snarls, a fender bender here or there, but those were normal.

He was on the 405 close to LAX when a black kid on a big hog whined past, doing eighty. Gridley smiled at the kid on the Harley. He knew who that was, even if the VR image was a little older and more muscular.

He upshifted, felt the Viper strain to be released and let it go as he pressed the accelerator to the floor. The big V-10 rumbled, roared, and the traffic around him turned into a painting.

He surged the little car from sixty to ninety in a couple of seconds. *Ka-wham!*

Born to be wild, and if you can't drive it, pal, *park* it!

He pulled alongside the black kid on the bike, grinned, honked his horn.

In reality, the two of them were linked via the net in a real-time on-line connection, much as twenty million or so other people did every day on the big commercial nets, but the VR visual mode made it so much more fun, when the software allowed for overlapping scenarios like this one.

"Hey, Tyrone!"

The kid looked over and grinned, showing bright and even teeth. "Hey, Jay Gee! What're you doin' here?"

"Looking for trouble."

"I'm with that program!"

"Yo, there's a truck stop up ahead on the right. You want to pull over and have a cup of coffee? I need to ask you something."

"Sure, nopraw, Jay."

The kid goosed the bike and leaned into the wind, the airstream ruffling his clothes and even his tight curly hair. He pulled away, and Gridley let him get ahead.

Nopraw? Jay considered it for a moment. Ah. *No problem.*

He wasn't *that* old, but the cutting edge was always moving, and he knew he wasn't on it anymore. The slangspeak hot when he was a kid was ancient history to somebody Tyrone's age. "Nopraw" would be like his "Sweat not," or his father's "No probleemo, Batman." The language shifted, changed and sometimes, circled around completely. "Cool" became "hot" became "bad" became "groovy" became "cool" again. No way you could keep up.

He was twenty-eight, but talking to a kid like Tyrone made him feel like a pile of dinosaur bones. He shook his head.

Then again, kids who rode the net seriously saw and heard things that adults missed, and Gridley wanted to use every resource he could get his hands on. This was about getting the job done, not about who lifted what.

He put his blinker on and pulled into the exit lane. If things kept going the way they were, by the time Tyrone was Gridley's age, he'd be doing stuff that would make this look like stick figures carved into stone.

12

It was a quiet Sunday evening, the fall air still warm and
sticky with humidity. Alexander Michaels's condo was
dark, save for a light in an upstairs bedroom. A plain-
vanilla, government-issue, black-tire fedmobile with two
FBI agents in it sat parked at the curb across the street.
They weren't trying to hide, and that was good, because
they might as well have a big flashing red neon sign
mounted on the car's top announcing they were who they
were: *Cops! Cops! Cops!*

The two men in the car listened to a radio playing country music at a low volume, and played chess using a small
magnetic board mounted on the dash. Now and then, one
of them would glance at Michaels's place, or up and down
the street, checking auto or foot traffic.

There weren't many cars or pedestrians at this hour in
this neighborhood on a Sunday. Most of the people in these
houses had to get up and go into the office on Monday
morning; most of them were home by now, watching TV

or reading or doing whatever else upper-middle-class people did behind their walls when tomorrow was a workday.

How odd it must be, to have to get up and go to a real
job every day. She wondered how people did it—worked
at places where they hated what they did, for people they
could barely stand. How could you make yourself spend
your life without any joy, any passion, any real satisfaction?
Millions did it—billions did it—but it was beyond her.
She'd rather be dead than forced to endure the mundane
lives most people led. What was the point?

A Mercury Protection Systems neighborhood patrol car
rolled slowly down the street. The uniformed driver in the
vehicle—offering "Fast Armed Response," according to
the door logos—nodded at the two FBI men as he cruised
past them. They nodded back.

A quiet residential street. Nothing out of the ordinary.
Moms and pops and two-point-three rugrats, dogs, cats,
mortgages, unending blandness. Everything in its proper,
boring, dull place.

Well. *One* thing was not quite as it seemed. . . .

The Selkie walked along the sidewalk approaching Michaels's condo. The condo was on the west side of the road,
and she was eighty yards shy of it, moving slowly north.
She had already examined the agents' car with a twelve-
power spookeye monocular. The tiny starlight scope was
state-of-the-art Israeli issue, made at the Bethlehem
Electronics plant. The scope had excellent optics, and offered a good view of the chess-players from a distance
where they couldn't possibly see her without using scopes
of their own.

The shotgun mike in her purse—a product of the wholly
owned Motorola subsidiary Chang BioMed, in Beaverton,
Oregon—had sufficient electronic amplification so that
from a hundred yards she had been able to hear the soft
twang of country music from the surveillance car. The mike

was disguised as a hearing aid, and the scope passed as a small can of hairspray. Anything less than a determined search wouldn't know these things for what they really were.

And who was apt to be searching her purse, determined or otherwise? Nobody.

When she was fifty yards away, she saw the agents glance in her direction, then back to their chess game. She kept her expression neutral, even though she wanted to smile. They had seen her—and dismissed her.

The dismissal was based on good reason. For what the agents saw was an old lady, easily seventy, hunched over and walking slowly, hobbling with a cane, while a small champagne-colored toy poodle trotted ten feet ahead of her on a Flexi lead, exploring the neatly cropped wilds of the sidewalk foliage.

The poodle, a well-trained neutered male, had been rented from the Not the Brothers Dog Kennel, in upstate New York. A thousand dollars a week, the pooch, and worth every penny.

The little dog sniffed the base of an ornamental cherry tree planted next to the walk, lifted his leg and watered the trunk.

"Good boy, Scout," the Selkie said. Anybody close enough to have heard her—and nobody was—would have recognized the tones of an old lady, the voice weakened by long decades of hard work and too many cigarettes.

She wore an ankle-length cotton-print dress, a thin cotton sweater and stout, sensible, lace-up Rockport walking shoes over black knee socks. Her hair was white and fluffed up into a rounded perm. The latex mask and makeup she wore had taken her an hour and a half to apply, and should pass inspection from five feet in broad daylight. She was in some apparent pain as she shuffled along—the right hip was bad—but she was bearing it for the sake of her good boy

Scout, who stopped to sniff every tree or bush, careful to mark as his own all those with scents from previous canine passersby.

She was also hot, her face itched and the stink of latex and face powder was thick, but there was no help for that.

The Selkie knew exactly what the watchers saw when they looked at her: somebody's arthritic granny, out walking her little dog before going home to bed. And home was only three blocks away, rented in a hurry, but using her current disguise. If she was stopped—and she wouldn't be—she had an address that justified her being here, and a pedigree better than the dog's. She was Mrs. Phyllis Markham, retired from her job of forty-one years as a bookkeeper for the state government, at the capital in Albany. Her husband Raymond had passed away last October, and Phyllis had finally moved to Washington so she could spend her spare time visiting the museums, which she loved. Have you seen the new Russian capsule on display at the Air and Space? Or that gray 1948 Tucker they confiscated from some drug dealer?

Mrs. Markham's daughter Sarah lived in Philadelphia, and her son Bruce was the manager of a Dodge truck dealership in Denver. Her background was all in place, and any kind of computer check would vet it. She could bore the leg off a clothes-store dummy reciting it in her dull and scratchy voice, too. She carried no obvious weapons, nothing to give her away, save the disguised electronics that nobody would recognize for what they were if they happened to see them.

Then again, the cane she pretended to need was a three-foot length of hand-crafted hickory, sanded furniture-smooth and lovingly oiled, made by Cane Masters, a small company in Incline Village, Nevada. Cane Masters specialized in building perfectly legal weapons for serious martial artists. An expert—and the Selkie was certainly that—

could beat somebody to a dead pulp with a walking stick such as the one she carried, and do so without breaking a sweat.

A mugger who looked at her and saw somebody's tired and helpless old granny and an easy score, well—that would be a big mistake. And possibly his *last* mistake if she chose to make it so.

When she was at the first condo past the target's, she whispered, loud enough for the dog to hear but not the agents: "Scout, dump."

The little poodle was very well trained. He stopped, squatted and left a little pile on the grass next to the edge of the walk. With some apparent effort, the old lady bent and half squatted, and scooped the poop up with a little cardboard-and-plastic container designed for that purpose. "Good boy, Scout!" she said, loud enough for the agents to hear this time. She proceeded onward, seemingly oblivious to the young men playing chess in the car across the street. She would bet dollars to dimes they'd be smiling. Aw, look at that, isn't that cute, old granny's little toy dog crapping on the grass.

She didn't know if the guards were permanent—probably not, but it didn't matter. Two men in a parked car on a street were not much of a threat. Now they had seen her as she wished them to see her. She would be back in the morning, and again at night, for at least the next week, perhaps longer. Soon, the day and night sets of guards would file her away under "harmless." Mrs. Phyllis Markham was but one of several shadows who might become an unseen part of the target's life. Another one was an office temp who could soon go to work for the Marines Civilian Liaison Office at Quantico. There was a new driver for a Taco Tio lunch wagon that sometimes fed part of the FBI, and half-a-dozen other possibilities, if necessary. She would chose the ones best suited, after she had done a little more observation.

And if it was Phyllis Markham who drew the assignment to delete the target, he would probably die quietly in his bed one night in the next week or two, with nobody the wiser. The old lady could circle around the condo after the deed was done, then walk right past the agents assigned to watch the target, and they would never have a clue.

By the time anybody knew the target was dead, the poodle would be back in upstate New York at his kennel, and the old lady would have ceased to exist.

"Let's go around the block and go home, Scout. What do you think?"

The toy poodle wagged his tail. He was a sweet pup. And just like the T-shirt said, the more she learned about people, the better she liked dogs.

Monday, September 20th, 8:17 a.m.
Kiev

Colonel Howard had just finished a field-strip and reassembly on the H&K G3A3Z assault rifle. This was a major piece of small-arms ordinance. It roared like a thunderclap and fired the big 7.62mm NATO round full-auto. The expended brass ejected so hard that anybody within fifty or sixty feet to the right and slightly back of a shooter risked having an eye put out by a spinning shell. Sometimes the empties flew so fast they *whistled* as air blew across the mouth of the fired cartridge.

He wiped excess dry lube from the weapon and put it back on the table. Maybe he should clean his handgun, too?

He pulled the S&W Model 66 from its holster and looked at it. It was a six-shot stainless-steel revolver in .357, with a four-inch barrel and Craig Spegel custom-wood boot grips. Hardly regulation, the sidearm—most of the teams carried H&K USP tactical pistols in .40, with high-density plastic slides and frames, laser sights and suppressors, and more than twice as many rounds per magazine as the old wheelgun carried. But it was his talisman, the Smith, and he trusted it. He could shoot it well enough to hit a man-sized target out to a hundred meters on a good day, and it never jammed the way an auto-pistol sometimes did. He opened the cylinder and checked the loads.

"Your hardware gets any cleaner you'll be able to do surgery with it, sir."

He looked at Fernandez. "You know, a less indulgent commander would have thrown you into the stockade years ago and left you there."

"Yes, sir. Your patience does you proud, Colonel."

Howard shook his head.

"Zero-eight-one-eight, sir," Fernandez said.

Howard raised his eyebrows. "I wasn't going to ask what time it was, Sergeant."

"No, sir, of course not, sir."

Howard grinned again. He closed the cylinder on his revolver and reholstered it. All right, he was fidgety. They had a location on the terrorists, and a meeting was supposed to take place for the leaders of the group at 1130 hours. Once the woman trooper had gotten the drunk to an empty room where he had been expecting something much more fun than what actually happened, he had been relatively quick to volunteer that information.

Which meant Howard and his troops wanted to be in place an hour and a half before then, by 1000. It was a fifteen-minute drive to the warehouse district where the meeting was set. Allow twice that for traffic problems, plus a half hour for X-factor, which meant they should roll at 0900. Most of the troops were already outside the embassy compound and assembled at the takeoff point.

Which meant that they had at least forty minutes before they should crank up.

Time flowed as it did when undergoing a root canal— slow. Very, very slow . . .

Fortunately, Howard's appearance wasn't going to be a problem. A local bus had been secured, of the kind used to ferry workers to and from various industrial sites in the area. He and Fernandez would leave the compound in a limo and meet the bus, and he could sit in an aisle seat where nobody would notice him from outside, if they bothered to look. And since everybody inside the bus was working for him—about twenty-five troops—that wouldn't be a problem. Combat gear was on the bus. The troops would wear civilian coveralls. They would be just another group of workers going to a construction site in the warehouse district on the river. In theory, there should be no problems. The CIA chief, Hunter, had the routes laid out, and the local police were supposed to be advised to turn a blind eye. It ought to run like warm oil on clean glass.

There was no reason for Howard to feel as nervous as he did, but that didn't matter. He had already paid two visits to the bathroom, and a third would be likely. The idea of eating made his stomach queasy, and the coffee he had already drunk had only added to his jitters. It might not be a major firefight in a jungle somewhere, but it was very possible bullets would fly and men would die. And it was his responsibility. He most assuredly did not want to foul it up.

"Oh-eight-two-two, sir," Fernandez said.

This time, Howard didn't reprimand the sarge. They knew each other too well. The colonel nodded. He picked up one of the H&K's magazines and checked the loads. Didn't want to overfill it, jam the rounds in so tight they wouldn't strip off and feed. That would be bad. Of course, he had counted them twice already. Probably the number hadn't changed since the last count.

Dentist-chair time, moving as slowly as five o'clock rush-hour traffic on the Beltway.

The way he felt right now, a root canal would be almost welcome.

13

Vladimir Plekhanov sat on a mossy rock next to an old-growth tree, drinking cool water from the bottle he carried, enjoying a shaft of early sunshine that had angled in under the thick fir canopy. He took a deep breath, smelling the sharp scent of evergreen tree sap. He saw ants scurrying up and down the Douglas fir, and watched them swerve to avoid the sticky ooze. One of the ants blundered too close and the rosin caught him. The ant struggled.

Given another few million years, some creature that had once been human might find a bit of amber with that ant in it and wonder about its life.

Plekhanov smiled, reached over and using his fingernail, carefully freed the struggling ant. The creature hurried along its way. What would it think, if it did think, about the giant finger that had come from nowhere to spare its life? Would it speak of it to its fellows? Of how the hand of a giant god had saved it from the deadly trap?

His musings were interrupted by the arrival of the

Ukrainian. The man appeared muscular, fit, dressed in hiking shorts and boots and a tight T-shirt. His footsteps made no sound on the soft path, but he did not look at ease as he moved. He spotted Plekhanov and nodded. "Greetings," he said in Russian.

The older man returned the salutation in the same language.

The Ukrainian came to stand next to Plekhanov's rock. He looked around. "Interesting imagery," he said.

Plekhanov snapped the cap back into place on the water bottle, and stuck it into his pack where it lay on the rock next to him. "I spend too much time in RW civilization—why bring it with me into VR?"

"A bit quiet for my tastes," the Ukrainian said. "But to each his own."

"Have a seat."

The Ukrainian shook his head. "I need to get back soon."

Plekhanov shrugged. "You have news for me?"

"The Americans have discovered the location of those planning the attack upon their embassy in Kiev. They will be acting upon this information shortly."

Plekhanov looked at the ants on the tree trunk. "Took them long enough. Perhaps we should be less subtle in our clues."

It was the Ukrainian's turn to shrug. "I don't understand why we did not simply allow the attack to go forward."

Plekhanov smiled. "Because damaging a perfectly good Ukrainian building serves no purpose. Why drain any more from your already sparse treasury to repair it? Why risk killing your innocent countrymen?"

"The plotters are also my countrymen."

"But hardly innocent. That band of fanatics is a loose cannon, overfilled with explosive powder. Sooner or later, it would have gone off and done as much damage to those nearest it as any target. We need such things removed from our deck—and the Americans will do that for us. The Americans have spent *their* time and money uncovering the plot, and it has also made them nervous in the process. They will be worried about such things, spending yet more time and funds to protect their other embassies. We kill several birds with one stone here, my friend. Do you still play pocket billiards?''

''Da.''

"Then you know that sinking a single ball means little, especially early in the game, unless one positions himself for the next shot.''

"This is true.''

"If we are to run the table, we must consider our next position with each play.''

The Ukrainian bowed slightly, a military gesture done mostly with the head.

"As usual, Vladimir, you are correct.'' He glanced at his watch. "I must get back.''

Plekhanov held up one hand, gesturing toward the trail. "Please. Good to see you again.''

"I'll call later.''

"It is not necessary, but thank you.''

After the Ukrainian had gone, Plekhanov watched the ants for a short time. He inspected his pocket watch. He had time before he needed to get back. Perhaps a quick walk on that side trail he had been meaning to explore? Yes. Why not? Things were unfolding more smoothly than even in his best-case scenarios. Indeed they were.

Alexander Michaels sat in the stern of the houseboat, watching a brown pelican dive for fish. Pelicans were salt-water birds, he believed, but he liked their look and so had included them in his scenario. He was on a southern Louisiana river, a large bayou, actually, and the brown water flowed sluggishly toward the distant and unseen Gulf of Mexico. A small, flat-bottomed green-anodized aluminum bateau approached from a side channel, the harsh drone of its outboard motor enough to shoo the diving pelican away. Michaels stood, walked to the railing, leaned against it, and watched the boat come.

Jay Gridley sat in the rear of the flat-nosed bateau, one hand on the motor's control arm. He throttled the motor down so that it popped and burbled, swung the little boat sideways as it drew near and allowed it to drift to a gentle stop against the houseboat's stern. Metal thunked against fiberglass. Gridley threw a nylon rope up to Michaels, who caught the rope and wrapped the end around a brass cleat under the rail. Gridley stepped to the short ladder and clambered up onto the houseboat.

"Permission to come aboard, Cap'n?"

Michaels shook his head in mild amusement. "Granted."

Once he was on the craft, the younger man looked around. "Funny, I'd have thought you'd be in the Prowler."

Michaels shrugged. "It would spoil the RW version for me if I did that. Car'll never run as good there as it would here."

"That's true. Well, it's not a bad scenario. Commercial software?"

"Yes." Michaels felt a little uncomfortable saying that, but the truth was, while he could have written his own program—he was, after all, a computer-literate operative— he had never been that absorbed in VR per se. True, it was more interesting sitting on the deck of a big houseboat, drifting past cypress trees hung thick with Spanish moss, than tapping commands into a keyboard. But it was not his thing, despite his position in Net Force. Probably people would have thought it odd, his take-it-or-leave-it attitude about VR, but Michaels liked to think it was kind of like a carpenter's attitude toward his tools—you didn't *love* your hammer or saw, you used them to do your job. When he wasn't working, Michaels didn't spend much time on the net.

He waved at a deck chair. "Have a seat."

"Thanks."

After Jay sat, the younger man said, "We've come up against a bunch of dead ends so far. The sabotage links bounce off in all directions, and that's real interesting."

"Go on."

"Well, what that means is that the rascals came from more than one locus, like we figured, so the actual piece is played by an orchestra and not a solo artist. Thing is, while we have multiple loci for the initiators, all of the firewalls are the same."

Michaels knew enough about systems to know what that meant. "So we're talking about one programmer or team, and a wide distribution of software."

"Yep." Jay looked up as they passed by a huge live oak whose branches hung low over the shore of the bayou. A fat reddish-brown king snake sunned itself on a big limb. "Or, given the setting you have here, maybe 'sho' nuf, y'all' is more appropriate?"

Michaels smiled. "You recognize the programmer's style?"

"No. The firewalls are off-the-shelf Netsoft bullet-proof; anybody could install 'em. But the trails *leading* to the walls? They're all different, but they're different in similar ways. They have a . . . rhythm. We're talking about a single conductor directing the orchestra, I'd bet my paycheck on it.''

"Not a major surprise," Michaels said.

A small town appeared on both sides of the bayou. A drawbridge linking the halves of the split town loomed ahead of the drifting boat. Downriver, a pair of weathered shrimp boats churned against the slow current toward the bridge. A warning horn blasted from the drawbridge as the center span clamshelled up. Traffic stopped on both sides of the interrupted road, parked behind red-and-white-striped barriers.

Michaels stood and walked to the pilot's chair inside, on the port side of the houseboat. He cranked the engines, waved at the bridge tender, throttled up and hurried the boat toward the opposite side of the bayou from the boats coming upriver.

Behind him, Jay said, "Build the bridges kinda low in this scenario, don't they?''

"He's not raising it for us. It's for the shrimp boats," Michaels said.

In reality, the passage was a rerouting of a multigigabyte information flow from one node to another server, a switching operation necessary when large amounts of data needed to move in bulk without interruption. The drawbridge was as good an image as any.

Once they were clear of the bridge and fishing craft, Michaels steered the houseboat toward the center of the bayou, then cut the engines and let it drift. He moved back to the stern. Normally, he'd be paying more attention to the channel around him, but he'd chosen this scenario in part because it didn't require his full attention on the straight and wide sections of the waterway.

Gridley said, "We're running the signature and looking

for matches, but there are hundreds of thousands of professional programmers out there.''

"Assuming he even is a professional and not some gifted amateur,'' Michaels said.

Gridley shook his head. "Guy's gotta be a player. Rascals are too clean to be some kid or duffer.''

Michaels nodded. "All right. Keep looking. Anything else I should know?''

"Not really. We've got rovers everywhere, looking for more trouble. You know Tyrone Howard?''

"The colonel's son?''

"Yeah. I talked to him netmail. He's checking with his friends. They spend a lot of time on the air, they might notice something. He and his buddies are even checking out CyberNation.''

"CyberNation?''

"A new VR abode. Supposed to be a whole country online.''

"Interesting. Is this something we need to worry about?''

"Someday, maybe, but I don't think it has anything to do with our current problems. CyberNation didn't erase the Commander, and I don't think it's them doing rascals on the net.''

"So about our problem . . . ?''

"Well. If this guy uses the same setup he's been using, we should be on him like ketchup on fries pretty quick.''

"But you don't think he'll use the same setup?''

"Nah. *I* wouldn't—and this guy is almost as good as I am.''

Michaels laughed.

"Hey, it's hard to be humble when you're great,'' Gridley said. He looked at his watch. "Oops. Better shove off. I have a VR staff meeting in half an hour. Probably take me twice that long to get there using this thing.'' He waved at the green bateau, then pointed at the bayou with a sideways nod. "Fortunately, I cleverly left my car just around that next bend."

Michaels cast off the rope as Gridley climbed down into the bateau and started the outboard motor.

"Bye-bye, you-all!" Gridley yelled.

Alex watched the young computer genius head toward the nearer shore. A red Viper convertible was parked at a small dock. As Michaels continued to watch, Gridley pulled the boat to the dock and tied it to a piling. He climbed out of the craft, turned and waved at the houseboat, then headed for the car.

Tuesday, September 21st, 11:50 a.m.
Kiev

The terrorists' meeting was supposed to begin at 1130 hours, but Howard had allowed twenty minutes more for late arrivals. That extra allotment of time was now up. There were eighteen men and three women inside the warehouse, and while none of them had openly carried weapons, several had worn long coats, and at least three had arrived bearing what appeared to be cased musical instruments—a cello, a double bass and some kind of large-belled horn, probably a tuba, to judge from the shapes.

Howard would be very surprised if those cases contained anything a musician would use onstage. More likely, inside the cases would be pistols, assault rifles and a rocket launcher, maybe even a few grenades or other explosives. Since this was the staging area for the attack on the embassy, there was a distinct possibility there were other armaments already hidden inside when the terrorists arrived.

The terrorists were in an office on the second floor of a small, and apparently otherwise unoccupied, two-story warehouse. No one was on the ground level, save for a guard at the building's south entrance. Howard's recon team, led by Fernandez, had done a quick scout when they'd arrived, and discovered that same guard just inside the big metal roll-up door on the south side of the building. While the stealthiest of the recon team could have easily slipped into the warehouse at another entrance and installed surveillance gear in the building itself, Howard chose not to risk it. Maybe these yahoos had set up some alarms of their own, and he didn't want to be tripping one of those and scaring them off.

Instead, he'd had his teams put cams, motion sensors and parabolics outside the building, along with digital radio and IR scanners. Each of the arrivees was photographed as they entered the warehouse, and vidcaps should clear enough to ID anyone who somehow escaped.

Not that escape was going to be real likely.

It was tempting to have his troops kick in the upstairs door, toss a few flashbang grenades inside, and then blast anybody not blind and bleeding from the ears stupid enough to go for a gun, but—no. Instead, he had his troops deployed around the warehouse, watching all possible modes of egress. He would prefer not to do any shooting outside; however, he was prepared for such an eventuality.

There was still just the one guard watching the only un-locked entrance to the building.

"Sarge."

"Sir."

"Do you suppose somebody in this unit of tripfoots might manage to take out the guard without raising the dead?" This was a rhetorical question. Howard already knew who had the assignment.

"Why, yes, sir, I believe that might be possible."

"Then make it so, Sergeant Fernandez."

"On my way, sir."

"You? You're going? A moth-eaten, tired *old* man like you?"

The two men grinned at each other.

Howard watched from his vantage point in the building across the alley from the south entrance as Fernandez approached the closed roll-up door. Fernandez did not wear any obvious weaponry, just dark and greasy coveralls and a battered yellow hardhat, and he carried an old metal lunch pail he must have scrounged from somewhere.

The parabolics picked up the sound of Fernandez whistling something as he arrived at the door. Sounded like something from *Swan Lake*. Nice touch, that.

Fernandez banged on the door with his free hand.

After a moment, he hammered on the door again. The door accordioned up about six feet. The guard, unarmed, stepped into view and rattled off something Howard didn't understand, but in a questioning and somewhat irritated tone of voice.

Fernandez said something in return, and it had a familiar ring to it.

Howard grinned. If he wasn't mistaken, Fernandez had just asked the guard where the men's room was. Before the man could respond, Fernandez said something else, and pointed behind the guard. The man turned to look, puzzled.

A tactical error on the guard's part.

Fernandez swung the lunch pail and slammed it into the guard's right temple. The man dropped as if his legs had suddenly vanished. Fernandez put the lunch pail down, grabbed the obviously unconscious man, and dragged him into the warehouse. After a moment, the sarge reappeared, and waved: Come on in.

"A and B teams, go!" Howard said into the LOSIR tactical com unit he wore. He grabbed his H&K assault rifle and sprinted for the door.

14

From the time Julio Fernandez knocked the guard cold until the two assault teams were in place inside the warehouse had taken slightly less than forty-five seconds. Not a glitch.

Now, they waited.

There was an elevator, but the circuit breaker working the lift had been tripped; it wasn't going to move. The only way down from the second floor consisted of two sets of stairs. The exit door on one set of those stairs was pad-locked from the outside—wouldn't *that* be lovely during a fire? Howard left two men watching that door anyhow, along with men outside watching the windows. Nobody was sneaking out of here.

The other set of stairs was wide and straight, the door unlocked. This was how they'd gone up, and this was how they would come down.

Howard deployed his men so they weren't visible from the base of the stairs. Everybody was to stay hidden until he gave the word.

Howard himself would have put on the unconscious guard's coveralls to stand by the front entrance—until the sarge reminded him it wouldn't be enough of a disguise— not unless these guys were *really* color-blind.

"Fine, fine, you do it. By the way, what was *in* that lunch box you hit that guy with?"

"Twelve pounds of lead shot, sir. Packed into a nice tight leather bag. Sometimes low-tech stuff is still the best way."

Thus it was that Fernandez wore the guard's coveralls, his face in shadow, so when the party broke up and the terrorists made to leave, they'd see that things were still fine downstairs.

Howard found a spot behind a stack of wooden crates in which to hide. There was enough of a gap between the boxes so he could see the base of the stairs. He could smell the pine-like scent of the unfinished wood, and the lube from the machine parts in the boxes. He could also smell his own nervous sweat.

Once most of the plotters were down, they'd move on them. He reasoned that the plotters wouldn't be showing weapons, since they were about to go out into public view, and unless they were real fast on the draw, they wouldn't have time to get their weapons out without getting cooked for their efforts. They'd see they were caught and that resistance was unwise. That was how he reasoned it. If he could take them all alive, that would be the best thing. Let the interrogators at them.

The sound of voices talking in Russian or Ukrainian drifted down the stairs, along with the clump of boots. This was it. He took a deep breath.

Don't screw this up, John—

Tuesday, September 21st, 12:53 a.m.
San Diego

Ruzhyó sat upright in bed, heart pounding rapidly. Despite the motel's air-conditioning, he was clammy with sweat, the covers tangled in a knot around his feet.

He kicked the covers off, swung his legs over the edge of the bed and stood. The room was dark, save for a thin shaft of light from around the edges of the almost-closed bathroom door. He padded in that direction, scratching at his damp chest hair. It was not fear of the night's gloom that caused Ruzhyó to leave a light on there, but practicality: The nightmare woke him frequently, and often in a room in which he had never slept before. Switching on a bright lamp with its hard glare to find his disoriented way to the toilet seemed . . . excessive. Over the years of cheap rooms and fast moves, he had learned the lesson: Leave a lamp burning near the toilet, close the door so only a gap remained, and relief was always in the direction of the light. Had he been a religious man, he would have perhaps considered some metaphorical significance in that, but faith in an Almighty Being was not in Ruzhyó's soul, if indeed he had such a thing.

No God worthy of the name would have ever let Anna die so young.

In addition to the one over the sink, there were mirrors across from, and next to, the toilet—a stupid place to put such things—who wants to watch himself urinate or defecate? The mirrors reflected his external image, which always came as something of a surprise, since he did not spend too much time looking at himself. To hear the mirrors tell it, he was a fit man, muscular, but not overly so, his brown hair now cut short, going gray at the temples. He looked at least his age of forty, perhaps a bit more, and his eyes, though bleary from the night's touch, were all too cold and knowing. Those eyes had seen many die. They belonged to a man who had caused more than a few of those deaths. But at least his method was quick. He did not leave the wounded to suffer slowly, in pain.

When Anna had been alive, he had not been so introspective. There had been no need. She had asked the deep questions, and often, she had answered them, too. It had been enough for him to listen, to smile and nod, to let her speak of such matters. For a time after she was gone, he had been completely shut down, had done nothing other than the barest survival motions, not wanting to remember, to think, to feel. It was only later, after the wound had slowed from a torrent to a slow but steady trickle, only then had he spent any time inside his own head. He had gone back to doing what he knew best and he was still good at it—but he no longer took any joy in the work. His pride at being able to deal death with expertise was greatly diminished. It was simply what he did. What he would continue to do until someone better did it to him.

He finished pissing, closed the toilet's lid without flushing and returned to his rented bed. He lay in the dark for a long time, but sleep did not want him back. Finally, he got up and turned on a light. He stretched, sat on the floor and began to do crunches, working his abdominal muscles. He would do a hundred of these, then push-ups, a hundred of those, then another set of crunches and push-ups, and another, until he could not do even one more exercise. Sometimes that helped. Sometimes he would be tired enough to fall back into exhausted slumber.

Sometimes it merely left him exhausted, but still awake. Those were not the best of times.

Nor, unfortunately, were they the worst of times.

Tuesday, September 21st, 11:54 a.m.
Kiev

"Now!" Howard said into his mouthpiece. As he spoke, he stepped out from behind his cover and raised the assault rifle to a hip point. "Don't move!" he yelled, using the Ukrainian phrase Fernandez had taught him.

For a heartbeat no one did. The terrorists, most on the warehouse floor, two still on the stairs, froze, startled no doubt by the sight of more than a dozen armed men in coveralls stepping or rolling out of concealment to point weapons at them.

Then one of the terrorists screamed something, certainly a curse, even if Howard didn't understand the words. The screamer dug his hand into his jacket pocket and pulled out a small chrome-plated pistol—

Somebody cooked off a double-tap—*pop! pop!*—and dropped the pistoleer.

It all went south. Most of the other terrorists tried to get their guns out.

One of them saw how stupid this was, yelled *"Nyet! Nyet!"* but too late.

Howard's orders to his troops had been clear—take them alive if possible, but if *somebody* is going to get shot, do *not* let it be you.

Time stalled, stretched, and Howard saw part of it in his suddenly tunneled vision, as if it were a movie being run in slow motion and he was in the front row. His vision narrowed, but there was nothing wrong with his hearing: Even amidst all the gunfire, obscenely loud in the enclosed warehouse, he distinctly heard the sound of men yelling, actions cycling, *chunk-chunk!* and brass clinking on the concrete floor, *tink, tink, clink*—

—a big bearded man pulled what looked like a World War I Luger from his belt and swung it up, only to catch several rounds from a submachine gun in a neat horizontal row across the center of his mass—

—the man yelling "Nyet!" dropped to the floor, covered his head with his hands, curled into a fetal position, still repeating his panicked yell—

—the men on the stairs turned to flee back the way they had come—

—a thin, balding man missing a front tooth came up with a sawed-off bolt-action rifle, a .22 maybe, and thrust it toward Howard. So keen was his vision that Howard noticed a ring on the man's right forefinger as he wrapped the digit around the trigger—

No time to raise the assault rifle to aim. Howard point-indexed the thin man, stabbed the weapon at him as if it were a bayonet and pulled the trigger. The big weapon bucked, once—twice—three times! and recoil lifted the muzzle with the second and third rounds. The first bullet struck at high solar-plexus level, the second the base of the throat, the third at the top of the receding hairline. Howard saw the spray of the head's exit wound, a balloon full of dark red fluid bursting—

One would have been enough. That was the thing with a .30-caliber rifle, a good solid body hit was a one-hundred-percent-fight-stopper. No handgun could claim that, but a 7.62mm, yeah—

The thin man fell, already dead, taking nearly forever to reach the floor. Land masses rose and sank, life came and went, time wore away mountains. . . .

By the time the dead man lay flat on the concrete, the battle was over.

Howard noticed his ears were ringing, and the stink of burned gunpowder filled his nostrils. Jesus!

His troops moved, covering the surviving terrorists. Two had made it up the stairs, only to find the other exits blocked. Hands raised, they came down the stairs again.

The yelling man had survived. When the smoke cleared and the counts were done, of the twenty-one terrorists, nine were dead, six were wounded—two seriously enough so that Howard's medics didn't give them much hope, four with survivable injuries. The unit's medical transports had already pulled up and were hauling the bodies and wounded out.

None of Howard's troops had sustained a scratch.

And he had killed a man, face-to-face, who had tried to kill *him*.

"Sir," Fernandez said, "we oughta skedaddle."

"Affirmative, Sarge." He glanced at his watch. Not yet noon. Amazing.

According to Hunter, they had about ten minutes before the local authorities would have to quit pretending they didn't know anything and take action. "Pack it up," Howard said to the troops. "Oh, and . . . good work."

That earned him a few grins, but his adrenaline was fast fading. He felt tired, old and suddenly depressed. He and his troops had been better trained, better armed, and they'd had surprise on their side. This wasn't a battle, it had been a complete rout. These so-called terrorists had never had a chance.

How much pride could you take in winning a battle of wits with an idiot? A footrace with a man wearing casts on his ankles? Not very much.

Still—he hadn't screwed it up. That was something.

15

Toni Fiorella was practicing *sempok* and *depok,* moves that allowed a fighter to go quickly from standing to sitting positions while keeping a defense. To do these properly required a fair amount of balance and leg strength, and she tried to include them in most of her workouts to maintain both. *Silat* had a lot of ground-fighting techniques, but being able to spring to one's feet in a hurry from a seated position was also part of the training. It was hard on the knees, however.

She was breathing hard and working on a pretty good sweat when Jesse Russell came into the gym. No spandex this time. He wore faded black sweat pants, an oversize black T-shirt and mat shoes.

"Hey," he said.

"Mr. Russell."

"Rusty. Please."

"All right. Rusty."

"What, uh, do I call you in class? As a gesture of re-spect? *Sensei*? *Sifu*?"

"The term we use for teacher is 'Guru,' " she said.

He smiled. "Really?"

"Indonesia got a lot of its culture from the mainland, some from the Hindu and Moslem religions."

He laughed.

She raised her eyebrows.

He said, "I was just thinking about telling my friend Harold about this: 'I went to see my guru today.' 'Yeah? You learning how to meditate?' 'Actually, she's teaching me how to kick some serious ass.' "

Toni smiled. "Are you serious, Rusty? About learning?"

"Yes, ma'am. I trained five years in taekwondo, and I'm pretty sure I can handle myself in most situations, but it's mostly outfighting, long range. This in-your-face stuff sorta came as a surprise. I'd really like to learn it."

"All right. There are three things you want to remember: base, angle and leverage. And one of the most basic prin-ciples works on taking the center line—you want to control the area in front of your head and body, and in front of an opponent's head and body. I'm going to demonstrate the first *djuru*. Watch me, and then we'll break it down."

He nodded. "Yes, ma'am."

Tuesday, September 21st, noon
Quantico

When Alex Michaels bothered to eat lunch, he usually ate it at his desk. The unit secretary would get his order, put it on the list and fax it to the deli guy, who would deliver the food to the reception guard just after noon. Before the deli had been approved as a supplier, Net Force had run a background on the deli's owner, his wife and grown kids and the guy who brought the orders. Even so, when the assassination protocols had been in place, if anybody wanted to order out, an agent had to hand-carry the order to the store, then stand and watch the food as it was prepared. Security was tight, and rightfully so—why bother to shoot somebody if you could poison his lunch?

Michaels was partial to the Reuben sandwich and potato salad, and the crunchy dill pickle, quarter-sliced lengthways, that came with it. That was what he usually ordered.

On days when he just had to get out of the unit for a few minutes, he skipped the deli order and the Net Force cafeteria and went to the new restaurant row a couple miles away. In good weather, he took his recumbent trike, a lowslung sixteen-gear three-wheeler he left parked in the covered bike racks.

Today, the weather was a little crisper than it had been, not quite so warm and muggy, a good day for pedal power. He could legally take the trike on the roads, but there was a jogging/bike path that wound from the edge of the fence, and while it was twice as long, it was a much prettier and safer trip. It had been two weeks since Day's murder, and since there had not been any more assassination attempts on federal officials—if you didn't count the Ninth Circuit Court judge whose wife had beaned him with a fishbowl during an argument about his alledged extramarital affair—the assassination protocols had been downgraded. Now, it was basically pay-attention-to-things, but not an active alert with bodyguards, at least not at his level.

He changed into bike shoes and shorts and a T-shirt in his office, stuck his taser into a small fanny pack with his ID and virgil and put his foam helmet on. He walked outside to the bike and trike racks, unlocked his trike and wheeled it out into the parking lot. The recumbent had set him back two weeks' pay, even used, but he enjoyed the heck out of it. In the lowest gear, he could climb the steepest grade around here, admittedly not saying much, and on a flat road without traffic, he could pump along in high gear at speeds pushing forty. Well, maybe a little less than that, but it felt like he was flying. It was a good way to keep a little tone going on the days he didn't jog, and he hadn't been doing much of that lately. Working out was usually the first thing to go when he got really busy. It was easy to rationalize it—he could always run or hit the Bowflex later, right?

He squatted and sat on the low seat, slipped his feet into the toe-clips on the pedals and put his riding gloves on. He grabbed the handlebars. He planned to stretch it out a little today—he felt stale. Lunch was pretty much an excuse for a place to go. Probably he wouldn't do more than grab a soft drink before he headed back.

He checked out at the gate, and headed for the bike path.

He stayed in a fairly high gear, even though it was hard to pedal that way at slow speed. The shift lever was on the seat frame next to his right hip, and easy enough to gear down if the going got too hard.

He passed a few people he knew from the base, out jogging on their lunch hour, and he waved or nodded at them. He came up behind one young woman in a red Speedo tank top and matching skintight shorts with a fanny pack slung in back, going at a pretty good rate in his direction. She was in great shape. He admired the play of her taut legs and backside as she ran. He checked her in the handlebar mirror when he passed, but he didn't recognize the face. There were a lot of people here. She could be a Marine, one of the new FBI recruits, maybe an office worker. Or maybe she lived in town and this was the return loop.

Lately, despite his feelings for his wife—*ex*-wife—he had felt a few stirrings that exercise and long hours working, or playing with the Prowler, couldn't quite quell.

He sighed, shifted into a higher gear and pumped harder. Sooner or later, he'd have to jump back into the pool; he couldn't really see himself as a monk for the rest of his life. It just didn't seem quite right yet. He was out of practice—and the idea of asking a woman out was still more than he wanted to think about.

The path, a nice smooth macadam, meandered through a small stand of hardwood trees whose leaves were fast changing from greens to yellows and golds, then swung past the back of a new light industrial park, mostly office buildings or jobbers' warehouses. A beeping forklift, painted a dark red, with a big silver propane tank on the back, carried a stack of wooden pallets toward a larger stack next to the chain-link fence. The fork's motor rumbled as the driver expertly lowered the shipping platforms and backed away.

Michaels smiled. He'd run a forklift in an aluminum warehouse one summer when he was in high school, moving plate and bar to big flatbed trucks for shipment. It had basically been a simple job once you got the hang of it, uncomplicated. You picked it up *here,* and you put it down *there,* and the only thing you had to worry about was dropping it. It made a hell of a racket when you let a couple thousand pounds of metal slip off the forks, and most of the guys in the warehouse would stop what they were doing and applaud when it happened. Just like dropping a plate in the high school lunchroom.

It was true what they said: Life was like high school—only bigger.

He came to the long straight stretch, a little over half a mile before it curved again, and he upshifted into top gear. He pushed and pulled hard on the pedals, the toe-clips allowing him to apply pressure in both directions. It didn't take but a couple hundred feet for his legs to get really warm, and halfway through the strip, his thighs and ham-

strings started to burn really hot. He checked the speed-
ometer. Thirty-three. Not bad. He had the windshield
mounted, but without the full faring installed, the drag
wouldn't let him get much faster sitting upright with just a
little backward lean.

He passed another rider on a two-wheeler, cruising along
at a steady, but slower, speed. The rider wore purple and
yellow gear, and the bike was one of those carbon-frame
Swiss jobs that easily cost twice what his trike did. He
waved at Michaels as he blew past. Probably going to crank
out forty or fifty miles, and save the sprint until the end.
And even after that distance, Michaels knew he wouldn't
be able to stay with him if the guy was a *serious* biker.
Those guys were all crazy.

The burn increased, but he kept pumping, holding on.
When he had about a hundred and fifty yards before the
curve, Michaels allowed himself to coast. He slowed, added
a little brake and made it through the curve. Not much bank
there—too bad. A couple more degrees and he could have
taken it at speed, but he guessed the designers didn't want
walkers or joggers sliding down the side of a hill if the path
got wet. It did rain here from time to time.

It felt good to get out, to do something physical. He
resolved to do it more often.

Tuesday, September 21st, 12:09 p.m.
Quantico

The Selkie slowed her run to a walk as soon as the target
was out of sight on his big trike. He had seen her, of course,
and given that he was a normal heterosexual male, he
would have noticed her in the tight red shorts she wore.
She was in excellent shape, and although running was not

her preferred method of keeping that way, she could go a few miles without collapsing when it was necessary.

That the target had seen her and very likely stared at her ass didn't mean anything. He would not see her in these clothes again.

She could have killed him when he went past. Could have easily pulled the snub-nose .38 S&W revolver from the fanny pack she wore and put all five rounds the little gun carried into the target's back as he sailed past oblivious. Knocked him off his tricycle, reloaded, calmly walked to where he lay and put a couple more in the head. Even if somebody had been there to see—and no one had been— it was unlikely anybody would have been able to stop her. She was adept with the Smith, could manage NRA Expert with it, or keep up with the IPSC action shooters and their tricked-out pistols in their combat scenarios, despite the short barrel and lousy sights. It was one of the tools of her trade, and she was the best there was at that business.

But such killings were . . . inelegant. Anybody could point a gun and blast away, and for an adept, there was no joy to be found in such a simple method. Of course, the needs of the client had to come first. Some of them wanted it known that the target had been killed. They wanted it done bloody. And some of them even wanted souvenirs—a finger, an ear—or some normally less-visible appendage. She didn't torture and she didn't take hurry-up contracts, but if the client wanted anatomical proof the target was gone, she would supply it. Those who asked for such things didn't usually offer her much repeat business. Clients who wanted body parts to put in a jar tended to piss people off and get into fatal trouble of their own.

She nodded at a jogger coming from the other direction, but didn't make eye contact.

Good assassins deleted their targets and got away.

The best assassins could delete their targets and arrange

it so nobody even suspected there had *been* a murder. That was much more satisfying. She hadn't been given instructions about the manner of this target's death, and she was toying with the idea of making it look like natural causes, or maybe suicide. She was in control, it was her choice.

Always.

16

The buzzer sounded and Tyrone Howard joined the exodus
of students from first-period class into the dingy green halls
of Eisenhower Middle School. Ahead of him, he saw Sean
Hughes lumber into a guy from behind and shoulder him
aside. The guy slammed into the lockers, hard. He recovered, turned, started to say something—then saw who had
hit him and changed his mind.

This was a real good idea.

Tyrone slowed, to avoid getting too close. Hughes was
an ox, pushing six feet tall and two hundred pounds, and
at fifteen was two years older than most of his grade class.
Hughes was a flicker screen who had flunked at least twice,
not including summer school and private net teachers, and
he got his kicks by bullying anybody who had more brains
than he did—which was everybody in the school except
MCMs—mentally challenged mainstreamers. And maybe a
few of them were smarter, too. They had a name for
Hughes, though nobody ever said it to his face.

"Essay is on a roll today, ain't he?"

Tyrone looked to his left and saw James Joseph Hatfield grinning at him.

"Essay" came from the initials S and A. Which came from "Sore Ass," which came from "Brontosaurus," which was what the computer set called Sean Hughes. Tyrone didn't know who had come up with the original nickname, but it was dead on. The guy had all the wit and grace of a big dino tanked on sleeping pills.

Jimmy Joe was a hillbilly from West Virginia, small, so white he was bright, with eyes so bad he had to wear thick glasses instead of contacts. He was also one of the best netriders in the whole school, and he held the record for completing the first ten levels of Black Mysts of Total Catastrophe fastest, not just in the school but anywhere. And he was Tyrone's best friend.

"Hey, Jimmy Joe. How's the flow?"

"Dee eff eff, Tyrone." This stood for DFF—data flowin' fine.

"Listen, I talked to Jay Gee. He needs our help."

"Jay Gee needs *our* help? Praw that."

"Nopraw," Tyrone said. "Somebody is poppin' strands."

"Tell me somethin' I don't compro, bro. Somebody is *always* poppin' strands."

"Yeah, affirm, but this is different. There's a C-1 grammer looking to rass the whole web."

"Nofeek?"

"Nofeek."

Jimmy Joe shook his head. "Eyes up, rider. If Jay Gee can't grope him, how are we gonna do it?"

He had a point. Jay Gridley's reputation among the set was large.

"We got links he doesn't scan," Tyrone said. "We can backline, OHT, little feek like that."

"Yeah, yeah, nopraw pross that. I can blip the aolers. Induct-deduct fine lines, do the One Horse Towns. Build a scoop. We could seine minnows. I know a couple of hangers in CyberNation, they got some pretty good nets there. You think about joining? CyberNation, I mean."

"I think about what my dad would say if I tried," Tyrone said.

"I copy that. My old man would blow a major fuse, but it looks like the place to live. Then again, this is too warm, slip. Us, riding with Jay Gee."

"Yeah—"

Tyrone ran into a wall. Only it wasn't really a wall, it was Essay.

"Watch it, tits!"

Tyrone backed up two steps fast. He hadn't been paying attention. Essay must have forgotten where he was going and stopped to puzzle it out. Stupid. But maybe not as stupid as walking right into his back!

"Sorry!" Tyrone said.

"Yeah, you gonna be," Essay began. "I'm gonna mush you—!"

But before he could finish the threat, Belladonna Wright walked past, trailing the scent of some musky, sexy perfume.

Essay shifted his thinking from his big stupid head to his small stupid head. He turned to watch Bella—as did Tyrone—and she was something to see in her green microskirt and halter top, walking high on her cork slope-plats. A grade up and the best-looking girl in D.C. easy. Essay had as much chance getting next to her as he did flying to the moon by waving his big old arms, but that didn't stop him from looking—though that was all he would do. Bella was currently hardlinked with Herbie "Bonebreaker" LeMott, the captain of the Epitome High School wrestling team. He was a senior, and *he* made Essay look little. When Theo

Hatcher had sneaked up behind Bella once and "accidentally" put his hand on her butt, Theo had spent six weeks with his arm in a blue fiberglass cast for his trouble, courtesy of LeMott. Bella could have any guy in school broken in half with two words into Bonebreaker's ear, and even Essay knew that.

Jimmy Joe grabbed one of Tyrone's arms and steered him back the way they came. "Ride, rider, ride! Time his brain clicks back on-line, we need to be scanning *elsewhere*!"

Tyrone understood—he definitely prossed *that,* nopraw at all. On some level, though, he was really pissed off. He wasn't ready to die, but sooner or later, he was going to have to do something about Essay.

What to do and *how* to do it—well, those were the problems.

Wednesday, September 22nd, 6 a.m.
San Diego

Ruzhyó did not much care for television, though he sometimes watched the international news to see what mention there was of his homeland. CNN droned in the background as he fixed coffee in the small pot provided by the hotel. The coffee was prepackaged and stale, but it was better than nothing.

It had been yet another bad night for dreams. After managing to get back to sleep for an hour or two, he came awake and knew it was pointless to try again. He had known a man in the army once who, it was said, could sleep while eating a bowl of hot soup. Ruzhyó was not that good, but he had learned to survive on a minimum amount of rest when he had been a soldier, catching naps when he could; two hours was enough to fuel a day.

He took his coffee and went back to stare at the television.

In Idaho, some cult had gone into a barn and set it on fire, to free themselves from the flesh to join their god. Ruzhyó did not know how free they were, but the flesh was certainly well-done, to judge from the pictures.

In France, student demonstrators had attacked a police line outside a hotel where the French President was scheduled to speak. Nine of the demonstrators had been hospitalized with wounds from rubber bullets; two others had died from the same cause.

In India, a flood drowned two hundred people, uncounted sacred cows, and washed away several villages.

In Japan, an earthquake on the island of Kyushu had killed eighty-nine people in collapsing buildings and done major damage to the city of Kagoshima. During the quake, the new bullet train that spanned the island had also crashed when the ground in front of it dropped twenty feet, killing sixty and injuring more than three hundred.

Of Chechnya, CNN had nothing to say.

Ruzhyó sipped his bad coffee and shook his head. Just as well that there was no news of home, given how dreary it all seemed. The world was a dangerous place, full of misery. All over it, people would be lamenting the loss of loved ones this day, family or friends taken by accidents or illness or murder. During those few times when he had felt qualms about the work he did, all he had ever needed to do was watch the television, or read the newspapers, or just talk to someone. Life was full of woe. He was no more than a drop in a sea of misery. If he took a man out, what did it matter? If not him, something or somebody else would. In the end, it did not matter all that much, did it?

His com unit cheeped. He sipped the coffee and stared

at the com. No, it did not matter. And just as well—more wetwork was surely about to be forthcoming.

Wednesday, September 22nd, 4:45 p.m.
Washington, D.C.

Naked, save for a sweatband around her head, the Selkie sat at the small kitchen table and examined her cane.

She checked the wood for nicks and gouges. Every couple of months, she would take fine sandpaper and Watco satin-finish oil to the cane, to smooth and polish the already smooth hickory. It was hardwood, but it scratched easily, and she liked to have it gleaming. The manufacturer recommended mineral oil, but Watco gave a tougher finish. Smelled better, too.

It was a couple hours work to do it right, the sanding and finishing, but one of the first things she'd learned from her father was to take care of her tools so they wouldn't fail her when she needed them. The guys who made the wooden weapons did excellent work. She owned five of their canes in three different styles, as well as two sets of *escrima* sticks, and a custom-made pair of six-inch *yawaras*.

The cane she preferred for work in places where she did not carry a gun was the Custom Combat model. It was hickory, thirty-seven inches long, blond in color, with a round shaft a little over an inch in diameter; it had a large crook tipped by a flamingo-beak design. Hickory was best for the street, heavier than the walnut tournament models, more sturdy than the oak. The end of the curved hook—called the horn—was sharp and wicked enough to do some real damage. The ground end of the shaft was a dull and rounded point, innocuous-looking, and with the rubber tip in place, perfectly usable as a support cane. There was a series of decorative notches carved into the shaft just below the crook, designed to serve as a handgrip.

That cane was at home. The one she inspected at the moment, the Instructor's model, was almost identical to the Combat style, same length and diameter, but the crook was a hair wider and the horn was rounded instead of beaked. It looked a lot more like the cane an old lady should be using to hobble about with. It wouldn't do for some eagle-eyed cop to see that pointed horn and think: *Why, Granny, what a sharp stick you have. . . .*

The weapon looked okay, so the Selkie left the kitchen and padded naked into the living room of her rental condo where she had set up her practice target. This was a section of an inch-and-a-half-diameter aluminum rod with a ring-bolt on one end. The rod was wrapped in a pad of biogel, the same stuff they used to soften racing bike seats and the insteps of running shoes; the gel was then covered with a stretched sheet of chamois leather and held tightly in place with duct tape. It wasn't exactly the same as flesh over bone, but it was close enough for her purposes. At home, she had a *wing chun* training dummy set up with similar wrapping, so she could work the full range of angles, with weapons or feet and hands, but on the road, one had to make do.

She got a sudden mental image of herself trying to check a *wing chun* dummy in at an airport with her luggage, with the reaction that would bring, and grinned.

A thin nylon rope ran from the target's eyebolt through a second eye hook she'd screwed into a ceiling rafter; the other end of the line was tied to a doorknob. This way, she could adjust the target's height. Right now, it was at knee level. Knees were great targets for a stick—a broken knee put a big crimp in anybody's fighting style.

She moved within range of the target, took a couple of

cleansing breaths and assumed her basic stance, cane in front of her, tip on the ground, both hands on the crook. She was aware she would look very interesting to a watcher were not all the curtains pulled closed: a naked woman standing with a cane in front of her crotch in the middle of a room empty except for something weird hanging from the ceiling. She grinned. She'd always liked working out nude, there was something so primal about it.

She cleared her mind. Wait. Wait . . .

She whipped the cane up from the floor in a short arc from her right, slid her right hand to mid-shaft to guide the strike, her left hand to the carved grip to power it.

The solid *thunk!* of the wood into the padded bar felt very satisfying. A good hit.

She spun the cane, caught the target in the crook, pulled it toward herself, then pivoted the stick and hit the padding from the opposite side.

One more solid hit and the target stopped cold, no swing. Yes!

She pulled the cane back, held it like a pool cue and thrust the tip forward. Hit the target high, knocked it back.

Yes.

It was just practice, but even so, the Selkie was in the zone—she was in the *killing* zone. And there was no place more exciting.

17

Plekhanov sat in an old stone bell tower, a long-barreled Mauser Gewehr Model 1898 rifle balanced across his knees. The piece weighed about four and half kilos, was intrinsically accurate, fired the 7.92mm cartridge at high velocity, and had an appropriate-period M73B1 telescopic sight mounted upon it. Even though the scope was American-made, used primarily on the Springfield 1903, some of the optics had found their way into Germany. This was somewhat ironic, given the uses to which they had been put. The long bolt made the rifle's action slow to operate, and it held only five rounds in the box magazine, but the range would be enough to allow plenty of time to escape despite the sluggish operational speed.

The church steeple was the tallest point in the picturesque and nameless little village southwest of Maintenon, and offered a good view of the approaching armies. The AEF—American Expeditionary Force—had come late to the Great War, but they were here now, and would help

turn the tide. Recent storms in the region had been torren-
tial, and it was one of their brigades now slogging its way
across the muddy fields even as Plekhanov watched.

Along with the Americans was a polyglot combined-unit
comprised of Russian, Serbian, Chechen, Korean, Japanese,
Thai, Chinese and Indian soldiers.

Plekhanov removed the clunky helmet he wore and ran
one hand through his sweat-damp hair. He grinned.
Historical accuracy fell down a bit in this scenario, since
no Oriental countries had fielded soldiers in this area during
World War I, even though Japan and China had been considered allies of the western Europeans battling Germany.
Certainly there had been no Koreans or Thais—still called
Siamese back then—nor Indians, unless perhaps the Brits
had sprinkled a few Gurkhas or Bengal Lancers in among
their troops. The British were odd ducks, so he supposed
that might well have been possible. Plekhanov's research
was not as thorough as it might have been, since it wasn't
really necessary. While writing the software, he did recall
reading a piece about how outraged the Brits had been
when the nabob of Bengal, one Suraj-ud-Dowlah, sacked
Calcutta in 1757. After the battle, the nabob had stuffed
146 captured Brits into a small and very hot room at Fort
William. When they were released the next day, only
twenty-three of them were still alive; the rest had died, most
of them from heat stroke. Thus was born the infamous
"Black Hole of Calcutta."

*Careful there, old man, you are drifting. Best you get
back to the business at hand.*

Plekhanov put his helmet back on, shifted his position
from where he sat upon the empty wine cask and propped
the rifle onto the ledge under the tower's opening. He could
have used the hiking scenario, but since he was taking direct action himself—there was nobody he could trust to do
this particular job—he thought a more active imagery was

appropriate. A German sniper picking off enemy troops at long range seemed eminently suitable. Poetic, even.

He chambered a round, and lined the scope up on a rather fat American officer who looked like a caricature of a Wall Street stockbroker, despite the military uniform. Even with the optics, the target was still somewhat small at the distance—nearly two hundred meters, he judged. The scope was zeroed in at one hundred meters, so he aimed a bit high, for the head, to allow for a little extra drop. He took a deep breath, held it, squeezed the trigger. . . .

In New York City, a currency tasking computer subcontracted to the Federal Reserve sent copies of all user ID codes admitted to every connected terminal—

Even as the fat American collapsed with a bullet buried in his chest, Plekhanov worked the bolt and shifted his aim.

Ah. There was the White Russian, saber in hand, leading his men. Plekhanov put the crosshairs on the man's throat, held his breath again, fired—

In Moscow, the computer interlink responsible for balance-of-trade statistics with the European Commonwealth scrambled and went down—

There was the Korean officer, trying to get his troops to duck and cover. Plekhanov worked the rifle's bolt, ejected another spent shell and chambered a fresh round. *Goodbye, Mr. Kim—*

A small setting inside the fabber making the new PowerExtreme mainframe computer chips at the Kim Electronics plant in Seoul altered, not enough to be noticed by the operators, but enough to change certain pathways in the chips' silicon circuitry. The virus had a time limit, so the settings would revert, but a thousand chips would be affected before that happened, turning the high-end systems they would eventually control into electronic time bombs waiting to go off—

And here on the muddy French field was an Indian looking for a place to hide. *Sorry, Punjab, old Wog, there's no cover there—*

The newly installed computer traffic system in Bombay blew its triple-redundancy circuits. All two hundred main traffic signals under its direct control turned green. All passenger- and freight-train track signals turned green. So did all light-rail crossing signals—

One unfired bullet remained. He had to use it before they got too close. He already knew his target. Plekhanov swung the rifle's barrel to the right. The Siamese commander held a pistol; he fired it wildly. He would not be able to hit Plekhanov at this distance, save by accident, even if he could *see* him, which he could not. Still, it paid to be cautious. Plekhanov recalled the last words of the American General John Sedgwick, speaking of the Confederate sharpshooters during the Civil War Battle of Spotsylvania: "They couldn't hit an elephant at this distance—"
Plekhanov grinned.
Aim. Squeeze—

The Thai Prime Minister's collection of personal pornography, most of which showed recognizable images of him in sexual congress with women not his wife—and some of which showed him in such congress with her, too—somehow uploaded itself from his home computer and into the mainframe of the Southeast Asian News Service. Then, two of these pictures went into the hourly edition of SEANS NetNews in place of scheduled images.

Plekhanov raised his face from the Mauser. An oily wisp of smoke drifted from the muzzle, the smell of burned powder entwined with it. Below and still a hundred meters distant, the enemy soldiers milled around in panic, then dropped prone, looking for targets. Some of them returned fire, but none of the bullets came close to where he was.

Enough damage for one day. He shouldered the rifle by its sling and headed for the tower's steps.

Monday, September 27th, 8:11 a.m.
Quantico

Everywhere Jay Gridley drove on the net, sirens screamed. The virtual highways were full of fire engines, ambulances, police cruisers, a whole shitload of activity as people went to repair the damage and to haul away metaphorical bodies. Within a few minutes, there had been major wrecks in at least three or four supposedly secure systems internationally, maybe more.

Jay drove the Viper at speed and got to the spots as best he could, legally when they allowed it, illegally when they didn't; what he saw was not good. It was the same guy dropping sharp spikes on the roads. The pattern was there, the same blurred and unidentifiable footprints as before, leading away and quickly dead-ending. Maybe the local operators couldn't see it, but Jay was sure of it. He couldn't ID the terrorist, but he knew it was one guy.

He pulled the Viper to a halt on a long and relatively straight stretch of the new Thailand-Burma Highway. A reporter stood next to a smoldering limo with a bunch of cops, making notes on a little flatscreen. Jay knew the guy slightly; he was a distant cousin a couple of times removed.

"Hey, Chuan, how's it goin'?"

"Jay? What are you doing here? Something I ought to know about?"

"Nah, just cruising."

The other man looked around, seeming to shift his gaze as he blinked. "Ah, your highway metaplay. I see you're still driving that bomb on wheels. I disremember what it's called, some kind of lizard or snake?"

"Viper. It gets me there." He looked at the limo. "So who's the cookie in the shake-and-bake portable oven there?"

"A mess, isn't it? Behold, our beloved Prime Minister Sukho. This is what's left of his career, anyhow. Somebody got past the OS security wards on his personal system, and then became very clever with the nasty pictures hidden therein. Gave them to my bosses. My service somehow managed to accidentally send a pair of them out with the feed—or so the editors say. I know a few would have happily done it on purpose.

"So, on the sports screen, instead of the photo of the Indonesian football team winning the World Soccer Cup in Brazil, we got our beloved Prime Minister being attended to by an enthusiastic professional girl well known in Bangkok as Neena the Cleaner. And two jumps later, on the international screen, instead of Malaysian Prime Minister Mohamad doing a nice ribbon-cutting with a bunch of dignitaries for a new rec facility at Cyberjaya, we gave our viewers Sukho on a big round bed with two other very naked Bangkok working girls seeing what will go where. Bet those pix raised an eyebrow or two at the old water cooler during break." He smiled. "Hey, you ever been to Cyberjaya? In RW, I mean?"

His cousin was talking about a nine-mile-by-thirty-mile

zone in Malaysia called the Multimedia Super Corridor. Begun in '97, the MSC stretched south from Kuala Lumpur, and included at the south end a new international airport and a new federal capital, Putrajaya. "Once," Jay said. "I spent a few days there a year or so back, a real-time seminar on the new graphic platform. Unbelievable place."

"They say that's where CyberNation's programmers came from."

"Yeah? I hadn't heard that. I heard nobody knew where they came from."

"Rumors." He shrugged. "So much for the sordid tale of a political career gone south. I gotta get back and file my story."

"Not a lucky man, your Prime Minister."

"Oh, he's *real* lucky—thing is, it's all *bad*. This ain't America where the politicians can get away with such things, you know. It don't play with the family vote over here. Plus it is well known that Sukho's wife's brother was one of the Secret Bandit Warlords before he died. Word is, the wife's still got a couple SBW nephews out in the jungle who would just as soon cut you in half as look at you. The Prime Minister's wife is in big shame over this. Some pictures were of her, taken from a hidden camera, and I bet she didn't know about 'em." He waved at the burned-out limo. "I was Sukho, I'd tap my Swiss accounts and retire someplace in a galaxy far, far away. And I'd do it under another name, and with fifty grand's worth of false teeth, hair dye, and plastic surgery, while I was at it."

"I'd have thought his computer security would have been better than normal, given what he had to hide and him being a PM and all."

"Yeah, you'da thought so. My guess is, next guy selling a pick-proof OS around here is gonna make a fortune."

"Here and everywhere else."

"I scan that. See you, Jay."

"Later, Chuanny."

After his cousin was gone, Jay considered the situation. So Thailand was going to get a new Prime Minister. That might or might not have much effect on the world, but he had to figure that whoever was doing this rascal had picked his targets carefully. To what end, Jay didn't know, but his gut feeling was that it was a real bad end.

He better get back himself. The boss would want to know about the newest developments.

On the way, however, something else caught his attention.

Holy *shit*!

"Alex? I think you better see this."

Michaels looked up and saw Toni in his doorway.

"In the conference room," she added.

He followed her. The big-screen viewer was on. CNN.

A newscaster was doing a voice-over as images flashed across the large screen.

"Bombay, India—known by the locals as Mumbai—is the capital of Maharashtra and *the* major economic power of western India. Located on the shore of the Arabian Sea, it is a city steeped in culture. From the Victorian facades of the British Raj, to the tourist ghetto of Colaba, to the pulse-of-the-city Fort, eighteen million people call Mumbai home. Most of them are dirt-poor."

There was an aerial shot of the city. Stock footage.

Michaels glanced at Toni and raised an eyebrow. Why did she want him to see a documentary on India?

"This is the sidebar," she said. "Wait a second and they'll get back to the main story." She sounded grim.

"Modernization has brought at least some of Bombay into the twenty-first century," the newscast continued. "And modernization has reared its ugly head here today."

The image shifted. Two buses had crashed together in an

intersection. One of the red double-deckers lay on its side; the other was tilted, resting against the back of a fruit truck. Some kind of yellow-orange melons were scattered and shattered all over the street. Bodies were laid out along the narrow street's narrower sidewalks. Rescuers ran to the buses, pulling more dead or injured from the wrecks. A man covered with blood wandered in front of the camera, yelling something over and over. A small boy sat on the curb, staring at a woman lying next to him who was obviously dead.

"All over the city, computer-controlled traffic signals apparently turned green at the same instant."

Another image. A major intersection with at least a dozen cars melded together by impacts. The cars were on fire, and an explosion rocked the scene, knocking the cameraman down. Somebody cursed in English: "Shit, shit, *shit!*"

Here was a high-angle helicopter shot—scores of cars, trucks, motor scooters and bicycles compacted into jagged masses. The voice describing the event was excited, but not overly so: "There are at least fifty known dead in a massive traffic pile-up on Marine Drive, with hundreds more injured, and estimates of other traffic fatalities in the city go as high as six hundred—"

Again the image shifted, showing a train station. A passenger train lay crumpled like a child's toy next to a stretch of track. Freight cars were scattered among the coaches, some of them turned onto their sides.

"At Churchgate Railway station, malfunctioning train signals apparently caused the collision of a Central Railways passenger train northbound from Goa, with a freight train heading south. At least sixty are known dead at this point, with more than three hundred injuries. We have unconfirmed reports of electric commuter trains colliding in suburban areas with fatalities, but travel in the city is impossible and we are unable to get to those locations except by air.''

Another scene shift. A twin-engine airplane, engulfed in flames. Bodies—and *parts* of bodies lay scattered around it like broken dolls.

''Air traffic control malfunctions have reportedly caused at least four plane crashes. This one, a sightseeing flight filled with Japanese tourists, crashed into the yellow basalt monument known as the Gateway to India at the north-eastern end of the Colaba tourist district, killing all twenty-four on the aircraft and at least fifteen on the ground, with dozens more injured. We have unconfirmed reports that an Air India jet with two hundred and sixty-eight passengers on board has crashed into Back Bay just south of Beach.''

''My God,'' Michaels said. ''What the hell happened?''

''The computer programmer.'' Toni's voice was grim.

''Somebody did this on *purpose*?''

''That's what it looks like. Jay is on it, but he's too busy to talk about it right now.''

Michaels watched a rescue truck, lights flashing, frozen in gridlock. Jesus. They were dealing with a madman. A homicidal madman. Until he was caught, nobody was safe.

18

No real progress had been made on Steve Day's death.

Oh, the labs had cataloged all kinds of hair and fiber and bullet casings, but in the end, none of it meant anything without the people, clothes and guns the things belonged to—and they didn't have any of those.

Alex Michaels was more than a little bothered. He sat at his desk, staring into the wall. He knew there was nothing to be done about it; the best minds in the FBI were hard at work looking for the smallest clue, and standing there yelling "Hurry!" wouldn't help.

It wasn't as if he didn't have other things to worry about. As head of Net Force, he'd suddenly found out what it meant to have the buck stop on your desk. Aside from having to assign high-level cases to make sure they were handled right, there was all the political bullshit. He had to justify what his organization was doing, why they did it, and how much it cost, first to the Director, then, if they were feeling snoopy—and they always were—to Congress.

He had to appear in front of Senator Cobb's Security Committee on Thursday to answer questions about something Day had done a year ago that had mightily upset the Senator. Cobb, unaffectionately known as Tweety Bird in intelligence circles—"I taught I taw a puddy tat!"—was always imagining conspiracies, no matter where he happened to look. Cobb thought the military was scheming to violently take over the reins of government; that the Germans were secretly re-arming themselves to eat Eastern Europe; that the Girl Scouts were Commies. He had been the bane of Steve Day's life, and it looked as if he was going to be giving Michaels the same grief.

And if that wasn't enough, the political side of the job required a lot more of something else Michaels hated—socializing. Since he'd taken over, he'd gone to four black-tie political soirees, suffering through vulcanized chicken or salmon cooked to blackboard-eraser consistency. All of these events had featured after-dinner speakers who could put a room full of dexadrine addicts into a suspended animation that made Sleeping Beauty look like an insomniac.

No, this was definitely not a part of the job he enjoyed.

At least he didn't have to worry about building appropriations. That was the Director's job. And given all the new structures that Net Force had recently constructed, was in the process of constructing, or was planning on constructing, that would be a major chore in itself. J. Edgar Hoover would never recognize the FBI Compound, it had grown so large in just the last five or six years. It was a small town unto itself.

He stared at the pile of hardcopy and the blinking To Do list on his computer screen. He had a stack of stuff to read, things to sign, all the minutiae of any mid-level office manager that had to be taken care of, regardless of the more important things that had to wait. And it wasn't going to get done if he just sat there and stared at it.

It was going to be a long day. And when it was done, he would go home to his empty condo, eat a meal alone, watch the news, read his mail and slog through reports on his flatscreen. Probably fall asleep reading—that was what happened most of the time. Either that, or get called out to one of the Nights of the Boring Politicos.

He missed Megan. He missed his daughter. He missed having someone to share his day with, to care that he came home, that he lived or died. . . .

He shook his head. *Poor you. You're just so damned* sad, *aren't you?*

Michaels chuckled. The Island of Self-Pity was a waste of time; he never could stay there very long. He had a job to do, and he was part of the solution and not part of the problem, wasn't he? Hell with the rest of it.

He reached for the hardcopy.

Monday, September 27th, 9:44 a.m.
New York City

"Yes, I'll be there," Genaloni said. His voice was curt and he was irritated, but he tried, as always, to hold onto his temper. "Good-bye."

He put the phone's receiver down gently when what he wanted to do was slam it into its cradle hard enough to break both. Women. Jesus.

As wives went, Maria was probably as good as any. She stayed home, took care of the kids, supervised the maids and butler and cook and gardener, was active in charity affairs. He'd met her in college. She was smart, and she'd been drop-dead gorgeous when he'd married her. She worked out, and had spent some time under the knife, so she was still damned attractive for a woman her age—hell, any age; and if anything, she had gotten smarter, too. She looked good on his arm, was always dressed better than anybody else in any room they went to, but she was a pain in the ass sometimes. Because she was smart and good-looking, and because she came from a rich family, she was used to getting her way. She wanted his time, and she always wanted it most when he least had it to give. He was going to have to break a date with Brigette, his mistress, to go to some cure-a-disease ball his wife wanted him to go to, and he wasn't happy about it.

That Maria probably knew about Brigette and had done this on purpose also crossed his mind.

There was a tap on the doorjamb. He looked up and saw Johnny the Shark Benetti standing in the open doorway. Shark was a good name for Johnny. He was young, quick, and could cut you to tatters with a knife no longer than your finger. The Shark also had a degree in business from Cornell. As people in his organization retired or went away for legal reasons, Genaloni replaced them with equally tough but more educated ones. Sure, smart people had their drawbacks—too much ambition was usually part of the package, but you could deal with that. Bury a guy chin-deep in money, and mostly he would think long and hard before messing with the golden goose. Ignorant people caused more trouble in the long run. And in any event, you always watched your back—you never totally trusted *anybody*.

Johnny the Shark was holding Sampson's place until he returned.

If he returned. Whatever was going on with that, it stunk, and Genaloni didn't like it a damn bit.

"Yes?"

"Hey, Ray. Nobody we can touch has anything to say about Luigi. We put some serious money on the table, reached out to everybody who owes us favors, nothing. He's invisible.''

"Keep looking." At least one fed was going to be sorry about this business, although there was no way to tell when the guy was going to buy it. The Selkie took his time, and it didn't do any good to try and hurry him.

The intercom cheeped.

"What?"

"It's your wife again."

"Jesus. I'm not here, okay? And I forgot my cell phone, too."

"Yes, sir."

Genaloni shook his head. He looked at Johnny, who was smiling.

Smiling. Jesus. "You're married, what, a year and a half?"

"Two years, come December 14th," Johnny said.

"Still on your damned honeymoon. Come back and see me in fifteen years and let's talk about women."

That brought another grin.

Genaloni shook his head. Johnny was twenty-four, which meant he still knew everything. Genaloni was old enough so that he realized he knew less every year that went by. "You study any history?"

"It was my minor."

Genaloni did know that, but it never hurt to let the help think you were a little slower than you actually were. And he was something of a history reader himself, when he had the time. He said, "You know who Mary Katherine Horony was?"

Johnny searched his memory. Frowned. "Doesn't ring a bell."

"She was Hungarian, a hooker, went by the name of Big Nose Kate."

"Oh. Doc Holliday's girlfriend?"

"Good to see that degree means something. Kate was a whore, a drunk, a brawler. She screwed and drank and fought her way across the Old West, ran with Holliday, the Earps, some other real dangerous dudes."

Johnny nodded. "Uh-huh."

"She could have quit once she hooked up with Doc, but she couldn't settle down. She kept going back to the life, even while she and Holliday were together. And even when she was at home, she wasn't your shy and demure type. She broke him out of jail once after he gutted a man with a Bowie knife, and she clubbed a guard half to death to do it. She had a whorehouse in Tombstone in the 1880's, first one in town. Did it in a big tent, ran a dozen girls and sold a lot of cheap whiskey. People used to fight and get shot up there all the time. Plus she and Doc also used to beat the shit out of each other—and he didn't always wind up on top.

"After Holliday croaked from TB, old Kate kept whoring around for years. Got married, left her husband, moved around, kept kicking her heels up until she wound up in a nursing home. Died in 1940. She was ninety years old."

"Fascinating," Johnny said. He raised an eyebrow.

"So, here was this woman, a whore—which in those days was a damned dangerous job—with these hardcases all around her who'd just as soon shoot you as look at you. A woman who used to punch out Doc Holliday, one of the stone-coldest killers ever, and she was living in neighborhoods where you could get raped and murdered and nobody would blink."

"And your point . . . ?"

"Kate outlived them all—the job, Holliday, the killers, the booze, the bad towns, everything." Genaloni smiled. "She died of old age." He paused, then said, "You know what the cavalry men used to say out in Dakota when they were trying to wipe out the Sioux? 'If you're captured by the Indians, don't let them give you to the women.'

"A woman can cut off your nuts, cook 'em with onions and make you eat them—and smile the whole time she's doing it. Remember that. No matter what your bride says, no matter how good she is in bed, you keep your *business* to yourself. The prisons are full of guys who blabbed shit to their women and then pissed them off. Women are good for a lot of things, but you don't trust one with your life. Never."

"I'll remember that."

"Good. Now go find out why the feds are hiding Luigi."

After the kid had gone, Genaloni smiled to himself. That wasn't a bad little lecture. He'd have made an okay professor, he always figured.

19

In her guise as Phyllis Markham, the Selkie gimped her
way toward the target's house, the little poodle doing his
imitation of a watering can on every other bush or tree
along the way.

The guards in the surveillance cars were gone. She had
been disappointed to see them leave. There were times
when she'd been set upon a mobster or gunrunner or po-
litico with a dozen guards crawling all around, and that had
made the job more difficult. But one guy, who didn't have
a clue he was a target, no protection except maybe a house
alarm? It took some of the fun out of it.

At her level, she mostly made her own challenges.

She'd been on this more than a week, and she was ready.
She knew the target's habits. When he ordered Chinese
food delivered, she knew he liked the hot and spicy chicken
with noodles. When he went for his morning run, she could
have run half a block in front of him and stayed with him
all the way. She knew when he went to a fund-raiser, where

he tried to sit if he wasn't assigned a table, and what time he would make his excuses and leave. She knew about his ex-wife and kid in Idaho, the car he played with in his garage, and that his assistant had the hots for him, to judge from how she looked at him. And that he didn't have a clue about that. She knew how tall he was, how much he weighed, where he got his hair cut and that he hadn't really wanted his current job. She knew much about the target— just not why he had been chosen.

Scout heard something in one of the bushes to the left. He yapped at it. Probably a cat. She let him bark a couple of times, then told him to hush. He did, but he trembled to go after the thing in the bushes. The dog didn't know he was a toy; he thought he was the son of a wolf and he wanted that prey. She smiled.

The worst dog bite she'd ever gotten hadn't been from a big beast like a shepherd, but from a dachshund who must have thought *he* was White Fang, too. Maybe the little ones had something to prove.

The target seemed like a decent enough guy. He was fairly attractive, had a nice smile and did a good job. As bureaucrats went, he was better than most. He loved his little girl out there in flyover country, and hadn't been active much sexually since his divorce, so he was probably still carrying a torch for his ex. He was a more useful member of society than most, an ethical, moral, reliable man.

That she was going to kill him didn't bother her at all.

Some professionals didn't let themselves know anything about their targets, didn't get involved any more than necessary to make the deletion. They stayed cool, didn't interact, didn't let themselves see the targets as people. She'd always thought that was chickenshit. If you're going to take somebody out deliberately, you ought to get to know him. It seemed only fair, and so much better than being killed by a stranger. Her way, at least she had some respect for people who deserved respect. There was a kind of honoring of the target involved.

She knew more than enough now. He wasn't a bad guy, but he wasn't that interesting, and there wouldn't be any surprises.

"Move along, boy. Go."

Reluctantly, the dog proceeded, looking back for the thing in the bushes as he walked, just in case it tried to break from cover and run for it.

Little Scout there, hearing the call of the wild, that was funny.

When would she hit the target? When you could choose any time, when you had all your bets covered, then you did it when it *felt* right. Not before. Not if you wanted it to be perfect. This guy's death would unleash an army of feds on her trail. It needed to be perfect.

She was approaching the target's condo. She glanced at her watch, an analog, battery-powered Lady Bulova, one Phyllis Markham would wear, since it had supposedly belonged to her dearly departed mother. She slowed a hair, letting the dog sniff a little longer at some other male's territory marking.

Tomorrow was trash pickup day—the collection mini-trucks came around twice a week here—and the houses and condos on this street did not have an alleyway in back.

The gate to the target's condo opened and the target came out, hauling a single compacted recyclable paper bag. Right on schedule. On the evenings before trash pickup, he came home, changed clothes and carried out the garbage first thing.

She arrived in front of the target's condo just as he dropped the sack.

He smiled at her. "Hi," he said.

"Good evening, young man," the Selkie said in her Markham voice. "A nice night for a walk."

"Yes, ma'am." He squatted, offered the back of his hand to the dog, who sniffed and then wagged his tail. The target scratched the dog behind the ears. "Good pup."

The Selkie smiled. She could drop him right here with one swing of the cane—he'd never know what hit him. Crack open his skull as he squatted there petting the dog, bend down, cut his carotids with the nail scissors in her purse. He'd bleed out in a couple of minutes.

Or she could ask if he'd mind giving her a glass of water, and of course he would invite her into his condo. He was too nice a guy to cause an old lady to finish her walk thirsty. She could do him inside without anybody ever being the wiser. It was too easy.

She smiled at the target. Now? Should she take him inside?

The moment stretched. She held the man's life in her hands. This was power. This was control.

No. Not tonight. It didn't feel quite right. Maybe tomorrow.

"Come along, Scout. The nice man doesn't want to fool with you."

The target stood, and the woman who would soon kill him limped away.

"Take care, ma'am," he said.

"Thank you, young man. I surely will. You, too."

Wednesday, September 29th, 3:14 a.m.
Somewhere over the North Atlantic

The drone of the 747's big engines was a steady, hypnotic thrum, and most of the passengers slumped in the dark, sleeping. John Howard's reading light was on, but the report on his flatscreen hadn't been scrolled for so long that the screensaver had kicked in and blanked the screen.

"You need some warm milk and melatonin, Colonel?" Fernandez said.

Howard glanced up at Sarge, on his way back from the head. "Just working on a report, Sergeant."

"Yes, sir, I can see that. A detailed study on the zen of the blank screen?"

Howard grinned, waved Fernandez to the seat across the aisle.

"It wasn't much of an operation, was it, Julio?"

"Begging the colonel's pardon, but what the hell is he talking about? We located a terrorist cell, took down a score of armed, bomb-throwing radicals while they were shooting at us, and did it without an injury to ours. That's batting a thousand where I come from."

"You know what I mean."

Fernandez looked around. Nobody was close to them, and the nearest passengers were asleep. He dropped the NCO-to-officer rap. "Look, John, if you mean it wasn't the beach at Iwo Jima, yeah, you're right. But the assignment was find the bad guys and stop them. We did it, protected our embassy, didn't cause a stink with the locals, and we're hauling all our boys back to base without having to peel a Band-Aid. That's as good as it gets."

Howard nodded. Fernandez was right, of course. Go, do the job, come home, all asses-and-elbows. He had carried out his mission by the numbers. That was what a soldier was supposed to do. They were thrilled with him back at Net Force. A couple of his old military buddies in the know had already sent him coded e-mail congratulating him. It was a win, all the way around.

So why didn't he feel better about it?

Because it had been too easy. Yeah, Rule 6P had worked—proper planning prevents piss-poor performance— but when it got right down to it, he'd never had any doubt they'd win. His troops were the best of the best, ex-SEALs, Green Berets, Rangers. Drop them in a jungle behind the lines with nothing but pen knives, and they'd build a castle out of enemy bones. The terrorists had been a bunch of out-of-shape gutter-scum with big ideas and almost no strategic or tactical experience. How could they have possibly lost to rabble like that?

He said as much to Fernandez.

Fernandez laughed.

"What?"

"Oh, I was just imagining what the commander of the British armies must have said to his field officers toward the end of the Revolutionary War: 'What? A bunch of out-of-shape gutter-scum with big ideas and almost no strategic or tactical experience just kicked the shit out of His Majesty's finest? How could we have possibly lost to rabble like that?'"

Howard chuckled. Fernandez had a way of putting a spin on things you wouldn't expect from a noncom who'd earned his rockers the hard way. And the posh British accent just added to it. And he had a point. The terrorists could have been more adept. The blood on the warehouse floor could have been that of *his* troops. There was always that possibility.

"Thing is, John, the glory might be a bit thin on this one, but a win is a win. That's why we went, ain't it?"

"Yeah. You're right."

"Damn, and me without a tape recorder? Can I wake up some witnesses for the colonel to repeat that, sir? The me-being-right part?"

"To what are you are referring, Sergeant? I don't recall saying any such thing."

"That's what I thought, sir." He grinned. "Guess I'll see if I can catch a few winks."

"Good night, Julio. Thanks."

"Sir. And if it is any consolation, I got a feeling this won't be the last episode in this particular war. Next time might be different."

Howard watched his best man amble toward a row of empty seats. Yes. There was always that. A small battle did not a war make.

Wednesday, September 29th, 10:54 p.m.
Portland, Oregon

Ruzhyó watched the front door of McCormick's Restaurant. The place was away from the main section of town, toward one of the bedroom communities to the west. It specialized in fish. The food was supposedly excellent, and it looked to be so from his brief visit to reconnoiter earlier. It was the best restaurant near the company that produced one of the fastest computer chips for home use, a company just up the road in Beaverton, a town named after the dam-building aquatic mammal.

Ruzhyó sat in the rental car across the street, parked in the shadows of a sign in front of a Korean travel agency. Sixty-two meters away from the door, according to the Ranging optical tape, an easy distance. The car was a full-sized one with a large engine, though he did not think he would need the power for his escape. With both eyes open, he looked through the large aperture of the Bushnell HOLOsight. What he saw was an unmagnified image of the door with a glowing red crosshair superimposed upon it. The scope was a state-of-the-art gunsight; unlike a laser, it emitted no light to the front, and thus did not reveal the user. The scope had cost more than the weapon upon which it rode, a 30-06 bolt-action Winchester deer rifle, itself an excellent piece of equipment. He had bought the sight at a gun store in San Diego; the rifle he'd purchased in Sacramento, second-hand, from an advertisement in a newspaper. He had assembled the rifle and scope, and sighted the weapon in at a rock quarry along an old logging road west of Forest Grove, Oregon.

With the sighted-in rifle, Ruzhyó could shoot consistently into a circle made with his thumb and forefinger out to a hundred meters. More than sufficient.

He had considered using a suppressor on the rifle, but the projectile would break the sound barrier and make a loud crack after it left the barrel anyway, so there was really no point in trying to damp the noise. Besides, in these conditions, the shot would echo, seeming to come from everywhere. And even if they knew exactly where he was, it would mean little. Executives of the local computer company did not go forth armed, nor with bodyguards. There had never been any need. Nor would there likely be a need after this night, though it was unlikely they would believe it to be so.

By the time police arrived, Ruzhyó would be miles away. He had three escape routes mapped out in his mind, and all included quick stops where he would not be seen, where he could lose the rifle. He wore waterproof thinskin synsilk gloves—there would be no prints or fluids left on the scope, rifle or bullets inside the weapon.

He glanced at his watch. Just after eleven, local time. The party had been in the restaurant nearly two hours. Their vehicles were parked in the front. The diners would be in sight for plenty of time.

He lowered the weapon.

Eight minutes later, the door to the restaurant opened.

Ruzhyó put the silicone earplugs into his ears. The sound of a high-powered rifle shot inside an automobile could easily destroy unprotected eardrums.

Six men emerged, talking, laughing, taking their time.

Ruzhyó raised the rifle. He took a deep breath, let half of it out, held the rest. He clicked the safety off, lined the glowing crosshairs up on the second man in the group, put the sight picture on the man's forehead, right between the eyes. . . .

He squeezed off the shot.

With a rifle, you don't hear the one that kills you.

The man was dead before the sound of the bullet reached him.

Ruzhyó put the rifle down on the floor of the car and started the engine. He pulled out of the travel agency's parking lot and drove away. Traffic was light this time of the evening. He was half a mile away, at the entrance to the elevated freeway, when the first police car flew past, lights flashing, siren wailing, going toward the restaurant.

He did not look back. There was no need. Nobody was following him.

20

"You have another call, Dr. Plekhanov," Sasha shouted from the outer office. The intercom still operated only sporadically, but that hardly mattered now. "Mr. Sikes, from Bombay Municipal Systems."

Plekhanov smiled. The phone had certainly been busy the last couple of days. Exactly as he'd expected it would be.

The plantings were beginning to bear fruit. After the computer foul-ups had killed hundreds of people in Bombay, those in charge would have called Bertrand, the second-rate programmer who had installed their security system. And while even Bertrand was skilled enough to see what had been done, he would be unable to offer a guarantee that he could stop it from being done again. So they had called Plekhanov—whom they should have called originally—and why, yes, he could most assuredly guarantee them that no such security breach would happen if *he* installed a new protective system. Of course he could make that assurance: There were only a handful of programmers expert enough to slip his wards, only one who would bother, and that one's interests—*his* interests—would best be served if the system stayed unbreached.

Given how people worried over such incidences, it would take only one or two more assaults on the stoplights and buses of big cities before most—if not all of them—came running to Plekhanov for his help. So by the time the movers and shakers of the municipal transportation systems for all of Asia's major cities met for their annual get-together later this year in Guangzhou, China, most of them would be in Plekhanov's camp. He would, after all, do excellent work for them, at better than reasonable prices. They would all owe him. They would all want to keep him happy, so as to avoid suffering fates similar to those unlucky enough to be the victims of what had to be terrorists. Who would bother to rascal a transportation computer save a terrorist? Where was the profit?

"Hello?"

"Vladimir? Bill Sikes, Bombay Transport."

"Ah, Bill, how are you?"

"Not so good. You heard about our problem?"

"Yes, I am afraid so. A terrible thing. I am so sorry."

"Yes, well, that milk is spilt, but we don't want to lose any more. Can you help us out?"

"But of course, Bill. Of course I'll help."

"Another call!" Sasha yelled from her desk. "From Korea!"

Plekhanov leaned back in his chair. His smile was truly a happy one.

Thursday, September 30th, 8:15 a.m.
Washington, D.C.

Tyrone Howard met his friend Jimmy Joe in the strip club called Big Boobs. It was off-limits to boys their age, and neither of them were within years of being old enough to be there, but they wore adult personas and had enough skill to pass a casual scan. Slipping into an R-rated VR room in a public newsforum was something anybody with half a brain could do. All you could see was naked women here; the XXX-rooms were harder to sneak into, and besides, Tyrone didn't want to risk that. His parents would flay him if they found out, and since his dad worked with a player like Jay Gee, he could find out if he wanted.

"So, Jimmy Joe, you scan anything?"

"No mucho, spiderboy. Lotta strand-poppin' on the FEN, though."

Tyrone nodded. Far East Net had been DFB—data flowin' bad—the last few days. He'd seen that himself. The mad programmer was kicking serious ass there.

On the stage in front of a flashing light show and a driving bass beat, a tall blue-eyed brunette showed the audience that her hair color was natural. *Boom, bop-a boom!* He stared. She smiled at him, not knowing that his appearance was a fake. Of course, *her* appearance could be fake, too. She might be a sixty-year-old fat man.

If you were hunting for truth, VR wasn't the best place to look for it.

"I'm gonna hit the OHTs and see if there's any feedback," Jimmy Joe said. "You just know some wirehead with a strainer program and no life is catching minnows. Maybe one of them can lead us to the big fish."

"Scan and download that," Tyrone said. The brunette stripper had left the stage. A new one came out. Well, well, look at that: Belladonna Wright herself. This was Jimmy

Joe's doing, the override and image-craft such that the new woman wore Bella's face and body. No way would Tyrone risk that, even in VR. If Bonebreaker found out, that would be . . . bad.

"I'm gonna ride," Tyrone said.

Jimmy Joe grinned real big. He made the sound of a chicken clucking: "Buck-buck-buck-buuucckk!"

"You right about that. I'm not ready to spend six weeks regenerating bone tissue, monkey-boy. Especially for an overlay that even isn't real."

"Your loss," Jimmy Joe said. "Who is gonna know?"

"Only takes two words in Bonebreaker's ear and you're pretzel-boy."

Jimmy Joe shrugged. "Better to burn it than bank it." He turned to watch the ersatz Bella shuck her costume.

"Me, I'm ridin'," Tyrone said. But he sneaked a quick look as he headed for the door.

Maybe he'd take a pass at CyberNation, see what was up there.

Thursday, September 30th, 8:20 a.m.
Quantico

Parked in the Viper across the street, Jay Gridley watched Tyrone Howard leave the strip joint. The boy didn't see him. He smiled. The colonel had asked him to check up on his son from time to time, and Gridley didn't mind doing so, but he wouldn't mention this. Teenage boys were curious, and a VR stripper was a lot less dangerous than some of the stuff a kid could get himself involved with, on- or off-line. If a teenage boy *wasn't* interested in looking at a naked woman, that would be the time for his father to get worried.

No harm, no foul.

Tyrone mounted his Harley and roared away.

Gridley watched him leave before he started the Viper's motor. He had plenty of other stuff to worry about.

Thursday, September 30th, 11:55 a.m.
Quantico

Toni Fiorella stretched in the gym, warming up her knees. She looked up and saw Rusty enter. He waved at her. He was already dressed to work out.

He was a pretty good student. Very flexible, if a bit too much addicted to speed and power, neither of which were necessary in *bukti negara*. If he got to the *serak*, he could use that, but that was years away, if he stuck to it. So far, at least, he had shown up for every practice, and his moves indicated he'd been practicing on his own. He was still a little leery of working close, he kept wanting to distance himself too much for the proper working of the techniques, but that would level out with time.

"Hey, Guru."

"Rusty. Let's get started."

He nodded. He stood with his feet apart, his hands by his side, palms forward, fingers pointed at the ground.

Unlike some of the traditional Japanese styles, there were only a handful of Indonesian terms you had to know to practice her version of *silat*; one was the word for "on guard." *"Jagah,"* she said.

She mirrored Rusty's pose. Her guru was right. Teaching helped sharpen your own skills. You had to think about things, get them right in your own head, before you passed them along. The ceremonial bow, something she had been doing for years, was a good example. For her, it was automatic, one long and smooth piece, but for a beginner, it was a series of small moves, and each move had a meaning:

I present myself before the Creator in the beginning—

The left foot came in, next to and slightly in front of the right foot, knees bent, hands moved to the left side, by the hip, palms down, left over right.

I present myself to the best of my ability in the knowledge of the Art—

The hands came up and out together as in supplication, palms up, almost as if holding a book. The right hand folded into a fist, the left hand wrapped around the right, both came back toward the chest.

I ask to receive from the Creator all those things which I do not see—

Another book-reading move, open hands coming back to cover the eyes.

—to engrave upon my heart—

The hands pressed together in *namaste,* the classic praying gesture, and touched the chest over the heart.

—until the end.

And the final move, a repeat of the second, the palm-down block by the left hip.

"Do your *djuru,* please," she said.

Rusty nodded, and began *Djuru One.*

It was the simplest of the dances, but from it, everything more complex arose. A metaphor for life, she had come to realize.

Thursday, September 30th, 12:30 p.m.
Quantico

The Selkie bought a Coke, sweet-and-sour chicken, and sticky rice from the Chinese place the target sometimes rode his trike to for lunch. It was a warm day, a little breeze keeping the humidity bearable, and she sat at one of the small white wrought-iron tables just outside the restaurant. She wore a baggy gray T-shirt and very loose black cotton pants, a baseball cap and dark sunglasses. The wig she affected was brunette, and even with most of it stuffed under the cap, was enough to add to her changed appearance so that she didn't look much like anybody the target had ever seen.

There he came on the raked three-wheeler, a sheen of sweat on his face and neck reflecting the hazy sunshine.

She opened the cardboard containers and dumped the chicken and rice together onto a paper plate. She stirred the combination with the split-apart-throw-away chopsticks, allowed the sauce to soak into the rice. There were a dozen other diners outside enjoying their lunches and the day, and she did not make eye contact with any of them, or the target.

The target parked the trike, pulled his gloves and helmet off and hung them on the handlebar, then walked into the restaurant. His legs were tight, pumped from the ride. The spandex shorts hid little an interested viewer might want to look at. And it was interesting. She was not a nun, though she put sex aside when she was working. Mora Sullivan could roll and break beds if she felt like it; the Selkie could not afford the risk.

It had not always been that way. Once, early in her career, she had picked up a target in a bar. He'd been a good-looking man, and she'd gone with him to his hotel and slept with him. It had been a very athletic encounter.

When he fell into a satisfied and exhausted sleep, she had taken a silenced .22 pistol from her purse and shot him twice in the back of the head.

He'd never known what hit him, and at the time, she'd felt pleased with herself. She had made his last moments very happy ones. If you had to die, there were worse ways to do so than making love to a passionate woman, falling asleep, and never waking up.

It had been foolish, what she had done. She had left hair and fluids at the murder scene, had been seen by hotel staff, even though she had been in disguise. Nothing had come of it—it was years past, the file long since buried—but it had been stupid. Another time, another place, and the target here might be fun to romp around with, but she was not willing to risk capture to be sentimental.

She ate the chicken. She'd had better. Had worse, too.

Was today the day? She glanced at the target where he stood in line to order.

The Selkie smiled.

21

Kiev had several decent restaurants, but the breakfast was catered in a private suite at the new Hilton hotel, not far from the banks of the beautiful Dnieper, in a site formerly occupied by a theater and row of shops. Unlike a public restaurant, such a suite could be—and had been—swept for electronic listening devices. The sixth-floor windows could be—and were—rigged with simple vibrators that would defeat a hidden laser reader aimed at them from half a block away. The food servers had been dismissed, the doors locked, the secrets thus kept among the players. Not that anybody would likely be spying upon them. Nobody outside this room had a real clue as to what was going on inside it. But one erred on the side of caution, always.

Plekhanov wore his bland smile, revealing nothing about his thoughts. This meeting was merely one of many. By now, the players were known quantities, their fortunes dependent upon him. Today, it was the politicians; tomorrow, it would be the military. In a few days, he would be in another hotel room, in another country, having similar talks with politicians and generals. Covering all his bets.

They finished the scrambled eggs and salmon hash, drank their juice and coffee. Plekhanov enjoyed the sharp and bitter smell of the brew, so dark it looked like espresso. He wouldn't have expected coffee this good in such a place.

"You all have your new transfer numbers?" Plekhanov asked.

There were three other people in the room, two men and a woman, all duly elected members of the Verkhovna Rada, the local parliament.

"Yes," they said simultaneously.

Plekhanov nodded. The electronic money he had given these three access to was inconsequential, a half million or so each in the local currency. Of course, it was a lot to a potato farmer, a part-time university teacher and an ex-Army officer. This particular money was oil for squeaky wheels, to smooth and lubricate rough spots, for bribes, gifts, political contributions, whatever it took. There would be much more later, and power to go with it. These three were to be the new President and his two most influential ministers, come the next election. He had yet to decide who would get which job, but it would be happening soon, so best he start making his choices.

Tomorrow, he would talk to his two tame Ukrainian generals, also about to be promoted in rank and prestige. There were many paths up the mountain, but the two that would give a man the most power when he got to the summit were to be found in the ammunition sacks of the army and the briefcases of the lawmakers. When you had those, you were practically invincible. With but one other, you were untouchable.

Too bad the churches were not as powerful here as once they'd been. . . .

"Comrade Plekhanov?" the woman said.

"Yes?" This was Ludmilla Khomyakov, whose parents were originally from Moscow, and once very active in Communist Party circles. He had not been called "comrade" in a long time—not in the way she meant the word.

"There has been some . . . difficulty from the trade union movement. Igor Bulavin threatens to have his members call a strike if the new reforms are passed."

"Bulavin is a Cossack and a fool." That was from Razin, the ex-Army officer. He'd retired as a major before going into politics.

"You are *also* a Cossack, Yemelyan." Khomyakov said.

"*That* is how I know," Razin said. "Do not worry about Bulavin. He can have a fatal accident in that ancient car of which he is so proud. It can be easily arranged."

Plekhanov looked at the woman. "Is it your feeling that this Bulavin is enough of a threat to warrant such an . . . accident, Ludmilla?"

She shook her head. She was forty, but still a handsome woman. "He is a threat, but perhaps killing him is not altogether necessary."

"Death is final," Razin said.

"*Da,* it is, but Bulavin is a devil we know. Alive and tethered to a pole in our tent, he could still be useful."

"And how do you propose to chain him there? He is too stupid to be afraid of threats, he will not accept a bribe and he has no skeletons in his closet to rattle at him. I say we squash him."

The third man, Demitrius Skotinos, an ethnic Greek who still ran a small potato farm up-country, said nothing.

"Perhaps we could put a new skeleton into his closet?" Khomyakov said.

Razin snorted.

Plekhanov raised an eyebrow at her.

"Bulavin is fond of both liquor and women," Khomyakov said. "He has been discreet, careful to keep his activities in these areas confined to those which would not irritate his union members if they found out. Not too much drinking in public, the occasional fling with a secretary. Men are men, and not bothered by such things. Perhaps we could supply him a woman willing to . . . doctor his liquor and engage in activities his members—and his wife— would find less than . . . tasteful? There are many possibilities along these lines. And our woman would, of course, have an excellent holographic camera.''

Razin said, ''Pah! You would put him in bed with a boy? A sheep? This is a woman's answer to everything! If it moves, screw it!''

''Better, perhaps, than a man's answer—if it moves, kill it,'' she said. She smiled.

Plekhanov liked both her response and her solution. Brutes could be found anywhere; subtlety was more of a prize. A live enemy in your pocket was sometimes better than a dead one in the ground. Sometimes.

Well, at least he knew who the new President of Ukraine was going to be.

Thursday, September 30th, 11 p.m.
Washington, D.C.

''I bet you've never seen anybody get killed, have you, Scout?''

The little dog wagged his tail, momentarily diverted from his sniffing and peeing. When it didn't seem as if the comment would lead to a command, he resumed his work.

In her old-woman disguise, the Selkie moved toward the target's condo. She had decided to do it tonight. The target was still awake, a bit late for him, but his reading light was on, and it was going to be simple, clean, in and out. By the time anybody knew he was dead, she would be home and Phyllis Markham would have vanished forever.

The Selkie bent down to pet the dog. As she did so, she unsnapped his leash, but said, "Scout, heel."

She adjusted her thin white cotton gloves, took a grip on the cane and came slowly and painfully to her feet. When she continued on her gimpy way, the dog stayed with her. Anybody from more than a few feet away would likely think the toy poodle was still on the lead, especially if they'd seen them together before. People saw what you gave them to see.

When she got to the target's condo, she forced herself to take several deep breaths. No matter how many times she did a job, the adrenaline rush always came. Her heart raced, her breathing speeded up, she felt tight, itchy, anxious to move. It was something she could use, the rush, and part of the allure. If it ever got to the point where she didn't feel the touch of stage fright, the roiling butterflies in her belly, she'd quit, no matter how much money she was shy of her goal. If she got that blasé, it would be too dangerous.

The darkness was alive with fall smells: foliage, grass, the perfume of a softener-sheet in somebody's clothes dryer's exhaust. The air was sensually cool on her skin where she was not covered with makeup. The stars glittered through the city glow, hard gems in a mostly clear sky. A moth fluttered by, and his flight left ghostly trails in the night air. Sensations always turned psychedelically sharp when the life-and-death game came to its final moves. This was another part of the attraction.

One was never so alive as when dancing with Death.

She looked around, and saw she was alone. She urged Scout into the bushes to the left of the front door, where he couldn't be seen. "Scout, down, stay," she said.

Obediently, the little dog sat, then stretched out. She'd tested him, and he'd held that position for at least an hour.

She wouldn't need but five minutes at the outside.

The Selkie moved to the door and rang the bell.

In bed, Alex Michaels dozed, the technical report balanced on his knees. The sound of his front doorbell jarred him awake. He looked at the bedside time display. Who'd be here this hour of the night?

He got up, slipped a robe on over his naked self and belted it shut.

The doorbell rang again.

He frowned, still half asleep. It was probably somebody from work.

Yeah? How come they didn't call? They have your numbers.

He opened the drawer in his bedside table, took his issue taser from the drawer and dropped it into the robe's pocket. Not that he was really worried, but there had been some robberies in D.C. where a couple of strong-arm types had knocked on doors and then forced their way inside. Better prepared than not.

When he looked through the peephole, he saw the old lady who had the poodle. He relaxed as he opened the door.

She looked upset. "I'm so sorry to bother you," she said, "but Scout got off his leash." She waved the little plastic roll-up case with the dangling clip. "I think he wiggled through your gate into the back. If you could open it for me? I didn't want to be yelling for him in the middle of the night, waking people up and all."

"Sure," Michaels said. "Why don't you just come on through the house to the back."

"Oh, I don't want to trouble you. I can go around."

"No problem." He smiled, had her come inside, then closed the door. "Follow me." He led her through the living room.

Behind him, the old lady said, "I don't know what got

into him. He never does this. I think he heard something in the bushes.''

"My neighbors all have cats," he said. "Though most of them are bigger than your dog. He might get in trouble if he catches one.''

They were in the small kitchen, almost to the sliding glass door, when Michaels heard the little dog bark. It sounded like he was out front. Probably had lost the cat and gone back looking for his momma.

"Oh, there he is," he said. He turned—

—and saw the old lady with her cane held over one shoulder like a baseball bat.

The expression on her face was cold but determined.

She swung the stick at him as if she were trying to belt one out of the park—

Shit!

Michaels tried to do two things at once. He dug for the taser in his robe's pocket and jumped backward. He didn't do either of them well. He hit the edge of the breakfast table, tangled his robe around one of the chairs and pulled it over. The chair fell between him and the old lady—and that was what saved his ass.

The cane whistled as she whipped it back and forth, but as she stepped toward him, she hit the toppled chair with her shins and stopped.

"Fuck!" she said. The word was not only unladylike, it was in a deeper, smoother, younger voice.

Still stumbling backward, Michaels banged into the sliding door. The crown of his head thumped against it hard—it made an almost metallic gonging sound, but the glass held—

The old lady kicked the fallen chair out of her way, started to take another step, the cane pulled back to brain him, but he had the taser out now and he pointed it at her and pressed the firing stud—

No, not the firing stud, he'd accidentally hit the laser sight instead! Damn!

A tiny red dot appeared—but on the *wall* next to the old lady. He moved the taser, put the gyrating dot on the old lady's chest—

She snarled and threw the cane—

It hit Michaels low, below his outstretched arm, across the belly. He didn't feel any pain, but it was hard enough to jolt his aim. The laser dot jerked to the side, off the old lady—

She spun and ran. By the time he recovered, she was mostly out of his line of sight, almost to the front door. Jesus, she was fast! Taser needles were only good for five or six yards, even if he could hit her this far away—

He started after her. He didn't know who the hell she was or what she was doing here, but this was *his* goddamn house and now his surprise gave way to rage—

Just who the hell did this woman think she *was*? How *dare* she?

He heard her yell something he couldn't make out, but by the time he got to the front door, she was twenty yards away and going strong. In the back of his mind, the sight of a seventy-year-old lady sprinting like an Olympic athlete was pretty amazing, even though he knew she was a younger woman in disguise.

He started after her, but she'd had too good a start. And she was fast. No way he was going to catch her wearing a robe and slippers.

The danger was over. He'd chased her off. Now what he needed to do was call the cops. Let them hunt for her.

Michaels started to step back into the house, but stopped when he heard something in the bushes. He leveled the taser, and swept the laser's red dot back and forth, seeking a target. "Who's there? Don't move, I'll shoot!"

He was ready to blast *somebody,* anybody who got in his face.

Nothing.

He stepped cautiously toward the bushes.

On the ground in a down position, front legs stretched out and looking up at him, was the little old lady's toy poodle. It yapped once. Wagged its tail.

Michaels shook his head. Jesus H. Christ!

He bent down. "C'mere, boy. Here, Scout."

The dog came up and hurried over, head lowered and tail going like crazy. Michaels picked the little dog up. It licked his hand.

Michaels frowned, realized he was breathing way too fast. He blew out a big sigh and tried to calm himself.

What in hell was going on here?

22

Goddammit!

In her clean-car, driving into the Maryland night, the Selkie's smoldering rage flared yet again. She pounded the steering wheel with the heel of her right hand. "Shit, shit, *shit*!"

She knew it was a waste of her energy, that it did no good at all. Done was done, and there was nobody to blame but herself. It was her fault. She'd put the damned dog into a down-stay, but she hadn't told him "quiet." One of the goddamned cats must have spooked the dog, and naturally, he'd barked at it because *she hadn't told him not to*!

Stupid. An amateur's mistake, so simple it never occurred to her. But even though it was a waste of her energy, it still pissed her off. She beat on the steering wheel again.

It was incredible, but that was how it always went when luck went bad. The smallest thing that could go wrong to screw up things always went wrong at *exactly* the wrong instant. That bark, just as she was set to strike, had ruined the deletion. A second earlier, and she'd have been a smiling old lady hobbling along behind the target. A second later, and the target would have been out cold on the floor, waiting for the final stroke—game, tip over your king.

If the dog hadn't barked. If the target hadn't had a taser in his pocket. If that chair hadn't gotten in her way—

If, if, *if*.

Damn!

So now they had the dog, her cane, and unless they were all a whole lot stupider than was likely, they knew that Alexander Michaels was targeted by an assassin. They'd find the place she'd rented in the neighborhood quick enough, though there was nothing in it to tie her real identity to it. They'd know she'd been stalking him. She didn't think there was much they could use from what they had, but one thing for sure:

Getting to the target was going to be a whole lot harder now.

That brought a smile, despite her anger. Oh, yes, she was still going to delete the target, no question of that. The obstacles would be bigger, the risks riskier, but she didn't take a contract and not deliver. Never.

Well. She'd wanted a challenge. She sure as hell had one now.

Friday, October 1st, 12:34 a.m.
Washington, D.C.

Alex was trying to pretend it was no big deal, but Toni knew better. He was rattled. He looked calm as he stood there, dressed in tan slacks and a T-shirt, with no shoes, holding the toy poodle that had been part of the would-be assassin's cover. He petted the dog absently as the cops metaphorically tipped their hats and left. They'd kept the local cops from lighting up the place with their flashers, but even so, there was a lot of activity around Alex's condo for this time of night. Neighbors peeped through windows or stood on door stoops, trying to puzzle out what was going on.

Toni was relieved that Alex was all right, that the assassination attempt had failed. And she was also gratified that he had called her first, before he'd called anybody else. That meant something.

Toni had lost no time in co-opting this investigation. It belonged to Net Force, part of the Steve Day case. The local cops had been called in only to provide a net to catch the woman, and it was probably too late for that. The woman wasn't going to be hiding under a bush a block away or anything. If it *was* a woman. Maybe it was a small man under the disguise?

"Alex?"

"Hmm?"

"We'll need the dog."

He looked down at the poodle, then back at her. "The dog? Why?"

"We'll want to run a scanner over him, see if there is an ID chip implant or anything."

"No, I think he'll stay with me. Have somebody from the lab come by, they can check him here."

"Alex, he's evidence."

"No, he is what kept me from going to fill a hole next to Steve Day's." He looked at the dog and scratched behind one of its ears. "He's a good boy, aren't you, Scout?"

Toni nodded. Anybody who didn't know him would think Alex was used to assassins coming into his house, no sweat, and isn't it a nice night? But she knew him. Maybe better than he knew himself. "I guess we can work on this for a while." She held up the cane, wrapped in no-smear plastic sheeting.

"She wore gloves," Alex said. "White, silk or cotton, probably. I bet it was wiped clean after she put them on. The gloves."

"Won't hurt to look," Toni said.

He shrugged.

The last of the D.C. police were gone, but there were four of Net Force's agents still there. A man on each entrance to the house, one in a car across the street, one standing by the sliding glass door. They'd stay with Alex until they got this sorted out.

Toni felt a surge of anger she had to hold on to. Whoever this person was, she—or he—was going to be sorry if Toni got to them before anybody else did.

"You okay?"

"Yeah. It was just such a surprise, seeing this nice little old lady from my neighborhood ready to knock my head over the left-field wall."

"I bet."

"I've seen her around for at least a week."

"So did the agents on your door during the protocol watch. This wasn't some spur-of-the-moment thing. You were being stalked."

He shook his head. "Because I sit in Steve Day's chair. This woman probably had something to do with that."

"Yeah, that thought had crossed my mind."

"Well. Take that stick into the lab."

"I can stay around if you want."

"No, go back to work. I'm all right."

She left, reluctantly, and the image of Alex standing there petting the little dog stayed with her as she drove back toward HQ.

Friday, October 1st, 7:37 a.m.
New York City

Johnny the Shark stood in front of Ray Genaloni's desk with a sheet of paper in one hand.

"Okay, what?"

"This just came from our guy in the D.C. cop shop," Johnny said. "I thought you'd like to see it first thing."

Genaloni took the paper, put on his reading glasses and looked at it.

Before he got six words into it, Johnny said, "Seems some woman tried to kill the Commander of Net Force."

Genaloni looked up from the paper, over the top of the reading glasses. "Tried? *Tried* to?" Then it sank in, the rest of it. "A woman? You saying the Selkie is a fucking *woman*?"

Johnny held both hands up in an I-dunno gesture. "This is what our guy in D.C. sent."

Genaloni read the paper. It was a copy of an incident report, and it was lean, not much to it. And it didn't look as if the cops were gonna stay on it, either; the feds had kicked them out.

Genaloni shook his head. A woman. He couldn't believe it. He'd talked to the Selkie on the phone three, four times, had never had a clue—she'd sounded like a man. A woman. That bothered him more than that she'd tried the hit and missed. And that bothered him more than a little. What if they caught her? What if she kept some kind of records, linking him to her?

He'd worried about this before, of course, but not really. The Selkie had always delivered. There was a lot of money to be made and it wouldn't serve him—no, *her*—to rat him out. But now? This was bad. Especially if she was a woman. You couldn't trust women with your ass.

"We got some computer geeks on the payroll, right?"

"Some of the best."

"Put 'em to work. I want them to run down the Selkie. Find her—if it really is a her."

"And after we find her?"

"Nothing. Just find her. I'll decide what I want to do once you get that part done."

Johnny nodded and left. Genaloni looked at the fax sheet. This whole thing with Luigi and the feds was a fuckup. He didn't like any of it, and it was getting worse. Maybe it was time to cut his losses and tighten up. Find Luigi and put him away, in case he'd said anything he shouldn't have. Find the Selkie, put her away. Take care of the guy she'd tried to kill himself, no loose ends anywhere.

Jesus. He didn't need this kind of crap. The damned road to legitimacy was going to be knee-deep in blood, the way it was looking right now.

Jesus.

Friday, October 1st, 12:12 p.m.
New Orleans

Jay Gridley downshifted from fourth to third, enjoying the Viper's muscular rumble as it slowed for the off-ramp to the right. He pulled to a stop at the light, waited for a couple of trucks to go by, then turned right onto the surface street.

Welcome to New Orleans. *Laissez les bons temps rouler*—let the good times roll. . . .

He'd heard a rumor he had to check out, that there was some kind of rascal going down, a chunk of money being rerouted, and the fingerprints on the deal were invisible. Might be the guy he was looking for.

He idled at another traffic signal, and while waiting for

the light to change, glanced at the newsstand on the corner. The hardcopy papers and magazines wilted under the heat and high humidity, covers drooping flaccidly. There was one of those big colorful maps pasted on the kiosk: *CyberNation!* He really was going to have to check that out a little more. A man in his position needed to know such things.

A headline caught his attention. He waved at the vendor, held up a dollar and pointed at the paper he wanted. The man next to the stand stepped into the street, took Jay's money and handed him the paper.

The headline said: THAI PRIME MINISTER DIES IN CRASH.

The vendor didn't offer any change.

Gridley had time to scan the first paragraph before the light turned green.

Apparently Prime Minister Sukho had driven his car off a bridge. He'd been alone at the time. A freak accident.

His widow had no comment.

Gridley blew out a sigh. Well, well.

The traffic was bad in the Crescent City, the roads jammed with locals and tourists coming to visit, to see the river, taste the spicy foods, maybe take in a strip show on Bourbon Street in the French Quarter. When you visited an officially sponsored city-site in VR, you had to live with the RW local conditions, and even in October, the heat and dampness were oppressive here.

The place he was going was called Algiers, and it was not the best of neighborhoods, despite years of trying to renew the district. He had done a little research on it, enough to know he wanted to get in and out quick. His Viper would move fast enough to keep him ahead of a lot of trouble, but it wasn't a tank. He depended on his speed and skill, and so far, he'd been able to outrun VR thugs, but even an expert could get trapped in a dead end.

He wove his way through narrow streets, keeping a careful watch on the other traffic. He also watched with care the pedestrians who lounged on corners, drinking beer from long-necked bottles or unknown liquid from pints hidden inside little paper bags. In this section of town, most of the faces he saw were dark, or at least swarthy, and none of them looked kind.

He saw money being exchanged for small baggies or vials, saw women dressed in short skirts and hooker heels leaning against bus benches or in the lee of bar doorways, watching for potential customers.

Even in VR, Gridley wanted no part of these women.

He glanced down at the directions he'd gotten. Another turn, a right, and he was on a street barely wide enough for two cars. Ahead was the branch of the Bank of Louisiana he'd come to find, what looked like a trailer without wheels, set in front of a lot full of building rubble.

Parked in front of the bank branch was a shiny new metallic-blue Corvette convertible with the top down, the motor running. A man came out of the bank in a hurry. He looked young, but he moved old, wore a nice suit, and he carried a briefcase in one hand. He would have passed for a customer, a businessman—except he was wearing a mask.

He looked up, saw Gridley, and ran for the Vette. He threw the briefcase into the passenger seat as he opened the driver's door and jumped into the car.

On some level, all of a sudden, Gridley knew. It was *him*! The programmer! He was sure of it!

He grinned, gunned the Viper. He'd cut the sucker off, block his escape.

The masked man got the jump on him, though. He pulled away from the curb, leaving rubber as he upshifted.

All right, all right, it didn't matter! The Vette was fast, but it couldn't touch the Viper, through the gears or topside—it didn't have the guts, no way!

Gridley stomped the gas pedal, felt the Viper surge as if it was goosed. Gained on the Vette. Aloud, he said, "Might as well shut it down, pal, you ain't goin' nowhere!"

The narrow street hadn't been designed with muscle cars doing eighty in mind. A curve to the right burned more tire rubber on both vehicles, but Gridley kept the Viper on the road, shifting, tapping the gas, still gaining. He was a hundred feet back and he'd eat that space in five more seconds—

The driver of the Vette threw a handful of shiny dimes into the air.

At least that was what it looked like at first. It wasn't until the dimes hit the street that Gridley saw they weren't coins at all, but some kind of spiked things.

Caltrops!

He stood on the brake pedal. The Viper's brakes locked, the car skidded and slowed, but not enough. The left front tire went first, made a noise like a firecracker going off. The Viper lurched to the left. Gridley jerked the steering wheel, partially straightened the car out, almost had it— then the right front tire blew. The Viper spun into the new flat, lost traction as it hit the curb, popped both rear tires and slammed into a storefront. Glass exploded as the Viper smashed through a big window and into a small bakery, shattering display cases. The car slid backward, knocked over a table and came to a stop against a counter. The impact tumbled the old metal cash register onto the Viper's trunk.

The Viper was going to need some major repairs.

Covered with glass and pastries, Gridley looked up at a startled baker in a white apron and hat standing a foot away from the Viper's door.

Gridley shook his head. The guy had suckered him, trashed his ride and gotten away clean. He looked at the baker, who stared at him wide-eyed.

"Hi there. Say, are your donuts, uh, fresh?"

23

Standing at his locker, waiting for the thumbprint reader to open the door, Tyrone Howard heard the Voice of Doom. It didn't sound the way he thought the Voice of Doom would have sounded. Instead, it was soft, throaty, sexy, not a hint of disaster connected to it.

"Hi. Are you Tyrone?"

He turned and saw Belladonna Wright, all fourteen years of her, standing there, the most beautiful girl in Eisenhower Middle School, probably the most beautiful girl in all of the District. She was smiling at him.

Smiling at him.

He was a dead man.

What did she want with *him*? If anybody said anything to Bonebreaker LeMott, he might as well kiss his ass good-bye now and avoid the rush later. *Jee-sus!*

"Uh, uh, yeah?" To his horror—and burned forever into his memory—his voice cracked.

"Sarah Peterson told me you were pretty good with computers, that you could make it so simple even a doof like me could understand it. I have to get at least an eighty in Basic Cee or I'm in trouble. Could you maybe help me?''

The voice of self-preservation screamed—from behind the big mind rock where it had run and hidden as soon as it realized who was talking to them:

No! Danger! Danger, Will Robinson! Warning, warning, run, flee, the dam busted, the volcano blew, the aliens are coming! No, sorry, no, can't do it, uh-uh, negative, negative, zipper-roo, count zero!

''Uh, okay, sure,'' came out of Tyrone's mouth.

Who said that? Are you insane? *Death! Dismemberment! Destruction! Aaiiee!* screamed the voice of self-preservation as it tried to dig a hole under the rock.

''Oh, thank you. Okay, here is my number,'' Bella said. ''Call me and we can set up a time, pross?''

Oh, yes, we pross! Bonebreaker LeMott taking us apart like an overcooked chicken, that's what we pross!

Tyrone took the slip of paper from her and smiled reflexively. ''P-p-pross.''

She smiled, turned and walked away. Well, she *swayed* away, something like a Polynesian princess on a white sand beach in the hot sunshine might sway as she moved. Ruler of all she surveyed.

Lust reared its head in Tyrone. At the same time, fear dried his mouth to a consistency roughly that of a pile of bones left to bleach a hundred years in the Gobi Desert sunshine.

That's our *future, fool! Run, hide, change your name, leave town!*

''Ty-*rone*! Was that *Bella* you were talking to?''

Tyrone stared at Jimmy Joe. All he could do was nod stupidly.

''Man! Way to go, Ty-*rone*! Studly Dudley! Oh, and congratulations on getting your black belt, too.''

Tyrone frowned at Jimmy Joe. "What? What black belt?"

"The one you're gonna need when Bonebreaker finds out you're trying to complete a hot circuit with Bella. Either that, or a gun. Me, I'd want the gun."

"I wasn't trying to make a circuit! She just stopped to ask me something! To help her with her Basic Cee stuff!"

"Uh-huh."

"No, really! She gave me her number, I'm supposed to call her, we're going to get together later, to—to . . . uh . . ."

"Somewhere private, like, say, oh, *her* place?" Jimmy Joe prompted.

"Oh, man. Oh, no."

"Oh, yeah. Here's how I scenario it: Bonebreaker drops by, sees you leaning over Bella's tasty shoulder with your hand on her . . . mouse, and it's *sayonara,* Tyrone-san."

"Ah!"

"Well, maybe not. You could, you know, get too busy to help her."

"Right. And she gets pissed off and tells Bonebreaker I insulted her, and *then* he kills me."

"Sounds like a no-win situation, all right."

"Why are you *smiling*?! This is not funny, Jimmy Joe!"

"Depends on where you're sitting, don't it? Listen, if you're gonna die anyhow, you might as well enjoy yourself, right? Be a happy man when you discom."

"I think I need to go to the bathroom," Tyrone said. Suddenly, he needed to do that *real* bad.

Jimmy Joe's barely suppressed chuckles followed him down the hall.

Friday, October 1st, 9:45 p.m.
Grozny

VR gear removed, Plekhanov sat in his chair, breathing hard. How had that American Net Force operative gotten so close so fast? Yes, he had stopped him, wrecked his program, but that had been too near a miss. It shouldn't have happened.

He blew out a sigh and calmed himself. Well. He was the best, but there had to be a second- or third- or tenth-best. The reason for the attacks on Net Force's Commander and its operations had been to keep their decent programmers busy elsewhere. Their best were not in his class, of course, but at the highest levels, skills were not galactic leaps apart. No, the top players were dangerous. If one of them happened to be in the right place at the right time, it could be a serious problem.

He rubbed at his eyes. He'd been spotted by the opposition. Of course, there hadn't been any real danger, he'd had his escape route planned, and several ways to discourage pursuit had the first one failed, and it had *not* failed. The reason those safeguards had been put in place was for just such an unlikely happenstance. He had escaped, had he not? The boy, that naturalized-American Thai orphan—what was his name? Groly? Gridley?—was a hotshot, but however fast his hands, he did not have the experience. Put the two of them into a VR ring with gloves on, and the boy would have an edge, but the Marquis of Queensbury rules did not apply in this arena. When the guidelines did not hobble them, the old and treacherous beat the young and quick every time. . . .

Still, he would exercise even more caution. The perfect crime was not in getting away once you'd been spotted; the perfect crime was one nobody ever knew had been committed. That had never been in the cards for this venture, but outrunning a pursuer was not nearly as good as staying out of his sight. He would have to work on that.

Meanwhile, the trips to Belarus and Kyrgyzstan were next on the agenda. He would continue to sow; soon, he would reap.

Friday, October 1st, 4:02 p.m.
Quantico

Michaels's boss was on-line, and what he had to convey was not happy news.

"The President is concerned, Alex. It's been more than three weeks."

"I am aware of that, sir." He was also aware of how stiff his voice was.

Walt Carver had not risen to FBI Director by missing the nuances. He said, "Don't get your back up. I'm just pointing out something you already know. The politics here makes all the difference."

"I understand," Michaels said.

"We need a victory," Carver continued. "It doesn't have to be a major one, just something we can wave at the big dogs to keep them from gnawing on us. Sooner you come up with something, the better, and when I say sooner, I'm talking about a couple of days."

"Yes, sir."

"I'll keep the Senate committee off your butt, but I need something on Day's murder by Monday. Tuesday at the latest."

"Yes, sir."

After Carver disconnected, Michaels stood. He needed to move, to burn off some of this nervous tension. It wasn't enough that he'd almost been killed last night. Now he had the damned President of the United States after his hide. If he didn't come up with something, he'd be dead in this town; if the powers that be thought he was a sludge, he could kiss his career good-bye.

Well, fine. He loved the work, it was satisfying, but hell, he could get another job, that wasn't the problem. As long as he got Steve Day's killer before they threw him out, he could live with it. He hadn't wanted to sit in the damned chair in the first place—not given the cost.

He felt a sudden urge to call his daughter. He glanced at the time. Just after four p.m. here, but Idaho was a couple hours earlier. Would she be home from school yet? He didn't know. He should know, but he didn't. Did she have a beeper? He shook his head. He didn't know that, either. And even if she did, he wouldn't want to upset her by buzzing her in class. She'd worry, and what would he tell her when she called? Hi, honey. Guess what—Daddy almost got killed last night and probably is going to lose his job.

Yeah, right. There was nobody he could tell about this, even if he'd really wanted to tell somebody. And he didn't want to tell anybody. He wasn't going to whine about how tough life was—that never solved anything and nobody wanted to hear it anyhow.

He was too nervous to sit still. Maybe he should go to the gym and work up a sweat. It wouldn't hurt anything, might make him feel better. And sometimes exercise cleared his head out enough so he got some good ideas. Sure, a session on the multiplex machine might be worthwhile. What the hell, he sure wasn't getting anything done sitting here.

Being stuck as an administrator, he had discovered, wasn't much fun.

Jay Gridley walked into the VR Cane Masters store in Incline Village, Nevada. Given his choice, he would rather
be hunting the robber in New Orleans, but the programmer
would have to wait. He had gotten a good look at the guy's
vehicle, a feel for how he moved, and after backwalking
the heist, he had a handle on the guy's MO. Some things
you could hide, some things tended to stand out. Mostly, it
was style that separated one good programmer from another, and Gridley knew one thing: If he found the guy's
trail again, he would know him when he caught up with
him. That was a big advantage, and he meant to jump on
it as soon as he could.

But somebody had tried to kill his boss last night and
that took precedence.

Inside the store, there were racks of gleaming, polished
oak and hickory and walnut canes lined up neatly on the
walls. Other martial-arts weaponry made from wood, too—
staves, *escrima* sticks, plus exercise rubber bands, videos,
books, jackets and T-shirts with "Raising Cane" on them.

An attractive Chinese woman behind the counter smiled
at Jay, who had the weapon used in the assault on Alex
Michaels tucked under his arm.

"Help you?" the clerk said.

Gridley handed the cane to her. "Is this one of yours?"
He already knew it was, having gone through product de-
scriptions and .GIF files of all the commercial cane man-
ufacturers in North America until he'd found a match.

The woman examined the cane. "Yes, it's the Instructor's model, in hickory. Is there a problem with it?"

"No, it works fine, far as I know. But I need some information about it. Do you keep records of your sales?"

"Of course."

"Is there any way to find out who bought this?"

The woman's smile faded. "I'm afraid our client records are confidential, sir."

"You have a manager I could talk to?"

"Just a moment."

A tall man wearing a frown appeared behind the clerk in a few seconds. "May I help you, sir?"

Gridley produced his Net Force ID and held it out. He waved at the cane he'd brought. "This stick was used in an attempted assassination of a federal government official," he said. "I need your sales records."

"I'm afraid we can't do that," the man said.

"Oh, you can. You can voluntarily give them to me, saving us both a lot of time and hassle, and earn my gratitude. Or I can get a federal subpoena and be back in an hour with a gang of IRS/CPA programmers to deconstruct everything your company has done in the last ten years. My guess is that these guys will almost *certainly* find some irregularities in the way you do business. I mean, given the tax code complexities and all these days, you can't be totally honest even if you want to be."

The man took Gridley's ID, ran it under a scanner and waited for the verification. When it came, he said. "We're happy to help the government in any way we can. Denise, would you transfer the records for this agent, please?"

Gridley nodded, but didn't smile. Too bad he didn't have this kind of clout when he wanted to get into a decent restaurant.

Outside the store, Gridley walked to his new Viper. Well, actually, since the program he was using was a backup for the one that had been trashed in New Orleans, it was the same age as his *old* Viper, and it also lacked a few bells and whistles compared to the wrecked one. He'd done a lot of fine-tuning on the wrecked unit, and he hadn't bothered to save the updates. No big deal, but it would require a little work to sharpen this one so it ran as well as the other.

In the car, he looked at the HC printout. Cane Masters had been around for at least fifteen years, and they had sold thousands of canes in that time. In the last ten years, they had sold several hundred of the particular model Net Force was interested in. Still, running down several hundred possibilities was better than running down *no* possibilities.

He started the car, frowned a little at how rough the engine ran. Definitely needed a tune-up. He put it in gear and headed away from the store.

24

Grigory the Snake had won three hundred in chips, playing at the five-dollar blackjack tables in the big pyramid-shaped casino; to celebrate, he was getting drunk and talking about looking for a prostitute. The drinks were free as long as he kept playing. The prostitute would likely take most of his winnings, in exchange for which he would have a few moments of loveless pleasure—and run the risk of catching a deadly disease.

Ruzhyó did not know how prevalent HIV was among American trulls. In parts of Africa and Southeast Asia, eight of ten whores would be infected. Of course, there were vaccines for the more common strains of the disease, but it seemed as if a new strain developed every week. And the Snake had bragged more than once that he did not use a condom under any circumstances. The Snake could catch something, rot slowly and painfully, and it was all the same to Ruzhyó. He did feel sorry for Grigory's wife, who might also contract the disease before her husband had the grace

to die. And sorry for her that she had married such a buf-
foon in the first place. . . .

Ruzhyó stood next to an electronic slot machine, listening to the jarring and obnoxious chords blare from the other
machines as people methodically and joylessly pumped the
handles or punched the buttons that operated the devices.
No one seemed to be having a good time. There were no
smiles, no backslapping, just intense manic concentration,
as if by so focusing, the winning bars would magically line
up and pay off. Now and then, they did, and along with
flashing lights, the cacophony of the machine forced to give
up its gold added more to the general noise, *Look,* it said,
people do win! Put in more money! You could be next!

Greed was supposed to be fun, but apparently it was only
fun if you were winning.

He did not know why he had gone along with the Snake
for this outing. Ruzhyó was not a gambler. Cards, dice,
wheels, these were things beyond his control. The risks did
not interest him. There was nothing to be gained but
money, no more pleasure for him in winning than there
would be in losing.

Perhaps he was trying to prove to himself that he could
still relax and have a good time; if so, this had not been the
way to demonstrate it. It was not yet midnight, and he was
tired, of the clamor, of the din of machines and unhappy
voices of people in the casino, and especially he was tired
of Grigory the Snake. Already the man had made it clear to
the other four players at the table that he was a Russian war
hero. Soon, he would be talking about his medals. Ruzhyó
did not wish to hear those stories again. Ever.

The days when Ruzhyó could party all night and then
work the next day without sleeping were long past. Decadent living was for the young or the stupid.

Winters came to stand next to Ruzhyó. The American
wore a black T-shirt with the logo of another casino, one

shaped like a lion, upon the back. He wore Levi jeans, a broad belt with a large, shiny buckle and black cowboy boots. He had a brownish, watery-looking drink in one hand. He looked as if he belonged here. He sipped at the liquid and frowned. "Lizard piss," he said. But he took another sip. "Welcome to the adult version of Disneyland, pard. You catch that whole River of Death and Boat business on the way in? Dog-headed gods and Ra and all? Christ, it looks like a ride in Yesterdayland. The Mummy's Pyramid Boat to the Other Side."

Ruzhyó glanced at his watch.

"Our boy racking up a few bucks?" Winters asked.

"He is ahead, yes. Three more hands and he plans to leave, to seek professional female company."

"Now there's an idea. Might as well blow your money on blow jobs. That way you could have a good memory to show for it. Not like gambling and losing."

"Grigory has a system."

Winters laughed, took a final slug of the drink, then put the glass of ice cubes on the floor next to his feet. "A system? Hell, you got money and a system, the casino will send a *plane* to pick you up. They'll give you your room and food and drinks for free. Only thing that works besides cheating at twenty-one is card-counting, and if they spot you doing that, they throw you out. And our boy Griggy ain't got the smarts to count cards past the three or four in his hand, much less the multiple decks in the shoe. I grew up over a bar with poker tables and slot machines in it. Trust me, you stay at the tables, the house always wins."

Ruzhyó looked at Winters, then back at the Snake. "I am going back to my room," he said.

"I'll watch Griggy here for a while. Maybe keep him out of trouble."

Outside, it was cool, even after a day when the afternoon temperature had been near body heat. A gusty desert wind stirred the dry, dusty air. The fronds of the palm trees planted around the parking lots of the giant black pyramid streamed like organic flags. A bright beam of light erupted from the top of the structure, right at the apex. So brilliant and hot was the beam that it sucked dust into itself and hurled it upward and into the night sky. A searchlight would be pale and anemic by comparison with this laser-like ray shooting from the pyramid.

Disneyland for adults. Yes. Decadent in the extreme.

And what was he going to do when this assignment was over? Where would he go? Not home, to the suffocating memories he could not help but have every time he looked around. Perhaps he would move into a desert like the one surrounding this artificial green spot. Away from everybody, to become a recluse, kept company only by spiders and scorpions and real snakes. To be parched dry during the day and to lie on a cot in the chilly nights and listen to the wind scouring the sand, with perhaps the distant howl of a coyote . . . ?

He smiled at his fantasy. No, he would not move to the desert. He would accept another assignment from Plekhanov—for there would always be more assignments from a man like Plekhanov—and he would do it. And he would keep on doing them until one day he came up against a younger, faster, hungrier opponent. And then it would be over.

He would not leap from a bridge, nor swallow his pistol barrel, nor would he run away and hide. He would continue to do the only thing he had ever really known how to do, and he would do it as well as he could. It was what he had. Aside from Anna, it was all he had ever had. It was his path, and he would follow it until it ended.

The dry wind followed him as he walked toward his hotel.

Saturday, October 2nd, noon
Quantico

Toni bent over, touched her toes, then dropped into a deep squat. Her knees popped. She stood, and shook out her legs. She was one of only three people in the Net Force gym. Most people didn't work Saturdays, and normally she wouldn't have worked, either, but until they had something on Day's death, plus the new business about Alex, she wasn't going to be taking any days off. Hardly anybody would.

She looked up, and saw Rusty come out of the men's locker room. She hadn't expected to see him here today. The FBI trainees usually got weekends off at this stage of their schooling.

"Guru," he said, offering her a short bow.

"Rusty. I didn't think you'd be here today."

"Well, I knew you'd be working and I didn't have anything else on my schedule. I mean, if it's okay?"

"Sure."

Toni found she enjoyed teaching. It did force her to think about her own form, to make certain it was right before she tried to pass it along. Guru had been right; the teacher learned as much as the student.

They loosened up for another five minutes, stretching and rotating joints. "Okay, let's begin," she said.

He faced her. They bowed in and she started him on the first *djuru*.

As Rusty went back and forth, repeating the simple block-elbow-punch combination, Toni corrected his form, demonstrated the footwork, adjusted slightly the positions of his hands. She had always had to do a motion dozens or hundreds of times before it sank in, but Rusty was a quick student. He picked up the lessons pretty fast.

After ten minutes of *djuru* practice, Toni stopped him.

"Okay, today we're going to work on *sapu* and *beset* moves."

He nodded, but looked puzzled. "Uh-huh."

She smiled. "*Sapu* is a sweep, uses the inside of the foot or leg. It means, literally, 'broom.' *Beset* is a drag, using the heel or back of the leg. Step in right side and throw a right punch."

Rusty nodded, and obeyed. He threw his fist hard, because to do less was to have to do it over again. She double-blocked with her open hands and then stepped in with her right foot just to the outside of his. "Okay, you see where our feet are? I am outside your attacking foot. We call this *luar*. Okay, back up and punch again, same way."

He complied.

This time, she blocked and stepped inside. "This position is to the inside, or *dalam*."

He looked down. "*Luar* is outside, *dalam* is inside. Okay."

"Right. In *silat,* there are basically four positions you can assume in relation to an attacker's feet. So I could have either of my feet forward in relation to yours—left or right on the outside, left or right on the inside. If you came in with a left lead, I'd have the same positions available for that foot, too. So, I've got four basic responses no matter which foot you put forward."

"Okay."

"Punch again, slow this time. The first technique I'll show you is called *beset luar*."

"Which hand?"

"Doesn't matter. What you can do right, you can do left. What you can do inside, you can do outside. What you can do high, you can do low."

"Sounds like something I should be writing down."

"Don't worry about it. You'll hear it again. And again. And again. *Silat* is not about hard and fast techniques. It is about laws and principles. It takes a little longer to learn it this way, but once you do, you'll have something you can use anytime. Obviously I have to show you specifics, but the goal is become a generalist. Punch again, slow."

He stepped in and threw a lazy straight right fist at her nose.

"Okay, here's the block, from the outside. Then I shove your arm out of the way and around, like so." She rolled his arm down and across his body to the outside, held onto it just above the elbow with her left hand. "Now, I step in, right foot, and put it right behind your foot. Straight step, not around, like this." She showed him the wrong way, then the right way. She exaggerated the step, turning it into a stamp. "I put my hip against yours, and I cork it inward, just like the *djuru* stance, do you see? Shoulders and hips square?"

"Yeah."

"This is my base. Then with my left hand, I pull your arm down and slightly behind me. This is the angle. Humans only have two feet, so no matter how they stand, they are always weak in at least two directions. You're strong right now forward or backward, but if I make a diamond pattern using your feet as the center line, you have no power at ninety degrees."

"Geometry," he said, grinning.

"Absolutely. So then I use my right hand up here on your neck. I could have punched or poked, but for now, I just put it there. Elbow down. This is my leverage. So now I've got all three—base, angle and leverage. What happens?"

"I go down?"

"Right. And if I add just a hair of drag with my right foot against your foot, the *beset,* then you go down a little faster."

She applied a little pressure, tugged with her foot, and

Rusty dropped flat onto his back. He slapped the mat hard.
He came up.

"One more time," she said. "Slow, so you can see it."

He punched. She blocked, stepped in, corked her hip
against his thigh. "It's important to get in close, so you
can feel your attacker move," she said. "In *silat*, you stick
to your attacker. It feels dangerous, especially if you are
used to outfighting, but if you know what you're doing,
inside is the place to be. Use your eyes for distance, your
body in close, so you can sense motion without having to
see it. You feel my hip, how it's pressed in there?"

"Oh, yes, ma'am, I surely do feel that."

She dropped him again. She'd caught the not-so-veiled
sexual tone in his voice. She grinned. If he liked that, wait
until she stepped inside and showed him the *dalam*.

Saturday, October 2nd, 12:18 p.m.
Quantico

Alex Michaels prowled the hall, too wired to eat. Gridley
was working the background on the cane the hitwoman had
tried to use against him, and he had people doing seines on
the net, following up on the New Orleans VR bank robbery.
All the information they could gather was flowing into Net
Force, and there wasn't anything he could do to hurry it
up. He had a meeting with his top people scheduled for
1:30 p.m., and until then, nothing new to pick at.

He knew Toni usually worked out at noon, and it gave
him a place to go, so Michaels headed toward the gym.

When he got there, he saw Toni and the big FBI trainee
she had taken on as her student in her martial art. They
were standing face-to-face, legs entwined, her waist pressed
against his crotch. As Michaels watched, the man reached

across Toni's chest, appeared to cup her right breast, then
twisted awkwardly and threw her to the practice mat.

Michaels stopped and frowned. For some reason, he felt
a stab of irritation.

Toni laughed, rolled up and faced her student again.
They moved, he punched, she ducked under his arm and
upended him with a move Michaels couldn't quite follow.
They both laughed as the feeb trainee came up again. She
said something to him, moved in close, pressed her hip
against the inside of his thigh.

At this point, the man saw Michaels and said something
to Toni. She turned and spotted him standing by the door.

"Hey, Alex."

Again, that surge of anger filled him. What was this?
Toni had the right to teach this yahoo anything she wanted
to teach him, it wasn't his business. He knew that. But still,
that nagging irritation in Michaels resolved itself all of a
second into something he could identify:

He felt *jealous*.

Bullshit. Come on. Toni was his second in command,
that was all. They didn't have any romantic notions about
each other. And even if they had, it would be stupid to act
on them. He was her boss, and office romances were dangerous.

Certainly if she wanted to spend her lunch hour rubbing
up against this feeb bodybuilder, that was her affair.

He shook his head, tried to rid himself of the thought as
if it would sling away like water after a shower.

"Alex?"

"Hmm? Oh, sorry, I was just passing by, on my way to
the cafeteria. I'll see you at the meeting."

He turned and walked away. Toni's personal life was her
own. Period. End of story. He had enough to worry about
on his own, thank you.

25

In the Miami identity, she had established that she was a recreational runner. Even though this was not something she particularly enjoyed, it was part of her cover, so she did it. Here, it was as much a part of her as the fake name and background. Oh, she'd never run a marathon, she'd say if anybody asked, but maybe a 20K someday, when she got into shape. . . .

Today, when Mora Sullivan came in from her noon run—six miles, the last two in a pouring subtropical thunderstorm—she found her computer flashing its warning-light signal.

The house alarm diodes were all green; nobody had come into the building itself. The computer warning was due to an electronic break-in—or somebody trying to.

She blotted her face and hair with the thick towel she had left by the door. It rained almost every other day here in the summer, and while hurricane season was pretty much over, early October had its share of storms. She stripped

off her wet shoes and socks, dropped the fanny pack with
the plastic and pretty much waterproof Glock nine in it; she
peeled the spandex bra and pants off, and finished toweling
herself mostly dry before she started for the computer.

She put the towel on the office chair, sat naked upon the
damp terrycloth and said, "Security program, log on."

The voxax brought the log up on-screen. Given her
choice, Sullivan preferred real-time computer work; she
didn't much care for VR, since it meant she had to effectively blind and deafen herself to ride the net.

She scanned the program. Somebody had probed at the
Selkie's com circuit. They had only gotten a couple of
bounces into the maze she'd constructed before they'd lost
the signal, but even that was something of a surprise. Whoever had tried it was pretty good, professional-class.

She hoped they weren't good enough to spot the leeches
she'd left for potential invaders.

"Security, backtrack the intruder."

A series of numbers and letters flashed on the screen,
followed by a map. Arcing, bright blue lines lit as the leech
program fed the intruder's initial signal back to her computer through the series of firewalls and shunts. When it
reached New York City, the dot representing the intruder
pulsed a bright light, and an electronic address lit and also
pulsed red underneath the dot.

So the invader was good, but not great. The leech had
been undetected. Given what she had paid for the leeches,
that was not a big surprise.

"Security, reverse directory, e-mail unabridged, cross-
check this address."

More letter-and-number crawl sped up the screen.

A name flashed: Ruark Electronic Services, Inc.

"Security, give me the names of the corporation officers
and any holding companies for Ruark Electronic Services,
Inc."

A moment passed. A list of names appeared. Heloise Camden Ruark, President and Chief Executive Officer; Richard Ruark, Vice-President; Mary Beth Campbell, Treasurer. A public company, incorporated in the state of Delaware, June 2005, blah, blah, blah—

Well, well, well. And look here, the owner of seventy-five percent of the outstanding shares was something called "Electronic Enterprises Group," which itself just happened to be—

—a wholly owned subsidiary of Genaloni Industries.

Sullivan leaned back and stared at the screen. So. Genaloni was trying to find her. She nodded. To be expected. The man wore a thin veneer of respectability, but under it, he was a thug. To a man like Genaloni, the response to a threat, whether real or imagined, was to burn all the bridges on any road leading to his castle, and then stand by the pots of boiling lead to cook anybody who might get past the rivers. Never use a needle when there was a boulder available. Genaloni would have heard about the attempt on her target's life. And since the target had seen her as a woman, and doubtless reported it so, the thug would be doubly worried. He did not trust women, and he could not abide failure. In Genaloni's league, strike one and you were out—strike two was a guarantee of bad things to come.

This was not altogether unexpected—she had halfway thought Genaloni might attempt to trace her before now—other clients had tried to get a handle on the Selkie. So far, her safeguards had been sufficient; nobody had ever gotten close.

As of now, the address and identity she had used when she'd taken the assignment from Sampson were history. Even if they found the place, there was nothing to tie it to Mora Sullivan, or any of the other aliases she used. But this was a bad sign. Genaloni was a thug, to be sure, but he was a smart thug, and a persistent one. If he was worried that the Selkie might be linked to him, he would do everything he could to remove the link. If that included having her found and killed, well, there it was. In Genaloni's jungle, self-preservation ruled. If he saw an aged, crippled lion half a mile away, going in another direction, he'd shoot it anyhow—because it might turn around someday. Who knew?

She scratched an itch on her bare left shoulder. She wouldn't be collecting anymore money for the target she had missed, but that was not really important. For her own pride, she would finish that job, payment or not. That was a given. And while she didn't think Genaloni's hackers could find her, even the smallest possibility that they might was too much to ignore. She would not spend the rest of her life looking over her shoulder. She would finish the job on the target in D.C., but she would also have to do something about Genaloni.

And after that? Well, maybe it was time for the Selkie to retire. When the winds of change blew up a line of tornadoes, a smart woman took cover—or moved elsewhere.

Saturday, October 2nd, 1:15 p.m.
Washington, D.C.

"Tyrone?"

Tyrone instantly recognized the Voice of Doom, even though the phone's visual was off. "Uh, yeah."

"This is Bella. Did you lose my number?"

"Uh, no, I was just about to call you."

That's good, said the voice of self-preservation, hiding behind its rock. *Lie. First a little one, then a big one. Tell her you have a fatal disease and you can't leave the house!*

"Standout. So, can you come over this afternoon?"

No! No! A million quadrillion times no!

"Uh, sure. I can do that. Come over. I mean, to your house."

"About three okay?"

No-no-no-no-nooo! Not good, not okay!

"Sure, three."

"You have the address?"

"Yeah."

"Okay, scan you then. And Tyrone? Thank you. This means a lot to me, you know?"

"Um . . . sure. Nopraw."

"Discom," she said.

Yeah, nopraw and discom, deadhead! Maybe because it means so much to her, Bonebreaker will make it quick, just snap your neck fast so you won't suffer too much! Asshole! Fool! Moron!

Tyrone stared at the cradled phone. He knew he ought to be terrified, but oddly enough, only a small part of him was. That part hiding inside his head behind its rock. The rest of him was . . . what, exactly? Thrilled? Yeah, that was part of it. That the best-looking girl in school had asked for *his* help, that he was going to her *house,* to stand and sit right next to her, to show her something he knew something about. . . .

Well, like Jimmy Joe had said. If he was going to die, he might as well get there by a fun route. Besides, RW-speaking, Bonebreaker probably wasn't going to actually *kill* him. Maybe hammer him into a bloody pulp, but probably he'd survive, right?

His mother wandered into the room, carrying a set of blueprints for the birdhouse she was building. "Hey, hon. Who was that on the phone?"

"A person from school. They want me to help them with a computer project. I'm going to go over to their house at three, is that okay?"

" 'A person? They? Them? *Their* house?' My, aren't we getting plural." His mom grinned. "Would 'this person' perhaps be of the . . . female persuasion, Ty?"

"*Geez,* Mom!"

"Ah. That's what I thought. What's her name?"

"Belladonna Wright."

"Is that Marsha Wright's little girl?"

"I think so."

"Oh. I remember her from the third-grade play. She's a cute little thing."

"She's not *nine years old* anymore, Mom."

"I would hope not. Well. Do you need a ride?"

"I'll take the Trans," he said. "It's not far."

"All right. Leave a number, and be back for dinner at seven."

"Yes, *Mom.*"

"Lighten up, Ty. I know I used to ride dinosaurs to school, but my memory hasn't all gone. It's not as dangerous as you think, talking to a *gurrul.* . . ." She laughed.

So much for what you *know,* said the voice from behind its rock.

Saturday, October 2nd, 1:33 p.m.
Quantico

For once, a meeting actually got started on schedule. Michaels looked around the conference room at his people. "Okay, let's not waste any time. Jay?"

Jay Gridley waved the presentation projector on. "Good news and bad news," he said. "The cane came from this store, made by a company that mostly supplies serious martial artists."

An image appeared.

"This is the model. . . ."

Another image, this one of the cane, flashed on-screen.

"After eliminating a whole bunch of customers—legitimate teachers, people who really need to use canes, collectors, and the usual number of loose nuts and bolts who buy things out of paranoia, all of whom could account for their purchases—we are left with eight possibilities."

Names flashed on-screen.

"Of the eight, our agents have so far interviewed five. Four of these produced the canes they are recorded as having purchased. One gave the item as a gift to a friend, and we have found that one."

Five of the names faded away.

"Of the three remaining subjects, one is a survivalist in Grant's Pass, Oregon, who refuses to allow local, state or federal agents on his property. The gentleman in question is seventy years old and according to his medical records, has had a surgical hip-replacement. We have a judge signing a search warrant as we speak, to look for the cane on his property. I'd guess they'll find him leaning on it when they get there."

The name on-screen began to blink, alternating red and blue.

"So that's pending. The remaining two names . . ." He shook his head. "Well, they are . . . interesting."

Michaels said, "Interesting?"

Jay waved at the screen. One of the names began to pulse in yellow. "Wilson A. Jefferson, of Erie, Pennsylvania. Mr. Jefferson, in the last three years, has bought a cane, two sets of *escrima* sticks and a set of custom-designed *yawara* sticks. These were delivered to a post office box. The cane is the right model. The *escrima* sticks are used in a Filipino fighting art called, oddly enough, *escrima*; the last items are used in several different fighting styles, but the name is Japanese. According to the post office box rental agreement and state driver's license records, Mr. Jefferson is a white male, forty-one years old, and he resides at this address.''

A street number and name blossomed.

"However, a check at this address came up negative. Nobody by that name has ever lived there. On the surface, Jefferson's credit records seem fine, but below the surface, they vanish. What we have here is an electronic man."

"So this is our assassin," Toni put in.

"Sort of," Jay said. "Then there is Mr. Richard Orlando.''

More screen action.

"Mr. Orlando has bought, over a period of four years, five canes, including two of the models we have in hand. All were delivered to a post office box in Austin, Texas. And a check of his background says he is an Hispanic male, twenty-seven years old, and as far as we can tell, also exists only in a few record computers and apparently nowhere else. The photographic image on his driver's license is blurred so badly he could look like anybody in this room. Oddly enough, so are the photographic records of Mr. Jefferson.''

"Same person, using two fake IDs," Michaels said.

"That would be my opinion," Jay said. "Very dissimilar and a thousand miles apart. Fakes, and unless you were looking for them, you'd never accidentally spot them.''

"Great," Toni said. "So, what's the good news?"

"That *is* the good news," Jay continued. "Nobody remembers either Mr. Jefferson or Mr. Orlando. We've interviewed postal workers, and come up blank. There are no trails leading away. As far as we can tell, the only reason these two E-men ever existed was to take delivery of some fancy but perfectly legal *sticks* half a country apart. And I'd give you good odds that the real person who has these things—if he or she still *has* them, knowing we'll be trying to trace him or her through them—isn't in Pennsylvania *or* Texas.''

"Dead end," Toni said.

"Deader than black plastic in the noonday sun," Jay said. "We'll keep on it, but whoever this is, he or she, they are real good. They went to a lot of effort for such a small thing."

"Seems to be paying off, too, isn't it?" Michaels nodded. "I'm still betting on a she, " he said. "It didn't feel like a man under that old-lady disguise. Okay, thanks, Jay. Toni?"

"We're running checks on all known professional assassins. So far, nothing substantial on anybody as good as this one seems to be."

"What about insubstantial?"

"Rumors about this shadowy figure or that. Usual stuff— the Iceman, who can kill you with a hard look. The Specter, who walks through walls. The Selkie, who can change shape. Urban legends. Problem with the really good hired killers is that they keep very low profiles. Pretty much the only time anybody bags one of them is when a client gives them up."

Michaels nodded. He knew this. He'd been thinking about it since Steve Day's murder.

"Anybody got anything else?"

Brent Adams, the FBI head of Organized Crime, said, "Something is going on inside the Genaloni organization."

Michaels looked at Adams. Raised his eyebrows.

The OC man said, "Our people went back and strained out a year's worth of everything with a Genaloni tag. A couple of weeks ago, the FBI regional office in New York City got an inquiry from one of Genaloni's lawyers regarding the detention of Luigi Sampson. Sampson is Ray Genaloni's enforcer—the head of his legal and illegal security operations."

"Yes?"

"Well, our agents in New York didn't detain Sampson. Genaloni's people didn't follow up on it, so nobody thought anything else about it. A mistake of some kind."

"Which means . . . ?"

Adams shook his head. "We don't know. But since then, our wiretaps and surveillance cams haven't heard or seen anything of Sampson."

"Maybe he went on vacation," Jay said.

Adams shrugged. "Maybe. Or maybe he pissed off Ray Genaloni and he's in a field outside Dead Toe, South Dakota, pushing up the daisies."

"I don't think they grow daisies up there. Too cold," Jay said.

"You'd be surprised," Toni put in.

Michaels said, "So, why would Genaloni's people be calling the FBI, supposedly looking for Sampson, if they deleted him?"

Adams shook his head again. "Establish an alibi, maybe. With these guys, you never know what they're going to do. They make some smart moves now and then; then they turn around and make a stupid one."

Toni said, "Maybe this Sampson was responsible for Steve Day's death and Genaloni got nervous? Wanted to erase the link?"

Adams said, "I don't know. It's possible. Ray Genaloni is a careful man. He doesn't step out on the street without having it checked for six blocks in all directions first."

Michaels stared at the table. Something was bothering him, rattling around inside his head. He couldn't quite put his finger on it. Something about all this. . . .

He sighed. "All right. If you'd stay on top of that, Brent? Jay, you run the cane stuff as far as you can, see if you can get anything. And check out those New Orleans links—

we can't spend all our efforts on the Day investigation. Anything else?''

Nobody had anything they wanted to put on the table.

"Okay. Let's get back to it."

Michaels headed toward his office. Things were not looking good for the home team. And the clock was ticking on his job. A few more days and this might be somebody else's worry.

Maybe it was time to get out of government service. Move back to Idaho, get a job programming game computers or something, spend weekends with his daughter. Just walk away from all this.

Yeah, right. Until Steve Day's killer was caught, he wasn't going anywhere, even if they put him in charge of counting paper clips in the underground storage bins. Whatever else he might be, Alexander Michaels didn't bail when the going got rough. No way.

26

He would have preferred a walk on his quiet trail, but because he was in a hurry and could not afford the time to dawdle, Plekhanov drove the car. It was the program that was loaded, and he had planned to trash it after the unfortunate interface with the American Net Force agent—such was only prudent. And he *would* erase the software eventually, but just at the moment, it was more trouble than it was worth to go off-line, degear, switch to a new scenario, then regear. It was one of the disadvantages of the old-style system he liked—with the newer VR units, you could do it on the fly without missing a step.

It didn't matter. This was just a short run to make a few minor adjustments on a legal scenario running in Canberra. The chances of Net Force seeing him were practically nil, and besides, there were a lot of blue Corvettes out there, probably tens of thousands of them.

He put the VR automobile into gear and pressed on the accelerator.

When Belladonna Wright opened the door to let him in, the first thing Tyrone noticed was that she wore tight shorts and a baggy sweatshirt with the sleeves and neck cut out to reveal a lot of bare skin.

A lot of beautiful bare skin.

The second thing he noticed was the hulking form of Bonebreaker LeMott sitting on a couch in the living room behind Belladonna.

Tyrone was pretty sure his heart stopped for at least five seconds. Then his belly rose up and lodged in his throat. And his bowels and bladder both threatened to empty. The end was near.

"Hi, Tyrone. Come in."

The voice of self-preservation couldn't even form words. It babbled and whimpered mindlessly.

His feet didn't seem to belong to him. They took him into the house.

"Tyrone, this is my friend, Herbert LeMott. Motty, this is Tyrone."

Motty?! He would have laughed—except that he was sure that would be the last sound he'd ever make through his own teeth.

Bonebreaker wore a tight T-shirt and cotton shorts that strained all their seams as he came off the couch. He had muscles on his muscles. He loomed like a human tyrannosaur; Tyrone expected to hear Godzilla's shriek any second. . . .

But Bonebreaker's voice was soft, quiet and actually fairly high-pitched. He said, "Oh, wow, hey, Tyrone, glad to meet you." He extended his right hand.

Tyrone took the giant hand, and was amazed at how gentle the grip was.

He had a sudden image of a cartoon mouse looking for a thorn in a lion's paw.

"It's real nice of you to help Bella out with her computer class. I never was much good at that stuff. I appreciate it a lot. If I can ever do anything for you, just lemme know, okay?"

If Bonebreaker had suddenly turned into a giant toad and begun hopping around looking for flies to eat, Tyrone could not have been anymore amazed. Holy shit!

"Okay, Bella, I gotta go, we got practice at the gym. I'll call you later." He bent down—a long way for him—and kissed Bella on top of her head. She smiled and patted him on the back, as if he were a favorite horse. "Okay. Be careful."

After Bonebreaker left, Bella must have seen something in his face, because she smiled at Tyrone. "What, did you think Motty was going to get *physical*?"

"The thought briefly crossed my mind." *Yeah, briefly— like a snail with a broken shell crawls over a salt flat briefly.*

"Motty is a big sweetie. He wouldn't step on an ant. My room is upstairs. Come on."

Unless the ant put its hand on your butt.

Still marveling over being alive, Tyrone followed Bella upstairs.

She had a standard home computer, and the VR gear was not top-of-the-line, but pretty decent. And it only took a few minutes for him to realize she was better at general systems than she'd let on.

He said so.

She said, "Well, I'm okay on theory and real-time, but my network is slow."

"You came to the right guy, then. You have another set of VR gear?"

"Right here."

"Gear up. Let's walk the web. We'll start on one of the big commercial nets—that's easy enough for anybody to do well."

"You're in charge, Tyrone."

Flushed with a sudden fearlessness, he took a leap: "Call me Ty," he said.

"You're in charge, Ty."

She geared up as he did, then sat next to him on the bench in front of the computer. She sat close enough that he could feel the heat from her bare leg. A hair closer and they'd be touching.

Man! He most surely did not want to forget this moment. Life might never *get* any better than this.

And even as he thought it, he realized that there were ways it *could* get better. If he could figure out a way to move half an inch to his left, it would get better instantly. That half inch might as well be a light year, though. He wasn't completely stupid with bravery.

Sunday, October 3rd, 6 a.m.
Sarajevo

"First squad, flank left! Second squad, take the rear!"

Small-arms fire rattled, bullets chopped bark from trees, dug furrows in the ground. They were in a city park—what was left of one—and the attack had been unexpected.

John Howard opened up with his tommy gun, felt it buck in his hands as the fat and slow .45's went off.

"Sir, we've got—ah—!"

The lieutenant went down, a stray round in the neck.

Where were they *coming* from?!

"Third squad, suppressing fire at five o'clock! Move! Shoot—!"

His men began falling, their armor wasn't working, they were getting their butts kicked—!

Washington, D.C.

John Howard jerked the VR gear off and dropped it in disgust. He shook his head. Crap.

Upstairs, his wife and son slept. It was still hours away from when they'd get up, get dressed and go to church. He hadn't been able to sleep, so he'd come down to the computer to run battle scenarios. He should have stuck to chess or *Go*—every combatsit he'd tried had been a loser.

He stood, walked to the kitchen and opened the fridge. He took out a carton of milk and poured himself a small glassful. Put the carton back. Sat at the table and stared at the glass of milk.

He was, he realized, depressed.

Oh, not clinically depressed, nothing to run to a shrink about, but definitely glum. He didn't understand it. There wasn't any reason to feel that way. He had a beautiful wife, a great kid, and a job most military officers would kill to have. He had just come back from a mission in which all of his objectives had been achieved, he had not lost a single soldier while under fire and everybody was happy with him. His civilian boss had put him in for a Presidential Commendation. What was the problem?

What was wrong, other than that he wanted to jump into the middle of an all-out shooting fracas?

What kind of attitude was that? No sane man wanted war.

He stared at the milk. It was the test, he knew. He'd never been tested, not really. He'd slipped between the cracks, missed the shooting in Desert Storm, been teaching when the police actions in South America got hot, gotten to the Caribbean dustup a day after the guns had gone cold and quiet. He had spent his adult life as a military man, training, learning, preparing. He had the tools, the skills and the need to use them, to see if they would really work— but there was no place for such things in peacetime.

It was why he had joined Net Force. At least there was a chance he'd get dropped into a hot spot. The mission to Ukraine was as warm as it had gotten so far, and while it was better than sitting in an office reading reports, it was . . . lukewarm. . . .

"Morning."

Howard looked up and saw Tyrone standing there in his pajama bottoms.

"Just after 0600," Howard said. "What are *you* doing up so early?"

"I don't know. I woke up, couldn't get back to sleep."

Tyrone walked to the fridge and got the milk out. Shook the carton, saw that it was almost empty, then drank from it. Grinned at his father. "Mom says it's okay if I'm going to drink it all," he said.

Howard grinned, too.

Tyrone took another sip of the milk, then wiped at his lips. "Can I ask you something, Pop?"

"Fire away."

"How do you deal with a force that's bigger and stronger than yours, if it already holds territory you want to occupy?"

"Depends on the objective, the terrain, the weapons and equipment available, transportation systems, a bunch of things. First you define your goal, then you have to come up with a viable strategy, then the tactics to make it work."

"Uh-huh."

"When did you get interested in such things?"

"Oh. It's what you do. I thought I ought to, you know,

kind of check it out. You know.'' He stared at the floor.

Howard held the grin back, kept his face serious. The boy was thirteen. Puberty. It had been a while but, yes, he knew.

He said, "Okay, let's talk about goals and strategy for a second. Your goal is to take the territory without destroying it, am I correct?"

"Oh, yeah."

"So you have to move carefully. The enemy's forces are bigger than yours, so he's stronger, but—is he smarter? You know you can't just charge in and engage in a stand-up fight if you are outgunned. You'll get slaughtered. So before you move, you have to assess the situation. You look for your enemy's weak points. In guerrilla warfare, you find a weak place, you hit it, then run. You do it fast, then hide, so not only can't he find you, he might not even know who you are.''

Tyrone leaned against the fridge. "Yeah, I can see that."

"Also, according to Chairman Mao, to win a guerrilla war, you have to get the locals on your side."

"How do you do that?"

"You offer them something they can't get from the enemy, something more valuable than what he is giving them. Allow them to compare you to him, and when they do, show them his shortcomings. You reveal how you are better for them. You can't match his guns, but maybe he can't match your brains.

"So you show them why brains are more important than brawn. You teach the locals stuff he can't. How to get more fish in their nets, grow better crops or . . . how to use their computers, for instance."

The boy nodded again.

"You have a goal, you move toward it most of the time, but not always. Sometimes you have to take an oblique angle, move away a little so you can come at it from another direction. Sometimes you have take a step forward, strike, then retreat a few steps, so you don't get hit with return fire. Patience is the key in this kind of war. You have to pick your targets carefully, make every shot count. Wear the enemy away slowly.

"Once you get the locals on your side, then it doesn't matter how strong your enemy is, because the locals will start to help you, to hide you from enemy forces. Sometimes they'll overthrow your enemy on their own, and you won't have to do anything. In the end, that's the best way."

"Yeah."

There was a moment of silence. Then Tyrone said, "Thanks, Pop. I'm going back to bed now."

"Sleep well, son."

After the boy was gone, Howard grinned at his milk. It had been a long time since he'd been that young. And the problems then had seemed just as big as any he had faced since. It was all relative. He needed to remember that. And that being here to tell his son what he needed to hear was as important as winning any battle in some foreign country halfway around the world. In the end, being a father was more important than being a colonel.

He tasted the milk. Warm. He walked to the sink, poured the milk into it, rinsed the glass and set it to dry on the rack. Maybe he could go back to sleep, too. Might as well give it a shot.

27

Alex Michaels stood by the sliding glass door and watched the dog wander around in the backyard. He'd been asleep when Scout came and hopped up onto the bed. It was a pretty good hop for a dog his size. Once up, he hadn't barked or anything, just sat there staring patiently until Michaels got up and went to let him out.

Michaels had some part of the alarm system lit all of the time now; a tech from the unit had come out and fine-tuned it, connected it to the voxax program of his house computer. All he had to do was say the word ''Assassin!'' loud enough for the house mikes to pick up, and the alarms would start screaming. He'd shut the system's sliding-door link off to let the dog out, but he had his taser in his robe pocket. He hadn't played with the taser much since it had been issued to him, but he was going to be spending a little more time at the indoor range practicing. He was going to work especially hard on getting it out of a pocket or belt clip in a hurry.

There was a car parked at his curb with a pair of agents in it. A third guard stood by the gate on the side of the condo. Michaels wouldn't have known about the third guard, except that the dog had seen the man and yapped at him until he'd been hushed. Better than the house alarm, the little pup.

The dog finished watering and fertilizing the lawn and, now sure the territory was secure from intruders, trotted back to the kitchen. He stood by Michaels' feet, tail wagging, looking up at him.

"You hungry, boy?"

Yap!

"Come on."

Michaels had bought some expensive canned dog food. He peeled the lid from the little aluminum container and dumped the contents into a small bowl, then put it down on the floor next to the water bowl.

As he always did, the dog waited. He was hungry, but he stood over the bowl looking up at Michaels, waiting for permission. Whoever had trained him had done a good job. "Go ahead, eat."

Scout bent and gobbled the stuff up as if he'd never been fed before.

When the dog was done with his meal and enough water to wash it down, he followed Michaels into the living room. Michaels sat on the couch and patted his lap. The little dog leaped up and into his lap, and began to lick one of its paws as Michaels scratched behind Scout's ears.

It certainly was soothing to sit and pet the little critter. Susie had always wanted a dog. Megan had told her she had to wait until she was old enough to take care of it. She was getting there—faster than he liked. Eight, his daughter was, going on eighteen. . . .

Michaels liked dogs. He hadn't gotten one after he'd moved to D.C. because he hadn't wanted to leave it alone while he was at work, but as small as Scout was, the house was plenty big enough to roam around in. The previous owners of the condo had owned a cat, and they'd left a litter box stuck up in the rafters. Michaels had bought a sack of kitty litter, and during the day the plastic tub full of litter sat by the sliding glass door. So far, the dog had used that faithfully when he couldn't get outside.

Scout licked Michael's hand. The man grinned at him.

"You don't care if I had a crappy day at work, do you? You're perfectly happy to see me no matter what, aren't you?"

The dog gave out a small yip, almost as if he understood what Michaels said. He snuggled his head under Michael's hand.

Michaels laughed. That was the thing about dogs—you didn't have to be anything special to impress them. He liked that. If you were as good a person as your dog thought you were, you'd be able to stroll across the Potomac without getting your ankles wet.

Well. Time to get moving. Better shower and shave and get dressed.

He had a thought: Why not take the dog with him to work? He could let him run around the office, take him out to pee once in a while. There wasn't any policy against it. He was the boss, wasn't he? At least for another day or two he was. Sure. Why the hell not?

Sunday, October 3rd, 7:40 a.m.
Quantico

John Howard wore an Army-green T-shirt and faded, frayed cargo-pocket fatigue pants over his Kevlar combat boots. He also wore a black headband—he sweated pretty good once he got going, and keeping a garrison cap on was hopeless—but otherwise, he looked like any of the other fifty troopers doing the obstacle course this early Sunday morning.

John Howard was no armchair commander ordering his troops to do something he wouldn't—or couldn't—do himself.

He was last up.

Fernandez blew his whistle. "Go, go!"

Howard felt his belt transponder buzz, starting his personal clock. He sprinted toward the water hazard, jumped, caught the thick rope and swung out over the pit, more mud than water. The trick was to let your momentum swing you back and forth, pump a little with your arms and crunch your body, then jump on the *second* swing. . . .

Howard released the rope, fell, landed two feet beyond the edge of the pit. He ran for the razor-wire tunnel. There was a backstop at the end of the razor-wire approach, enough to stop machine-gun bullets. The gunners had the day off, but during the graduation run, a steady stream of jacketed full-auto fire, every tenth round a tracer, laid a roof over the wire. This would scare the crap out of a green recruit, but most of his troops were old hands: They knew you couldn't catch a bullet unless you stuck your head up through the razor wire, a difficult proposition even if you wanted to do so.

"Clock is running, Colonel!" Fernandez yelled.

Howard grinned, dropped prone, began knee-and-elbowing his way under the razor wire. As long as you stayed low, the only thing you'd get is dirty. If you got uppity, the razor wire *would* bite you.

Clear!

Ahead was a fifteen-foot-high wall with a rope draped over it. If you got there at speed and jumped high as you caught the climbing line, you could make it over with two or three pulls, roll and hit the sawdust pit in three seconds. If you had to climb eight feet of rope, it took longer.

Howard leaped, grabbed the two-inch hawser with both hands a good ten feet up, reached high with his right hand and caught the rope again, did it on the left side, and was over.

The next obstacle was essentially a forty-foot-long telephone pole lying in a series of six-foot-high, X-shaped, four-by-four supports. You had to boost yourself up on the end—there was a short step built in there—mount the pole and walk the length. If you fell, you had to go back and start the walk over. The trick was to move steady, not too fast, not too slow. It wasn't that high, but a fall from six feet could sprain an ankle or break an arm. Once, they'd had a man break his neck when he slipped and landed on his head.

Howard reached the step, bounced up, stood on the pole. He had walked this hundreds of times, he had the pace down. Steady—not too slow, not too fast.

At the other end, there was another sawdust pit, though the archaic term was not really appropriate—the dust was not wood, but reconstituted buckyball-plastic. The best way to land on the stuff without sinking to the bottom, a good three feet, was to do so in a sitting position or stretched out and supine.

The colonel reached the end of the pole walk, jumped outward, lay back and hit flat on his back, hands extended, palms down. Buckyball-plastic splashed, but quickly settled back. Howard rolled, sank a little, but reached the edge of the pit and came to his feet.

The trooper in front of him was slower than he was. He had just gotten free of the pit himself, and was on the way to the minefield.

Howard came up behind the man. "Track!" he yelled. The trooper moved to the side and allowed Howard to pass.

He was making good time. Not his best, but not bad, he felt.

The minefield was a twenty-foot-wide corridor of sand thirty yards long. The mines were electronic, about the size of a softball, and not dangerous, but if you stepped on one, you knew it—it let out an amplified scream that would wake a man six days dead. Every one you hit cost you fifteen seconds. You could see where the mines were; there were little depressions that dropped the sand a half inch or so over them. If you were first through, it was easy, you could see them and run the field in ten or fifteen seconds, but after a few people went through ahead of you, it got harder to spot the mines among all the boot prints.

There were two troopers still walking the sand when Howard got there. Newbies tended to think they could run in the old boot prints and get home free, and if the mines had been real, that would have worked. But the traps reset randomly every two minutes, and stepping where somebody had gone before might earn you fouls. You couldn't be sure.

You couldn't learn a pattern, because Howard had his techs change it every week or so.

Again, steady was the key. Try to hurry, and you'd get sonicked good. Too slow and you started worrying, seeing traps where there weren't any.

He stepped into the sand.

Forty seconds later, he was clear, without triggering a sonic blast, and feeling pretty good since he had passed one of the troopers in the sand and caught the other on the way to the final obstacle.

The last test this day was Sergeant Arlo Phillips, a six-foot-four-inch 240-pound hand-to-hand-combat instructor. Phillips's role was simple: You tried to get past him to slap a buzzer button mounted on a post in the middle of a white circle marked on the soft ground; he tried to knock you out of the circle before you did it. Troopers were only allowed to enter the circle one at a time, and if you got thrown out, you had to go back to the end of the line and try it again. While your timer stopped when you reached the circle— your belt transponder clicked it off when you lined up in the quay zone—and resumed only as long as you were *in* the circle, this was where most testees hurt their scores. The combat instructors did not like to lose. They took turns in the circle, and they were all good, but Phillips was strong, skilled, and he loved this. One-on-one, face-up, Phillips would hand you your head if you tried to outmuscle him. There were troops who swore they'd seen Phillips lift and pivot the front end of a Dodge pickup truck into a too-tight parking space. The only way to beat him was to keep out of his range, and that wasn't easy.

When Howard's turn came, he went straight in at Phillips, jinked left, then right, faked high, then dived to the left and rolled. Phillips got his hand on Howard's right ankle as he came up, but too late—the colonel swatted at the buzzer, barely brushed it with his fingertips as Phillips jerked him prone on the ground. It was enough—the buzzer went off. His timer stopped, his run over.

"You got officers' luck, sir," Phillips said.

Howard rolled up, brushed himself off and grinned at the larger man. "I'll take it. Better to be lucky than good."

"Yes, sir." Phillips turned away. "Next!"

Howard walked around to where Fernandez and a couple of techs were scoring the exercise.

"You must be getting old, Colonel, sir. You're gonna come in third."

"Behind . . . ?" He pulled off his headband and used it to wipe the sweat from around his eyes.

"Well, sir, Captain Marcus is first by a good sixteen seconds. You missed him throwing Phillips with that jujitsu move he likes."

"And second . . . ?"

Fernandez grinned. "Modesty forbids, sir."

"I don't believe it."

"Well, sir, I was first up."

"How long?"

"Two seconds faster than you," Fernandez said.

"Jesus."

"I do believe He favors me, yes, sir."

"If you were first up, you should have flown through the minefield."

"I stopped to have a beer, sir. Since I figured I had plenty of time and all."

Howard shook his head and grinned. "How are they doing?"

"Pretty good overall. I'd put all our A1 boys—and girls—up against any SpecForce outside of maybe the SEALs' best, and they'd give *them* a pretty good run."

"Carry on, Sergeant."

"Sir."

Howard walked toward the new officers' dressing room—hell, it was all new, none of this had even been here a few years ago—to change his clothes. If he hurried, he'd just have time to get home and join his wife in time for church.

Sunday, October 3rd, 8:45 a.m.
In the air over Marietta, Georgia

Mora Sullivan looked through the jet's window at the ground far below. She had both of the first-class seats to herself this flight, and that was not due to chance—she usually bought two tickets to each destination, in case she needed to change identities before she boarded the flight.

Coach was only half full, so nobody was getting a free upgrade to take the empty seat next to her.

Fall colors were up—the hardwoods in the Georgia mixed forests below were shades of orange and yellow and red among the evergreen pine trees. She tended to sleep on plane trips, but she was too awake and edgy for that this morning.

During all her years in the biz, she had only deleted two of her own clients. The first, Marcel Toullier, had been for a contract from a different client six months after she'd worked for the Frenchman; being one of her clients did not confer immunity, and it had been strictly business, nothing personal. She'd liked Toullier.

The second deletion, the gun dealer Denton Harrison, had been because Harrison had done stupid things and gotten himself arrested. The authorities had enough on him to put him away for fifty years, and Sullivan knew he was a talker, he'd be willing to give up what he knew to stay out of prison. Sooner or later, Harrison might have gotten around to mentioning that he had hired the Selkie. The numbers he had for her were, of course, dead ends, disconnected and untraceable, but the authorities did not know for certain there even *was* such an assassin. She did not want them to find out.

Wearing class-two body armor, on his way to a safe house, Harrison had come out of a courthouse in Chicago, surrounded by federal marshals.

She had made the shot from six hundred yards. Class-two Kevlar didn't much slow the sniper rifle's .308 bullet: it had punched through Harrison's aorta and left a fist-sized hole in his back when it exited his body. He was effectively dead before the sound of the shot reached him.

And now there was Genaloni.

A flight attendant came by. "Coffee? Juice? Something else to drink?"

"No, thank you."

Did she have to take the crime lord out?

If she had reflexively thought she must, she would hardly be any better than he was. Yes, she had to do *something*, and since what she did for a living was delete people, that was where her strength lay, and naturally, she had to consider that an option. But there were other ways. Having made the decision that it was time to retire, all the old IDs, the houses and rentals, all of those were going away. She could lay a trail that ended in a car crash or other accident that would convince any pursuers she was dead. Or she could set Genaloni up for some criminal rap and know he'd get put away. He would still wield power from a prison cell, of course, these guys always did, but he'd have other things on his list. Even somebody like Genaloni would probably forget about her after five or ten years in the gray-bar hotel.

Men like Genaloni tended to die relatively young, or wind up in prison. They made a lot of enemies on both sides of the law, and the odds were that one of those enemies would get to them.

Of course, there were ninety-year-old ex-mobsters rolling around in wheelchairs, sucking oxygen from portable bottles and pretending to be feeble or insane, who had beaten the odds. Old Mustache Petes who, despite the dangers, were still free.

She sighed. Which was the best way to go? She had to decide pretty quick. After she paid for the lost dog at the kennel upstate, she'd go to her place in Albany and think about it.

Sunday, October 3rd, 1:28 p.m.
Washington, D.C.

Tyrone stood at the door to Bella's house, taking deep breaths, trying to calm himself. Yesterday's session had gone pretty well. She was not a great net rider, but not that bad.

Twice, she had brushed her hip against his. Once, when she reached across to grab a stylus, he had felt the weight of her breast on his arm.

The memories might cool someday, but just at the moment, they did *not* help slow his pulse rate.

He touched the buzzer.

Bella opened the door. Today, she wore a less-revealing outfit—a sweatsuit. She had her hair pinned up, and she looked scrubbed fresh, smelled clean, and a little bit soapy.

"Hey, Ty. I just got out of the shower. Sorry I look so undone."

There was an image he could imagine all too clearly, Bella in the shower. "No, no, you look fine," he said. And he said it too fast, his voice too high. He was too stupid to live. Man!

"Come in."

Upstairs, they donned VR gear and got started. He said, "Okay, let's use my program today. You mind riding double on a big motorcycle?"

"Nopraw," she said. "Whatever you want to do."

Yeah, right. What he wanted to do had nothing to do with the net. No, sir, definitely not. But he said, "Okay. Here's how scenario translates. . . ."

Sunday, October 3rd, 9:45 p.m.
Grozny

Plekhanov settled in, lit his VR, then realized he still had not deleted the car program. The shiny blue Corvette sat parked at the curb in front of him. He mentally shook his head. He really should get rid of this thing. All right. As soon as he finished the little drive over to Switzerland, he would dump it. Definitely.

Sunday, October 3rd, 1:50 p.m.
Washington, D.C.

Riding the Harley along the curvy road through the Swiss Alps, Tyrone yelled over the wind noise: "You see how this works? My program translates their programs into compatible visual modes. That truck over there? If we were in a water scenario, it would probably be a barge or a ship."

"But how does it do that?" Bella yelled.

He glanced back at her. Her hair streamed free behind them, whipping back and forth in the wind.

"Easy. If we're in totally different modes, my program just overlays the other guy's imagery. Angle and relative speeds will be the same—air, water, land, even fantasy. If we are in similar enough modes—like the truck is doing roads and not water or something else—my program will take his image and stet it, to keep the VR speeds up. Most people who meet pick one program or the other and use it. Otherwise, you get a couple of microseconds lag on the refresh rate."

"Ah, I see."

"That truck? It's really a big info packet. It contains a lot of code, so it moves slow. Watch."

He twisted the throttle and the Harley's powerful engine roared. They passed the lumbering truck, and whipped back in front of it as a car approached from the other direction.

"Wheee!" Bella said.

Oh, he liked the sound of that.

"So this is all off-the-shelf software?"

"Well, I've modified this one a bunch."

"You can do that?"

"Sure. I could write one from zero, but it's easier to alter an existing one."

"Could you show me how to do that? Write my own program?"

"Yeah, sure, nopraw. It's not that hard."

"Exemplary!"

In that moment, Tyrone remembered talking to his father. *Offer the locals something they can't get from your enemy,* he'd said. Although Tyrone didn't really see Bonebreaker as an enemy, exactly, the old man was right. Tyrone had something LeMott didn't have, a skill, a talent, and right at this moment, Bella wanted it. This was dee-eff-eff for sure, data flowin' fine to the fourth power!

They came to an intersection with a stop signal. CyberNation was to the left. Maybe he should take her there? It was interesting the few times he'd explored it, but they didn't let you see the really good stuff unless you joined, and that wasn't gonna happen. He could hear his father: "Give up your citizenship to join a computer country that doesn't exist? I don't think so."

Cross-traffic rolled past, and Tyrone was so much in his own head that he almost missed the Vette when it zipped across the intersection.

Almost. A mental alarm went off. Corvette . . . Corvette . . . what—?

Oh, yeah, Jay Gee's bulletin in yesterday's Email. Keep

your eyes open for a young guy in a business suit driving a blue Vette.

The car was past before he had a chance to see the driver, and there were two cars and a small van lined up in front of Tyrone at the light. Probably it was nothing.

On the other hand, maybe it was something. He ought to at least check it out, right? And if Bella asked, he'd have to tell her why, wouldn't he?

Bonebreaker wasn't helping out a major federal agency, was he?

Tyrone tapped the Harley's gears into first and gave it a little gas. He pulled over onto the shoulder and zipped past the waiting cars, earning a couple of horn blasts for his trouble.

"Whoa! Is this legal?"

"Well, not really," Tyrone said, "but we gotta do it." They reached the corner, and he leaned into it, straightened it out, upshifted and goosed the bike. "You see that blue Vette up there?"

"Yeah?"

"I need to check it out. I'm, uh, helping out a buddy of mine at Net Force."

"Net Force? Really?"

"Oh, yeah. Jay Gridley, he's their top computer guy. I do stuff for him every now and then."

"Wow. Exemplary, Ty!"

Was that his imagination, or did she tighten her grip around his waist a little?

"Can we catch him?"

"Nopraw. There's not much that can outrun me in this scenario. Hang on."

Definitely, she was holding him tighter. *Yes!*

Sunday, October 3rd, 9:58 p.m.
Grozny

Plekhanov was on his way back from the bank in Zurich when he saw the motorcycle coming up fast behind him. He frowned, felt a moment of worry. He watched the bike in his rearview mirror. It wasn't long before the vehicle caught up with him. It swung out into the incoming lane, then started to pass, apparently oblivious to the lorry bearing down from the opposite direction on the narrow two-lane feeder road. He watched the motorcycle peripherally. Two riders, teenagers, a boy and a girl, neither of whom appeared to take much notice of him. After a few seconds, the motorcycle passed, cut back into his lane and accelerated, missing the oncoming lorry by what seemed like centimeters. The two-wheeler quickly left him behind.

Plekhanov shook his head at his paranoia. It was nothing. A Kaffir boy, showing off for his pretty friend by blowing past the fastest vehicle on the road, risking the dangers of oncoming traffic. He had been that young once, although it had been aeons ago. He would not go back to those days, exchange his hard-earned knowledge and wisdom for the hot hormones and reckless *carpe diem* philosophy of youth. Teenagers thought they would live forever, that they could do anything in the world. He knew better.

Always, there were limits to such things. Even the richest and most powerful men who ever lived eventually went the way of all flesh. Another fifty or sixty years, and his time would be up. But at least in his case, it would be quality time. Quality time indeed.

28

Jay Gridley was on the net, piloting the Viper at high speed through the middle of Nowhere, Montana, when the override cut into the scenario. What he heard was the chirp of the unlisted landline phone in his apartment. He did a cycle-and-bail from the VR program, degeared and voxaxed the incoming call.

"Yeah?"

"Mr. Gridley?" said a young woman's voice.

Jay frowned. Nobody who had his private code for the landline should be calling him "Mister." He said, "Who is this?"

"My name is Belladonna Wright. I'm a friend of Ty Howard."

Before Gridley could wonder too much about that, the girl said, "Ty is on-line in a scenario. He said to call you and give you the coordinates. He thinks he might have found the blue Corvette you're looking for."

"Jesus! Where?"

She rattled off the coordinates. Gridley had the computer feed the numbers directly into his VR program. "Thanks, Ms. Wright. Tell him I'm on the way. Discom."

Gridley immediately started back to VR, but as he was about to initiate mode, he stopped. Probably it wasn't, but if it *was* the right car, the driver would surely be suspicious of the Viper. Better switch programs, no point in taking any chances. Something not so flashy.

Gridley called up the gray Neon.

The most common car on the RW roads was a two-year-old Neon, and the most common color of such automobiles was gray. For newbies and people who didn't care what they drove on the net, it was the default vehicle. No doubt Dodge had paid the big servers a whole bunch for that default setting. A Viper was a standout ride, stylish, classy, you got noticed in one. But another gray Neon? Driving such a car made you more or less invisible. And if you knew what you were doing, you could hide something more powerful than a stock engine under the plain-vanilla hood. It wouldn't be as fast as his usual mode of choice, but it would trade off speed for anonymity. If this was the guy, he most definitely did not want him to spot him too soon.

He cranked the program and set it for the coordinates.

The coordinates turned out to be a truck stop-style service station in western Germany. As Gridley pulled the car into the parking area, he saw a pretty girl walk from the public fresher toward Tyrone, who stood by his parked Harley, next to a big Volvo electric van sucking a torrent charge. This was a realistic scenario. Tyrone didn't see him as he drove up; he was looking at the restaurant's parking area.

Gridley glanced at the restaurant, and saw the Vette parked next to the building. It was the right model and color, but that didn't mean much by itself. He pulled the Neon to a stop close to Tyrone's bike, getting quick notice from the boy and girl. He killed the engine and stepped out of the car. It was cool, crisp, a perfect fall day. The smell of diesel hung in the air, along with the ozone odor of the big step-down charger feeding juice to the van. This was a *very* realistic scenario.

"Hey, Tyrone."

"Hey, Jay Gee. Uh, this is, uh, Belladonna. Bella, meet Jay Gridley."

Gridley said, "We spoke on the phone. Nice to meet you. This a persona or Real World Appearance?"

"RW," the girl said.

"She actually looks better in person," Tyrone said. Then he developed a sudden fascination with the tops of his shoes.

Gridley smiled. Good thing the kid's skin was dark; otherwise he'd be blushing so bright red you could use him for a taillight.

Tyrone knew it, too. Quickly, the boy pointed. "There's the car. The driver is inside."

Gridley nodded. "Thanks for the call. You check the license plate?"

"Sure, first thing. Quikscan says it belong to a Wing Lu, out of Guangzhou, China. But a cross-index number check doesn't match."

"So the plate is probably a fake," Gridley said. "Big surprise."

To the girl, Tyrone said, "A lot of people want to be anonymous on the net, so along with fake names and personas to mask their appearance, they layer in other fake ID—ersatz vehicle registrations, addresses, comcodes. One of the first rules of webwalking is—"

" 'Never trust anything you see,' " the girl finished. "I *have* been on the web before, even if I'm not a total spider, Ty."

"Sorry," Tyrone said.

Gridley shook his head. Puppy love. It was painful to watch. "So, what else?" he said, to steer the conversation back to the Vette.

Tyrone said, "He drives fast, changes lanes without hitting the centerline bumps, never gets caught behind a slow packet or boxed by traffic."

"A lubefoot," Gridley said.

"No doubt," Tyrone said.

"What's a lubefoot?" the girl asked.

"Somebody who slides along the web without much friction," Tyrone answered. "Means he's real good with this particular mode, probably used it a bunch, or else he's spent enough time on the web so he can probably use any mode well."

"Which means?"

"Probably he's a programmer," Gridley said.

"So, can I ask why you're looking for him?"

"I really can't tell you that just yet. It's part of an ongoing investigation."

"But it's a big deal?"

"Oh, yeah, if this guy is the one we want, it's a gargantuan deal. More we can collect on him, the better." Gridley glanced at Tyrone. "He see you?"

"We passed him to get a closer look. It was a narrow road. We've hung back pretty far since then. I don't think he spotted us following him, but if he sees us again, he might recognize us from when we went around him."

"All right. You want to stay on it, you ride with me, leave the bike here. We'll see how long we can run with him."

Gridley walked to the car, the two teenagers behind him. He had a sudden thought. "Better get in the back," he said, "I've got stuff piled up all over the front passenger seat."

That wasn't strictly true, but it would be by the time they got to the car. He could do that from here easily enough.

What the hell. He'd been that young once. Seemed like a long time ago as he looked at Tyrone and his friend Belladonna, but unless his memory had blown a fuse, getting to sit next to a beautiful girl in the backseat of a small car was still a pretty big thrill at that age.

Shoot, when you got right down to it, it was still a thrill at *his* age.

They had just entered the car when Tyrone said, "There he is!"

Gridley looked. Sure enough, a man was exiting the restaurant. He headed for the Vette. Jay got a good look, then grinned. Yes! It was the same persona he'd seen in New Orleans! The guy was sure cocky, to keep using it. Stupid to keep using it, too. Here at last was the break they needed.

"Way to go, Ty-*rone*! I owe you one."

"It's him?" Bella said.

"Oh, yeah."

"Exemplary, Ty!"

It sounded as if somebody's stock had just gone up in the backseat. " 'I have you now,' " Gridley said in his best Darth Vader imitation. He reached under the Neon's dashboard and came out with a com mike. He keyed the mike. "This is Jay Gridley, Net Force operative, ID number JG-six-five-eight-nine-nine, authorization Zeta one-one. I have a Priority Five at these coordinates, that's a Priority Five. Stand by for particulars." Gridley put out the code, the fake tags on the Vette, and a description of the vehicle and persona.

In the back, Tyrone quietly told the girl, "He's alerting law enforcement agencies. Any cop on the net who sees the Corvette will log in a time and location. We might be able to get a location pattern after we lose him."

She said, "After we *lose* him? You don't think we can keep up with him?"

"Not if the guy is a lubefoot running guilty. He'll be

checking. He'll spot a tail sooner or later. If he just cycles and bails, that leaves his lines open and a trail that we can follow. So when he spots us, he has to outrun us, or lose us some other way.''

"Not with these tires,'' Gridley said. "They're puncture-sealers.''

"Huh?''

"Never mind.''

Tyrone said, "If slip comes to slide, the guy can bail out of VR with a gear peel or a power cut. Probably crash his system and damage his VR program if he does it on the fly, but if he does, he's gone.''

"Would he do that?''

"I would,'' Gridley said. "First rule of computers is to back everything up. Might take him a little while to reinstall his software and sharpen things back to where they were, but that sure beats having Net Force kick in your RW door to arrest you.''

"Whoa,'' she said.

Gridley cranked the Neon's engine. "Yeah, well, that's later.'' He looked at the Vette as it pulled out of the lot and onto the highway. "Until then, he's not gone until he's gone. Buckle up.''

Sunday, October 3rd, 3:00 p.m.
Albany, New York

As a matter of course, Sullivan paid for the lost dog. She did it the long way. The company that dropped the envelope full of used hundreds at the kennel was the third in the chain; it got the envelope delivered to it by a second company. The second company had it brought to them by a first. The first picked it up from the lobby of a hotel where it had been left by an underage kid who Sullivan had bought a six-pack of beer for, and she had done that transaction in disguise. It was unlikely anybody would trace any of this, even if they were looking, and it dead-ended with the boy, who would remember little more than a forty-year-old woman with a warty mole on her chin.

So now she was in Albany, and now she had made her decision. She was a young woman. She might have another sixty or eighty years, given the state of medicine, maybe more. Yes, it was true, she was at her peak—mentally, physically, her skills as good as they were likely to get. After all the years of dancing on the edge, she had developed a feeling about things, almost an instinct. She had learned to trust those feelings. Right now, on some level, she knew: It was time to leave the party. Hanging around like an over-the-hill boxer to get decked by some big kid with an iron jaw was not a good idea. So. As soon as the missed target was deleted, the Selkie was going into early retirement. She would shut down all the Selkie's lines. If wasn't as if she was poor. She had eight million dollars tucked away. With careful investments, the money would generate all the income she'd ever need. Ten million had been a goal, but never more than a hypothetical number. And there were a couple of high-risk, but very-high-return, ventures she could invest in that were likely to pay off. She wouldn't starve.

But the one big dangling problem was Genaloni.

Probably her employer would wind up like most of the wise guys, dead or in stir. But "probably" wasn't good enough to risk sixty or eighty years on. She did not want to be spending any big part of those years sneaking looks over her shoulder, worrying that Genaloni might lurk behind her in the shadows.

No, Genaloni had to become part of her past. Her dead past.

It wouldn't even be that hard. The criminal types surrounded themselves with muscle and guns to protect themselves from each other. They had lawyers to take of the cops, and they figured they were immune from anybody else. Genaloni was maybe the brightest of the bunch, but he had weaknesses. The Selkie made it her business to know all about her clients before she ever took a job from them. Genaloni had a small army of thugs and lawyers, but he also had a mistress. Her name was Brigette, and while she was well off from Genaloni's care, she had neither lawyers nor bodyguards between her and the world.

So. First Genaloni, then the bureaucrat in Washington. Then off for a month in beautiful Hawaii, maybe. Or perhaps Tahiti. Someplace warm and sunny and without clocks or work to order her day.

The Selkie smiled. It was good to have a new goal.

29

He had, Plekhanov realized, a tail.

He cursed briefly in Russian, vented his anger, then put it away. Done was done, the past but prologue. He had to make adjustments.

The car shadowing him was one of those ubiquitous little sedan things, like millions of others on the net and in the Real World, and he wouldn't have noticed it, save that he was doing a standard side-road loop-the-loop to check for just such problems. This was the third of his evasive maneuvers, and while he had not spotted the tail before, he had to assume it had been with him for some time. How long had he been under surveillance? That was merely the first of several questions, wasn't it? Who was it? How had they found him? What was the best way to rid himself of them?

He swung the Corvette back onto the main road. Best to pretend he did not see them. Better the devil one knew than the devil one did not.

The gray car followed, maintaining a fairly long distance, but assuring him he was right. They would be gathering information generated from his vehicle—vectors, construction, code modules, all things that, in the hands of an expert, could eventually point to him. VR was a metaphorical place, but the images had real underpinnings. They could be recorded and perhaps traced—especially since if it was Net Force, they had enough computer power to brute-force their way through programmer profiles. The longer they stayed with him, the fewer possibilities they would have to sift. Before, he could have been one of tens or hundreds of thousands; now, every minute they stayed with him, that number fell. Every programmer had a style— and the best of them had styles that were as nearly as individual as fingerprints or DNA profiles. If they stayed with him long enough, they would suck his true identity out— or get so close they'd find him on a first or second pass through their strainers. It was a matter of knowing what to look for, of which questions to ask the search system.

Damn!

He was on the North EuroAsian Highway now, already through the Baltics and almost home. He couldn't go there, of course, but a sudden course change would engender suspicion in his pursuers. Too, he had to assume they weren't alone. There could be cars rolling ahead of him, others waiting at intersections for him to pass. If the little gray car was that of a Net Force or affiliated agent, then there almost certainly would be others around.

All right. He could turn off on the India Highway a hundred kilometers ahead, lead them south and away from home. He could park the car, go into a restaurant, bail from the scenario—

No, what was he thinking? That kind of panicky reflex would leave them the car and a possible way to trace it.

Something else . . .

It had worked once. Maybe it would work again. Maybe he could lose the chase car, take a side road, maybe duck other pursuit. Get away from this scenario and dump it.

Certainly worth a try.

He slowed, allowed the following car to draw a bit nearer. When he was ready, he drew the spikes from the pouch he carried, and with a quick and practiced hand, scattered them across all four lanes behind him, a sharp-pointed shower—

The pursuer swerved, missed most of the caltrops, but still ran over a few.

Aha!

His bright flare of triumph went dark quickly. The gray car's tires did not deflate, nor did it slow. If anything, it speeded up.

Damn, damn! They must suspect who he was, at least in this persona and vehicle. They knew what to expect, had hardened their program against his defense. Unfortunately, he didn't have much else in the way of armament—at least nothing that would stop people as good as these had to be. He had plenty of smoke-and-mirror programs, but they wouldn't do the trick here.

If he couldn't shake them, he couldn't lead them very far, either. They already knew too much. He could not take the risk they'd pull enough more information by osmosis to further narrow down their search. He wouldn't be able to make the India Road.

He had to get out of VR now!

The damage-to-system warning light flashed on his computer, along with the vox: "Warning! System Failure! Warning! System Failure!"

Plekhanov degeared and slapped at the power switch, killed the juice to his computer, not bothering with the emergency shut-down procedures. Data would be corrupted, the OS would be mangled and the VR was probably a total loss. None of that mattered when seconds counted for escape or capture.

Damn, damn, *damn*! How had they found him?

How much did they know?

Sunday, October 3rd, 3:10 p.m.
Quantico

Ahead of them, the Corvette exploded into a bright flash of light, then vanished.

"Shit!" Jay said.

"There he goes," Tyrone said to Bella. "He spotted us and crashed out." To Jay, he said, "You get anything useful?"

"Yeah, yeah, I think so. He was on the road to Central Asia—Russia, one of the CIS, maybe. He might have turned off at the India Road up ahead, or been going on through to the Orient, but if he was planning to head south, he should have cut that way a hundred klicks back. Besides, he doesn't drive like any Japanese or Korean I've ever seen. I think he was going home, and I think he drives like a Russian."

"What is he talking about?" Bella said.

Tyrone explained it to her, about programmers' styles.

"We're gonna have to take what we've got home and study it," Jay said. "Maybe we got enough to nail this sucker."

Sunday, October 3rd, 3:23 p.m.
Quantico

Michaels waved his phone circuit to life. "Yes?"

"Boss, Jay Gridley. We got something on the guy who has been giving us fits in Europe and Asia."

Michaels felt a quick stab of disappointment. Steve Day was higher up on his personal priority list right at the moment; still, the other business was more important for Net Force, even if his career did go down in flames. "That's great, Jay."

"I'll be in there as soon as I've tied up the loose ends," Jay added.

As soon as Michaels discommed, the phone cheeped again.

"Hello?"

"Hey, Dadster!"

"Hey, Kidster."

"You sleeping late?"

Three-thirty in the afternoon and she wanted to know if he was still in bed. He smiled. "Nope, I'm at work."

As a matter of course, Net Force had an agent keeping an eye on Susie, plus the local cops had been alerted, but there hadn't been any signs of trouble so far.

"Mom got the visual fixed. Scope it out."

The image of his daughter blinked onto his computer screen. She wore blue coveralls and a red T-shirt. Her hair was shorter than he remembered; she must have gotten it cut. What a beautiful child she was, a younger image of her mother. That was a totally objective thought, of course, her being beautiful. He grinned, tapping the camera control to send his visual to her.

"Whoa, Dadster, you look like Drac's old granny."

"Who is Drac's granny?"

"Come *on*, you don't watch *Drac's Pack*? It's only the

number-one entcom *any*where, Dad! Vince O'Connell is
Drac, Stella Howard is his wife, Brad Thomas Jones is the
son? The old granny is the mom from *Chunk Monks*? Are
you living on the moon?''

He grinned again. ''I haven't had much chance to watch
the entcom casts lately.''

''It's a great show, you should watch it. Anyway, you
look awful. You're not sick, are you?''

''Nope. Just tired. Working too hard, not getting enough
rest. But I got a dog, though.''

''A *dog*? An *RW* dog, not a sim?''

''Yep.''

''What kind? When did you get it? Will you bring it
with you when you come for my play? How big is it?
What's its name? What color is it? Is it smart?''

He laughed. ''It's a toy poodle, his name is Scout and
he's about as big as a medium-sized cat. He's pretty smart.
I think he'll like you.''

''Too *shiny*!'' She glanced off camera, then yelled:
''Mom! Dad got a *dog*! He's going to bring it when he
comes to visit!''

He heard his ex-wife mutter something in the background.

''You think he'll like me?''

''I'm sure he will, sweetie.''

Watching her, the thought about leaving Washington and
moving out West came up again. It sounded better all the
time. Of course, he would rather go out with his banner
held high, not dragging in the dust. But still. . . .

Well. The clock was running. He needed to finish this,
whatever else he did. Steve Day wasn't going to be forgotten. No way.

Sunday, October 3rd, 4:00 p.m.
Long Island, New York

Ray Genaloni glanced at his watch. Traffic, even this far out on Long Island on a damned Sunday, was terrible. Of course, he was in the back of a limo with his driver having to deal with it, but even so, it pissed him off. Every minute he spent stuck in a crawl of cars and trucks was one more he wouldn't get to spend with Brigette.

It wasn't as though he didn't get out here once or twice a week. And it wasn't as if Brigette was the best thing ever to pull off her skirt. He'd had better, a couple of times, actually. On the other hand, she was drop-dead gorgeous, ten years younger than he was, and willing to do anything he asked—stuff he would never *think* about mentioning to his wife, much less trying to *do*.

When he got to Brigette's place—a little house he'd bought for her on a cul-de-sac in a quiet neighborhood among far bigger and more expensive houses—Genaloni sat in his car until his guards in the car in front of his got out and did a quick check of the area. When he came out here, he always had two or three guys in a car in front of the limo, and a couple more in a car behind it. They stayed outside until he was done, even though nobody had ever tried to follow him out here as far as he could tell.

He rang the bell, and his mistress opened the door, dressed in a transparent black silky thing that went from her neck to the floor but hid absolutely nothing. Her grandparents had come from Sweden or Denmark or somewhere like that, and she was big, busty, and fit. You could also see she was a natural blonde. She had two glasses of champagne in her hands, the glasses still frosted from the freezer.

"Hi, handsome. My husband is out. Want to come in and have a drink?"

He smiled. Sometimes they played games. He took a

glass of champagne and stepped in past her. He knew she was giving his bodyguards a show, and he liked that. *Suffer, boys,* he thought.

As soon as she closed the door, he slid one hand underneath the silk thing and cupped one of her breasts. No silicone here, just smooth, warm boob.

"Well. If that's what you want, we'd better hurry before my husband gets home."

"He can wait his turn," Genaloni said.

Sunday, October 3rd, 2:01 p.m.
Las Vegas

Even in the airport, there were machines: slot machines, poker machines, keno machines, electronic beggars lined up to take your money as you walked to your flight. The walls were plastered with giant viewscreens showing dazzling stage magicians, wild-animal acts, and showgirls clothed only in glitter.

Ruzhyó watched as the Snake stopped and fed a dollar bill into one of the slot machines, then cranked the big handle and waited expectantly. The machine whirled its bright colors, then clicked to a stop. Grigory the Snake shook his head, grinned, shrugged. He was not a winner.

"Don't know when to quit, does he?" Winters said.

Ruzhyó did not speak to that, though it was certainly true. In three days here, Grigory had lost at least five thousand dollars gambling. His one small winning streak at the blackjack tables had ended quickly. In addition to his losses, he had probably spent another two thousand dollars on whores. Of course, it was his money, and he was well paid by Plekhanov; still, seven thousand dollars would provide food and shelter for an average family back home for, what? Nearly two years? Grigory was a fool, a waste of oxygen.

"I have a call to make," Ruzhyó said. "Let him spend whatever he wants until the plane leaves. We have more than an hour."

"I'm gonna mosey on over to that gift shop, pick up a magazine."

Ruzhyó nodded. He moved to a bank of public telephones, clamped a one-time scrambler over the mouthpiece and dialed the emergency number. The call took a few seconds, since it was being rerouted five or six times around the world on its way. He was not worried, at least not much, but Plekhanov had missed the last two scheduled calls, on Friday and Saturday, and this was the procedure in such a case.

"Yes," came Plekhanov's voice. It was terse.

"All is well?"

"Basically. There has been an unexpected glitch. A small thing, but a bit worrisome."

Ruzhyó waited to hear whatever it was Plekhanov wanted him to hear. It was not long in coming.

"That . . . engineering matter you began has not been completed to my satisfaction."

Ruzhyó knew they were speaking of the action to divert Net Force's attention—the assassination of its leader, the dragon's teeth sown to put that organization at war with the criminal group. He said, "It is early, yet."

"Nonetheless, we need to bring that matter along. The small glitch of which I spoke has arisen from that direction, and requires an earlier completion date for the overall project."

"I see."

"An attempt was made to, ah, duplicate your first experiment. By someone in the employ of the Italian company. They were unable to match your end results."

So. The Genaloni organization had tried kill the new head of Net Force and failed. Most interesting. He had not seen anything on the news about this.

"And you want me to take care of that?"

"Very likely. However, I would like you to wait for my signal. It might be premature. I should know in a day or two."

"As you wish."

"It would perhaps be prudent to locate yourself close to that area."

"Of course."

"Good-bye, then. I will speak to you tomorrow."

"Good-bye."

Ruzhyó removed the one-time scrambler and stared at it. The visual-purple biomolecular matrix that was the brain of the device would begin dying the moment the pressure switch left the phone's mouthpiece. In twenty seconds, the device's memory would be blank, the circuitry dead. It was a nice toy, a slopover from fighter-jet research. If one had a jet crash in enemy territory, one did not wish for the computer systems to be recovered. Electronic storage was difficult to wipe completely clean, but a bio-unit, once it was completely dead, was impossible to bring back.

He stood there holding the scrambler for a full minute, then dropped it into the trash.

So, they would be going to Washington again. Actually, to a motel in Maryland, less than an hour's drive away.

Grigory wandered over, away from the row of slot machines.

"Are you done gambling?" Ruzhyó asked.

"*Da.*"

Ruzhyó could not resist a small verbal jab. A needle, just enough to sting. He said, "Your system apparently needs some refinement."

The Snake frowned. Ruzhyó took a certain amount of pleasure in the expression.

30

Toni Fiorella stepped out of Net Force HQ into the cool evening air and headed for her car. The parking lot was nearly empty, of cars or pedestrians, but angling toward her, carrying a briefcase, was a figure she recognized.

"Rusty. What's up?"

She saw him take a deep breath. "I've been doing some research on *silat,* got into some material on the net, a couple of books and old tapes. I was, ah, wondering, could we, you know, go over some of the stuff? I'd like to get your opinion on it." He waggled the briefcase.

"Sure. I'll look at it."

"Well, good, thanks. But you know, I could show it to you at supper. I mean, we, that is—you want to get something to eat?"

Toni stopped and blinked. He had obviously been waiting out here for her to leave. It certainly sounded as if he was asking her out on a date. And the question that brought up was, *if* he was, did she want to go down that path?

Ever alert, the voice of rationalization popped up: *Dinner couldn't hurt. You have to* eat, *don't you?*

She grinned to herself. A quick test of Rusty's resolve might be in order. "Are you asking me out?"

If he wanted an escape hatch, there it was. *Why, no, I was just suggesting that we eat while we discussed this here* silat *stuff I have here in this here briefcase.*

"Yes, ma'am, I guess I am."

She laughed. "Ask a woman out and then call her 'ma'am.' That's probably as polite as I've ever heard it."

So. What is it to be, Toni? He's a student, but he is also an attractive man. Fit, bright, relatively adept. Got a nice legal degree to go with his FBI trainee status. Dating him might do bad things to the teacher-student relationship. And it certainly would put a kink in the line she wanted to establish with Alex.

Jesus, girl, if you wait for Alex to notice you as a woman, you might die of old age before it happens. Besides, it's just supper—he didn't ask to you bear his children or anything.

"All right. I suppose we can have something to eat. Where is your car?"

"Home. I came in on the Trans."

"Okay. We'll take my car. You have any place in mind?"

"Nope. It's not the food, it's the company. You pick."

She smiled again. He was charming, in his flattering Southern way.

Despite herself, Toni felt a little surge of adrenaline. Outside of work, it had been a long time since she'd been out with a man socially. And it was always nice for the old ego to be asked.

Dinner wouldn't hurt anybody.

Alex took Scout for a walk in his neighborhood. This was much against the wishes of his new security team, so actually what he wound up doing was sponsoring a small parade though the streets around his condo. And the party was somewhat larger than he had realized. There were four agents in two cars, one in front and one in back, inching along at walking speed. There were four men on foot, one in front, one behind him and the dog, and two more across the street forming the corners of a moving box. In addition, he'd been told, another two cars roamed the streets that ran parallel to his, and two *more* cars covered the cross streets. Some of the cars only had one person in them. Fourteen agents in all, the chief bodyguard had told him.

It seemed like an excessive use of the taxpayers' money to have that many people guarding him, but his boss had signed the order personally.

Scout didn't seem to mind the company. He watered lawns, signposts, and fire hydrants. Growled at hidden dangers in clumps of bushes that couldn't possibly hide anything any bigger than he was. Had himself a fine old time.

Michaels enjoyed the walk himself. It was a bit cooler than it had been, still not cold enough to need a jacket, though he wore a windbreaker so he could carry his taser in the pocket, close at hand. If somebody did manage to breach all his security, at least he could defend himself.

Caution—fear—was a new feeling for him. It was not something he'd ever worried about before, actual physical danger. He was a fair-sized man, in pretty good shape, living in the hub of civilization. He'd had some training, years ago when he'd joined the agency, in unarmed self-defense, with guns and with the taser, but right now that wasn't much comfort. He was not very good at such things, and, he knew, he was not at heart a violent man.

The last time he had been in a fight had been in the seventh grade. It had been with a boy named Robert Jeffries. They'd bumped into each other in the hall between classes, and though it had been Jeffries's fault, he had gotten pissed off and told Michaels to meet him after school. That was the last thing Michaels wanted to do, but he was too afraid of looking bad to skip out. In those days, like most of his friends, he believed it was better to get beaten up than to be thought a coward.

So, with his gut churning, terrified and almost paralyzed with fear, he met Jeffries by the bike racks.

They took their jackets off and circled each other, neither wanting to make the first move. This close, he could see that Jeffries was pale, sweaty, breathing fast, and it dawned on Michaels that Jeffries had had time to think about things, and *he* was also afraid.

So, if neither of them wanted to do this, why were they fighting?

They might have talked the talk, pushed each other a couple of times, then backed off, but some boys in the crowd gathered to watch shoved them at each other.

Jeffries came in swinging, wild, wide, looping roundhouse punches.

What exactly happened had never been clear in Michael's mind. One moment, there were fists bouncing off his shoulders and head—fists he couldn't feel, and couldn't seem to avoid, even though they came at him in slow motion and dead silence.

The next moment, he had Jeffries on the ground, was sitting on his chest, his knees pinning the other boy's arms.

Thus holding his opponent trapped, Michaels could have pounded his face to a pulp—Jeffries couldn't have stopped him. But he hadn't hit him, he'd just held him down.

Jeffries had squirmed, bucked, twisted, screamed for Michaels to let him up.

No fucking way, Michaels had said. *Not until you call it quits. I'll sit here all night.*

It had seemed like hours, though it was probably only a minute or so. When Jeffries realized he couldn't buck Michaels off, he agreed to end the fight. They called it a draw, and Michaels was thrilled to let it go at that. . . .

Scout stopped, marked a weed as his territory and scratched some grass over it with his hind legs.

Michaels smiled at the memory of his boyhood fistfight. He'd been what, all of thirteen? A long time ago.

But the smile faded at the more recent memory of Scout's former owner and the look on her face as she'd prepared to brain him with her cane. It wasn't a bloody nose or a black eye she'd had in mind, but a corpse. *His* corpse. That knowledge made Michaels feel a vulnerability he had never known before.

He could have died. Whack! A cracked skull, just like that, and he'd never have woken up. Ever.

Intellectually, he knew he was going to die someday. Everybody's path led that way. But emotionally, it had never come home to him until he'd sat there in his kitchen after the would-be assassin had fled, sat trembling, the taser gripped in his hand, waiting for his people and the police to arrive. He hadn't been afraid during the actual fight. But afterward . . . ?

He *had* been afraid. He'd felt . . . helpless.

He hated it, that sick feeling of helplessness. Yeah, he had chased the would-be killer. He hadn't run away or anything, but even though he had *done* the right thing, he hadn't *felt* brave. He realized he didn't have the skill he needed. And now, he needed to do something about that lack of skill, get a handle on it somehow. Maybe he should talk to Toni. She was an expert—he had seen that for himself. Before, he hadn't been interested. But now? Maybe she would teach him some of what she knew.

What was that definition he'd heard? A conservative was a liberal who had been mugged?

Yes. The idea of being able to take a stick away from somebody and keep himself in one piece while he did it had a great appeal to Alex Michaels just now. He wasn't always going to have a platoon of armed guards protecting him. He needed to be able to do that himself, or he wasn't going to be able to leave his home without feeling fear. And being afraid was no way to live. He wasn't going to bow to that. No way.

Sunday, October 3rd, 8:09 p.m.
Washington, D.C.

It had been a long and exciting day for Tyrone. As Bella walked him downstairs to the front door, he wondered how a day could get much more exciting. First there was Bella, then the business helping Jay Gee with the mad programmer in the Corvette. It wasn't every day you got to take a beautiful and bright girl out on a VR chase that was also an official Net Force investigation. His dad had been right—let Bonebreaker match *that,* if he could.

At the door, Bella said, "Thanks for the help, Ty. And letting me go with you on the Net Force thing. It was giganto excitamento. Let me know how it turns out, okay?"

"Sure. I don't think you'll have any trouble with the class, now. You got this stuff glued tight."

He opened the door and turned to say good night.

Bella leaned over and kissed him on the lips. It was soft, quick, but if he lived to be a million, he would never forget that warm and unexpected touch. He couldn't have been more stunned if she'd whacked him on the head with a hammer. "Call me sometime," she said. "We'll do something. Mall rawl, BurgerBarn, something."

His brain stalled, his mouth shorted out. When he got partial control back, he managed a stammer: "Wh-wh-what about Bonebr—uh, I mean what about LeMott?"

"He doesn't own me. We aren't *married*." She smiled. "See you." She closed the door.

Tyrone stood there, staring at the door, unable to move, to think, maybe even breathe. When his brain came back he had no idea how long he'd been a statue. Could have been a few seconds, could have been a couple of centuries. How could time mean anything after what she had said?

"Call me sometime," she said. "We'll do something. . . ."

Oh, *man*!

His feet must have been on the ground as he walked toward the Trans station, but Tyrone could hardly tell.

So this what it was like to be in love.

Sunday, October 3rd, 10:01 p.m.
Washington, D.C.

In her apartment, Toni looked at the black plastic tape box Rusty handed her. "Where did you get this?"

"I found it on the webpage for a bookstore in Alabama a couple of days ago. It just got here this morning. I don't have a VHS player, so I haven't had a chance to see it yet."

Toni looked at the box. The pictures on the back of the box showed a short-haired man in a light shirt and tan slacks doing a block and *sapu* against a large, ponytailed man in jeans and a dark jacket. The box had apparently gotten wet at some point, because most of the rest of the back was so water-stained and faded it couldn't be made out. She could see that it was a production of Paladin Press, copyright 1999. She knew about them. They produced off-beat books and vids, everything from a dozen ways to kill somebody with common items in your kitchen cabinet, to hardcore gun and sword texts. They were out in Colorado somewhere, if she recalled right.

On the front of the box, part of the faded illustration had been torn off, but the title, *Pukulan Pentjak Silat: The Devastating Fighting Art of Bukti Negara-Serak, Volume Three,* was still readable. She felt a quick rush of excitement. She hadn't known anybody had made tapes of her art. And this was the third in a series. ''Well, let's see if my player still works, I haven't used it in a while.''

She moved to the multimedia player, and pushed the tape into the VHS slot. The machine lit. She clicked on the television, and went back to sit on the couch next to Rusty.

The tape opened with a credit sequence, followed by the guy in tan slacks walking into an alley. A man in the alley was moving something, asked for help, and all of a sudden, three more attackers jumped out from behind Dumpsters or doorways. One of the muggers had a knife, another a baseball bat. All four went for Tan Slacks. What was his name? She had missed it in the credits. Never mind, she'd get it later.

In five seconds, all four of the attackers were on the ground, having gotten there with considerable impact. Toni watched carefully. She would want to see this again in slomo, the guy moved so fast. *Silat* wasn't pretty, there weren't any fancy stances artfully held, but it certainly worked.

The scene changed, and the guru stood on a mat against the background of a pastel blue wall. He wore a black T-shirt with cut-off sleeves and a classical sarong. The shirt had the *Bukti* emblem on it: a *garuda* bird with the tiger face on its chest, over a pair of *tjabang* tridents. The guru looked fit, fairly muscular, and very confident. She wondered what he'd be like now, more than ten years later.

Toni turned to Rusty. "This is great. I'm glad you let me see it."

"I bought it for you," he said. "I figured you'd appreciate it more than I would."

She smiled. "Thank you. That was nice of you." She put her hand on his arm.

The moment stretched. The gesture was a simple touch, nothing more, and it meant nothing more than a slight emphasis to her thanks.

Unless she left her hand there.

The moment continued.

Toni decided.

She did not pull her hand away.

31

Suddenly aware of how stiff and tired he felt, Jay Gridley looked at the clock.

Wow. He'd been up all night.

He had scanned enough material to fill a tanker, but now he had a better sense of the programmer they'd chased. Before, they hadn't had diddly, but now that they'd gotten a closer look, a picture was starting to resolve. The guy had the earmarks of somebody trained in the CIS, and Gridley was betting he was a Russian. Not a firm ID, but it sure narrowed things down considerably.

He tapped at the keyboard, using RW mode instead of VR. This was slogwork, basic number- and word-crunching, and he wanted the raw data where he could see it for what it was. He had the Net Force scanning main-frame winnowing possibilities and feeding him those that were within the parameters. Currently, the computer was going through all registered programmers living in Russia.

They were gonna get this lubefoot. It was just a matter of time. . . .

The priority incoming e-mail chime sounded. Gridley shook his head. The tags were in place on the winnow; if something showed up, his station would scream at him. He shifted to the mail and opened it.

Hmm. The incoming was from one of the field teams. They had, they said, something on the Day assassination.

Well, okay, that was important, too. Not as important as the programmer, at least not in Gridley's mind—Day was dead and he'd be dead forever. Nobody could hurt him anymore, but the net was still taking hits. Then again, catching a killer was nothing to turn one's back on. And everybody knew that if they didn't come up with something soon, the boss's head was gonna roll. That was how things always worked around here.

Gridley downloaded the attached file and opened it. It didn't take long for him to see the meat of the message.

Well, well. Look at that. . . .

Monday, October 4th, 5:05 a.m.
Washington, D.C.

Megan Michaels was on the front porch of their house, holding hands with a dark-haired, burly man. The two of them kissed. The man slid his hands down her back, cupped her buttocks. She moaned softly, then turned and saw Alex standing there. She smiled at him. "I'm his now," she said. "Not yours." She reached over, put her hand on the man's crotch—

Michaels came out of the nightmare, thick with jealousy and anger.

Dammit!

Scout was asleep, curled into a tight little ball near Alex's feet. There was a new dog bed on the floor next to the TV console, a top-of-the line hand-woven basket with a pillow full of cedar shavings, but the dog declined to use it unless Michaels made him. Somehow, ordering a dog who'd saved his life to sleep on the floor didn't seem right; besides, if Scout wanted to sleep on the bed, well, it was plenty big enough. It wasn't as if he was a mastiff.

When Michaels awoke, Scout raised his head and looked at him. He must have decided nothing was wrong, because he relaxed and recurled himself after a moment.

Walt Carver had a ten a.m. meeting with the President. If Net Force did not have anything new for him to bring to the table regarding Steve Day's assassination, Net Force would grow itself a new head—as soon as Alex Michaels's got lopped off. . . .

Hell with it. He got up and shuffled toward the bathroom.

Scout stood, stretched himself like a cat, hopped off the bed and came to stand next to Michaels. The dog sat, then watched intently as the stream of urine splashed into the toilet bowl. What was Scout thinking? That this was a bit of territory the man was marking as his own?

"Yep, this is my toilet, all right," Michaels said. "Mine, mine, mine."

Scout yipped in acknowledgment.

Monday, October 4th, 5:05 a.m.
Washington, D.C.

Toni lay in her bed, staring at the ceiling. Naked next to her under the covers, Jesse "Rusty" Russell slumbered on, breathing heavy.

Oh, Lord. Why had she done this?

She glanced at the man next to her. Rusty was attractive, smart, sexy. She had certainly enjoyed the taste and feel of him, and it had been quite an athletic and satisfying romp. The bought-long-ago condoms she had dug from under the panties and bras in her dresser drawer were still a few months shy of their expiration date. She and Rusty were adults, they weren't married to anybody else, so—who got hurt?

This was all true, and yet, it still wasn't right. Why did she feel so guilty? What was she doing here with this . . . *stranger* in her bed? There was a sense of unreality about it, as if it were a dream, not really happening to her. A feeling that also bordered on the edge of nausea. She felt a kind of sick dread. As if she had done something terribly, terribly wrong.

It should be Alex lying there, sated, happy, in love with her. It should mean something. She liked Rusty okay, he was a nice enough man, but he wasn't somebody she was going to spend her life with, or even any big piece of her life. She knew that. He'd been a considerate and experienced lover. The sex had been fun—she'd be lying to herself if she pretended anything else—but sex by itself wasn't enough, no matter how good it might be. There needed to be more, a lot more. She liked Rusty, but she didn't love him.

She loved *Alex*.

Right. So how could she have done this? And how was she going to be able to look Alex in the eye now? She had been unfaithful to him.

Wait just a second, girl, the voice of rationalization began.

Shut up, she told it.

Next to her, Rusty stirred.

She should get up, shower, get dressed. She didn't want

him to awaken and expect a repeat of last night. It had been enjoyable, but it had also a mistake—and she was not going to repeat it.

Monday, October 4th, 5:05 a.m.
Columbia, Maryland

Ruzhyó sat cross-legged on the motel bed, staring at nothing. He was not bored—he did not get bored anymore, hadn't for years—but he was not very interested in much of anything. It did not greatly bother him, but he was aware of his lack of connection to the world.

Plekhanov would eventually call; today, tomorrow, the day after. Likely when he did call, the Russian who had adopted Chechnya as his own would, using the fugue of non-specific and indirect language, order Ruzhyó to go forth and kill again. It would be part of Plekhanov's grand plan to become a powerful man who could run countries as he chose. In the beginning, Plekhanov's reasons had been important to Ruzhyó. Now, that Plekhanov wished a thing to happen was sufficient in itself. Ruzhyó was the tool that did the deed; it was his only reason for staying alive.

Live. Die. It was all the same.

Monday, October 4th, 7:30 a.m.
Quantico

Jay was waiting when Michaels arrived at his office. He was smiling.

"You have good news?"

"Oh, yeah."

"Come in."

In the office, Jay said, "Take a look. If I may?" He waved at Michaels's workstation.

"Be my guest."

Jay lit the system, called up a file.

"This is the report from our field team in New York State," the younger man said. "And this—"—he tapped keys, and an image flowered on-screen—"—is the Not the Brothers Dog Kennel. Located on the beautiful eastern shores of Great Scandaga Lake, between the hamlets of North Broadalbin and Fish House."

Michaels stared at Jay.

"That's north and west of Amsterdam, which is north and west of Schenectady, which is north and west of Albany, which is—"

"I got it, Jay."

"Mm. Anyway, this is where the little champagne poodle was trained."

"Really?"

"Yep. One of a handful of places that do such things. They'll train your dog, sell you one already educated, or even rent you one. That's what happened with yours. He's a rental." Jay smiled.

"Of course, they never saw who they rented the dog to. This woman is really sharp, Boss. Cash and instructions came by courier. The note was a computer printout, and the FBI doc-jock says the font and paper probably originated at one of the big print-copy places—Kinko's, LazerZip, no way to backwalk it to which one.

"Our ops traced the dog's delivery to another courier, then a third delivery service, which wound up giving it to somebody waiting in the lobby of a new Holiday Inn in north Schenectady. The courier remembers that a man signed for the dog, paid more cash. Average-looking guy, courier wouldn't know him if he saw him again."

"This doesn't sound too promising to me."

"Ah, but wait. The Holiday Inn is one of the new computer-controlled modules. They've got hidden surveillance cams built in all over the place. Take a look at this."

Jay touched more controls.

"Here's the guy who picked up the dog."

There was a image of a man holding a small plastic travel kennel. He was obviously outside, in some kind of courtyard. A lot of greenery and flowers were in the background. The man was medium-height, medium-build, medium-haircut, wore a shirt and slacks and dark shoes. Albert Anybody.

"And *here* is the woman he gave it to."

Another image, a three-quarter-front view of a woman standing in front of the man with the kennel. She looked about forty, had graying brown hair worn long, was a little dumpy, sported sunglasses, a baggy, long-sleeved shirt, baggy pants and running shoes. Angela Anybody.

"The hotel security cams shoot three frames a second, so if we let it run, it looks pretty jerky, but we've got six or eight real good images of the woman.

"She doesn't look anything like the old lady," Michaels said. "And what's to say she's not wearing a disguise here?"

"Our guys in ID say she probably *is* disguised—the size of her neck and wrists, the thinness of her face and hands don't really go with the weight of her torso and hips. Probably she's padded."

"So how does this help us?"

"Well. Computer-enchanted imagery says she probably didn't alter the shape of her ears or her hands, and using objects in view that we know the measurements of—that planter there, or those decorative bricks—we can tell her shoe size, her height, we can come pretty close on her true weight if we extrapolate from wrists and neck diameter. The hair is probably a wig, so that's no help, but the images give us a good view of her wrists and hands, and the techs in the FBI Skin Lab tell us that she's not wearing makeup there, so she's probably a natural redhead, to judge from her skin tone.''

''They can tell that?''

''It's still more art than science, but they say they are about eighty-five-percent sure.''

''Hmm.''

''There's a little more. Watch.''

Jay played the recording. The woman took the travel kennel, turned and started away. An image from a different viewpoint appeared—must be another cam, Michaels reasoned. This was a higher angle, looking down at the woman coming head-on. As he watched, the woman carrying the kennel slipped on something.

''See how the floor is wet? They had just mopped the exitway there,'' Jay said. ''Didn't put up the warning sign yet.''

The next image showed the woman lurch to the left, put out her arm, stop herself with her free hand against the wall at shoulder height. She shoved off the wall and continued on her way.

''Nice recovery, hey?'' Jay said. ''Me, I'd probably have fallen on my butt, but she just hit that wall, pushed off like nothing, kept going, even carrying a dog. Didn't even slow her down.'' His grin was really big now.

Michaels made the connection. He looked at Jay. ''Prints?''

''Yep. How many people do you suppose slipped on the wet floor and fell against the wall at just that spot in the last month or two?

''She left a palm print, a clean index, middle, and ring fingerprint and a smudged pinky.''

Michaels nodded. This was a big deal. This might just save his ass.

"Oh, and did I mention? We got a few cells and a little useable DNA?"

"Dammit, Jay—"

Jay laughed. "Well, I didn't want to get your hopes up, Boss. It's hardly anything to play with, a few stutters—just enough to know it *is* a woman, what her blood type is, that's all."

"Jesus! Why didn't you say so to begin with?"

"That's not how you tell a story, Boss. You save the best for the end. Anyway, we don't have a match from the FBI, NCIC, UPolNet or AsiaPol files on prints or DNA profiles yet. It takes a while to run them all, but even if we don't get her that way, she's probably on record somewhere—DL, BioMed, BankSeal, somewhere. If she is, sooner or later she is going to pop up with red flags and sirens screaming. It's just a matter of time."

"This is outstanding work," Michaels said. "You did good, Jay."

"Nopraw."

"Excuse me?"

"Just an expression, Boss. It means 'no problem.' You gotta keep current, you know. And did I mention—she paid for the lost dog? Sent the money by courier again. We couldn't backtrack it this time, but that was nice of her, wasn't it?"

Michaels was elated, but he tried not to let it overwhelm him. "What about the other thing, the programmer?"

"Getting close to him. He's a Russian, Ukrainian, something like that. I got Baby Huey—the SuperCray mainframe—winnowing possibilities, checking profiles."

"I thought you said he could mask his profile."

"Oh, yeah, he can, but only partially. I got enough of his style down, I'll know him when I see him. It's like a painter. Everybody knows a Picasso when they see one, and how it doesn't look like a Renoir. Style is what gives it away. He's too good to hide all his talent. Some of it will seep out of any bushel he buries it under."

"Truly outstanding work, Jay. Thank you."

"Well, Boss, it *is* my job. But, uh, if you remember this when you do performance reviews and raises next time, I wouldn't mind."

Both men laughed.

"I should get back to it," Jay said. "I've dumped this into your folder, and I'll check in when I get something new."

"Thanks again."

After Jay left, Michaels called up the material and scanned it again, ordering it in his mind. When he was comfortable with it, he reached for his com to put in a call to Walt Carver. The Director was not going unarmed to his meeting with the President this morning. It might even be enough so Michaels would get to keep his job for a little while longer. His sense of relief was a surprise. It was a lot stronger than he would have thought. Maybe he wasn't quite as ready to chuck it all as he'd rationalized.

"Director Carver's office."

"Hey, June, it's Alex Michaels. He in yet?"

"Since six, Commander. Hold on a moment, I'll put you through."

As he waited for Carver, Michaels looked up and saw Toni pass by his window. He nodded at her, but she didn't make eye contact as she headed for her office. Well. Probably she was tired—they'd all been working without a break for too long. He'd call her in and let her know what Jay had found, as soon as he was done telling the Director. She'd be happy to hear the news.

"Good morning, Alex. You have good news for me?"

"Yes, sir, I believe so. Very good news."

32

The Selkie stood on the doorstep, holding a small box wrapped in expensive paper. She wore crisp, dark blue cotton slacks, a matching long-sleeved shirt and a baseball cap the same color. A few wisps of the blond wig peeped from under the cap, and she had on just enough makeup to look five years older than she was. The wrapped package was the size of a box a diamond necklace might fit into. The van parked behind her on the street was a rental, plain, white, with stolen tags in place. She looked the part of a delivery woman in the upscale neighborhood.

She rang the bell.

A minute passed. The Selkie rang the bell again.

"What?" came a sleepy voice from the intercom.

"I have a delivery from Steinberg's Jewelers for a Miz Brigette Olsen?"

"A delivery?"

Jesus, honey, which part of that didn't you understand?

The Selkie glanced at the clipboard she held. "From a Mr. Genaloni?"

"Hold on a sec."

The woman inside opened the door only as far as the chain latch would allow. From what the Selkie could see through the gap, Brigette was young, blond, busty, what the Irish called a fine strapping girl. She wore black silk pajamas and a faded blue bathrobe. And if the phone call that the Selkie had listened in on last night was correct, Brigette would receive a visit sometime today from Ray Genaloni. The Selkie was ready. Brigette extended one hand for the package. "Give it to me."

"I'll need you to sign for it, ma'am," the Selkie said. She waved the clipboard. She glanced at her watch, as if she had places to go, things to do.

Brigette hesitated.

The Selkie could probably boot the door and pop the safety chain loose. Those things were nearly always tacked on with short and useless screws, but she didn't really want to take the risk of somebody seeing her—kicking in the front door of a gangster's mistress in broad daylight was not the smart way to go. Or she could pull the small .22 pistol she had tucked into the inside-the-waistband holster, under her shirt, behind her right hip and threaten the woman—Open up, honey, or get drilled. But that was risky. And she definitely didn't want the woman dead.

One more bit of business and neither way would be necessary. "Oh, sorry, I almost forgot, there's a note I'm supposed to read." She unfolded a piece of paper from the clipboard. "Says here, 'Ray says wear this and nothing else for me this evening.' "

The Selkie stared at the ground, as if embarrassed.

Brigette laughed and undid the safety chain. "That's Ray, all right."

She opened the door.

People were so gullible.

Wednesday, October 6th, 11:46 a.m.
Quantico

Alex Michaels was on his way to the cafeteria, though he wasn't really very hungry. The hot leads of just two days ago had petered out. Jay Gridley's winnow of programmers living in Russia had come up blank. And the DNA and fingerprints of the woman who had collected Scout at a Schenectady, New York, hotel hadn't found a match on any of the systems they had checked.

Gridley had moved his search for the programmer into the surrounding CIS countries, and was also widening the net he'd thrown for the assassin, but so far zip on either.

Toni Fiorella had, it seemed to Michaels, been avoiding him. She'd missed a staff meeting, left early and generally looked at him as if he'd developed some highly contagious disease she didn't want to get close enough to catch.

Well, at least he still had his job. Once the Director had told the President they had pictures of Day's assassin and were going to be able to run her down in the near future, that had been enough.

Whether that was true or not was another matter, but certainly they were better off than they had been. It *was* going to happen sooner or later.

Ahead of him in the hall, Michaels saw John Howard walking toward the cafeteria. Howard saw him as he reached the entrance. He nodded. ''Commander.'' He was polite, but no more.

Michaels didn't understand why the colonel didn't like

him, but it was apparent he did not. "Colonel."

Howard moved off, not offering to eat and visit with his boss.

But Jay Gridley came bustling up, grinning, and Michaels filed Howard away to deal with later.

"Tell me you've got good news and that raise is a done deal," Michaels said.

"Well, I dunno how good it is, but, lemme see, I, uh, got the programmer. How's that?"

"No!"

"Yep, yep, yep! I was right, he's a Russian. Emigrated to Chechnya, been living there for years, that's why we missed him on the first passes." Jay held up his flatscreen so the image on it was visible.

"Commander, meet Vladimir Plekhanov."

Wednesday, October 6th, 3:30 p.m.
New York City

Genaloni glanced at the clock on his desk. Enough. He needed to get out of here. Shuffling forms, electronic or paper, was enough to drive you nuts after a couple of hours. He waved the intercom on. "Roger, get the car. We're going out to Brigette's."

"Yes, sir."

What he needed after being cooped up with the pressures of business all day was a place to unwind and somebody to cut loose with. Nothing like getting your ashes hauled to mellow you out. And if they left now, they'd beat most of the rush.

Being rich had its perks, all right.

Wednesday, October 6th, 3:40 p.m.
Long Island

Brigette had been extremely cooperative. As soon as she'd gotten over her surprise at seeing the pistol in the delivery woman's gloved hand, her first words had been:

"Oh, shit."

The tone hadn't been one of fear, but of irritation. As if she'd just discovered it was raining when she'd planned to lie in the sunshine.

Now, the van was parked a block over, in the driveway of a vacant house for sale—a chore the Selkie had done while Brigette had been handcuffed to her kitchen plumbing.

Back in place, she'd uncuffed the woman and allowed her to dress.

As she had been slipping into her black silk panties, Brigette had turned those sweet cornflower-blue eyes on the Selkie and said, "Are you going to kill me, too?"

No doubt in her mind as to why the Selkie was here. No brainless bimbo, this one.

"No, why should I? You do what you're supposed to do, Genaloni goes down, I'm gone."

"He'll have bodyguards with him. They'll be out front."

"How many?"

"A couple."

Apparently being cooperative again—but lying. Genaloni would have at least four guards, five if you counted his driver. One of them would be watching the back, too. Brigette was trying to cover her ass—more than the silk G-string she had on did. If her sugar daddy took the hit, she could hope his killer would let her live because she'd helped her. If Genaloni survived and the delivery woman fell, sweet Brigette could tell him how she'd lied to protect him.

"You don't seem too upset that your ride is about to get erased."

The blonde slipped on a natural-colored raw silk blouse, no bra under it, and buttoned it. She noticed the other woman's look. "He likes to see my nipples," she said. Then she shrugged. "He's a mob guy. It's a risky business. I have a little put away, and I don't figure I'll have much trouble getting another honey. If it was good enough for Genaloni, there will be other mob guys who'll want a taste."

The Selkie grinned. No sentimentality for this girl. She knew what she was and meant to make the most of it. The Selkie kind of liked that about Brigette, her being straight up and no bullshit.

"Somebody might blame you."

"Why should they? I'll let them wire me with a stressbox and I'll tell them the truth. You stuck a gun in my face— what could I do?"

"I guess that means you'll tell them what I look like, too, right?"

There was a moment of hesitation as Brigette scanned that, tried to put some spin on it. Then she said, "Yeah, I'll tell them. But that's a disguise, right?"

"What if they ask if it's a disguise?"

"I can get by that one."

This was getting interesting. "Really. How?"

Brigette pulled a microskirt up over her long legs, zipped it and tucked the blouse into it. "Depends on how you ask the question. If they ask, 'Do you think Ray's killer was wearing a disguise?' I can say, 'No,' and it'll scan as truth."

"Really?"

"Sure. Because I don't *think* you're wearing one, I *know* you are. I've been around makeup before."

The Selkie grinned. ''Why would you do that? Cover for me?''

''You could come back later and delete me if you think I ratted you out.''

Her logic was frail, but the Selkie didn't point that out. If Brigette did a good enough job ratting her out, the mob might find and kill Ray's assassin, and she wouldn't be around to threaten sweet Brigette's peace of mind.

Could she trust her? Uh-huh. Right. The Selkie had no doubt that her target's mistress would sing an entire opera when asked by those who wanted to hear it.

Brigette found a pair of silk stockings, bunched one into gathers, then slipped it onto her left foot and up her leg. The Selkie watched, intrigued by the woman's complete lack of modesty and emotion regarding the upcoming deletion.

Brigette caught the look. She smiled. ''You like women? I can show you a good time while we wait.''

The Selkie shook her head. ''Thanks. Not while I'm working.''

Ray's girl was a cool one, all right. The Selkie wouldn't want to be dangling over a cliff with sweet Brigette on the other end of the rope—not unless she had a wad of cash in her hand to bribe her to hang on to the lifeline.

Still, Brigette would be helpful. The Walther TPH .22 pistol the Selkie held was kind of a scaled-down version of James Bond's PPK. It was an excellent example of the gunmaker's art, the TPH, high-grade stainless steel, small and compact, very accurate. But the tiny .22 round was not a man-stopper out of a pistol unless it hit the central nervous system. A spine or brain shot was necessary for a certain kill. If, as Ray came up the walk, Brigette started screaming, a head shot would be difficult. Not impossible—she could make that shot with this piece out to twenty yards—but by that time, the TPH would be wearing the suppressor, to cut down on the firing noise. The barrel wasn't long enough to let the Stinger ammo achieve supersonic speed, and the suppressor would cut the velocity even more as it absorbed the exhaust gases with the sound. Unless you put the round into an eye, the target might survive. The skull was hard, bullets had been known to glance right off. And hitting an eye with the suppressor blocking the sights, well, that was iffy.

No, with a .22 handgun, you wanted to put the muzzle an inch or two from the back of the target's head, and pump three or four sound-suppressed rounds into the hindbrain while his bodyguards were sitting in their cars unaware. And be long gone before anybody came knocking.

She needed privacy to do this right. Brigette would get Genaloni into the house. Once the door was closed behind him, the Selkie would handle the rest.

Wednesday, October 6th, 6:00 p.m.
Quantico

The five o'clock meeting began an hour late. This was a small group—Michaels, Toni, Jay, Colonel Howard, and the new FBI computer liaison, Richardson—though the FBI guy couldn't stay long. From here on out, the information concerning this case was going to be NTK—need to know—only.

"All right," Michaels said. "You've all gotten the info-packet Jay put together. Any questions?"

Richardson said, "Yes. Once you've done a verification that this . . . Plekhanov is for certain the programmer we want, how do we proceed?"

Michaels said, "It is a little tricky. Ideally, we would contact the Chechen government and ask to have him extradited under the Net Criminal Agreement of 2004. This might not be a good idea. Jay, if you would?''

Jay nodded. ''Plekhanov probably has a standby security program for his most sensitive files. If the local police go barreling into his office or house and start tapping keys or pulling wires, chances are his system will lock itself up tighter than spandex before they figure out how to pull the plug. And even if not, his sensitive files are certain to be encrypted, 128s or maybe even 256s. He used to write the Russians' military ciphers. Without a key, it would take our SuperCray going full blast something like ten billion years to break the code. That's probably a little longer than we want to wait, so we can't get his system files without the key. If we don't get the files, we can't prove it's him, not enough for the legal guys to ask for indictments.''

''So, how do you do it?'' Howard asked.

''The ideal way is to look over his shoulder while he's got his system lit. Either that, or get the key.''

''And that's only part of the problem,'' Michaels said. ''Jay?''

''I've done a little background on this guy. Turns out he's got links to some pretty high government officials all over. He's done a lot of legitimate security work, for the Russians, the Indians, the Thais, the Australians, you name it. He's got money—a nice chunk on the legal books— talking a couple of million personal net, and no doubt a lot more illegal money stashed. That bank robbery in New Orleans probably wasn't his first.''

''So we have a rich guy with clout,'' Toni said. ''And even if the Chechens were willing to nab him and hand him over, we can't nail him without evidence we can't get?''

''That pretty much sums it up,'' Michaels said.

Howard said, ''If this guy is rich and powerful, why is he doing this? Why take the risk?''

Michaels nodded, glad to see his people were paying

attention. "There's the big question. What does he want?"

"*More* money, *more* power," Richardson said. "He's greedy."

"Probably," Michaels said. "But I've been going over the information, and what it seems like to me is that he's driving at something specific. Some of the system crashes have been directly beneficial to him—Jay has the particulars—but some have not. Even if some of that is just blowing smoke to cover his trail, there seems to be a pattern. He's going someplace in particular. Before we try to grab him, it might be wise of us to see if we can figure out where that place is. He might have help, and it would be good for us to gather them all in."

Before he could continue, the door to the conference room opened. Michaels's secretary stood there. She wasn't supposed to interrupt unless it was an emergency, and Michaels's first fear was that something had happened to his wife—*ex*-wife, dammit—or his daughter. But before he had more than a flash of panic, his secretary put that to rest:

"Commander, there is some news from New York you need to hear. It's about Ray Genaloni."

33

Brigette's doorbell rang. "Oh, Jesus," she said.

"Go let him in. Remember, I'll be standing where I can see you and he can't see me. If there are any sudden moves, anything at all, I'll drop you before I do anything else."

"Okay. I understand."

Brigette headed for the door.

Here was where it got dangerous. The Selkie didn't think Brigette would do anything stupid—she was betting a lot on that. If it went sour before Genaloni got inside, she had four .22 magazines loaded for the Walther, twenty-four extra rounds, plus the seven in the gun. And the remainder of a box of Stingers in her pants pocket, though if it came to her needing more than thirty-one rounds, she was going to be in deep shit.

"Hey, baby. Come in. My husband just left."

Genaloni laughed and stepped into the house.

The Selkie moved back out of sight, the pistol held in both hands by her right ear, muzzle pointed at the ceiling.

She now wore surgical gloves, had not touched the pistol or magazines with her bare hands since she'd scrubbed and cleaned them last night. She took a deep breath, let it out slowly. Adrenaline surged over her in warm rushes.

"I can't get the wire thing off the champagne bottle, Ray. The little round part twisted loose."

"I'll get it. In the kitchen?"

"Uh-huh. In the ice bucket." Oh, she was cool. Not a hint of nervousness in her voice.

The Selkie moved into the open closet behind her, smelled the fresh scent of new, unworn dresses that still had the tags on them. She pulled the door almost closed. Genaloni and Brigette walked past her hiding place, never glanced in her direction.

The Selkie stepped out behind them as they entered the kitchen.

"Don't move," she said.

Genaloni knew what was going down from those two words, and he knew Brigette's part in it. "Shit. You lousy fucking whore."

"I'm sorry, Ray, she made me do it! She has a gun!" This was the most excited-sounding Brigette had been all day.

"Hands high and wide, Genaloni."

He obeyed. "Can I turn around?"

"Sure."

He did. When he saw her, he nodded. "So. You must be the Selkie, right? Why this?"

"You know why. Your people tried to find me. You were told a long time ago that's not allowed."

He didn't try to lie. "Shit. They were supposed to be good."

"Not good enough."

"All right. So you spotted them. What's the deal? Money? A guarantee we won't try to look for you again?"

She already had the pistol lined up on his right eye. At this range, she didn't need sights. She could point-shoot a marble off a tabletop all day long without scratching the finish, just using the gun and suppressor to index the target.

"How much money are we talking about?"

He grinned, thinking he had her number.

He was wrong.

The pistol's hand-polished action was honed to a crisp three-pound pull for the single-action mode, no creep. The Selkie squeezed the trigger gently. The shot broke like an icicle under her finger. It sounded like an air rifle, a *spat!* nobody would hear outside this room.

The tiny bullet hit Ray Genaloni in the white of his right eye. He went boneless and fell, his brain shorted out by the lead bouncing around inside his skull.

"Oh, Jesus!" Brigette said. "Oh, Jesus!"

Because she liked Brigette a little, and because she wasn't a cruel woman, the Selkie said, "Calm down. You're all right. I'm going now, take it easy—who's that at the door?"

Brigette turned to look.

The Selkie fired twice—*spat! spat!*—and double-tapped Brigette in the right temple. The blonde fell. She kicked spasmodically as damaged brain connections triggered a last frantic try to run away. It was an instinctive reaction— the mind that had been Brigette wasn't home any longer. And she had checked out thinking she was going to survive this.

The Selkie moved fast. She bent, put two more shots into the back of Brigette's head, then two more in the back of Ray's skull. The gun worked perfectly—she had polished the feed ramp with steel wool until it gleamed like a mirror, then coated it with TW-25B, a fluorocarbon-based military-spec lubricant. She never had a failure to feed, even with the hollowpoint Stingers. She pressed the heel catch on the pistol, pulled the empty magazine out and shoved another magazine home. She put the empty magazine into her pants pocket, racked the slide on the TPH, stripped and chambered a round. Then she changed magazines again, putting a fresh six-rounder into the gun. One up the spout, magazine full. Seven shots on tap.

She looked around. She hadn't left any prints anywhere. The empty cases from the .22 were clean—she'd loaded them fresh from the box while wearing gloves. They could make something from the extractor and firing-pin marks on the brass rimfire empties, but since she was going to dump the gun as soon as she could, that didn't matter. Even if some diver found the piece twenty years from now, there wouldn't be anything to link it to her—she'd bought it clean on the gray market. Too bad. She really liked the Walther, but you didn't keep murder weapons around once they were used. The prisons were full of shooters who got attached to favorite pieces and kept them after they'd cooked somebody with them. Stupid.

She looked down at the bodies. They both had thought they were going to walk away when she'd dropped them, and they'd been effectively dead before they had time to realize any different. There were worse ways to go.

Okay, now the second part.

She moved to the back door, peeped through a gap in the blinds covering the window next to the door. A big man in a gray sweatsuit stood inside the fence, next to the gate. He was smoking a cigarette, and he had a belly pouch drooped heavily over his crotch. That was where he'd have his gun. Good. A belly pouch was a lot slower than a holster.

She needed to get him away from the gate and closer to the backdoor, out of line of sight from the front, in case anybody was looking at him.

She had spent the better part of the day with Brigette.

She could do enough of an imitation of her voice to fool somebody who might have heard it no more than a couple of times.

She took a deep breath. Opened the door. "Excuse me? Could you come here a second? Ray needs a hand."

The sweatsuited bodyguard ambled toward the back door. As soon as any view of him from the front was blocked by the house, the Selkie stepped out into the yard.

Sweatsuit frowned. The Selkie wasn't what he expected to see.

His reaction time was pretty good, but his tactics were bad. Instead of ducking his head, bolting and trying to hop the fence, which might possibly have gotten him clear with a couple of small-caliber rounds in the back, he dug for the pistol in his pouch.

The fastest gunslinger who ever lived couldn't move fast enough to outdraw a gun already lined up on him. The reaction time, plus the mechanical time it took to come from the holster—even from a quick-draw rig, he'd need at least a third of a second, even if he was really fast. Coming out of a belly pouch, this guy was going to need two seconds to get his piece on-line, and he didn't have two seconds.

The Selkie squeezed off her first shot before the guy got past the frown. The second and third rounds followed so fast they sounded like one long *brap!* She tapped him three times in the head, then ran for the back fence before the bodyguard even hit the ground. Her van was on that block, two houses down, to the left, and there weren't any dogs in the neighbor's yard—she had checked.

The barrier was a cedar-plank, good-neighbor fence, six feet tall. She got to it at speed, put her hands, including the pistol, on top and jumped and levered herself over it. A pretty good hop.

The ground was soft, the neighbor's yard empty. Nice grass, recently mowed.

She ran to the gate next to the house, opened it, closed it behind her. Unscrewed the suppressor from the Walter's threaded barrel, shoved the suppressor into her back pocket, slipped the gun into the horsehide waistband holster, pulled her shirt out and over the gun.

Forty-five seconds later, she was at the van. Across the street, two little girls played hopscotch on a pattern chalked on the sidewalk. The Selkie smiled and waved at the girls. Got into the van, started it, backed out into the street, then pulled away. She drove without any particular haste, stopped at the stop sign, put her blinker on to make the right turn. A model driver.

Ray Genaloni was no longer a worry.

Now, she had to go back to Washington, to finish one more little chore. . . .

34

As he was rebuilding his system, damaged in the sudden VR bail he'd been forced to take, Plekhanov came across bad news.

Somebody had snapped a couple of his trip wires.

It was late, he was tired and his first reaction was panic.

He forced himself to take several deep breaths. *Easy, Vladimir. All is not lost.*

He re-ran his security scans. There were no other signs of the intruder, so he was good, whoever he was. But there was no way to avoid breaking the trip if you went down certain electronic corridors. Like very fine strands of spider silk, the trips were always placed with utmost care, put in places short of where most would begin to look for them. Even a passer-through looking for such wards would usually miss them. They'd be strung across at knee-level, nearly invisible, offering so little resistance they'd never be noticed. If you stepped over one, chances were you would then break the next one. Once broken, the threads could not be restrung.

It could have been a coincidence, some hacker exploring, but he did not believe that, not for a moment. No, hc was sure that it was a Net Force operative, using the information gathered during the chase. Had the positions been reversed, had he been tailing somebody in VR, he could have tracked somebody with what he would have gotten during that run. As much as it galled him to admit it, if he could do it, so could someone else.

He had underestimated them once. He would not do so again.

So. Either they knew who he was, or they were close to figuring it out. If it was still the latter, with the resources of Net Force at their disposal, it would be only a matter of time.

And then? Ah, then was when it would get interesting. They had no hard evidence, he was certain of that. And in order to get such evidence, they would have to probe a lot deeper into his system than they could possibly have managed thus far. And if they did know who he was, they would know how impossible that was going to be. They would know his capabilities. The key to his cipher existed only inside his brain, it was not written down anywhere, and they couldn't legally force him to divulge it. Without the key, his coded files might as well be blocks of iron—nobody could open them, nobody.

Plekhanov leaned back in his chair, steepled his fingers and considered the problem. Knowing who he was was not the same as proving what he had done. He had, of course, run scenarios in which Net Force or some other law enforcement organization had uncovered his identity before his plan came to full fruition. As unlikely as that possibility had seemed, he was too old and too experienced to have not at least *considered* it. In his worst case scenario, they knew who he was and they had *proof* of what he had done—the net rascals, the bribery, the killings, all of it.

There was a point beyond which even that would not matter. Once his people came to power, he would be practically invulnerable. Extradition requests would not be denied outright. That would be impolite. An investigation into the charges against the valuable and honored friend of the people would, however, eventually come to the conclusion that it was not in the best interests of the country to turn him over to the Americans. Not that his people wouldn't throw him to the wolves if they thought they could get away with it. They would. Fortunately, the newly elected officials would not only owe him for their jobs, there would exist also a detailed record of how they *got* those jobs. To abandon him to the beasts would mean those responsible would fall off the sleigh with him. He had learned a long time ago that self-interest was more dependable than any amount of gratitude.

This was distressing, of course. A blot on an otherwise perfect plan, but not crippling, not this far along. He would keep a careful watch on things, proceed with extra care, but keep going as before. Ruzhyó was in place. Any sudden activity from Net Force, and the Rifle could be fired to offer them more confusion. Past a certain point, nothing they did would matter, and that point was fast approaching.

Wednesday, October 6th, 7:06 p.m.
Quantico

Michaels was still chewing on the news that Ray Genaloni was dead, along with his mistress and a bodyguard, as he wound the meeting down. Richardson had already gone.

Alex had a couple of final assignments for his own people.

"Jay, run scenarios on what Plekhanov might be after. Tie all the pieces you have together. Is there any way to figure out where he's been, who he's seen, both in VR and RW?"

"Maybe. He'll have his files locked, but we've got an ID and we might be able to backwalk some of his movement."

"Do so, please."

Jay nodded. He left.

Michaels said to Howard, "I need you to do something for me. Work up a plan that would involve a sub-rosa extraction of Plekhanov from Chechnya."

Howard stared at him. "Sir?"

"Assume for a second that we can't get the Russian legally extradited. What would it take for a team to go in and get him? Could it be done?"

Howard didn't hesitate. "Yes, sir, it could be done. How sub-rosa are we talking about?"

"We wouldn't want our troops marching down the main street in full dress uniform waving the stars 'n' stripes; on the other hand, if something went wrong, we wouldn't leave them hanging. Dog tags under civilian clothes. Some kind of contingency plan if the extraction went sour. This is your area of expertise."

"I see. I can work this up, sir, but realistically speaking, what are the odds of getting such a go-ahead?"

"I'd say the chances are slim and snowball, Colonel, but as far as this scenario is concerned, we're talking the NRA slogan about guns and self-defense here."

" 'Better to have it and not need it, than to need it and not have it'?"

"Exactly."

"Sir. I'll work it up ASAP." Was that a new sense of respect in his voice? Even a little warmth?

"Thank you, Colonel."

Michaels went back to his office. Toni walked along with him.

"If Genaloni had Steve Day killed, he's beyond our reach now," she said.

"Somebody saved the people the cost of a long and expensive trial, yeah. What I'm wondering is—who did it? And why?"

Toni shrugged. "He's a mobster. They swat each other like people at an outdoor summer barbecue slap mosquitoes."

They got to his office. Toni followed him in.

He frowned. "This wasn't a casual, reactive swat. Somebody very professional did this, an expert. Three dead people in a quiet neighborhood and nobody saw anything. They capped Genaloni and his mistress inside the house, came out, dropped the bodyguard in the back, knowing there were four hardwared bodyguards out front. We're not just talking cool, we're talking about somebody with supercooled liquid in their veins. Anything I don't have here?" He waved at his computer screen.

"Our forensic report is still preliminary. All we got is a boot print in the neighbor's yard. He's a little guy, whoever he is."

Michaels raised an eyebrow.

She called up the prelim: "See. Print looks like a man's size four or five. Depth in the ground says he weighed maybe one-fifteen, one-twenty. Cat-burglar build."

Michaels shook his head. There was something about this rattling around in his mind. . . . "I don't like it," he said, "it's too neat."

"Sometimes things just . . . happen, Alex, and they aren't directly connected. You can't predict them. Somebody turns up in the right place at the right time, the circumstances are ripe, things just get out of hand."

He looked at her. What was she talking about? It sounded more like an apology than an explanation.

She looked uncomfortable. She said, "What I'm saying is, somebody had it out for Genaloni. Maybe the timing is a coincidence."

Something occurred to him. He tapped his keyboard, called up a file.

"What?"

He didn't look up. "What size did you say this killer's shoe was?"

"Four or a five. Forensics will know better when they get the cast back to the lab and do a like-surface comparison."

"Let me ask you a question. Women's shoes and men shoes, how do they compare size-wise?"

"Depends on the cut and maker, but usually the woman's shoe will be a couple of numbers larger than the same size in a man's. Why do you—? Oh."

"Yeah. According to the computer extrapolation on the woman who picked up the dog in New York—and who came back and paid for *losing* it a few days ago, using a series of couriers like before—that woman wears a six. And weighs between a hundred and fifteen and a hundred and twenty-five pounds."

"You think it's the same person?"

"Coincidence only stretches so far. Our theory assumes that the woman who tried to kill me, who we think might have killed Steve Day, works for Genaloni. We know she was in New York to pay for the lost dog, and a few days later, Genaloni is killed by an expert who is about the same size. What does that say to you?"

"Could be the same person. But if she was working for Genaloni . . . ?"

"Exactly. Why kill him?"

"Maybe he didn't want to pay her for missing you," she said.

"Maybe, but it doesn't feel right, all of this." He thought about it for a second. "What if we're wrong about who had Steve Day killed? What if it was somebody who wanted to blame it on Genaloni? So maybe he found out and this woman deleted *him*. Maybe she's working for somebody else."

"That's a stretch."

"Yeah, it is, but consider: Day's assassination was by a team, and it was planned okay, but the execution was sloppy. A bunch of guys with submachine guns spraying all over the place, and even so, Day got one of them. Doesn't seem like this woman's style. She seems more adept than that."

"She missed you."

"Only because the dog barked. A second later or earlier, I'd be history."

"So what are you saying here? There are two sets of killers?"

"I don't know. But it's a possibility. We assumed that Day's death was due to his long battle with organized crime. The way it was done, his history, that would make sense. But what if we're wrong? What if somebody else did it? What if it wasn't connected to OC at all?"

"Okay, let's assume for a second you're right. Who? And why? Why would anybody want to take *you* out?"

"What do Day and I have in common?"

"Net Force. You took over as Commander when he died."

"Exactly. What if the attacks weren't on us personally, but on the heads of Net Force?"

"From two different sets of killers?"

"Yes."

They both thought about that for a moment without saying anything else.

There was a quick knock. They looked up to see Jay Gridley standing there.

"What's up, Jay?"

"Put in for my raise, Boss. We got her. The assassin. A positive ID."

35

Toni sat in her office, looking at the information Jay had developed. There was no photo or holograph to go with it. It was old material, and not much of that.

The fingerprints of the suspected assassin, lifted from the wall of a Holiday Inn in Schenectady, New York, had a match: They belonged to Mora Sullivan, an Irish national, the daughter of an IRA man killed by the British. When the prints were taken, little Mora had been eight years old. And from then on, there was no further record of the girl or woman in any of the computer systems linked to Net Force—which was most international police systems. She had vanished. Or, as Jay had said, somebody who knew what they were doing had cracked her records and *vanished* them, leaving no trace and no trail. The only reason they had these prints was luck, because they were hardcopy from an Irish police station that hadn't gotten around to being uploaded until they'd been discovered with a few hundred other sets of prints years after they'd been taken.

So what they had was her age, nationality and natural
hair and eye color, along with her prints. Not a lot of help
in recognizing her, given her ability with disguises. With
wigs or hair dye, contact lenses and gloves, she could hide
all of that; a little makeup and padded clothes, and her true
age changed. She had already demonstrated that she could
look a hefty forty or a frail seventy, and according to her
records, she was only thirty-two. Even if they'd gotten a
picture of little Mora, she and whatever she called herself
now weren't going to look much alike.

Still, more was better. When they finally ran her down,
they'd be able to get a positive identification.

Toni's phone announced an incoming call. The caller ID
strip lit with the name.

Her stomach twisted. Rusty. She'd been expecting the
call, since he was returning hers, but even so, it tripped her
fight-or-flight reactions. Sleeping with Rusty had been a
mistake, she knew that, but she hadn't been able to figure
out a way to tell him yet. She had put him off, but it wasn't
fair to keep spraying fog at him. And it wasn't something
she could tell him over the phone.

"Hello."

"Guru Toni. How are you?"

Why did he have to sound so cheerful? "Fine. Busy. The
usual."

"What's up?"

"I'm not going to be able to get to the gym for a workout
today," she said. "Too much going on."

"No problem. I have studying I ought to be doing. Tomorrow?"

"Listen, I can break loose for a few minutes around
lunch today, if you want to grab a quick cup of coffee?"

"That would make my day."

She winced at how happy he seemed when he said it. It

would make his day, all right, but not in the way he thought.

"How about Heidi's?" This was a coffee shop near the complex. It was a small, quiet place. They had lousy coffee and worse food, so there wouldn't be a crowd around when she told him.

When she *dumped* him.

"Great! See you then," he said.

They discommed.

Toni blew out a big sigh and stared at nothing. Yeah, *Great*.

Somebody somewhere had surely written a book on how to tell a man you still liked, but didn't want to sleep with again, that you still liked him—but didn't want to sleep with him again. She wished she had read it. How did you just up and blurt it out? *Look, it was a lot of fun screwing our brains out, and I like you and all, but I don't want to have sex with you anymore because it was a spur-of-the-moment mistake and, nothing personal or anything, but I love somebody else. Even though he doesn't think of me in that way. Sorry. So, how about them Orioles, huh?*

Toni tried to think how she would feel if the roles were reversed. It would be hard to be dumped, especially if she was in love with the man blandly telling her they should just be friends from now on. That was close enough to the relationship she had with Alex to be painful. If *they'd* slept together and *he'd* said it to *her,* she didn't think she'd be able to stand it.

Did Rusty love her? He had not said so in those words, but he certainly was attracted to her strongly. And since the sex had been good, he might have trouble understanding. The problem was, *he* hadn't said or done anything wrong; it wasn't his fault. But no matter how she polished and shined it up, no matter how many pretty flowers she covered it in, it was still going to be a rejection: *I don't want you anymore.*

Worse, it didn't matter what Rusty thought—he didn't have any choice. It was a done deal, not open to negotiation, end of discussion. So sorry.

That it was already decided didn't make it any easier. She didn't want to hurt him, but it was either cut him off clean with a sudden slash, or poke him with a needle and let him slowly bleed out. That was the easier way. She could be too busy to see him, too busy to work out, too busy to answer his calls. His FBI training would end soon. He'd be posted as a junior agent to some field office a thousand miles away—a nasty part of her realized that if she wished it, she could even pull a few strings to *arrange* a distant posting—and that would be the end of it. A slow leak, eventually running dry, with Rusty probably wondering all the while what he'd done wrong.

That was the coward's way, to stand back at a distance and avoid the confrontation. She had been taught to face things head-on, to move in close and do what was needed to finish things. It was more dangerous, but it was quicker and cleaner.

Quicker. Cleaner. Harder.

Then again, maybe all he wanted to do was get laid. He was male, she wasn't so ugly people crossed the street to avoid her—maybe sex was all he had in mind? That would make it easier.

She wished she had somebody to talk to about this, a girlfriend to ask for advice, but there was nobody locally. She thought about calling her friend Irena back in the Bronx, but it didn't seem fair. They hadn't talked in months, and it didn't feel right to call her just to cry on her shoulder. Besides, Irena had never been a heavy dater. She'd had a couple of boyfriends before she got married, and she was madly in love with Todd. Toni had never told

her about Alex, how she felt, and she would have to do
that, to put the Rusty thing into context. Otherwise, why
would she *want* to dump him, with all he had going for
him?

No, she'd have to do this on her own.

She was not looking forward to it.

Thursday, October 7th, 8:56 p.m.
Quantico

John Howard paced in his office while the computer put
together yet another scenario for the theoretical snatch of
the Russian programmer. So far, Howard had run five operation plans, with the computer's estimates of their
chances at success ranging from sixty-eight percent down
to less than twelve percent. He did not like these numbers.
Given his knowledge of ops out of the standard Strategy
and Tactics modules, without at least an eighty-percent success estimate, people were likely to get hurt, maybe die.
Could be the enemy lost troops, could be *he* did. The former was better than the latter, but in this particular combatsit, both were bad.

Sometimes you had to fight the battle, no matter what
the odds, but he didn't like going in knowing he was going
to lose people.

The big elements were stable, but the small variables
were always the problem. The more of those he had information on, the better he could program the Op S&T mod,
but—how to determine some of these? A straight-up firefight in a big field in the middle of nowhere was easy. But
what, for instance, could you do to predict the traffic pattern
on the streets of any large city during a covert operation?
An unexpected wreck on a major artery during rush hour

could cause a total stoppage; you had to figure on alternate routes, and you had to assume that if you wanted to take those routes, others caught in the jam would also want to use them. But even if you planned on a big truck overturning, how could you figure out *where* and *when* it might do so?

You could not, unless you put it there yourself.

If you reckoned on an assault during off-peak hours, early in the morning or in the middle of the night, say, that offered other problems to replace the ones you solved by choosing that option. Local police noticed activity in the middle of the night they might ignore during the day; if discovered, it was much harder to hide, and outrunning air pursuit on the ground for any distance was nearly impossible. They had helicopters everywhere now, even in countries where most of the population still lived in grass huts.

Plus, the snatch was only one element. A small unit, three or four troops, no more, would handle that. An escape route, preferably by air, would have to be arranged. Something that could fly fast enough to get away quickly, and yet stay under enemy radar while so doing, was necessary.

But if the operation went south? How many men were necessary for a backup team? Did the Net Force team want to begin a firefight with troops of a supposedly friendly nation? What were the repercussions of that?

Howard shook his head. It was a lot to chew on, and no matter how well he did it, he knew some bit would be missed. It might be small enough to pass through the system undigested. It might be just large enough to block a windpipe and choke him. There was a pleasant thought.

The computer chimed. The new op was done. Chance of success, fifty-four percent.

Might as well flip a coin for that one.

"Computer, retain previous parameters, change operation begin-time to 2300 hours and run."

The computer chimed again and began cross-checking the op.

He paced again. It was probably all going to be moot. He did not have much confidence that Michaels would give the order to use military intervention in this situation. He had too many people to answer to higher up the chain of command, and they were all civilians. It was one thing to go into a foreign country with the locals knowing you were there but pretending you were not there, thus offering a tacit approval of your actions. It was another thing to put troops on foreign soil with the expressed disapproval of the locals. The Chechens had been touchy about such things since the Russians had invaded them years ago; they would not welcome an American StrikeForce team wandering around in their country, no matter how covert. If it hit the fan, there would be major noise. Heads would roll, and likely his would be the first to hit the ground.

Still, he had his orders. He would carry them out to the best of his ability. He was a soldier. That was what he did.

Thursday, October 7th, 9:02 p.m.
Washington, D.C.

The Selkie couldn't expect the teams guarding the target to use the same route to his condo twice in a row. However, the closer they got, the fewer options they had. There were only two main approaches to the neighborhood, and if they wanted to drive there, they would have to use one or the other. If they didn't use this one today, they would likely use it tomorrow.

She got lucky. Today, they picked this route.

She stood at a public phone kiosk next to a stop-and-rob a mile away from Michaels's place, her new bicycle on its kickstand next to her. She was dressed as a man in boots, baggy jeans, an oversized jacket, with a short and well-trimmed fake beard, and while the bodyguards saw her, she had her back to them as the procession passed, watching them via the small rearview bicycle safety mirror attached to the helmet she wore. They paid little attention to her.

As she'd expected, they had ramped up the level of protection. There were two close-in outrider cars, one in front, one behind, and the target rode in an armored limo. She hadn't wanted to risk a drive-by look at his condo, but she had to assume the place was covered with a tight net of security. She wasn't going to granny her way down the street, nor be able to slip over a back fence and sneak into his house unseen. And these guys would be quicker on the draw than a mobster's bodyguard. They'd be firing as soon as they spotted her.

She stayed at the kiosk for another minute, and was rewarded by a second tail vehicle, with two more guards in it. There might have been a fourth, further out in front, too—she hadn't noticed.

Given the location and logistics of the neighborhood, the Selkie eliminated the target's condo as a place to do the deletion. She might be able to set up to make a rifle shot as he left or entered the limo at home, but that would be risky. Likely the guards had thought of that and had any decent vantage points covered. She wouldn't be able to get outside their coverage and line up—there weren't any tall buildings around, no good angles. And even if she made the shot, getting away afterward would be the bigger problem. Escape was a primary goal, more important than the deletion.

No, the condo was out.

She hung up the phone, climbed onto her bike and headed for the motel where she'd rented a room. It was a couple of miles away and she'd used the male identity to register, in case they were looking for any single women checking in.

Trying for a hit on a convoy was also risky. The only practical way was explosives. A Stinger missile, maybe an antitank rocket or a bomb. To use a rocket or missile, she would have to expose herself to the guards for a line-of-sight shot. If they spotted somebody with a rocket launcher standing on the side of the road or leaning from a window, she would bet heavy they'd shoot first and ask the body questions later. And rockets were iffy. She had heard of cases where missiles had hit ordinary windshield glass at an angle and bounced off without exploding. Bullets did it all the time.

And as for a bomb? She would also bet that the FBI or Net Force teams in charge of protecting the target sent somebody along the route to check manholes and garbage cans for strange packages, once they were down to one or two routes to the condo. Besides, a remote-controlled bomb might not dispatch somebody inside a well-armored limo. A big enough charge to be sure of a kill would probably be picked up by an electronic sniffer or even a bomb dog. If they knew for certain she was still after the target, they would stick him into a secure facility and he'd camp out for weeks or months. She didn't want to wait for that. Once, she would have been as patient as necessary, but having made the decision to retire, she was ready to finish this and move on. A few days, a week maybe, that was all she had to give it. And given how she had failed before, she wanted to do this up close and personal. The cane was out, but a knife or bare hands had a certain appeal.

A car honked at her as it swung around to pass the bike. She waved, trying to give the impression she was sorry for blocking the road. The car passed. The driver yelled something at her, the last part of which was ''—stupid bastard!'' He didn't slow down.

The Selkie grinned. The driver of the car had no idea how dangerous it would have been to pull over and beat on a small bicyclist who'd slowed him down more than he wanted. She didn't want to have to use the pistol in her fanny pack on some angry motorist, but it was always an option if she couldn't beat his head in with all her training.

No, the only viable alternative for a deletion now was to do it where the target wouldn't be constantly surrounded by guards, and in such a way that nobody would know he'd been hit until she had plenty of time to get away.

Given her options, the only place that fit was a place considered secure.

She'd have to kill him inside Net Force Headquarters.

36

Getting yourself—or some illegal object—into a secure area when you weren't supposed to was not as hard as most people would like to believe. Offhand, the Selkie knew of at least four ways to smuggle a firearm onto a plane, even without resorting to a ceramic one, like the little pistol she now had tucked into the waistband of her panty hose. The pistol was a three-shooter with triple-stack-two-inch barrels. The weapon had been illegally made in Brazil, for their foreign service operatives, from the same hard-ceramic the Japanese had developed for those ever-sharp kitchen knives. The caliber was 9mm short, and the ammo was caseless boron-epoxy, no cartridges, fired by a rotating piezoelectric igniter. Propellant was a more stable variation of solid rocket fuel. The thing even had a rudimentary rifling in the trio of snub-nose barrels, though the bullets were light enough so long-range target shooting wasn't an option. The piece had a twenty-meter effective accuracy range; outside that, it was fire and hope you had a patron deity if you wanted to hit anything on purpose.

At close range, the non-metal gun would kill a man as dead as the biggest steel cowboy six-shooter ever made.

The gun had been cast in two main pieces, barrels and frame; the pivots, hinges, screws, trigger and firing mechanism were also ceramic. In theory, the weapon could be reloaded and used again, but in practice, it was a throwaway. Once it had fired its initial load, the internal ceramics got a little fragile. It made a lot more sense to use a new gun than risk having the old one misfire at a critical moment. The trivalent metalloid boron in the three composite bullets contained less metal than a tooth filling. The piece wouldn't pass a Hard Object scan, but standing on its end it would likely skate by a fluroscanner because it didn't look like a gun from that angle, and it would go through any standard security metal detector on the planet without a blip. Lying on a table, the pistol would look almost as if it had been carved from a bar of Ivory soap.

Strapped to her right inner thigh, almost to her groin, was a sheath knife, also of ceramic, full-tang, with a plastic handle. The blade was a *tanto*-style, with the angled point, and was both short and very thick. Ceramic tended to be brittle, and it needed thickness to keep from snapping if it was going to be used for stabbing, and not just throatcutting.

The standard security setup at most government buildings, which were, after all, limited in their funding for such things, involved picture or fingerprint identification tags, metal detectors and uniformed guards. If you had business in such a place and were not an employee, the process could be as detailed as the security force was willing to use. A computer check of your ID, a search of your carry-in and your person, somebody from inside assigned to accompany you wherever you went—these were all standard for basic Level Three access. Net Force was a Level Three through

Level One building; that meant that getting into the building itself needed only L3 techniques. More private areas would have tighter wards—palm or retinal scanners, knuckle readers, vox codes and such. She wasn't going to slip through those to her target's office and knock on his door, not without a lot more time to prepare. But, then, she didn't really have to.

Getting to a hard target wasn't necessary—if the target made itself easy and came to you.

With even the smallest computer knowledge, it was easy enough to find low-level employees—secretaries, receptionists, maintenance people—who had worked for Net Force only a short time. Choosing one who was unmarried and living alone that she could look like, was even easier. The Selkie, after all, could look like almost anybody. . . .

Thus it was that Christine Wesson, a not-too-ugly brunette with brown eyes, age twenty-nine, came to the end of her short and probably undistinguished life. And now, a woman who looked enough like Wesson to pass for her to anybody who didn't know her very well, wearing her clothes, came to the southwest entrance—the busiest one— of Net Force HQ. It was a thank-God-it's-Friday, and a crush of day-shift employees arriving for work stood in line at the reader, waiting their turns to slide their ID cards through the scanner slot. It went fast. One swipe, a green light, and you were in.

The Selkie already knew the card was valid, since it had gotten her into the parking lot—in the late Christine Wesson's eight-year-old rattle-infested Ford.

Christine herself was wrapped in plastic bags in her bathtub, under a hundred or so pounds of melting crushed ice that should keep the neighbors from complaining about the smell—at least for long enough that the Selkie could finish her work and be gone.

Once inside the facility, there were several places she

needed to check out, and several other places the Selkie could stay to avoid hanging around in the halls.

Two years ago, security people at the interim Pentagon had been found enjoying vids surreptitiously taken of women—and a few men—using the rest-room facilities in the building. Public outcry had been loud and immediate— but the military was long-used to ignoring whatever whim-of-the-moment the uninformed civilian public wanted. However, the idea that somebody might see a four-star general's wee-wee as he took a whiz had bothered the brass no end. And who knew but there weren't similar spy-eyes in Congressional johns? It was amazing how fast some laws could get written and passed when they were really important. As a result, surveillance gear in federal buildings had been restricted—at least the cameras were supposed to be kept out of bathrooms. The fake Wesson could park herself in a stall with a book and kill a couple of hours. She could dawdle over lunch in the cafeteria. She could go to the outside smoking area for a frowned-upon, but still legal, low-tar-low-nicotine cigarette, a pack of which had been in Wesson's purse. With her ID tag twisted on her blouse, she'd be anonymous. Nobody knew her, and it was a big bureaucracy.

While the target was safe in the high-security area, he would surely come out to a less-secure area, if she could find the right reason.

Somehow, she had to figure out the right reason during the next few hours.

Sooner or later, of course, the office where Wesson worked would probably notice she had not shown up. They might call her apartment, and get the answering machine. No problem, unless, for some reason, those concerned thought to check the building's security computer. If that happened, they would see that Christine Wesson had arrived for work at her normal time—which might cause some raised eyebrows. If she was here, where was she? To stall that, the Selkie had asked more or less politely if Christine would do something for her. She had been more than willing. So, Christine Wesson had called her supervisor in the Office Supply Section in which she worked, and told her she would be a few hours late, that she had an important personal medical errand to run. The supervisor had no problem with that, and a few hours could easily stretch to noon. Then a timed-e-mail would show up at the supervisor's terminal from Wesson, explaining that things had run late. A lot later than anybody but the Selkie knew.

At the least, the e-mail would buy the rest of the day. Which should be more than enough.

•

Friday, October 8th, 12:18 p.m.
Quantico

Toni went through her *djurus,* pausing after each one to do the corresponding *sambut.* She was the only woman working out. There were a few other men in the gym today, but Rusty was not among them. When she'd told him she wasn't going to be sleeping with him anymore, she thought he'd taken it rather well. No obvious anger, no tears, just a kind of surprised acceptance. "Oh?" It had gone much better than she'd hoped or expected.

Except that she hadn't heard from him since. She'd said she was going to try to be in the gym today and she expected him—he hadn't missed a class before—to show up.

Surprise. So maybe it hadn't gone as well as she'd thought.

She came up from the squat in *Djuru Three,* threw the right-vertical-forearm strike, then punched, continued to rise, alternating the next two punches.

She hoped Rusty wasn't going to quit class. She had been enjoying having a student, and learning a lot in the process of teaching.

But of course, it was his choice.

What was it with men that they could be your friend, then your lover, but they couldn't go back to just being friends if the other didn't work out?

She finished the series and shook her hands out. She was still tight.

A brunette in office clothes walked to the water fountain and smiled and nodded at Toni. Toni didn't recognize the woman, but she nodded absently back. Solving the Rusty problem didn't solve the Alex problem. How was she going to get him to notice her?

The brunette went into the locker room. Toni dismissed her from her thoughts, but a moment later, the brunette came out, all upset.

"Excuse me, miss," she said. "There's a lady having some trouble in there—she looks like she's having some kind of seizure! I called Medical but, oh, I'm afraid she's going to hurt herself! Can you help?"

Toni nodded. "Sure."

She followed the brunette into the locker room.

Friday, October 8th, 12:18 p.m.
Quantico

Jay Gridley and John Howard had joined Michaels in the small conference room. He knew protocol said he should keep these two meetings apart, the need-to-know business the spooks were always hammering at everybody, but he figured his top people needed to know what each was doing. Besides, if he happened to feel like it, there wasn't much Jay Gridley couldn't find out from a computer system he'd helped design and install.

"Jay?"

"Okay, Boss, here's the way it lays out." He waved the presentation computer to life. "We've been able to piece together some of Plekhanov's itinerary over the last few months. I can give you the details and show how brilliant we were in making some connections, if you want."

"I'll stipulate to your brilliance," Michaels said. "Let's hear a bottom line."

"All right. This is iffy, you understand, but what it looks like is, he's trying to buy himself a government or two."

Michaels nodded. Lobbyists did that all the time, and as long as they kept within the legally established limits, that was acceptable.

"Some of the people he connected with are less careful than Plekhanov. We think he's got a good chance of deciding who the President and Prime Ministers for two, maybe three CIS governments are going to be in the next elections, including those in Chechnya, where he lives. We don't have any direct proof, of course. We'd need his files for that."

Howard said, "What do you suppose our chances are of getting him turned over to us if the head of the government we ask owes Plekhanov big-time?"

It was a rhetorical question. Michaels said, "I don't much like this, Jay."

"Well, then, you're really going to hate this next part. Some of those people we were able to put in Plekhanov's vicinity? There are a couple of generals in there."

Howard looked at Jay. "Great."

Michaels said, "You think he's planning some kind of coup?"

Jay shrugged. "No way to be sure. But given the way this guy moves, yeah, I'd have to say it's a possibility."

Michael turned to Howard. "Colonel?"

"It would make sense, sir. Getting himself elected into power would be easier, but if I were him and willing to stage big-time computer theft and sabotage, maybe worse, I'd want a backup plan. Sometimes when ballots don't work, bullets will. A key military commander on your side, control of the media, nobody knows what's going on until it's too late—it would be good insurance."

Michaels stared at the other men, each in turn. "So, even if we could come up with proof that this guy was about to buy himself an election and then get somebody in power to believe us. . . ."

"He'd probably bag the election and start a civil war instead," Howard said. "By the time anybody from outside got there, the party would be over, a done deal."

"Shit."

"Yes, sir," Howard said. "I believe that about sums it up."

Michaels blew out a big sigh. Jesus. What a can of worms this was turning out to be!

"Okay, Colonel. You have some happier news for me?"

"Relatively speaking, sir. My best-case scenario for the operation to, ah, *collect* Mr. Plekhanov comes in at seventy-eight percent."

"That's good, isn't it?"

"I would prefer a higher percentage from the S&T computer, but anything over seventy percent is considered militarily acceptable. Although no battle plan survives first contact with the enemy."

"I'll want to see it," he said.

"Sir. Right here."

Alex's secretary came in. "Commander? Toni Fiorella on the private line."

He waved her out. "Gentlemen, let me take this call."

The colonel and Gridley nodded, and went back to looking at their presentations.

"Hello?"

"Commander Michaels? This is Christine Wesson, from Supply? I was working out in the gym and Deputy Commander Fiorella asked me to call you—this is her virgil unit. She's had an accident, Medical is on the way, but I think maybe she's got a broken leg."

Toni was hurt? "A broken *leg*?"

"One of the exercise machines fell over on her. She says she's okay, she just wanted to let you know she'd be late for her meeting. But between you and me, she's in a lot of pain."

"I'm on my way," he said.

The two men looked up at him, having heard his end of the conversation as they pretended to be busy.

"Is Toni okay?" Jay said.

"Apparently. Some kind of exercise equipment failure. Medical is on the way, but I want to check on her. You two put your heads together and see what more sense you can make out of this mess. I'll be back in a few minutes."

"Sure thing, Boss."

"Sir."

Michaels started for the hall.

Friday, October 8th, 12:28 p.m.
Quantico

Half in and half out of the shower stall, the Selkie held the gun aimed at the woman sitting cross-legged on the tile floor inside. If anybody came in, they would not see Fiorella, nor would they see the gun. The Selkie was tempted to shoot her, but she didn't want to risk the noise—or to waste any of her precious ammunition. If something went wrong, she might need the gun to escape. She also might need the woman to get the target in here; after that, Fiorella was as dead as Michaels. The Selkie would use the stubby ceramic knife strapped to her thigh under her skirt to do both of them. Shut them up in a shower stall, rinse away any blood spatter, and she could be halfway across Maryland before anybody discovered the bodies. A double deletion inside Net Force HQ—they'd be talking about that forever.

Fiorella twitched.

"Keep your hands on your head," the Selkie said.

"You can't get away with this."

"If you wiggle crooked, it won't matter to you."

"We know who you are."

"Uh-huh."

"You're not as good as you think—Mora Sullivan."

That surprised her. How the hell had they found that out? She had a quick spasm of panic, fought it down. Sullivan was just another name now, one more disposable ID. Still . . . "We're going to have to have a little talk before I leave," the Selkie said.

The woman was scared—and well she should be—but she said, "I don't think so."

Another gutsy woman. Damn. Too bad she had to kill her.

"Toni?" came a voice from outside the locker room's door.

"In here!" the Selkie said. "Hurry!"

She heard the sound of fast footsteps. She grinned.

37

Plekhanov didn't need to use VR to see that trip wires were broken all over his walkways. They knew who he was, and they were probing every aspect of his life they could reach. He didn't think they could find much, but he was worried a bit more than he had been. This damnable *child* who worked for Net Force might be faster than he was smart, but somebody brighter might take notice of some of the patterns and draw a conclusion Plekhanov did not want them to draw. Or they might feed all the bits they had to an AI-analog, and have the computer make a connection a human might not be clever enough to see. This was very much not to his liking.

And he was so close; it was but a matter of days until the special election was to be held. All he needed was to stall them just a little longer. Then it truly wouldn't matter what they knew. Even now, it was probably too late for anybody to thwart him, but he was a careful man. People had told him that he was *too* careful, that he lingered for another look when he should be leaping, but they were wrong. Those who had uttered such stupidities—where were they now? Not where he was, poised to control the destinies of millions.

No, he would add one more piece of insurance, something to make them think. One more obstacle to make certain they stumbled and could not recover in time to catch him.

He put in a call to the Rifle.

Friday, October 8th, 12:37 p.m.
Quantico

Give him credit, the Selkie thought. As soon as he saw the gun, he knew what was going on. She quickly pointed it back at the woman in the shower. "Move and she dies."

The target nodded. "I understand. I'm not armed." He spread his hands wide, to show they were empty.

The Selkie shook her head. How stupid of him *not* to be armed.

"All right. Slow and easy, over here."

Michaels felt the fear in the pit of his belly like shards of cold glass, but he knew he was going to have to go for the assassin anyway. He had to keep her from shooting Toni. And if he was going to die, he was going to go out on his feet, moving toward the threat and not away from it.

He took a slow breath. Held it—

Toni sat very still, watching. She was going to have to make her move soon. She tried to keep her breathing calm and steady, but it was hard. This was the assassin, the woman who had erased Ray Genaloni, tried to do the same to Alex, and who might or might not have murdered Steve Day. For sure, if Toni didn't do something, the woman was going to kill her and Alex. The gun was one of those ceramic things, but that didn't make it any less deadly.

She could come up from a cross-legged sit, had done it in practice thousands of times. A *silat* player had to be able to work from the ground. If the woman was six inches closer, she could reach her with a kick.

If, *if*.

Alex said, "Toni? You okay?"

"Yes," she said.

Alex was getting closer. The gun was still pointed at her, and Toni knew if she moved, she was certainly going to get shot, but that would buy Alex a second or two. She had to do it.

Toni inhaled slowly, a long breath. Held it. Made herself ready—

"Don't move! FBI!" somebody yelled.

Toni looked at the reflection in the shower door.

Rusty—?!

The Selkie reacted without thinking, almost a reflex. When the man at the locker room entrance jumped into the room, pointing what looked like a gun at her, she swung her own pistol over and fired. The little gun bucked hard in her hand, light as it was, but she saw the man react as the shot took him in the center of mass. He went down. No vest—

The target lunged at her, screaming something.

Too fast to get to the knife. She thrust the pistol at him, fired—

"No!" the woman in the shower screamed. Then she slammed into the Selkie and they both went flying. She lost the pistol, hit next to a bench, managed to roll up as Fiorella also got to her feet.

The Selkie kicked away her shoes, ripped her skirt off,

grabbed the knife and jerked it from the thigh sheath, gripped the blade in front of her to slash or stab. She glanced at the target—he was down, hit in the leg, it looked like—no threat to her. The Fiorella woman was the danger. She was up, trained, prepared.

The Selkie turned to face her, knife held ready. She would have to hurry. The shots would draw attention.

She had first learned street fighting from her father, who had survived several hand-to-hand encounters. She had trained with half-a-dozen fighters since, including a couple of Filipinos who were experts with a stick or blade. She would cut the woman down, finish the target and run. If she hurried, she could still get free in the confusion.

She moved toward Fiorella—

Michaels felt the bullet hit him—it was a hot ball-peen hammer smashing against the front of his right thigh. He fell. It didn't really hurt, but he couldn't get back to his feet. The shot leg didn't want to work.

In front of him, Toni faced the woman, who had torn off her skirt and pulled a white-bladed knife. The assassin edged toward Toni. It wasn't over. He had to do something—

The gun! She had dropped the gun. Where was it—?

Toni actually felt calmer now. An attacker with a knife— this was something she had dealt with in practice, over and over again. High, low. The most important thing was to control the knife. You couldn't trade a punch for a stab, so you had to take high line and low line, you had to stop the knife arm at two points, high, low, to control it—

The Selkie moved in, keeping her balance. Fiorella stood and watched her, waiting, and she looked as if she knew

what she was doing. It didn't matter. She had to finish this
and go.

The Selkie feinted with a kick, then lunged—

Back of the arm, back of the arm, where there were fewer
vessels to get slashed! Guru's instructions came back, crys-
tal clear, as sharp as the approaching blade: *Against an
expert, you* will *get cut. Give him a sparse target.*

The kick was a feint, but the slash was also a feint. When
Toni threw up her left arm to block, the assassin jerked the
knife back. The edge scored a deep line along the outside
of Toni's forearm, just above the elbow.

It didn't matter. She wouldn't bleed out from that. Her
hand still worked. She shifted her feet, waited—

Fiorella didn't react to the cut, didn't look at it, kept watching the attacker. The Selkie grinned. She was good, but
time was running out.

There was a sequence attack, two feints, a shift of the
knife to the other hand, then the heart stab between the
ribs, followed by the backslash to the throat. It always
worked in practice, and she had also killed a man with it
in real combat.

The party was over. It was time to do what she did best,
then leave.

The Selkie moved—

The attacker came in again, feinted, faked, thrust, then
flipped the knife to her other hand as Toni went for the
block. Toni would have been impressed watching from
elsewhere, but she didn't have time to be impressed now.
All the years of practice had to take over, no time to think
anymore—!

Toni shifted her stance, passed the fake and did the block
and break on the attacker's knife arm. Her right arm

stopped the thrust at the wrist—low. Blood flew from the cut on her arm as she slammed the back of her left wrist under the woman's elbow—high.

The arm broke, the knife fell. Toni moved in, went over the wrecked arm and slammed her elbow into the woman's face. Followed her as she stumbled back and hit the lockers, drove a knee into the attacker's belly, then did *sapu luar* and dropped her to the floor. The attacker hit hard, her head bounced, but she rolled, dove for the knife, caught it in her good hand, came up and cocked the blade for a throw. Her nose was broken and bloody, her eyebrow split—

She knew now she couldn't take Fiorella in a one-on-one, even if her arm hadn't just been broken. One chance. The knife wasn't the best for throwing, but it would back the other woman off if it hit, point or butt. She'd lost, but she could still get away—

The Selkie aimed her elbow at the target, knife held by the blade next to her ear—

Michaels found the white gun, rolled over his bad leg— *now* it hurt!—and shoved the weapon out in front of him. He yelled to distract the woman about to throw the knife: *"Hey!!"*

She didn't waver, started to make the throw—

He pulled the trigger.

The recoil twisted the gun from his grip, and the sound was so loud it was like a bomb going off next to him.

A long moment held. Aeons passed. Nobody moved.

The knife flew—but clattered to the floor five feet away.

He'd hit her. Right in the middle of the back. The woman dropped to her knees, tried to reach the wound in her back with one hand, could not. She turned to look at him, her face puzzled more than anything. Then she toppled over onto her side.

• • •

Toni ran to where Alex lay. "Alex!?"

"I'm okay, I'm okay, she just got me in the leg."

The sound of approaching and excited voices rolled over them.

"You're hurt," he said.

"Just a cut. Looks worse than it is," she said. "Stay there, I'll get us some towels."

"I'm not going anywhere."

She got to her feet. Remembered Rusty. She hurried to where he lay. His eyes were open wide, not blinking. He had a bloody wound in the center of his chest—wasn't breathing—there was no pulse in his neck.

Two of the men from the gym ran in. "He needs help!" she said, pointing at Rusty. She dropped to her knees.

The two men were joined by a third. "We got it, Toni," one of them said. "Go wrap up that cut."

Alex had dragged himself to where the woman lay. He rolled her onto her back. The assassin moaned. She looked at him. Toni moved back toward Alex and the assassin, found a towel, pressed it against the wound in Alex's leg.

"Ow." He looked at Toni. "Thanks." Then he looked back at the woman.

"Son-of-a . . . bitch," the woman said. Her voice was burbly. Probably bleeding into a lung.

Alex said, "Who paid you to kill Steve Day?"

The woman was dying. But she laughed, a bubbly, liquid noise. "Who?"

"Day. Steve Day."

"Don't know the name," she said. "I never . . . forget a . . . target. He's . . . not one of mine."

"You didn't kill Steve Day?" Alex said.

"You deaf? I was hired to . . . do you. I—Genaloni. I did him. And some others. I don't—"

And just like that, she blinked out. Whatever she'd intended to say was chopped off in mid-sentence. There was a final outrush of bubbly air, and she was gone.

Alex and Toni looked at each other. Somebody from Medical ran in. The place seemed filled with people. Toni felt an overwhelming urge to hug Alex. She did.

He let her. And he hugged her back.

38

Bureau Medical had a doctor and several nurses on staff in
the main compound, and their own ambulance for anything
they couldn't handle on their own. The in-house medic su-
tured the cut on Toni's arm—it took eighteen stitches inside
and out—sprayed it with clear statskin, gave her a tetanus
shot, and told her to have the sutures removed in five days.

X-rays of Michaels's leg showed that his bullet wound
was a through-and-through. It had hit him slightly to the
outside of the right thigh, glanced off the femur without
breaking it and exited just under the outer edge of his but-
tock, all without doing any major damage—except for a
couple of holes the size of his little finger's tip. The doctor
cleaned and bandaged the wounds, but didn't sew them up;
gave him a tetanus shot and a pair of crutches, and advised
Michaels to avoid playing soccer for the next couple of
weeks. He had his nurse give them samples of pain tablets,
and told them they would hurt more tomorrow than they
did right now. If they wanted to go and spend a couple of

hours in the local ER to get a second opinion, that was up to them.

Both Toni and Michaels declined the ER trip.

Instead, they were back in Michaels's office. He sat on the couch, resting on his good hip. Toni stood by the door.

"Something bothering you, Alex?"

"Other than getting shot?"

"Yes."

He said, "I didn't feel particularly heroic in that locker room."

"Excuse me?"

"I should have done more."

"You came to help me. You charged a killer with a gun and you were unarmed. You managed to shoot her after you were wounded. How heroic do you think you need to be? You planning on leaping tall buildings in a single bound?"

He gave her a small smile. "Yeah. Well. Still, it kinda felt like Larry and Curly catch a killer," Michaels said.

She looked blank.

"Two of the Three Stooges," he said. "Hey, Larry! Hey, Moe! Woowoowoowoo!"

"Oh, yeah. My brothers used to watch those old vids. They must be a male thing. I never thought they were funny. Too violent." She smiled at the irony.

"I'm really sorry about your friend, the FBI trainee."

"Yeah."

There was a long pause. Then: "You believe her?" he said. "About Steve Day?"

Toni shrugged. "I don't know. She confessed to Gena-loni and 'some others.' Why would she lie about Day?"

"Maybe to screw with our heads," Michaels said.

"We have to consider that. Did *you* believe her?"

He nodded. "Yeah, I did. I didn't think Day's murder was her style before, and this confirmed it for me."

''At least she won't be coming after you again.''

''No. But what that means is, somebody else is responsible for Day.''

''Somebody who apparently wanted us to think the mob did it,'' Toni said.

He nodded. ''Remember that business about Genaloni's lieutenant up and disappearing? That they thought the FBI had taken him?''

''Yes.''

''I bet whoever swiped his enforcer did it to piss Genaloni off. And whoever it was knew to point the finger at us when he did it.''

''Looks like it worked,'' she said. ''If Genaloni thought Net Force was gunning for him, he might have hired somebody to hit back. In his world, any problem can be solved with money or violence.''

He shifted his weight slightly. His leg was beginning to throb pretty good. He considered taking one of the pain pills, then decided against it. He needed his mind to be clear more than he needed to be doped up and pain-free.

''So, we're back to square one on Day's killing,'' she added.

''No. I know who did it.''

She looked at him. ''Who?''

''The Russian. Plekhanov.''

She thought about it for a second. ''How did you come to that?''

He said, ''It was part of his plan all along, to give Net Force something else to look at while he pulled off his power grab. The attacks on Day, our listening posts, all the rascals he threw in our paths all over the world. He wanted us busy, so we wouldn't notice what he was doing. It all makes a kind of warped sense.''

''I don't know, Alex. It's possible, but—''

''It's him. I know it. He was willing to crash systems

that caused deaths. It's not that big a leap to hiring a shooter. We were looking in the wrong direction—right where Plekhanov wanted us to look. He's smart.''

Toni looked at him. ''Assume you're right. How do we prove it? If his computer skills are as good as Jay says they are, we can't get into his files. Without some record, all we have is some very circumstantial evidence, and not much of that.''

''Plekhanov could open the files for us. He has the key.''

''He has no reason to do that—even if we had him, which we don't.''

''We'll have to figure out the right way to ask. After we collect him.''

She shook her head again. ''Uplevels won't go for it, Alex. Walt Carver is too much a political animal to risk it. And even if he wanted to, he couldn't convince the Foreign Covert Operations Committee or the CIA to go along. FCOC has been burned too many times with this kind of thing. They haven't greenlighted anything military in two years that doesn't have the locals willing to go along, or at least look the other way—like the operation in Ukraine.''

''This man had Steve Day *murdered*. And is responsible for the deaths of others. He's about to rig an election that will make him legally untouchable. And we can't get him because of some bureaucratic crap?''

''I know how you feel, but we'll be wasting our time to even ask,'' she said.

''Fine. So we won't ask,'' he said.

She stared at him. ''Alex . . .''

''There is a difference between the law and justice. The only way this guy skates is over my dead body. We never had this conversation, Toni. You don't know anything about this.''

She shook her head. ''Oh, no, you don't. You don't get rid of me that easy. You want to do something stupid, I'm going to make sure you do it right. I'm in.''

''You don't have to do this.''

''Steve Day was my boss, too. I want his killer to pay for it.''

Neither of them spoke for what seemed like a long time. Then Michaels said, ''We'd better get John Howard in here.''

''You think he'll go along?''

''We won't tell him, either. He works for me. If anything happens, it's my head that will roll. What he doesn't know won't hurt him.''

''You think that's fair?''

''It protects him. He gets what he thinks is a legitimate order, he's covered.''

''Your decision.''

''Yes. About time I made a couple of decisions that *do* something.''

Saturday, October 9th, 5:00 a.m.
In the air over Hudson Bay

''All right, Sergeant Know-It-All, let's hear it.''

Howard knew the plan—he had devised it—but it never hurt to burn it into long-term memory. Another pass to spot any errors.

Julio Fernandez grinned and affected his recruit-to-drillmaster voice: ''Sir, Colonel Howard, sir!'' More quietly, he said, ''Chechnya is landlocked, bounded by Ingushetia on the west, Russia on the north, Dagestan on the east and Georgia on the south. The western border of the country is about three hundred kilometers east of the Black Sea, give or take. The capital and largest city is Grozny, of which the colonel will see detailed CIA maps of the surface streets in his flatscreen file, when and if he cares to look.

"The population is largely Chechen or Russian, that is to say—"

"Skip the geopolitical history, Sergeant. Let's get to strategy and tactics, please."

"As the colonel wishes." He grinned, relaxed. "Our two vintage UH-1H Hueys are scheduled to be off-loaded at 1900 hours from jet transport at Vladikavkaz, in North Ossetia, a favor for which the locals hope to obtain certain reciprocal courtesies from the U.S. Since we want friends in that area, such courtesies will no doubt eventually be extended.

"Once on the ground and operational, we will have to violate about fifteen kilometers of Ingushetian airspace to reach Chechnya. Our command post will be outside Urus-Martan, which is another twenty-five klicks inside Chechnya. All in all, we're talking about flying over forty kilometers of unfriendly territory.

"Of course, both countries have radar and something of an air force; however, at treetop level in the dark, it is unlikely that anybody but a few goats will even notice our choppers' overflight. It should be a milk run, if a bit crowded.

"We have a truck waiting in Grozny, which our four-trooper collection-team squad will reach from Urus-Martan upon the two Russian motor scooters we'll bring with us on the black copters. Vespa knockoffs, I believe. They aren't very fast, but it's only a dozen kilometers from Urus-Martan to Grozny, and they'll be coming back in a truck. Pretty good trade, actually, leaving the two scooters for one murdering Russian. The locals come out way ahead."

Howard made the keep-it-rolling sign.

"We arrive, all things going well, at about 2200 hours, set up our tactical base in an old dairy farm owned by our friends the spooks. The spooks don't know we'll be using the place, as per our DTNS-policy on this mission."

Howard frowned. A new acronym. "DTNS?"

"Don't tell nobody squat," Fernandez said. "Especially the CIA." He grinned widely.

"You just made that up, didn't you?"

"I am hurt that the colonel believes I would do such a thing."

"Sergeant Fernandez, I believe you would give a polar bear a poodle cut and call him Fifi."

Fernandez laughed. "Sir. This farm—there's no neighbors within shouting range. Everything going as planned, our CT squad putt-putts into town, collects their ride, grabs the Russky, comes back, and a few minutes after midnight, we're all airborne and on the way back to this here comfortable 747, which is by then all gassed up and waiting for us at the Vladikavkaz Airport. As a gesture of goodwill, we leave the transport copters for our new friends the North Ossetians, climb on our ride and fly away home. Everything by the numbers."

"*If* everything goes as planned," Howard said.

"You worry too much, sir. Our squad speaks fluent Russian, and a bit of the local dialect. They got the proper travel and ID papers, they can shoot the balls off a gnat at ten paces. They'll get him. And if there is any problem they can't handle, that's what the two dozen of us sitting at the farm cleaning our weapons are for, ain't it?"

Howard nodded. He had been surprised the mission had gone forward, given how cloudy the politics were in Washington. He did not want to get into a shooting war with the Chechens. No matter whose fault it might be, he was the man in charge, and the fallout would all settle on him. No, he didn't want a war this time. He wanted a nice clean insertion and retrieval, and as Fernandez had said, to fly away home. This one was too touchy for anything else.

Saturday, October 9th, 10:00 a.m.
Springfield, Virginia

Ruzhyó and Grigory the Snake were at a petrol service station off I-95, not far from the Springfield Regional Shopping Center. According to the map Ruzhyó had, the old Fort Belvoir Proving Ground was a few miles ahead, on the way to Quantico. What, he wondered, did an American proving ground look like? It must depend on what they were trying to prove, which weapon or vehicle they were testing.

Winters, the Texan, had gone home, to Dallas or Fort Worth or wherever it was he claimed he was from. Should they need him in the next few days, he'd said, he would check for messages at the secure number.

They had stopped at the station because Grigory had an urgent need to use the toilet. From the muffled groans he had made as he urinated, Ruzhyó guessed that Zmeyá's own . . . *personal* snake was afflicted with some ailment. Gonorrhea, probably, since that was the venereal disease most likely to manifest itself with pain while peeing. As a soldier, Ruzhyó had heard many men groan while dribbling thus, usually a day or three after returning from the whores they had enjoyed while on leave.

Here was the Snake's reward for his adventures in Las Vegas.

Grigory came out of the toilet, his face flushed. "I need some penicillin, Mikhayl."

"Was she worth this?"

"Then, yes. Now, no."

"I do not believe you can buy penicillin without a doctor's order here," Ruzhyó said. He kept his face bland, even though he felt much like smiling. It served the fool right.

"There is a pet store nearby," Grigory said. "We can get it there."

"A pet store?"

"*Da.* The Americans have rules against selling antibiotics for people, but not for animals. You can buy penicillin, tetracycline, streptomycin, even chloramphenicol for your pet fish. You open the capsules, sprinkle the medicine into the water. The drugs are not so pure as those intended for people, and they are expensive, but they work just as well."

Ruzhyó shook his head. Amazing. Not just that the Americans would do such a thing—Americans no longer surprised him with how stupid they could be—but that the *Snake* would know this? That was truly fascinating. How had he come by such knowledge?

Ruzhyó asked him.

"I have been unlucky in love a few times," Grigory allowed.

Ruzhyó stared at the Snake. A man who knew no better was merely ignorant, a thing that could be remedied. Someone who *knew* better, but proceeded anyway? That was stupid, and not so easily repaired. "Very well. We shall go to your pet store, so that you may buy fish medicine to fix your sick *zmeyá.* Then we find a way to get within range of Net Force HQ. I am thinking we will become U.S. Marines. What better disguise in a place like Quantico?"

"Anything you like, Mikhayl, once I get my penicillin."

Saturday, October 9th, 10:48 p.m.
Urus-Martan, Chechnya

Howard looked at his watch, then through the dilapidated farmhouse's window. The troops had managed to roll both the copters into the massive, if decrepit, barn. There had once been stalls for rows of cows to be milked, but the spooks had gutted enough of the barn to allow for such things as hiding two beat-up Hueys. They didn't look pretty, but they were in fine mechanical condition. They were painted a dark, dead military green and not black, but they were covert birds. They didn't carry any weapons, not even machine guns. They were strictly transport. Not very fast transport—a loaded Huey might hit 120 knots—but the craft were sturdy and dependable. You weren't going to outrun an air-to-air or ground-to-air missile in anything that had a top rotor anyhow. They couldn't fight and they couldn't run too fast, but nobody could shoot you if they didn't see you. Hiding was better than shooting in this scenario.

Howard turned away. "Status, Sergeant?"

Julio stood behind three TacComp Specialists, who sat on stools in front of a bank of five field computers set up on their own telescoping legs. They were opened like big suitcases with the monitors in the hinged lids. The systems were also ugly-looking—lean-mean-GI-green—but when it came to this kind of hardware, pretty was as pretty did. These were state-of-the-art 900-MHz machines, with the new FireEye bioneuro chips, massive amounts of fiberlight memory, and fourteen hours of active battery power if the local plugs didn't work.

"Sir, our squad's GPS sig puts them here." He pointed at a map on-screen. There was a tiny red dot flashing in the approximate middle of it. "Two kilometers from their destination."

"Report?"

"Their coded signal-bounce three minutes ago stetted a continued ASG—all systems green."

"Good."

One of the TCS operators said, "We got on-line vid from

the Big Bird spysat footprinting the locale. Check this out.''

A ghostly phospor-green image of a truck rolling along a dark street from above appeared on one of the screens. As they watched, the truck made a right turn. It passed under a streetlight, and an image appeared on the truck's roof. The TCS op laughed.

''What's funny?'' Howard asked.

The TCS op touched controls. The image freeze-framed, and increased in size. ''A little unsharp mask . . . thus,'' the op said. ''Look here. A message from the squad.''

A crude hand-drawn image on the truck's roof sharpened enough that Howard could make it out. It was a hand, holding up the two-finger sign for the letter V.

V for victory. Howard smiled.

''You owe me five, Sarge,'' the op said.

Howard raised an eyebrow.

Fernandez said, ''We had a small wager as to what the unit would draw on the truck roof, sir. I believe TCS Jeter here must have gotten to them with a bribe.''

''What were you betting it would be?'' Howard asked.

''An, uh, illustration somewhat like, uh, this one, sir. Slightly different.''

''One that featured *one* finger, sir,'' the TCS op said. He kept his face deadpan.

Howard grinned again. No matter where they were, no matter what they were up against, soldiers always found some way to relieve the monotony—or the tension.

''Carry on,'' Howard said. He walked back to the window.

Saturday, October 9th, 11:23 p.m.
Grozny

Plekhanov was getting ready for bed, brushing his teeth, when the doorbell to his house rang. His house was small, but nicely appointed, and in a neighborhood of such houses. Soon he would have one twice as big in a much better neighborhood. Everything in its own time.

The bell rang again. It had an insistent quality.

It was awfully late for someone to be calling. This could not be good news.

He rinsed his mouth out, dried his face, then put a robe on over his pajamas. He stopped at the small writing table near the entrance, opened the drawer and removed from it the Luger pistol his grandfather had brought back from the German front in 1943.

Pistol in hand, he peered through the fish-eye lens into the door.

A very attractive young woman stood on the stoop. Her hair was in disarray and her lipstick smeared. Her dark blouse was pulled out of her pants, unbuttoned and wide open, revealing her unfettered breasts; her pants, blue jeans, were unzipped, and she held them up with one hand, clutching a wadded bra in the other hand. She appeared to be crying. As he watched, the young woman rang the bell again. He saw her sob.

Goodness. A rape victim?

Plekhanov lowered the gun and opened the door. "Yes? May I help you?"

A man appeared from out of nowhere. He also wore jeans, a dark T-shirt and a blue Windcheater. He pointed a gun at Plekhanov's face. "Yes, sir, you *can* help us." He spoke Russian, but it wasn't a local accent.

The gunman reached over and gently relieved him of the Luger. "Nice gun," he said. "Probably worth a lot."

A moment later, two more men joined the woman and the gunman. They seemed to materialize from the bushes and darkness. The other two looked to be cut from the same pattern—young, fit, casual dress.

What was going on? Was this a robbery? There had been a lot of criminal activity of late. What did they want?

The woman zipped up her pants and clicked the snap closed. She slipped her shirt off, put the bra on—some kind of one-piece sport thing—adjusted it, then slipped her blouse back on, buttoned it and tucked it in. One of the other men handed her a dark blue Windcheater.

"No need to do any of this on *our* account, Becky," the young man with the gun said.

"In your *dreams,* Marcus," the woman said.

"If you would step back inside, Dr. Plekhanov?" the gunman said.

His speech was correct, but Plekhanov still had not placed the accent. "You aren't Russian, nor Chechen," Plekhanov said.

"No, sir," he said. This was spoken in English.

Plekhanov's stomach twisted. They were *Americans*!

He gestured with the gun. "Inside, Professor. You'll want to change into something more appropriate for travel. We're going on a long trip."

Saturday, October 9th, 11:28 p.m.
Urus-Martan

"They got him!" Fernandez said. "They are en route, ETA twenty minutes."

The men in the room cheered. Howard let them, then said, "All right, let's not get ahead of ourselves. Get the birds on-line. We'll celebrate when we're back on our own soil.''

Ten minutes later, Howard was outside in the dark, watching the pilots preflight the copters, when Fernandez came out of the farmhouse double-time.

"Sir, we have a slight problem."

Howard felt his belly lurch and fill with several hundred butterflies who all wanted out, now. "What?"

"Our squad's ride just broke down. Squad Leader Captain Marcus says he thinks it blew a head gasket."

Howard stared at him. The *truck* broke down? That wasn't even *in* the scenario! Jesus Christ!

39

"Where are they?" Howard asked.

TCS-op Jeter was all business now, nothing funny in his voice. "Sir, GPS puts them in the city, south of the old Tets Komintern, in the new Visok Stal Oil Storage Area, close to the Sunzha River."

"How far from here?"

"A long walk with a reluctant prisoner in tow, sir. I make it eighteen kilometers."

"Wonderful."

"Uh-oh. We've got incoming vox transmission. I'm unscrambling." Jeter tapped keys.

If the squad leader was willing to break radio silence, even with a coded transmission, that meant things either had gone, or were about to go, right to Hell.

"Wolf Pack, this is Cub Omega One, do you copy?"

"This is Alpha Wolf, Cub. Go ahead."

"Sir, we're broken down in the middle of a giant oil-tank farm and we've got two security officers a hundred meters away, approaching us on *bicycles*."

Bike cops. Great. "Follow planned procedure, Omega One. Smile politely and wave your documents, thcy will pass muster."

"Yes, sir—oh, *shit*!"

"Say again, Cub Omega One?"

The captain's voice came back, but he wasn't talking to Howard: "Somebody shut him the hell up!"

"Omega One, report!"

There was a dead silence that stretched long.

"Cub Omega One, reply."

"Ah, Alpha, we have a, uh . . . *situation* here. Our passenger started screaming bloody murder and these stupid damned cops just up and *opened fire*!"

Next to Howard, Fernandez said, "Jesus, what kind of trigger-happy bastards are they? They can't know who they're dealing with."

"Alpha, we have returned fire, repeat, we have returned fire. Omega Cubs are all uninjured, say again, no injuries our squad, but we have one local down and the other has—has—" Proper report terminology failed him. "Has hauled ass behind a big fucking oil tank, sir. Stand by. Barnes and Powell, flank right, Jessel, left, go, go!"

Howard waited for what seemed like another couple of thousand years. He exchanged glances with Fernandez.

Captain Marcus came back on-line. "Sir, the downed local is . . . ah, defunct. He had a belt phone, and we have to assume the other one also carries communication gear, but we lost him. I would guess that we are going to have unfriendly company soon, Alpha. Please advise."

Howard looked at Fernandez. There was no choice. Nobody was leaving anybody out here. "Bag it up, troops! We lift in three minutes!"

To the squad leader waiting on the other end of the scrambled comline, Howard said, "Stand fast, Omega. The pack is on the way."

"Copy that, Alpha. Thank you, sir."

"Let's go, Julio."

"Yes, sir!"

Howard and Fernandez ran for the helicopters.

Saturday, October 9th, 4:10 p.m.
Quantico

Michaels and Toni were in the small conference room, working on their second pot of coffee. As the doctor had predicted, Michaels was a lot more sore than he had been right after he'd been shot. It hurt to move, it hurt to stand still, it hurt to sit. He'd taken pills at home, to sleep, but he wanted to stay sharp while Howard's operation was in progress. He had finally popped a couple of the pain tabs from their plastic-and-foil blisters, and washed them down with his fifth or sixth cup of coffee an hour or so ago, and the sharp stabbing pain had faded to a more-bearable *dull* stabbing pain. And despite all the coffee, he felt relatively mellow.

"How's your arm?" he asked Toni.

"It was a nice clean cut. It doesn't hurt much," she said, "but it itches."

He had thanked her after it had happened, but he'd had plenty of time to think about it since. "You saved my life in that locker room," he said. "If you hadn't jumped that woman, she would have killed me."

"Rusty saved us both. I'd never gotten to her if he hadn't come in and started yelling. Holding an ink pen and pretending it was a gun." She shook her head.

"I'm really sorry about Agent Russell," he said. "I knew you were teaching him your fighting art. Were you, uh, close?"

She hesitated for a moment. "Not really, no." She stared into her coffee cup. "His parents are having the body flown back to Jackson, Mississippi, for the funeral and burial. That's where he was from. They seem like nice people. I'd like to go, if that's all right. It's in a couple of days."

"Sure. After we get though all this—if we get through it—I wonder if I might get you to show me some of what you do—the *silat*?"

She looked up from her coffee.

"Lately, I don't know why, I've kind of felt the need to know a little more about self-defense."

He smiled, and she matched his expression.

"I'd be happy to show you."

"Might take a few weeks for me to stop gimping around." He touched his bandaged leg.

"I'll wait."

He sipped at the coffee, then decided if he had anymore, he was going to have to have a bladder transplant. He put the cup down. "I wonder how it's going. They are supposed to be done about now."

"I'm sure they'll call as soon as they can."

"I'm sure. And I am confident that Colonel Howard will execute his mission."

She smiled again.

"What?" he asked.

"Nothing. I was just remembering something from a long time ago."

"Yeah?"

"Between my junior and senior year at John Jay, I moved to an apartment with two other students. My brother Tony had lost his job, so his wife and two kids moved in with my parents while he went to Maine to find work.

Things were a little crowded at home. We lucked into a rent-controlled place that actually had heat *and* windows that would open. Building is probably a parking lot by now, but it was perfect for three girls away from home for the first time.

"Anyway, one of my roomies was an Eye-tie like me, that was Mary Louise Bergamo, from Philadelphia; the other was a tall, lanky black woman from Texas, a volleyball player, Dirisha Mae Jones. She was the funniest person I ever met. She was always coming up with these little homespun homilies she'd gotten from somewhere. One night we were drinking cheap wine and making a lot of noise and she defined 'confident' for us.

" 'Well, girls, listen here. There's this black man, name of Ernest, who is married to this here beauuutiful woman, Loretta, but Loretta is gone up and leave him 'cause Ernest got fired from his job—even though it wasn't no fault of his own.' "

Michaels grinned. Her imitation of her friend's Texas accent was pretty good.

Toni continued: " 'So Ernest gets up one morning and puts on his best tie and his only white shirt and his Sunday-go-to-meeting pants, and leaves the house to go to this job interview. Ernest knows he don't get this job, his woman is gone leave him. He also know the good old boy doing the hirin' don't particularly *care* for men of color, so he got to be sharp.

" 'By now, though, it's lunchtime. On the way to the interview, Ernest stops at Rick's Pit Barbecue, where he orders a double helping of pork ribs and a beer to wash 'em down. So while he's waiting for Rick's boy James to dish up the ribs—which are drenched in about half a gallon of hot, greasy barbecue sauce, and which are the absolute best ribs anywhere in East Texas, and pretty much in Central or West Texas, too, and that's *sayin'* something—while he's waitin', Ernest walks on over to the phone and calls up Loretta. Says to her, ''Honey, shake out your blue dress—we gone go out dancin' tonight to celebrate my new job.''

'' 'Now, a man that eats ribs wearing a white shirt he *knows* got to stay clean, *that's* a confident man, girls.' ''

Michaels laughed.

''I like seeing you do that, Alex. Laugh. You don't do it enough.''

Michaels felt a little stab of something through the pain medication. Something in her voice. She liked him. It made him feel a little uncomfortable, but not *too* uncomfortable. ''There have been better times for it. So, what happened to them? Your roommates?''

''Mary Louise went to law school—Harvard—then home to go into practice with her father's firm. She was on the team that took the State versus Pennco Housing to the Supreme Court last year and won.''

''And the woman from Texas?''

''Dirisha joined the Woman's Pro Volleyball Tour right after she graduated. Played for three years, was on the Nike Team that won the Four Woman Outdoor Championships a couple of times. She retired from the circuit, wrote a book about her adventures, got a job as a sports columnist for *The New York Times*. Got married a few years ago, had a baby, a boy. Want to guess what she named him?''

''Come on.''

''Yep. Ernest.''

''You're making this up.''

She raised her hand, made the scout sign. ''Not a word, I swear.''

He chuckled again. She was right. He needed to laugh more.

Right now, though, he was a little nervous. Where was

Howard? He should have called by now. He looked at his watch.

Even if it all went as smooth as silk on silk, Michaels was going to have to do some fast and fancy dancing to keep Carver from going for his throat when he found out. If they went through all this and *failed* to retrieve Plekhanov, well, he was definitely going to be in crap up to his eyebrows.

If this operation failed, he'd sure as hell get a lot of time to practice his laughing, probably a long, long way from anything connected to Net Force. Though he didn't think he'd feel much like yuk-yukking it up for a while.

Sunday, October 10th, 12:12 a.m.
Grozny

"She's at top speed now, sir," the pilot yelled. He had to yell to be heard over the Huey's rotor and wind noise. All those action vids where they showed people having normal conversations inside a big chopper with the doors open, like two aristocrats sharing tea in an air-conditioned Rolls Royce, were pure fantasy. Those vids were produced by somebody who had probably never even *seen* a helicopter close up. Even the radio chatter in the headphones was hard to hear.

"How long?" Howard shouted.

"Two, three minutes," the pilot yelled back. "There's the edge of the tank farm ahead, to the right. And there's the river. I'm going to take us right over the main road."

The ten men assigned to this craft carried H&K subguns and holstered side arms—9mm Brownings, along with Cold Steel sheath knives. They wore plain coveralls, but they also wore flak vests and generic Kevlar helmets and boots. The gear was all over-the-counter commercial—the subguns were from Germany, the pistols from Belgium, the vests Israeli, the knives Japanese. This was not supposed to be a stand-up fight, and if any gear got left behind, it wasn't going to point to the United States.

The troops did wear dog tags, but that didn't matter—they weren't leaving any personnel behind. Either they all left or they all stayed.

"There's the truck!" Fernandez yelled.

"And there's trouble," Howard said.

A convoy of military-style vehicles, three of them, was fast approaching the dead truck from the other direction. The lead vehicle was a Jeep-clone with a light machine gun mounted on it amidships, and a figure in camo manning the weapon. The second vehicle was a police car with a flashing blue light. The third vehicle was a large SWAT-style van, also with a light blinking atop it. Even over the roar of the noise in the copter, they could hear the sirens.

"Well, shit," Fernandez said.

Howard yelled at the pilot. "Will my headset reach C2?"

"Yes, sir, it should."

Howard trigged his com. To the commander of the other copter, Howard said, "C2, this is Alpha Wolf, do you copy?"

"Alpha Wolf, we copy your trans."

"C2, I want you to stand away, repeat, stand away. Circle back and we'll call if we need you. No point in giving them two targets."

"Yes, sir."

To his pilot, Howard said, "Put it down, Loot. Between our truck and the incoming."

"Yes, sir."

Howard's stomach lurched as the bird dropped toward the road. He felt his skin tighten. "Nobody fires unless fired on! Deploy in a staggered grid and stand ready."

Howard looked at the uprushing road. No cover, but he wouldn't start blasting in the middle of an oil-tank field if it was *his* property. He was banking on the Chechen force commander's surprise and sense of responsibility. If it was Howard running some out-of-the-way post, and he got a call to investigate a shooting in the middle of the night, and an unmarked copter put down and disgorged armed and unidentified troops, *he* would hesitate before opening fire— as long as they didn't shoot first. There would be some important questions he'd want answers to: Who were they? What were they doing there? Could they be his own, doing some covert deal? Before you started blasting, you needed *some* information. It was one thing to shoot at some criminals in a truck you thought might have a hostage, but if you cut your own troops down, that would be bad for your career. If you riddled a bunch of oil tanks with AP rounds and created knee-deep pools of the stuff, that would also be bad. In the Chechen's place, Howard would be making some fast calls, trying to figure out what the hell was going on.

The Huey touched down. "Lock and load!" Howard yelled.

He checked his own weapon to make sure it was ready, then went out to collect his squad and their catch.

40

The three Chechen vehicles skidded to a halt as Howard and his troops piled out of the Huey and spread out, weapons held ready but not locked on targets. The Chechens had the advantage as they bailed from their rides—they could use their vehicles for cover. There were fifteen, maybe eighteen, Chechens in military gear, and they deployed, pointing their weapons from behind the Jeep-clone, the van and the police car.

Howard's men were in the open, and the pucker-factor here was extremely high. A car body would stop a lot of small-arms fire; thin air would not.

"Marcus!" Howard said, quietly enough so he hoped his voice wouldn't carry to the Chechens. "Get the package into the bird and then get out here."

Behind him, the squad hustled Plekhanov toward the Huey. Marcus was the language expert, and as soon as he had the Russian onboard, he hopped back out and came to stand next to Howard.

Sixty meters away, somebody in the Chechen force began yelling in Russian. Howard had a few words and phrases, enough to recognize a "Who the hell are you?" query when he heard it.

"What is the name of their secret police force?" Howard asked Marcus, sotto voce.

"Zhálit Kulk, sir."

"Tell them that's who we are. Tell them we're on a secret mission. Tell them to get the hell away from here or we'll have their balls for breakfast." Howard didn't think they'd buy it, but they'd have to think about it. What if it was the truth? Could they take the chance?

"Sir." Marcus turned and loudly rattled off a fast string of Russian.

Howard kept his voice low, but loud enough for his troops to hear over the Huey's twin engines. "Fall back into the transport by twos. Last out, first in."

As the first pair of his troops climbed into the Huey, the Chechen commander yelled something, and his men took more precise aim with their weapons.

"I don't think they want us to leave," Fernandez said.

Howard's belly was suddenly full of dry ice and liquid nitrogen. He nodded. But the longer they stayed here, the more dangerous it got. Somebody might get nervous, his finger might slip, and the first round that went off would trigger a fusillade from both sides.

Slowly and carefully, Howard triggered his com headset, opened the opchan to the second Huey. He hoped they weren't too far away to hear him on the portable. "C2, this is Alpha Wolf."

There was a moment of dead air.

"C2, respond."

"Copy, Alpha, this is C2."

Howard repressed the urge to sigh in relief. "We need a distraction here. There's a big van with a flashing blue light about sixty meters north of our position next to C1. I would appreciate it if you would approach from the north and have somebody lean out and put a couple of magazines of hardball into the roof of that vehicle.''

''Consider it a done deal, Alpha. We're coming in.''

''Give me an ETA.''

''Forty-five seconds, sir.''

They hadn't gone far, a thing for which he was extremely thankful at the moment.

''We are *leaving,* troops,'' Howard said, loud enough for his force to hear. At this point, he didn't much care if the opposition heard him. ''On my command, by twos, as fast as you can.''

He saw a few of the Chechens glance away from their sights, looking up and behind. They'd be able to hear the oncoming Huey's engines—the big Pratt and Whitneys could put out almost 1200 horsepower in a pinch, and at full bore, quiet they were not.

''Stand ready. . . .'' Howard said.

In the reflected light from the Chechen vehicles and the yellow sodium lamps outlining the oil tanks, Howard saw the Huey roar in and swing into a drifting broadside turn eighty feet up. After a beat, the rapid yellow-orange flashes of two or three submachine guns blasted from the open doorway.

His troops could shoot. The roof of the van rattled under the jacketed hail.

The Chechens turned to face the new and more active threat.

''Go, go, go!''

Howard's troops piled into the Huey—

The Chechens opened up on the hovering copter—

The last of his troops scrambled into the grounded bird. Only Howard and Fernandez remained outside.

''Get in, Julio!''

"Age before beauty, sir."

Howard grinned, and leaped for the copter. Fernandez bumped him from behind as he cleared the door.

"Lift, lift!" Howard yelled.

The pilot powered up, and the Huey lurched into the sky.

The Chechens realized the attack from the air was a diversion. They turned their fire in two directions. Jacketed bullets chunked into the copter.

"Keep their heads down!" Howard yelled.

Fernandez, closest to the door, opened up, waving his H&K back and forth like a garden hose. The Chechens ducked behind their cover. Bullets hammered their vehicles.

The command Huey canted and fell away at a sharp angle, climbing slowly and spiraling upward. A couple more incoming rounds hit and clanged, but a moment later, they were clear.

"C2?" Howard yelled into his mike.

"Right behind you, Alpha."

"Casualties your way?"

"Negative, sir."

"Sergeant?"

"Anybody hit?" Fernandez yelled.

Apparently nobody was.

Howard blew out a big breath and grinned. They had done it! Man!

"This is kidnapping! You can't do this!"

Howard regarded the indignant Russian. He felt a cold hatred fill him as he looked at the man.

"You fools will create an international incident! I have influential friends! You cannot expect to get away with it!"

Howard stared at the man. "We already *have* gotten away with it."

The Russian began cursing, in Russian. Howard recognized a few of those words, too. He was not disposed to listen to them. He held his hand up for silence. The Russian fell silent and frowned at him.

"Mister, you killed a man I liked and respected. If you don't shut up *right now,* you might accidentally fall out of this thing. At this speed and height, you will bounce like a rubber ball when you hit the ground."

The Russian apparently decided he had nothing else to say.

Saturday, October 9th, 6:54 p.m.
Quantico

The phone rang in the conference room. Alone, Michaels grabbed it. "Yes?"

"Sir, patching through Colonel Howard," said the voice.

"Commander?"

"Right here, Colonel."

"Mission accomplished, sir. We're in the air and on the way home."

Michaels felt an immense welling of relief. "All right! Congratulations, Colonel. Any problems?"

"Nothing to speak of, sir. A walk in the park."

Toni came back into the room. Michaels looked at her, pointed at the telephone's receiver and gave her the thumb-and-forefinger sign for "okay."

"We should see you in about sixteen hours, Commander, give or take."

"I will look forward to it. Congratulations again, Colonel. Well done."

Michaels broke the connection and grinned at Toni. "They got him. On the way home. Be here tomorrow."

"I'll give Jay Gridley a call," she said. "He wanted to know how it came out."

"Do that."

"So, now what, Alex? If you're right, we have the man who killed Steve Day, even if we can't prove he did it. The woman who muddied up the waters is dead."

"Back to business as usual, I guess," he said. "If I survive the meeting with Carver when I tell him what I did."

"You will. The Director looks at the bottom line. This is like Bush's Noriega deal, or that Iraqi snatched from Baghdad during the last days of the Clinton Administration. Our current President wanted this guy caught, he's caught. He's the DOJ's problem now."

"After we have a few words with him."

"Of course. But basically, it's all over."

"Yes," he said. "All over. And all in all, we didn't do too bad, did we?"

"No. We didn't do too bad."

They grinned at each other.

EPILOGUE

Ruzhyó, dressed in the fatigues of a United States Marine sergeant, stood outside and next to the chain-link fence that surrounded the Net Force HQ building. He was three hundred meters from the front entrance, but the deer rifle inside the duffel bag on the ground next to his feet was more than accurate enough to make that shot on a man-sized target. The rifle was a Remington, and not a Winchester, but it was also 30-06 caliber, and also a bolt-action, like the weapon he had used in Oregon to kill the computer businessman. The main difference was that the scope was optical and not holographic, with a ten-power magnification, and zeroed in at three hundred meters. He had picked this spot for the shot before he set up the rifle.

There was a bus stop here, still so new there was no graffiti drawn upon it. He could dawdle for a few minutes before anybody noticed him. Even on a Sunday, there were people coming and going in enough numbers so that nobody would worry overmuch about another Marine waiting to catch a bus.

If the Net Force Commander did not come out for lunch, Ruzhyó would leave, then cycle back later, to see if he could catch him departing for the day. If he did not spot him then, perhaps he would set up along his route home. There was always somewhere.

A plain white Dodge van with government plates pulled up near the entrance. Ruzhyó had a tiny eight-power Bushnell monocular in his pocket, a device small enough to conceal entirely in one hand. He leaned sideways against the fence and cupped the monocular in front of his eye.

The door to the building opened and an attractive brunette emerged, moved to stand by the van. Immediately behind her was Alexander Michaels, and two men who looked like guards flanked him.

Ruzhyó's luck was good. This would have to be fast. A man standing at the fence aiming a rifle would draw attention, Marine or not. He bent, unzipped the duffel bag. The rifle was ready. All he had to do was lift it, stick the barrel through the fence, which would offer an excellent shooting platform, line the crosshairs up and squeeze off the round. A five-second operation if he hurried, perhaps ten if he took his time.

Smooth movements were the key. Nothing jerky. Just lift the weapon, push it through the link, take the deep breath and hold it, find the target. He moved.

The scope, a Leupold, had excellent optics. The sight picture was clear and sharp.

There he was.

Ruzhyó placed the wavering crosshairs on the man's chest. . . .

At this distance, the scope's circular field was large enough so that Michaels did not fill it. Ruzhyó could see the woman, one of the guards, and a military man in uniform stepping from the van.

He allowed half of his indrawn breath to escape. Began his squeeze . . .

Shit! Ruzhyó took his finger from the trigger. The military man, a black, held another man by the arm.

The man he held was Vladimir Plekhanov!

Ruzhyó was aware that he had to decide to shoot or not, and he had to do it fast. He could not continue to stand here.

So, for all his skill, they had figured out that Plekhanov was their enemy, and they had not only done that, they *had* him.

Plekhanov, captured. Ruzhyó had spoken with the Russian only two days ago. Amazing.

The moment held.

Should he shoot Michaels? Or should he shoot Plekhanov? The man might give him up when questioned. Ruzhyó knew well there were drugs, instruments that could pry secrets from the tightest lips. The Americans did not often use such things, but they could, if they chose to do so.

So. Shoot?

No. He would not kill Vladimir. If the Russian wished to give him to the Americans, so be it.

And as for the Net Force Commander? There was no point in shooting him now, either. It would not help Plekhanov. It would serve no purpose. Even as he was, Ruzhyó did not kill without reason.

He pulled the rifle from the fence, bent and put it into the duffel bag. He looked around. Perhaps fifteen seconds had passed since he had removed the weapon from its concealment. No one appeared to notice him. He zipped the bag closed. Stood.

A bus approached. He would take it, rent another car in the next town, drive and find a place to sit and think. He had the other rental car, of course, but he did not want to use that one again. It was a warm day for October, and already the interior of the car's trunk would probably be beginning to smell bad.

The bus hissed to a stop. The door accordioned open. The driver smiled at him. Ruzhyó returned a smaller smile, but it was more for the thought that crossed his mind than anything else.

At least he would never again have to listen to Grigory the Snake brag about his Medal for Action in Chechnya. And by the time somebody opened the car's trunk and discovered what lay therein, Ruzhyó would be far, far away.

In the desert, perhaps.